Watch for More Second Wind Publishing
Novels from Heidi Thurston

Author of
The Duchess, The Knight and the Leprechaun

www.secondwindpublishing.com

The Duchess
The Knight
&
The Leprechaun

By

Heidi Thurston

Running Angel Books
Published by Second Wind Publishing, LLC.
Kernersville

Cut Above Books
Second Wind Publishing, LLC
931-B South Main Street, Box 145
Kernersville, NC 27284

First Cut Above Books edition published
February, 2014
Cut Above Books, Running Angel, and all production design are trademarks of Second Wind Publishing, used under license.

For information regarding bulk purchases of this book, digital purchase and special discounts, please contact the publisher at www.secondwindpublishing.com

Cover design by Curt Thurston

Manufactured in the United States of America
ISBN 978-1-938101-90-8

For Elinor

I gratefully recognize the following people without whom this book could not have been written: Jean Stevens, Pat Green, Dolly Joyner, Sarah Wilson, Teresa Koons, Linda Collins, Gitte Mikkelsen, Bibs Oervad, Jens Oervad, Karin Frey, Ritt Bjerregaard and in memoriam; Elizabeth Bresee. Thanks also to my many Danish School friends who inspired much of the story.

Special thanks go to my children, Mark, Curt and Kristine for their lifelong support.

My gratitude and love goes to my husband, Chuck who, from the start, encouraged and supported my writing efforts.

"Worry never robs tomorrow of its sorrow, but only saps today of its strength."

—A.J. Cronin

TABLE OF CONTENTS

Heidi Thurston

INTRODUCTION

"Do You Remember?"

"Anna dear, I can't tell you how happy I am to have found you. I have so much to tell you and even more I want to ask you. In the meantime, I send you all my love—this is Christian, signing off."

The words caught me off guard and caused my heart to skip a beat. Of all the voices I might have expected to hear that evening—Christian's wasn't one of them.

It was a simple sentence—found late one night on my answering machine—part of a message by a voice I hadn't heard in nearly four decades.

It wasn't so much the message itself that affected me; it was the memories the voice brought back: laughter, running hand in hand on a beach, studying together after school, enjoying a cup of tea in my parents' home, sitting on a bench in a darkened park as passion flared, and dancing to one of "our" songs; wonderful memories from long ago.

But, along with the happy thoughts came the reminder of pain the day I boarded a plane heading for another continent, leaving behind the young man to whom I had given my love, my hopes, and my heart.

Christian's short sentence was simple; the impact anything but. It pulled me out of the safe cocoon where I had so neatly arranged my life, and threw me into a world I thought left behind. It opened old wounds, brought to light massive guilt, and some deep hurt. But in the end, it also brought healing and closure and caused my life to change forever.

This is a tale about three people who, for the sake of the

story, I've dubbed the Duchess, the Knight, and the Leprechaun. Through the strands of fate, they connected, lived and loved with a great deal of passion and pain, but also vast amounts of joy. The story brings to light their secrets and what eventually brought them all peace.

Let me introduce the cast:

First there is the Duchess. A duchess, one might rightfully ask? There are, after all, not too many of those around. Just the same, my paternal grandmother was the daughter of a Prussian Duke who at a tender age, eloped from Prussia to Denmark with the head coachman of her father's estate. This woman was *not* my grandmother Aggie—the stately woman with the proud bearing—that my school friends knew. I had two paternal grandmothers, you see; the duchess was the other one—the one I was *not* supposed to talk about. So much was kept secret while I was growing up. But now that most of the players have died and gone to their heavenly rewards—at least I hope that's where they've gone—I guess it is all right to finally tell the truth.

My grandmother was christened Elisabet Augusta Theodora Fredericka Von Ludwig but—for reasons only she knew—was called Clara. She danced at the palace of Kaiser Wilhelm back at the turn of the century and, as the only girl in an aristocratic family, grew up and lived her early life in luxury, waited on by attending servants, and pampered by devoted parents and her four older brothers.

As her granddaughter, I've taken on her title, if not legitimately, then for the sake of this tale, and like my "duchy" grandmother, I too have a long row of names. She received hers at birth; I came by mine through birth, an adoption—after my mother, Lilli, married the second time—and finally at the time of my own marriage. As Anna Elisabet Drener Wiinter Thornberg, I've done all right.

Next, comes the Knight. He is Christian, the young man I left behind so long ago. He actually knelt before the Queen of Denmark as she touched a sword to his shoulders and decreed him a Knight of the Order of Danebrog. He earned the honored title through some outstanding research, but long before that, through the years we dated, he was my Knight in Shining Armor.

Finally, there is Robert, the Leprechaun—the man I married. He hailed from Ireland, had dark blue eyes that sparkled, a smile to die for, and a brogue that could charm you out of your pants—it did mine. He was bright and charismatic and could spin a yarn that would captivate any audience. But he also had a dark side; one that at times made him withdraw from those around him, caused him to struggle with inner torments and—from time to time—seek refuge in a bottle. A trip to Ireland, following his death, brought to light his true story, a story that left me a wiser, but sadder person.

I've introduced the cast. What comes next—from the beginning—is the story that started with an email, followed by a long-distance message from Denmark—left late one evening—on an answering machine in my home in North Carolina.

Heidi Thurston

PART ONE

How It Began

Chapter 1

"Anna, my dear, I am so glad to have found you."

The words caught me off guard and caused my heart to skip a beat. Of all the voices I might have expected to hear that evening, Christian's wasn't one of them.

I reached over and stopped the answering machine—I'm not sure why. Then I dropped back in my easy chair, picked up the drink I had fixed earlier, and stared at the button still blinking on the machine.

I don't know how long I sat there staring, but I acknowledged that I had connected with my past and whatever was in that message was apt to affect my future.

It was past midnight but I knew sleep would not come soon; so I went out to the kitchen to replace my drink with a cup of herb tea, hoping to calm my racing heart.

My mind began to wander and the teakettle whistled for a while before I turned it off, made my tea, and walked back to the den. I sat back down, inhaling the soothing fragrance of mint, looked out the sliding doors, and watched the moon light the backyard. Lost in thoughts, I suddenly became aware of Jo Stafford's soft rendition of the "Tennessee Waltz" floating out from the radio.

It had been one of "our" songs; as a matter of fact, that

tune "belonged" to most young people living in Denmark during the fifties. It always signaled the last dance at every ball or party our group attended.

"It's an unspoken rule," my mother told me before my first dance, "that even if you dance with others, you always save the last dance for your 'someone special.'"

Christian and I had spent long moments in each other's arms while dancing, knowing the evening—and our time together—would soon be over. The song also signaled the start of our walk home, a special time in an era where private cars were nearly non-existent for young Danish couples, and bicycling not practical transportation to a dance.

We lived twenty minutes apart in opposite directions off a main thoroughfare in the southern part of Copenhagen. Strolling home, arms wrapped around each other, we stopped often to kiss and embrace until our parting point where Christian saw me board a streetcar. Then he walked to the home he shared with his parents and younger brother.

As the song ended I eyed the answering machine, chose to ignore it, and sipped my tea. I let my eyes stray to the flat, little box—a gift from my parents to Robert on his thirtieth birthday—sitting on the table in front of me. It was an engraved silver cigarette container that back in our early years of marriage had been filled with whatever brand Robert smoked. Later, when I took up the habit, I made the box mine; Robert was perfectly happy to carry his smokes in his coat pocket or in his briefcase. When we finally kissed the "coffin nails" farewell, the box became the home for small items of memorabilia and still held an assortment of sentimental nonsense including old theater ticket stubs and small post-it-note drawings done by our grandchildren. It had become a family treasure my children all wanted to inherit. For now I kept it close as a reminder of Robert and the many great times we shared during our tumultuous marriage.

I pushed back the thoughts of the past and decided to

play Christian's message from the beginning.

"Hello, this is Christian Raabensted. Are you there Anna? Is this the right number? I'm sorry to call this late, but I'm on my way to the airport and just wanted to let you know I've received your email. I sent you a short reply and just wanted to make sure you received it. I also wanted to touch base with you in person."

I stopped the machine for a minute.

He spoke English, perhaps not sure who might check the machine, and as I listened to the message his handsome face and charming grin reappeared and brought a smile to my lips. He sounded like he was on a car phone and I heard, ever so softly, John Coltrane's rendition of "My Favorite Things"—one of *my* favorite recordings—playing in the background. A coincidence, perhaps; I took it as an omen.

The answering machine indicated there was more to the message. It had come in at eleven fifty, just before I arrived home, so I knew Christian had been on the road right before six o'clock in the morning—Danish time—to catch a dawn flight. Thanking my good luck star for the Sunday ahead, I hit "play" again.

"Anna my dear," the voice said, this time in Danish, "I'm so glad to have found you again. Your email brought back wonderful memories of my lost youth and gave me a much needed lift and hope at this time in my life."

I stopped the message and smiled. At least I wasn't alone in experiencing re-found youth. Who knew; perhaps there was room for us to rekindle an old friendship. Love wasn't anything I needed to think about at this time.

The light on the answering machine kept blinking like a piece of dark amber caught in the rays of the sun, and I decided to listen to the end of the message and then make myself go to bed. Sleep was not part of my plan; there was far too much going on in that middle-aged brain of mine. But I knew I needed to get some rest so, with some hesitation, I hit the play button again and listened as Christian talked to me.

"I've just reached Kastrup Airport, Anna. I'm not sure you'd recognize it from when we rode our bikes out here to watch the planes land and take off; but perhaps you've been home and seen the changes. I'll be in France at a conference for the next two weeks and have a weekend free in the middle of the event. I planned to email you again at that time, but the more I thought about you the more I wanted to talk with you. I'm sorry not to have caught you at home. In my next email I'll let you know where I am in my life and what I'm doing. I'll tell you about myself and reminisce about our years together."

There was a short pause and then, with a hesitant voice, he said, "Here's my email address in case you feel like writing me while I'm in Paris."

Another moment passed; then he quietly added, "You have no idea what hearing from you means to me. I'm sorry about my first short email and the fact that it took me so long to reply. I'll explain all that later. Anna dear, I can't tell you how happy I am to have found you. I have so much to tell you and even more to ask you. In the meantime I send you all my love. This is Christian signing off."

I went out to the kitchen with my empty mug. Then I walked back through the house turning off lights and the radio, and finally settled down at my desk in the den. I played the message one more time all the way through and caught myself smiling. I pulled out a pad and pencil and wrote down Christian's email address before I finally turned off the machine and went to bed.

To my amazement I went right to sleep and dreamt about Robert and one of my old girl friends. The three of us were on a side street in New York City chasing a man we couldn't identify but who evidently was an important part of our mission. Suddenly, I heard the "Tennessee Waltz," emanating from a restaurant. I stopped and looked in and saw Christian dancing with my girlfriend as others stood around swaying to the music. Then he saw me, smiled, left my girlfriend and I went inside to meet him. The music changed into a fast rock and roll song, Robert grabbed me and we danced out of the building and down the street.

I woke to total darkness, looked at the clock on the nightstand without registering the time, and fell back into a deep sleep.

Well rested, I woke up early the next morning and decided to stay in bed listening to the birds sing. Contemplating last night's message—and the impact it might have on my life—I thought back to how I had re-connected with Christian.

Chapter 2

It started one afternoon when I was playing around on my IBM Think Pad. I was a woman a the nineties, I reasoned, and decided that if I were ever to contact any of my old friends from high school, email would be the way to go. You can hide so well behind the screen and not suffer embarrassment or rejection should you encounter a person who doesn't remember you—or perhaps chooses not to.

Actually, the story started late one Sunday morning in the early spring when I ran across the diary I kept during my school years. I was in my attic sorting through stuff intended for a rummage sale when, in a weak moment, I decided to go through an old box I had ignored for years.

After putting away some old pots and pans with the other items, I opened the box and, on the top, wrapped in newspapers dating back several decades, found the long forgotten diary. I immediately decided to skip cleaning out the rest of the crates and boxes; they had waited this long and could well stay unpacked for a while longer. Instead, I brought the worn and somewhat tattered diary down to the den, curled up on a couch, threw an afghan over my feet, and spent the next couple of hours re-visiting another time in my life.

I'd faithfully kept a daily journal during my last four years in Denmark. Not only did I record most of my own experiences and feelings, I also wrote detailed accounts about the clothes I wore, books I read, music and movies I enjoyed.

The diary offered a visit back to the late 1950s, a more innocent age, perhaps, but one filled with anxieties and fears different from those of today's youths, and while reading, I became engrossed in the story of my love life during those tender school years. I use the term "love life" guardedly— back in the mid-fifties, a love life did not always equal a sex life the way it often does today.

Oh, we had yearnings and desires, but the post-World War II era was also part of the pre-pill years and so, no matter how much we wanted to "go all the way"—and truth be known a lot of us did—it rarely happened. The reason was quite simple—most girls lived in deadly fear of the big "P"—Pregnancy! Just the same, there were those among us who eventually succumbed to love and passion.

As I turned the pages in the diary, I became aware of stirring feelings entering not only my head but also lower regions of my body.

"You've been without a man too long," my best friend Reenie (Maureen), said a few weeks ago.

"Robert died several years ago and you need to get laid," she laughed.

"I admit I miss a physical relationship, but I've not yet felt the desire to hop into bed with any of the several, and otherwise agreeable, men I've gone out with in the past year," I told her.

"You just need to find the right guy," Reenie added and poked my arm.

I had quickly changed the subject.

I finished reading the diary and got the urge to contact Christian. Over the years, I'd wondered what happened to him and since his last name was uncommon, I easily found it on a Danish search-site.

The good news was not only did I find Christian's name and home address, but his email address as well. The page also provided his phone number, but I quickly decided that calling would be much too personal—we had, after all, not talked to each other in nearly forty years. Besides, I knew nothing of his current circumstances.

I was contemplating what to write Christian, when my front door opened and I heard someone enter.

"Mom, are you home? We dropped by to ask you over for dinner" my daughter called out as she let herself in with her spare key. I put the diary on top of my desk and went out to greet Becca and her family.

"We just came from a movie matinee and would like you to join us for an early Sunday dinner, Mother T," Forrest, my son-in-law, said.

"We're having sgetty," Charlie, my young grandson said and flashed me a grin, "Not Lizzy—she's having baby stuff." He wrinkled his nose, reached up and took my hand and led me to the foyer where Forrest held out my coat.

I had my usual good time at Becca and Forrest's home playing with my grandchildren and chatting with my daughter and son-in-law over dinner and when I got back home I chose to ignore the diary—still at a loss over what to write.

For several weeks it lay on my desk daring me to go ahead and write Christian; reminding me that a trip down memory lane might be a nice journey. However, I never was all that brave, and fear of rejection was part of my life, so it took until Easter to summon up courage to write.

I got up at dawn Easter Sunday to watch the spectacularly sunrise at the back of my yard and went to early church service. Breakfast followed with a long-married couple and one of the eligible single men from my church. According to most of the single women at St. Peter's Episcopal Church, any unmarried male between the ages eighteen and eighty qualified as eligible.

I declined my friends' invitation to join them on a trip to the mountains and was faced with the rest of the day to myself. My North Carolina children were out of town celebrating Easter with their in-laws, having been assured by me that "I already have plans."

I put on the teakettle, sliced up a lemon and made myself a cup of tea. Then I took out a couple of imported, and sinful, shortbread cookies from a box stashed at the back of my freezer and wandered around the house before going to the den to check my email. During the early spring my study is by far the friendliest room in the house with sunshine coming through the sliding glass doors.

I had, for the most part, become used to living by myself and with Tessa around I never really felt alone. A large Airedale Terrier makes for great company and comfort.

Converting the master bedroom into a den had also turned out to be an excellent idea. Sleeping in the old bedroom without Robert had not been good and it proved much easier to retire across the hall in Becca's old room. Paint and a new set of bedroom furniture made it mine and enabled me to make it through the nights alone. Then I converted my former bedroom into a combination den and study.

"I love the soft colors in this room, Mother T," Hunter Lee, my daughter-in-law, drawled in her deep southern accent when she first saw the den.

"The subtle earth tones are *so* you; quiet and tasteful, but full of life," she said.

Shortly after the conversion of the two rooms, my two younger sons and daughter had trouped in with their families for a tour of "the new digs" as Patrick, my bachelor son, called the den.

Hunter Lee and Luke, our middle son, eyed their twins, Mary Margaret and Jackson Lee, as they tested the sand-colored futon to see if they could make if bounce. Finding it too firm, they went on to explore the items on the old sea chest that served as a coffee table.

"The baby obviously finds your leather chair and footstool very comfortable," Luke whispered, and looked with affection at Annabel Grace, his small daughter fast asleep in the corner chair, one foot dangling over the side. Bored with the new furnishings, the twins joined their older brother Luke Junior. and cousin Charlie and went outside to play.

Becca shifted baby Lizzy from one arm to another and pointed to the paintings on the wall. "Nice quiet beach scenes—it suits you, mom. I also like the fact that you have a full view of the backyard when you're on your computer."

"It's such a quiet and peaceful room," Hunter Lee repeated. "Except for the green plants and the books in the bookcase, the room has no primary colors."

"Strictly speaking the plants really don't count since green is *not* a primary color," said Patrick, an artist who, until now, had been quiet.

They all laughed at his observation. I told them that Reenie had dubbed the room "The Sanctuary" after the renovation—and Sanctuary it remained.

On that Easter Sunday afternoon I took a sip of tea, fired up my computer and checked my email. The first was a note from my granddaughter Acy (Anna Catherine) reminding me she was coming down for the latter part of her spring break asking me to rescue her English project due by the end of the month.

A student at Cornwell High School in upstate New York, Acy planned to continue her education at Corrier Hill, a small private college located in a town a few miles up the road from where I live.

I scrolled down through the messages and found a note with "Happy Easter" from Hunter Lee, an invitation to "come visit" from my friend Tess in New York, and a "Happy Spring" message from my daughter, Becca. There were also a couple of "forwards" with jokes and stories from various friends and an assortment of junk mail I quickly deleted.

With surprise, I found a note from my old school in Copenhagen. The school was preparing for its 100th anniversary the following year and was working on a chapter for a memorial book regarding former graduates. I had no idea how they traced me, but was intrigued. So I took a sip of tea and a bite of my sinful shortbread and read the whole message.

The school wanted to know my marital status, number of

children, and if and where I worked. They asked for a couple of paragraphs about my most memorable school experiences. They promised to reply and offered to sell me a copy of the memorial book, when printed.

I thought about it for a few minutes and quickly answered the questions. I let them know I looked forward to their response and would love to buy a copy of the book.

The note made me think about my school days and, without worrying whether or not this was a smart idea, pulled out Christian's email address and began to write:

"Please do not faint when you get this email with a 'voice' from your past." I went on to give a sketchy background of myself. I told him about my four children, adding I was the proud grandmother of nine wonderful grandchildren; I briefly mentioned Robert's death, what I did for a living, and listed some of my interests.

It was a friendly, but not terribly intimate note. It had been a long time since my whole life revolved around Christian; I wasn't at all sure how he would feel about hearing from me again.

I quickly reread the note and had I taken more time, I might have hit the delete button. Instead, I held my breath and sent it out on that mysterious information highway.

By now it was two in the afternoon—eight in the evening in Denmark. I had no idea whether this email went to his home or work or *when* Christian checked his email. I felt a little silly after I sent it off but reasoned what was done was done; besides—what could be the harm?

Instead of sitting and stewing about it, I put Tessa on a leash and went for a long walk in my neighborhood admiring the many shades of daffodils that brightened the otherwise barren yards. Before I went inside, I picked a bouquet of the most exquisite salmon-centered daffodils from my own garden and, feeling full of spring, went inside and placed them in an old earthenware pitcher.

By that time the email note had receded to the back of my mind.

Chapter 3

"I'm sure I've inhaled at least a pound of dirt," Reenie said, stamping the ground. It was Easter Monday, a holiday at the Chamber of Commerce where I worked part time as events coordinator, so I was off and Reenie had offered to help me buy and plant shrubs and flowers in my yard.

Reenie and I were best friends and had been since we met shortly after my arrival in North Carolina working as volunteers in the annual fall campaign for the local United Way. I'm an only child and Reenie grew up the only girl in a family of five children. By the time the goal was met in October, we each felt we had found the sister we never had.

As we worked in the yard I thought of telling her about my email to Denmark, but by now felt sort of foolish about the whole thing. So I kept quiet.

We had found what we were hunting at the new Lowe's Store right before lunch and since Reenie's husband was out of town, she had offered to come home and help with my landscaping efforts and stay the night.

"We look like a pair of rag-dolls," Reenie said around five o'clock, "but at least your yard now proudly sprouts four new yews, a dozen azaleas, and a ton of annual flowers," she added with pride.

I thanked her for all her work and suggested we quit for the day, send out for pizza, shower, and crash on the deck with two tall, cold gin and tonics. She agreed.

I admit my curiosity nagged at me throughout the day as I dug, planted, and wiped sweat off my face. When would there be a response to my email, and what would Christian say? My curiosity grew, but I made myself stay away from the computer.

We ate more pizza than we should and watched "Thelma and Louise," yet again. It was our favorite movie and we often used the two title-names as nicknames—I was Thelma. Around eleven o'clock we called it a night and Reenie headed for my guestroom where I'm sure she went to sleep right away.

I checked to make certain all the doors were locked, let out Tessa for her night-whiz, and turned on the alarm system. Then I returned to the living room and made myself a scotch and water. I felt restless and knew I was stalling.

I finally walked back into my den, turned on the computer and entered my email program where I found nothing—absolutely nothing—coming up on the In screen. Not even an ad or a silly forward, and certainly not any return letter from my old love. So I took my drink, grabbed my current New York Times Best Seller and headed for bed.

To heck with Christian! So what if he was laughing himself silly over my attempts at reconnecting. Men! Who needed them? Why was I even trying to contact him?

I'd like to say I never again looked for Christian's reply, or that his devoted letter greeted me on the screen the next day. Not so. For the next several days, I checked my email first thing in the morning, during breaks at work, and as soon as I came home in the evening. Each day I found the same thing—notes from family and friends, but nothing from overseas. There was not even a response from my old school thanking me for my wonderful contribution.

I did take time out during this period to enjoy my granddaughter's visit and helped her with her paper on the pros and cons of journalism. I was after all a journalist from a bygone era.

"I want to become an anchorwoman on national network and eventually take the place of Barbara Walters, if and when she ever retires," Acy stated.

"Don't get your hopes up," I laughed, "It's my opinion that good old Barb will be around for a long time."

But Acy is young and bright. There was hope, yet.

I was delighted she had chosen to come down on her spring break, and pleased that she seemed to enjoy spending time with me.

She'd been Grandpa's girl since she was five and began

spending summers with us, roaming the area with Robert. Rummage sales, bargain stores, hardware centers, car auctions and fiddlers' concerts—it didn't matter—during every summer vacation the two of them took it all in and laughed the days away. Even after she bloomed into a lovely teenager, turning the heads of all the neighborhood boys, she still took time out to go exploring with her beloved grandfather.

After Robert's death, Acy came down for a couple of weeks during her summer vacation. We mourned together and grew close. We also re-visited some of the places where she and her grandfather had gone. When the time came for her to think about college, she informed her parents she wanted to be close to the neighborhood and surroundings of her childhood summers in North Carolina.

One whole day was spent looking over the college where she planned to go. We investigated dormitories, the college bookstore, the campus grounds, and some of the shops in town. A couple of evenings we worked on her journalism paper and on her last night I took her to our country club just outside of town for a quiet dinner. I enjoyed showing off this petite and vivacious young woman, who with curly dark hair and sparkling blue eyes, resembled her Irish grandfather.

Acy left the next morning and I prepared for the week ahead.

Monday morning I met with a crisis at the Chamber regarding a new project, and for the next week, I put in long hours. I came home late each night, warmed up some soup, had a glass of wine, watched the news, and poured into bed. I quietly thanked my neighbor's son, David, who came over every day after school and walked and fed Tessa. By the time I stumbled through the door she came running, jumped up, licked my face and settled down at my feet until it was time to go to bed.

The upshot was that I quit worrying about my email. The memory of a park-bench on late spring evenings and young blood pounding through tender bodies passed through my head at fleeting moments, but that was all. I'd been foolish to send Christian the letter and was through with attempts to re-visit my past. I would just forget about him! What did I expect any way? Roses? By now, he was probably bald, fat, and happily married with five kids and numerous grandchildren. I reasoned that he, in all likelihood, had forgotten about the girl whose all he'd been several decades ago; I was just a young woman who had left him in order to accompany her parents to the other side of the world.

At eighteen, the United States *had* seemed like the other end of the globe. I had *not* wanted to come here, but as an obedient daughter, I followed my parents when they immigrated to America the year I graduated from school, shedding tears only when I was by myself.

Christian and I corresponded for several months after I left, but on one of the last days in September, I received what I later considered a Dear Jane letter. He wrote he still cared deeply about me, but was not sure I would ever return and felt it best for us to go on with our lives and date others.

I was devastated!

My mother understood. She told my father who tried to act sympathetic, but he couldn't hide his pleasure. He wanted me close by and told me not to worry about a boy miles away.

Two weeks later, I met Robert at a barbeque party held in the garden of friends of my parents. He was the nephew of the family next door and had arrived that morning on a month's leave from the Navy. He noticed the party and decided to crash it, he explained, and since he was polite and charming, no one minded.

"I'm twenty-six, a Navy pilot, serving aboard an aircraft carrier stationed at Corpus Christi in Texas," he said. "Graduated from Syracuse University and joined the Navy in order to see more of the world."

I took the offered drink and asked him to tell me more.

"I was raised in Ireland, the second oldest of nine children including two sets of twins and, except for me, they are all red heads like my father."

He had come to the States at age sixteen and after high school attended college, "on a full scholarship," he added with pride. During this time he lived with another aunt and uncle and their son in Syracuse.

"Why did you leave Ireland?" I asked.

For a moment he looked troubled, dodged the question, and instead asked me about *my* recent immigration. As the afternoon went on, we discussed our likes and dislikes regarding our new country. We found we had something in common, and by the time the stars came out I thought perhaps I had found a soul-mate.

Robert was just short of six feet tall, well-built, with curly dark hair, bright blue eyes and the most irresistible smile and dimples. His brogue—when he chose to use it— was charming and he sang Irish songs with gusto all night, waving a beer mug with one arm; encircling me with the other.

He told me his relatives next door had invited him to spend his leave with them and asked if he could call me for a date. I quickly agreed and for the next four weeks we went out almost every night and my despair at being cast aside by Christian subsided.

Hurt and on the rebound I threw myself at Robert feeling sure this was love. I pushed aside caution and sometime before his leave was up I finally gave myself to this wonderful and warm Irishman. After he went back to Texas he wrote me often, called me once a week and we planned to meet again at Christmas.

Then on a frosty November morning, right before Thanksgiving, I woke up and realized my period was late, and was afraid the "Big P" might have caught me. The following Monday I went by myself to a doctor who confirmed my suspicion—I was pregnant.

I told my parents and offered to go back to Denmark and have an abortion in order not to disgrace them. My father agreed and told me of a doctor, a friend of his mother, who could "take care of things;" my mother told me privately to think it over and let Robert know before doing anything.

When he called two days later, I told him I was going to have a baby and explained my thoughts of ending the pregnancy. He immediately voiced strong objections. Born Catholic, he was adamantly against it—it was a mortal sin he said, adding he would come back up north and marry me.

We were married in a quiet ceremony at St. Andrew's Catholic Church in upstate New York; Matthew arrived in the summer at the Navy military hospital in Corpus Christi. The three of us lived in a small rented ranch house in a neighborhood filled with other young military couples until Robert finished his tour of duty. We became friends with Tess and Tom O'Donnell and after Robert's discharge— three months following Tom's—we joined them in Cornwell, New York where both men had been offered jobs at the new Cornwell Tools Manufacturing Plant. We bought a house near the O'Donnell's and settled down to family life.

Chapter 4

On an early Saturday morning, sometime after I sent Christian the email, I decided to do some correspondence knowing I had no plans until later.

I threw on a sweat-suit, made a trip to the kitchen for some freshly brewed coffee, went to the den, and fired up my computer. My intent was to write a couple of notes to some cousins in Denmark and a letter to Tess telling her my new shrubs, including the rose bush she sent for my birthday, were doing well.

Neither the letter to Tess, nor to the others, ever got on their way.

As the screen came into focus and the emails began filling the monitor I saw, at the bottom of the list, the name of my first love popping up like the sun rising over the beach at dawn.

I opened the email wondering what his long awaited response would be. The note was brief and did not explain why it took him so long to answer. It read as follows: "Dear Anna, it was absolutely great hearing from you. I have never forgotten you—you never forget your first love. I am in my fourth marriage, have three grown children, and work at the university just outside Charlottenlund where I reside with my 'for the time being wife.' I am tied up for the next several weeks, but I promise I'll write you as soon as I can. Again, I am so happy to have heard from you.

Love, Christian."

That was it!

The top of the email read Dr. Christian P. Raabensted so I knew he had acquired a MD and worked at one of the largest medical universities in the country.

He was brilliant in school, always in the number one or two spot and graduated with top honors. Christian's intelligence and wit had been part of his appeal to me. He was good looking with golden hair and deep brown eyes that eventually had a powerful effect on me. I fell for him in my early teens but my heart was not true at that tender age.

I was crazy about him one day, and another day infatuated with a boy named Benny who was born in England and played the guitar. Now and then I yearned to hold hands with Bo, the cute and proverbial class clown, and sometimes I thought I would like to date George, our star soccer player. It depended on who paid me the most attention at the time. Not until a dance the night he turned sixteen did I fall hopelessly in love with Christian. It turned out to be a love that lasted a long time.

Reenie once asked me what I had found most attractive in the young men in my class.

"That they were attracted to me, were intelligent, tall, and had wonderful smiles. Once combinations of those things were in place, I was generally sold; brown eyes helped," I had laughed.

Christian was six foot four, had a dashing smile, was bright, and best of all—he liked me. In our early grades, he also liked other girls; danced with all of them and walked home any girl needing male protection. This was the fifties in Europe and girls did not walk home alone late at night.

After we became a pair, the night of his birthday—and the year I turned fifteen—that courtesy ceased. I learned that instructions from his domineering father had obliged him to do this gentleman-like thing. Mr. Raabensted, Sr. did not want his son to become serious about any one girl and told Christian to pay attention and "act like a gentleman" with all the girls in his class.

I read his email and sat by my computer, for what seemed like hours, staring at the screen. My heart pounded and my head felt light. I realized I was smiling from ear to ear admitting it was silly to sit here, at my age, and smile because of a short email from a friend I hadn't seen for years. But the smile would not go away, and I used restraint to keep from hitting "reply" and answer Christian's letter right away.

I made a hard copy of the email, opened the sliding doors and went out on the deck with the note still in my hand and walked around. After a while, I went into the kitchen grabbed a Diet Coke, went back outside, dropped down in a deck chair, and re-read the short note three times.

A train-whistle from the railroad going through the nearby town brought me to my senses, reminding me that in an hour I was to meet Becca at Reenie's. Then the three of us were to drive to Charlotte, pick up my daughter-in-law, and attend a charity fashion show put on by Luke and Hunter Lee's church in downtown Charlotte. The last thing I needed was to be late.

I tore off my sweat-suit, jumped into a pair of khakis, a black silk blouse and black high-heel sandals. To this I added a silver chain with a large chunk of amber—a gift from my mother on my twenty-fifth birthday—and was halfway through the hall before I realized that I had not put on make-up.

At my age, you do not leave your house without make-up, especially if you are going to a fashion show in an upscale part of town. I took a deep breath, took the last sip of coke and slowed down. After carefully applying make-up and running a brush through my hair, I grabbed my handbag, folded the email and stuffed it into a side pocket.

I backed my Mazda out of the driveway, popped in a tape, and as I pulled out onto the road the voice of John Fogerty's "Proud Mary," filled the car. It never failed to remind me of Robert and of all the good times we had shared during our years together.

The song added to my upbeat feeling and, although I was alone, I felt there was life ahead; probably not with Christian, and most likely not with any of the other men I knew at the moment—perhaps not with any man at all. But the email, in its simplicity, had brought something back to me; something I thought had died with Robert. I sailed off in my car feeling young and alive again looking forward to spending the afternoon with three of my favorite women.

Life was going to be all right.

Chapter 5

On my way to Reenie's, I reflected on my family and the period after we came to North Carolina, and thought of the things I wanted to write Christian.

Robert and I arrived in the Charlotte area at a time when a lot of Northern companies found it beneficial to expand their operations in the southern states where the absence of unions made it more profitable to operate. We found the people here to be friendly, but not nearly as driven as their counterparts in the north; if a job took a little longer than planned, that was all right. As we began building our house we came to know their particular interpretations of time. If told something would probably be done in an hour, we could usually count on it taking a day. Likewise, if informed it would take a day or a week, we planned on several of either—it was just a slower pace. For the rushing folks from the rust belt, it was sometimes a difficult adjustment.

While Becca was in high school and Patrick in middle school, I took a job as full time assistant to the school superintendent. After coming south I decided to work regular hours and not around the clock as I often had on the editorial staff up north.

Becca liked having me at the school. "It gives me a certain amount of clout," she told me. Patrick, on the other hand, was careful not to let his friends know his mother was part of "the system."

I did miss the newspaper, now and then, and sometimes longed for the rush I felt when interviewing people for a feature story, or the thrill meeting celebrities that came to our town. At times, I even missed the search for new ideas for my weekly column. Once in the south I did, from time to time, submit pieces to the local paper in order to quench my desire for the smell and the look of ink and print, and was fortunate that the local editor encouraged guest columnists.

I toyed with the idea of writing a book, but never found the time or the right subject, so I put it off to *someday* when, for sure, I would write my first novel.

I came to an abrupt stop for road repair work and while waiting for the Stop sign to turn to Slow, I thought of my children.

My two oldest sons and my daughter all resemble the Scandinavian side of our family—tall and lanky. It's a trait they inherited from my ancestors and not from me; I am of medium height and have spent most of my life trying to keep a slim figure. But like me, they have wide set bright blue eyes and—until late in their teens—very blonde hair. By grace, they also have my high cheekbones and narrow nose and could easily go to Denmark and pass for natives.

Our youngest son, Patrick, on the other hand, is the image of his father from his curly dark hair falling down over his eyes to the dimpled cheeks and the same winning smile.

I often see my three children living near me, but I miss our oldest son, still in New York.

Matt married in college after getting his girlfriend, Ellen, pregnant during their first spring break. Right after their wedding, they moved in with her grandmother who had raised Ellen since she was orphaned at an early age. Matt and Ellen continued college and worked part-time jobs while Ellen's grandmother took care of Acy who made her arrival the night before Christmas Eve.

From the start, it was not a good marriage and after they graduated, Ellen filed for divorce. She left Acy with Matt informing him she wanted "to be free" and took off for New Zealand with an aspiring artist. A few years later we heard from her grandmother that she had died in a skydiving accident.

After Ellen left, Matt rented a small farmhouse south of town and began work at Cornwell Tools Manufacturing Plant where Robert was head of the engineering department.

He threw himself into his job, worked his way up in the company and spent every hour away from the plant with his daughter.

Later, he met Camilla who worked in the human resources department at the Cornwell plant and following a short courtship they married and bought the farm where Matt and Acy lived. After they had the twins, David and Danielle, Camilla gave up her job to stay home to raise the children and tend a large flock of sheep they had acquired before the twins were born.

Luke, our second oldest, was still in college when Robert and I moved south. He did graduate work in Boston and, after receiving his MBA in finance, was hired by one of the city's large financial firms. After a few years he transferred to Charlotte, North Carolina where he is an investment banker at one of that city's many financial institutions.

Luke and his wife, Hunter Lee, met in Georgia during one of his business trips, and married a few months later. They settled in Charlotte in one of the fashionable suburbs, just south of the city, where they reside with their four children, Luke Jr., twins Jackson Lee and Mary Margaret, baby Annabel Grace, plus a housekeeper and a nanny, in a place big enough to house an army. They live not far from me and I see them often.

After high school, Becca received a degree in business administration and married Forrest, a local young man who, with his father and brother, owns and operates a small construction firm just outside our town. They have two small children, Charlie, four, and Lizzie (Elisabet Anna) just a year old. Like their nearby cousins, they frequently spend time with me.

And then there is Patrick—a dreamer all his life. He served as an acolyte during his teen years and after graduating from high school thought he wanted to become an Episcopal Priest. During his second year in college he took several art classes and discovered his real passion— painting—and graduated with a double major in art and philosophy. He has talent, but his break has yet to come; he is presently one of the many starving artists living in a loft on the outskirts of Charlotte with Madison, his long-time girlfriend. In addition to his art work, Patrick does odd jobs and makes a little money while Madison works at Presbyterian Hospital in downtown Charlotte and for the most part supports them.

I was thrown out of my reverie by an angry sounding horn and realized I was getting waved on by the young man from the road crew. A glance in my rear view mirror told me I was holding up half a dozen cars so I quickly stepped on the gas and headed right on a road not much traveled Saturday mornings and let my thoughts go from my children to Robert.

After leaving the Navy, he began work at Cornwell Tools Manufacturing Plant and worked his way up in the company. In 1979 he was offered a high ranking position in Charlotte and was there until the company decided, yet again, to promote him. He was transferred to Wilmington to help start up a new fiber plant Cornwell was opening.

For a year he commuted on weekends while I stayed at home with our two youngest children. Then after one harrowing trip at the onset of a hurricane—Patrick thought the whole thing an adventure—he decided to take a good look at what he was doing.

We survived the hurricane, losing only two scrub pines in the back yard, but Robert decided it was time for a change in careers. He didn't want to travel and it made little sense for us to move again.

He had been with Cornwell for a long time and felt ready to start his own firm and begin work as a consultant. So he set up office in town, hired a part-time college student and began, what soon became, a lucrative second career. With his knowledge of the industrial world, he was able to expand his operation and after a couple of years hired a full time secretary, a bookkeeper, and a junior partner.

I had resigned from the school system a few years earlier when the school merged and my position changed. After Robert died I was left with enough income and did not have to work, but when the part time job as events coordinator for the local Chamber of Commerce became available six months later, I jumped at it. I liked the flexibility of the position realizing that sometimes I might work around the clock and at other times be quite idle. The job was set up for twenty hours a week and turned out to be just the sort of work I needed. It kept me in touch with the community and still provided me time to myself.

Absorbed in my thoughts, I arrived sooner than expected at Reenie's where she and Becca were waiting. I pulled into the driveway feeling sure I would be able to compose a good reply to Christian's email—soon—real soon.

Chapter 6

I was a lector at church that Sunday and after the service chatted with Father Benjamin about his sermon. With my usual group, I went to brunch and on to an outdoor concert at Freedom Park in Charlotte. Then I hurried home to get things ready for the coming week. I read the email from Christian several times during the day and finally decided to wait a week before writing back - still not sure.

That turned out not to be difficult as the chamber's annual Summer Festival was scheduled for the coming weekend and I found myself working from eight in the morning until late at night.

By the time I arrived home, Tessa was ready for a walk. Then I showered, had some fruit, and closed out evenings watching old Kathryn Hepburn movies featured on TV that week. I checked my email each night and was relieved to find only forwards and assorted junk.

The Chamber put up its own festival booth at seven o'clock Saturday morning and from then on the day was an endless round of small crises.

An elementary grade dancing group, scheduled to go on stage at nine, lacked its accompaniment, but an innovative parent quickly came through with a portable tape recorder, and the little girls danced like the wind to the delight of parents, grandparents, and assorted early birds. The small drum corps that was to lead the parade at eleven o'clock had misplaced its drums! You figure how a dozen drums can disappear. It turned out, two minivans carrying the equipment had made a wrong exit on Hwy I-77; but after a call with correct directions the drums arrived just in time for the march.

By noon I was exhausted, by late afternoon, wiped out, but I did take time out to attend church at five thirty, enabling me to sleep late Sunday morning. I quietly thanked the Episcopal Church Counsel for joining the Catholics in offering Saturday evening service, jokingly termed "Sinners Mass," generally attended by those wanting to party Saturday night and sleep late on Sunday.

Partying was the last thing on my mind when we began taking down our booth shortly after nine. I did, however, go with the Chamber crew for a late night drink at a nearby Bistro where we discussed the event and the possibility of extending it to a two-day affair next year. Due to excellent planning and sensational weather, it had been a great day with lots of good PR for the chamber and profits for all the vendors. We could now begin to plan the next big event—the Fall Harvest Fair.

After finishing my drink, I said goodnight to Reenie and told her I planned to sleep in, having slipped away earlier to St. Pete's.

I arrived home close to midnight and was grateful to David who had taken Tessa with him on a weekend Senior Scout trip, relieving me of a midnight walk. I have a fenced in back yard with a doghouse under a huge Sycamore which provides a cool place for her to rest and a large area in which to play, but she still wants a walk every night before settling on her cushion at the foot of my bed. During stormy nights—and there are plenty of those in the Piedmont area—she invariably sneaks up on my bed; I have to admit I let her. I am scared of thunder and lightning and miss Robert's comforting hand reaching over to assure me "everything's all right Anna."

It was late and I was weary, but found it hard to settle down after an active day. Besides, the house felt empty without Tessa.

In my tiredness I chose to ignore the answering machine although I did see the message button blinking. I'd called home to check just before going to the Bistro, and found it empty and felt sure this was just another wrong number. I am one digit off from an all-night Italian take-out place and often get calls from someone wanting "an extra large pizza," delivered; so I delayed checking the message.

After a quick shower, I wrapped myself in my terry-cloth bathrobe and walked to the bar. I fixed myself a scotch and water and relished the fact that I could sleep late. Then I wandered back to the den, flicked on the radio and turned to the local jazz station. As John Coltrane's "My Favorite Things" filled the room, I sat down in my easy chair and I hit the button on the answering machine.

There was a moment's silence and then a voice came on.

"Hello, this is Christian Raabensted; would it be possible to talk to Anna Thornberg?"

And that's how it all began—really began.

Chapter 7

I woke up early Sunday morning and sat up to watch the sunshine through the sliding glass doors. The warm rays tickled my nose and for a moment I forgot about Christian's call. I sank back in bed luxuriating in the knowledge that I had some lazy days ahead. My boss didn't like me to work much more than the twenty hours a week his budget allowed and I had put in a lot of time during the past week. I was not due back at the Chamber until a board meeting Wednesday afternoon.

I turned over in bed and caught sight of the answering machine and remembered Christian's message. I was tempted to hear it again but after a moment's indecision decided not to. The truth was I didn't know how to deal with it.

Feeling restless, still thinking about Christian, I looked out at the yard where a slight breeze danced through the sycamore leaves. It was June, my favorite summer month, and the call of the beach was suddenly strong; I wanted to be by the ocean. The beaches in North Carolina and Denmark held part of my heart; it was where I went to relax and to think—this morning I needed to do both.

In years past Robert and I rented cottages in June at one of the Carolina beaches and brought along the children, their girlfriends (later wives) and grandchildren.

As the years went by the clan grew as did the houses and prices of the cottages, but it was money well spent. We had more fun than could be bought; times none of us would ever forget. Acy was two the first time we went to the beach and her joy in discovering the ocean, or the "big pool" as she called it, was worth more than a drawer full of money.

I considered driving to the beach for a couple of days, perhaps staying at a B & B in Wilmington, and decided to give it some serious thought after I dressed and had some coffee. I finally got out of bed, hopped in the shower, singing "Proud Mary," at full volume and nearly missed Reenie's call.

The phone was ringing as I turned off the water and I quickly grabbed my bathrobe and dashed out to catch it.

"I knew you went to church last night and figured I'd find you home this morning," she said without any introduction; none was needed.

Without a lead up, Reenie explained that Paul had been asked to go to Texas the evening before and had left Charlotte Airport early this morning.

Paul DeNero, fifteen years older than Reenie, is a former Marine, and has a PhD in Nuclear Engineering. After his service years he went into private business and has done extremely well. He is semi-retired, does some work at Corrier Hill College, and is in great demand on the lecture circuit. He adores Reenie and whenever she comes up with one of her crazy ideas and wants to move a wall or add another room to their home, he just smiles and says, "Whatever makes you happy, dear." There are some not so pleasant sides to Paul and his family that Reenie rarely talks about, but on the whole, theirs is a good marriage.

"Paul took the call from Texas while we were at the festival," she said as I towel dried my hair.

"Seems one of the presenters at a conference in San Antonio had a stroke early Saturday morning leaving the program with slots to fill. One of the organizers knew Paul and suggested they call to see if he could pinch hit."

I brushed out my hair and wondered where Reenie was going with this.

"Paul told me about the trip after I got home last night and while I packed his suitcase, he prepared his papers; someone at the conference had already made travel arrangements.

"After he left to catch the red-eye this morning, I felt an urge to go to the beach and decided to head for Topsail Island—*and* I want you to come with me."

Paul and Reenie own several properties along the Carolina beaches; mostly condominiums they rent out, but when they want to get away by themselves they head for their place just north of Wilmington. It is a rambling five-bedroom cottage just a walk up from the ocean with few neighboring homes.

Over the years, hurricanes have raced up and down the coastline and from time to time many of the island places suffered damage, but "Idle-a-While," the DeNero cottage, has held up against every storm. The cedar-shingled cottage sits uniquely protected by natural barriers formed years ago by high sand dunes overgrown with scrub bushes and ground cover. A few shingles have been lost in storms and on occasion a window shutter detached itself, but that's about it.

I've been there many times and will never forget Reenie taking me there shortly after Robert died. She drove me down and stayed the week-end to make sure I was all right and was with me late Sunday evening when I spread Robert's ashes into the sea. Then she left me to collect my thoughts, but came down to pick me up a week later.

We got trashed on "Fat Girl Margaritas," a Reenie concoction, the evening she came back and, with awful hangovers, went out for breakfast the next morning. But my life began to take shape after that and I started to make plans for my future.

"We can relax after the festival rush and regroup. We've not had any girl's days alone since Easter and I think it's about time we spend some quality time together," said Reenie.

Although I rarely do things on the spur of the moment, I didn't have to think long about going—I was more than ready. The fact that we both thought of the beach at the same time was not unusual. We often shared thoughts—perhaps another reason we were close.

"It's almost eight o'clock," I said. "I'll need an hour to get ready and make arrangements for Tessa. I'll call David's parents and let them know my whereabouts for the next few days and ask them to pick up my paper and mail."

Tessa would not be home until Sunday afternoon when David's Scout troop concluded their two-day dog training session at Camp Julian. I would tell David's parents my daughter would pick up the dog that evening.

Tessa is crazy about Reenie, who in turn is a sucker for animals so we rarely go to the beach without bringing at least two or three dogs along. But this was to be a girls only trip so Coal and Sukie, Reenie's two labs, would be taken care of by her dog sitter and Tessa would be with Becca and her family who are always glad to have her stay.

After the call to my neighbors, I threw khakis and white slacks and several pairs of shorts in my travel bag along with an assortment of cotton T-shirts. I added my new black silk shirt and batik skirt with its matching shawl, both bought with Hunter Lee two weeks earlier.

My toiletry bag is always on ready and needed only my prescriptions. I was out of sunscreen, but reasoned Reenie would have some in one of her well-stocked bathrooms; if not, I would pick it up in the small town within walking distance of the DeNero cottage. I packed the book I was currently reading, added a few girls' night essentials, and at the last moment decided to bring my Think Pad. I gave the house a final check-over, watered the green plants and set the timers on the radio and lights. Then I went down to the cellar to check the washer and dryer—I'm a worrier by nature—picked up a couple of choice wines from our small wine cellar and loaded the car. Finally, I put the printed note from Christian in my pocketbook and got on my way just before nine.

On an impulse, I decided to drive the Jeep Wrangler. It had been Robert's, and I just couldn't bear to part with it. It reminded me of the many trips to the mountains Robert and I had made looking for property for a future retirement place before we found and bought a couple of acres six month before he died. It also gave me a sense of security to have two cars; this way there was always a vehicle in front of the house making it look like someone was at home.

As I drove away from the house, I called Becca on my car phone and asked would she mind picking up Tessa that evening, after the dog got back from camp with David, and keep her until Wednesday afternoon.

"I'm heading to the beach with Reenie," I told her as I pulled out of the driveway. "I'm ready to play at the beach, have a few drinks, and eat a lot of crab legs fixed by Reenie, the way we all love them."

"You sound in high spirits and I'm betting you're driving dad's jeep," Becca laughed; "I hear 'Proud Mary' playing so you must be feeling really good.

"I'm a little envious, but happy you are taking some time off. Have a great time and bring me back a box of salt-water taffy or two; I'll pick up Tessa and keep an eye on the house," she added.

I sailed out of our development, windows down, singing along with Fogerty and arrived at Reenie's home feeling great.

Chapter 8

Reenie was in the driveway inspecting a flat tire on her black Chrysler Town and Country. The hatch was up and I saw her duffel bag already in the car along with a cooler, bags filled with groceries, and a new beach umbrella. She held a beach bag in her hand and she was *not* smiling.

"This car came back from the garage two days ago," she said, with a voice full of disgust. "They were supposed to give it an oil change and take a good look at the tires. That, apparently, is exactly what they did—just took a look. I drove this car yesterday—thought it was in great shape. Turns out I have a slow leak! Those bozos never really checked it—and the spare is also flat!"

She eyed Paul's truck with its extended cab and oversized tires parked next to the garage.

"Paul took his Lincoln to the airport and I really don't want to drive that big old thing to the beach. The guy at the garage said they could send someone over early tomorrow morning, but by that time I hoped to be at the beach making ass prints in the sand," she said, and gave me an agitated look.

I took a deep breath and offered to drive the jeep to the beach. Reenie stared as if I'd just landed from another planet. For me to make such an offer was not norm, and she knew it.

I never learned to drive in Denmark but began lessons early in my marriage. I went to instructions at St. Anthony Catholic Church to convert to Robert's religion during the same period and though the religious instruction, despite the language difficulty, went quite well, the driving petrified me. I was afraid of the car, of highway driving, and especially crossing bridges. Many a bridge still features paint marks from my close encounters years ago. I eventually did learn to drive but never conquered my fear of highways.

41

Reenie and I have a standing agreement—anywhere we go, she drives. I pay for the gas, or pick up the tab for lunch, but I do *not* drive long distances, and especially not to the beach. I'm terrified of that drive—snaking through a number of small towns or flying along the interstates. On this morning, however, high from the call last night, I felt full of myself, and the idea of driving to Topsail Island in the jeep seemed enticing.

"Since we have few alternatives, I agree, albeit with hesitation," Reenie said and laughed.

"Let's load my stuff into the Jeep and we'll still be at the beach in time for drinks. I'll leave the umbrella for next time.

I helped transfer her stuff to the Wrangler and noticed a couple of bottles of wine in her bag. "Oh, yes," I thought, "this is going to be a fine trip."

We cruised down the two-lane highway and sang along with the "Oldies but Goodies" station; in between songs we discussed yesterday's festival.

"With the help of Uncle Vince and Babe I did great; sold a dozen expensive gift baskets and several cases of high-priced wine *and* they've agreed to mind the gourmet shop while we're gone," Reenie said.

I asked her to tell me about the uncle she adored. I already knew Vincent Altieri was her father's youngest brother, a retired Navy chef, who came to the Charlotte area a few years back. He never had children and considers Reenie partly his; I was curious to know more.

"Uncle Vince is the black sheep in the family. I guess every family has one," she said as I negotiated a turn that took us out of town.

"He was way too young to enlist during World War II, but fiendishly followed the action abroad. He turned seventeen a couple of years after the war ended and asked his parents for permission to spend the summer in Europe. He told them he would pick up culinary skills to bring back

42

to the family's restaurant business and my grandparents agreed, thinking he might settle down after the trip.

"He headed overseas, and planned to take a train from Germany down to his father's family in Italy. He was to stop at various taverns and restaurants along the way and learn new ways of preparing meals," she said.

"But, he arrived in Hamburg, fell head over heels in love with an entertainer several years his senior, and never got any further. He wrote his parents that he had found 'my first true love,' and told them of his plans to marry her. He informed them that he was working as a chef's helper at the time, and would remain there until his love finished her engagement in Hamburg. Additionally, his parents were not to expect him back any time in the foreseeable future.

"No sooner did the family receive his letter before my father was dispensed—on a fast-boat to Europe—with instructions to bring back the wayward son," Reenie laughed,

"As it turned out, they needn't have worried. The singer, though mad about Vince, had made her own plans to leave her love after she learned his true age.

"She had no idea Vince was a minor until he confessed his true age. He was tall with dark good looks, a muscular build, and appeared to be more like twenty-four than seventeen. The woman also wanted to further her career and in the kindest way—I was told by Uncle Vince years later—encouraged him to return to his family, and then come back to her in a few years, when he was a little older, and the age difference wouldn't matter so much.

"Vince, of course, never returned. He joined the Navy when he got back and within a year fell in love with the first of many entertainers in New York City. But I think that first young love is the reason why he's never married.

"He once showed me her picture. It was old and faded from being in his wallet so long, but I could see she was a beauty."

Reenie's family very much disapprove of Babe, the trice divorced, former stripper, who has been Vincent's flame for the past ten years. Reenie and I found her charming and one of the funniest persons to be around. She kept her age a state secret but we guessed she was somewhere in her mid-sixties going on twenty. Babe loved the interchange with Reenie's customers and they in turn enjoyed her. Uncle Vincent, still a charmer, never lost his love of cooking and was an expert on food; so whenever the two of them took care of Reenie's gourmet shop, sales increased.

Reenie talked and miles flew by without my ever feeling tense while I drove through long stretches of twisting roads and small towns.

Shortly after eleven o'clock I suggested we stop for a break in Fayetteville at a small coffee shop that, in the midst of an old textile town, thrives against all odds. We often stop there to eat and decided coffee and an early lunch might be good. I was just pulling off the road when, out of the blue, Reenie turned to me, took me by the elbow, and said, "What is it you're not telling me?"

"I have no idea what you are talking about," I said and feigned surprise. It didn't fool her.

"Anna, this is Reenie—your best friend. I'm the one who cries with you, laughs with your, gets trashed with you, and with whom I share my inner most secrets. Do you honestly think I don't know when something's on your mind?

"The very fact that you are driving to the beach is a dead giveaway. First of all, you never, ever, drive on highways, not even on these little dinky ones. Second, there is something about you that wasn't there yesterday during the festival. So 'fess up."

I parked the jeep and gave her a long look. Without talking we got out and went inside and sat down in one of the back booths. We placed our orders for coffee with a handsome young man on duty that morning, and I pulled out my note from Christian and read it to Reenie.

She listened, and with her eyes dancing, looked at me and said, "You wanna tell me just what this is all about?"

Just then the young waiter brought the coffees enabling me to delay my story. Reenie told him we'd look at the menu and order later.

"I know we share almost everything, Reenie, and I feel guilty having kept this from you, but the whole thing seemed rather silly until the phone call last night."

She gave me a questioning look; I took a sip of hot coffee. Then I leaned back in the booth and told her how, on an impulse, I had sent Christian an email. Reenie listened and the time passed without either of us taking notice. I told her of the memories his note, and especially last night's phone call, had brought back; like a good friend she never interrupted.

When I stopped talking half an hour later she grabbed her handbag and pulled out money to cover the coffee and a large tip.

"Let's get out of here—we need to discuss this in detail. We'll head for the beach and not bother to eat now. There's enough stock at the cottage and in my bags to see us through lunch and we'll go to Charlie's Place for dinner tonight."

Then she gave me a significant look and said, "*I'll* drive the rest of the way—*you* talk."

We got back in the car, pulled out into the traffic, and I began to tell Reenie how I met Christian in school, fell in love, and finally left him knowing it would break my heart. Although she has known me a long time, and despite the fact that we have been through thick and thin together, there were still things she didn't know about me.

By the time we arrived at Idle-a-While, I was talked out. There were still parts of the story missing, but Reenie had gotten the basic facts of young and lost love and my newfound feeling of youth.

Chapter 9

We arrived at the DeNero cottage an hour later, and as Reenie opened the windows, I watched the noon breeze begin to play with the white muslin curtains. I unloaded the groceries, taking out several good bottles of white wine, a pound of grapes and some delicious looking foreign cheese. I smiled as I put it all in the refrigerator—it pays to have a best friend who owns a gourmet shop.

We lunched on cheese and crackers while we unpacked, and after turning down the beds, changed into shorts and tees. Then with gin and tonic drinks inside inconspicuous plastic mugs—alcohol was not allowed on the beach—we sauntered down to the ocean.

It was an absolutely glorious day, warm and breezy, with powder puff clouds sailing along the beach, empty except for a couple of lone fishermen and a woman painting a seascape.

We left our sandals at the bottom of the boardwalk and walked along the edge of the surf enjoying the cool water playing with our feet.

We didn't talk much—there was no need. Our friends would be astounded to see us both so quiet, but at the beach we often walked without conversation.

Reenie comes from a large family; Irish on her mother's side, Italian on her father's. They are warm and gregarious people and conversation is their breath of life. I, on the other hand, was an only and talkative child who, at times, was paid not to talk. But at the beach we often enjoy the quiet in each other's company.

We came back to the boardwalk an hour later and sat down on the bottom step with what was left of our drinks.

"So, what do you plan to do about it?" Reenie finally asked.

"I honestly don't know," I said, knowing she was referring to my re-acquaintance with Christian.

"It's not like a whole lot has happened, although he did sound *very* affectionate on the answering machine. But in all likelihood, he is probably still happily married."

"Somehow, I don't think so if what you told me is correct; I believe there's more to this," Reenie said.

"I assure you I quoted the phone message nearly word for word; I did, you recall, listen to it several times. You are just imagining things," I protested.

"Well, we'll let it rest for now," she said. "I'm hungry. Let's go change and head up to Charlie's. Paul and I discovered a new and absolutely fabulous dish on their menu when we were down a few weeks ago. They've hired a great jazz trio that plays week-nights until midnight, so dress up my friend," she said, and with a wink added, "and oh, yes, the group takes requests."

A shower and shampoo did wonders, and in high spirits, I decided to break in my long multicolored batik skirt. It was quite unlike anything else I owned and looked well with my black sleeveless silk blouse with the revealing neckline. I added silver loop earrings, my amber necklace and black high heel sandals. Then I threw the matching shawl around my shoulders and looked in the full-length mirror standing in a corner in the guestroom I like to call mine.

"For a middle-aged woman, you don't look bad," I assured myself and fluffed my hair. A month ago my hairdresser—while waving his hand at me—said, "Anna, darling, with your Carolina blue eyes and wheat-colored hair, you could look years, just *years* younger if you let me cut it in a shag." So of course I let him cut to his heart's delight. Most of us like to look younger and I still enjoy approving looks.

I turned away from the mirror and with melancholy thought back to all the times Robert and I argued over weight—more specifically my over-weight.

"When I'm gone you'll probably get reed thin," he threw at me during one of my many fat periods. I cried during our early marriage, yelled back for years, and finally ignored his remarks. I never gave up trying to stay in shape, but it remained a struggle.

I hit thin times now and then and had clothes ranging from size eight to sixteen stored in my closets. The fact that I bought classic styles in basic colors—"boring," my children assured me—allowed me to wear them again whenever I dropped or gained ten or twenty pounds.

Now, at five foot five, I had the size I always wanted with an hour glass shape I developed at age twelve. It had happened without any credit to me.

Despite his two earlier heart attacks, Robert's death still came as a shock. I was accident-prone and fully expected him to outlive me. I was not prepared for his death and grieved a long time.

Immediately after he died I functioned all right. Robert had said he wanted his ashes cast into the ocean, so I talked to the people at the funeral home and told them he was to be cremated. I wrote his obituary, arranged for a memorial service and a dinner afterwards, and managed sleeping arrangements for the family that came for the funeral—all on "auto pilot."

The first several days I hardly ate - I drank gallons of coffee. My ever-loving Becca stayed with me right after Robert died and made me sip soups she made.

Then immediately after the funeral I ate non-stop for a week consuming huge amounts of leftovers from all the dishes my caring neighbors—in true Southern style—brought to our house for the family to share. Sweet potato casserole buried in marshmallows, coconut cake so loaded with saturated fat my doctor would have fainted, creamed potatoes swimming in pure butter, green beans cooked in tons of ham fat, and most everything else left in the refrigerator.

After that I became violently ill and threw up for days. My system, although fond of sweets, no longer tolerated this sort of "pig eating," a phrase Robert and I picked up from our Danish relatives meaning continued eating long after one is full.

About this time Reenie took charge and took me to the beach for what she called "restoration of body and soul."

The days of up-chucking removed most of what I had engorged but it also killed my appetite. I used to joke that I would know it was time for lunch on the way to my own funeral and loved a good lunch and dinner with wine, rolls, and dessert. Resisting over-eating had been a struggle since the day I had Matthew. Now, I occasionally forgot meals.

So here I was a couple of years later keeping my weight down with little effort. Oh, I worked out most mornings and took Tessa for runs. I also ate a lot of salads and few heavy meals, but it was not a sacrifice anymore; I just lacked interest. Perhaps it had something to do with the fact that Robert had been such an excellent cook. I've no idea. I only wished this disinterest in food had arrived years earlier.

Chapter 10

"Are you taking a nap or what?" Reenie called from downstairs. "I've just been on the phone with Paul who's having a great time in Texas. Let's you and I go out and do likewise!"

Going out with Reenie is always fun. At five foot two with a figure to die for, she attracts men wherever she goes. She still has jet-black hair and lavender eyes that turn most men to putty. She likes to flirt, but that's as far as it goes. She has been propositioned many times, often in my company, but she laughs the men away in a way that doesn't make them feel like fools.

Tonight would be no different. Reenie wore a white jump suit with gold trim that showed off her figure and revealed just enough cleavage of her amble bosom to keep men staring. Her only jewelry was her wide wedding band with its large square-cut diamond. She never wore high heels and had on thin-strapped gold sandals and, as always, looked exquisite.

"Let's get the show on the road, sister," she said, and as we went outside I noticed she had removed the canvas top from the jeep.

"I thank my hairdresser for giving me a cut that'll survive a trip in the open sea air with you at the wheel," I laughed.

It turned out to be a great evening. Dinner was sumptuous and the wines delicious. The jazz trio was marvelous and played a great version of "But Not for Me," at our request. Reenie and I discovered early in our friendship that we both loved this song.

The music filled the room with a sensual atmosphere and

although we declined several offers to dance, we did flirt shamelessly with Marines young enough to be our sons.

Camp Lejeune is just a few miles away and on most evenings the area restaurants and bars serve military men not on duty. With only a few women at Charlie's that evening, we received a lot of attention and both had a good time.

We arrived back at the cottage shortly after midnight and quickly changed into our "girls' night" night-gear—thin sweat pants and men's tee shirts. Since we were not ready for sleep, Reenie made coffee and poured us each a brandy. We opened the doors to the deck to let in the sea breeze, walked out to the deck, and flopped down in the couch facing the ocean. After a few moments Reenie took a sip of her drink, looked me square in the face and said,

"Now, to quote a famous radio personality, tell me: 'the rest of the story', the part about meeting Robert, getting married, getting over loving Christian—if indeed you ever did—and how you ended up sitting in Idle-a-While all perplexed."

"I'm not perplexed," I said recognizing the defensive tone in my voice.

Reenie gave me one of those piecing looks that turn her eyes nearly purple.

"On an impulse *you,* who like to plan things months in advance, come with me to the beach at the drop of a hat. You even *offer* to drive down here. You step out tonight in an outfit that makes you look ten years younger; an outfit you never would have bought, let alone worn, a couple of months ago. You even flirted with the young Marines. Then you try to tell *me,* Reenie, that you're not perplexed. Give me a break," she sighed.

I tried to protest.

"I did not flirt much. After all, they were just boys," I said piously.

"Boys, my ass! They were full grown Marines and they were not blind either," she added.

We both laughed. For years, one of our private jokes is a promise to find a couple of "BBBMs"—our code word for big, blind, and buff Marines—and bring them back to Idle-a-

51

While. The Marines had to be big and in great shape of course; otherwise what would be the point? But we also figured they would have to be blind so as not to notice that we were old enough to be their mothers.

Reenie became serious and said, "Just for the record, you've got all the right in the world to be confused. You got your life together after Robert's death and have found a comfortable groove. In other words, your life's ok—even if it's a little dull sometimes.

"Anna, let's face it. You are intrigued more than anything else. Add to this the fact that your hormones, long time on ice, are beginning to move. Go with it lady. What's to lose?"

I looked at the ocean and was soothed by the steady sound of the waves. I had grown up minutes from a beach and spent all my summers in and around water; the nearness always gave me comfort. I knew I had to face whatever it was Christian's call had brought to mind.

So I began to tell her about my marriage, my children, and early life in the States realizing I'd never told her much about this. There was always so much current stuff that needed discussing, plus the fact that there were times and places in my life I wasn't sure I wanted to visit again.

We made another pot of coffee, poured another brandy and decided to go back out on the deck. It was an unusually balmy night without any invading sounds, save for the murmur of the ocean. The weekenders left Sunday afternoon and since it was still early June, the vacationers had yet to arrive.

I went in to the living room and picked up blankets from the cedar chest and, wrapped in throws, we settled down in comfortable chaise lounges. I talked, Reenie listened, and by the time I looked out over the water, the sun had begun its slow rise looking like a birthing star coming from the deep waters. It was going to be another glorious Carolina day.

Chapter 11

Although wrapped in warm blankets, we suddenly realized it was cold.

"There is absolutely no point going to bed this late and I'm famished," Reenie announced and got up from her chair.

This early hour at the beach means only one thing—breakfast at the "Mourning Dive," a place that's a nightmare for anyone on a diet, planning to live to a ripe old age, or trying to heed doctor's orders to eat right. But, oh, it serves the tastiest French toast and Canadian bacon you ever wanted to put in your mouth.

Leo, who owns the place, is a master short-order cook and makes the best coffee on the island. When there you can count on getting an accurate weather forecast, a couple of raunchy jokes, and all the local news not fit to print.

The name of the place is Leo's idea of a little joke. It's the only place on the island opening up at four in the morning in time for the fishermen to get a bite before the shrimp boats head out. Leo comes in around three thirty and fires up the grill and around nine thirty, after the crowd thins out, he quits for the day.

He doesn't have to work. Like many in this area, he retired from the Marines and invested his money well. But Leo loves to cook and talk, and at seventy plus this life-long bachelor thoroughly enjoys making passes at any women who walk into his place. He worships Reenie and shamelessly flirts with her whenever he has the chance.

So with Leo's place as our destination, we threw on jeans and sweatshirts and hopped in the Jeep.

We arrived at Leo's, located at the far end of the island, but instead of Leo behind the counter, we found a handsome young man in his mid-twenties, turning over French toast and bacon.

"Looking for Uncle Leo?" he asked when he saw our puzzled looks. He flashed us a winsome smile and added, "He's gone to Raleigh for the day so I'm holding down the fort this morning."

He poured us each a mug of scalding hot coffee and took a long look at Reenie, who even at five in the morning, and without any sleep, still looks good. I do not weather lack of sleep as well, so I did not take offense when he only gave me a passing glance.

"I'm Leonard, and you must be 'Dolce.' Grandpa's told me all about you. He's mad about you, you know, and says he can't wait, as he puts it, till he 'has his way with you.'" Leonard grinned, showing off a row of perfect teeth.

Leo's knowledge of Italian is limited, but he saw Fellini's "La Dolce Vita" back in the 60's while visiting New York City and since then associates the title with anyone Italian, sexy and vivacious. In this case, my best friend qualifies.

"Neither Maureen nor Reenie suits you; you're Dolce to me," he would drawl in his charming southern accent and open his arms in hopes of receiving a hug.

"I've told your uncle I'll let him have his way as soon as you-know-what freezes over," Reenie laughed. They had joked about this for years.

A couple of fishermen came in so we gave the young man our order, settled down in a booth near the window and inhaled our coffee.

The kid was as good as his uncle when it came to making coffee—and not bad to look at either. I stole another look at his firm butt as he turned back to the grill. Reenie was right; I had been on ice too long.

We left the diner after breakfast and briefly considered a walk along the beach, but Reenie declared that after three slices of French toast, bacon, orange juice, and coffee, she was pooped and ready for sleep.

"You can crash in your bed or stay out on the deck if you like, but I'm headed for the king size upstairs to catch some shut-eye," she yawned.

It was nearly six, and as I looked out across the ocean I saw the sun reflect on the rippling waves. The sight added to my well-being, and I turned and gave Reenie a hug and thanked her for taking me along on this trip.

"I feel I've begun to make some needed internal adjustments," I said, and told her I planned to stay up a little longer.

She kissed my cheek and drifted upstairs to the spacious bedroom she and Paul shared. It faces the ocean and I knew the sound of the breakers would put her to sleep before long; it always did.

Chapter 12

A few pelicans were hunting their morning meal and from the deck I watched them circle the water before diving into the ocean and expertly bring up small fish. While watching the birds, I decided I wanted a cup of tea and some fruit and went in and put on the teakettle. I remembered I had yet to take my morning meds and quietly went up to my room. Passing Reenie and Paul's bedroom, I heard her soft even breathing and knew she would be asleep for a while.

As I put away the pill bottles, my eyes fell on my ThinkPad and suddenly an idea hit me. Now would be a good time to write Christian and tell him how happy I was to have heard from him.

I picked up the computer and got down to the kitchen just in time to remove the kettle from the stove before the whistling penetrated the cottage and woke up Reenie.

I fixed myself a tray with a pot of Earl Gray tea, an apple from the refrigerator, a mug, and a linen napkin. Then I picked up the afghan from last night and put it on the chaise lounge, slightly damp from the morning dew.

After pouring the steaming tea into the mug, thinking about what to write, I wandered to the end of the front deck. A rattling noise from up the street reminded me—like others who regularly vacation at the beach—that the garbage truck was on its way. They always run Mondays and Thursdays and start early.

From the north side of the beach the sound of hammers began their steady rhythm. At the beaches, someone is always putting up a new cottage or repairing an established place; it's no different on Topsail Island.

Down from the south side of the cottage, a couple of fishermen sat beside their coolers patiently waiting for a fish to bite; the fish most always did. But if the morning turned out to be fruitless, that was all right too. Like myself, they just enjoyed being by the ocean.

Suddenly a bell sounded from the Catholic Church located a mile from the cottage. Early daily Mass at Our Lady Star of the Sea, I thought, and said a prayer.

I brought out my computer, sat it down in front of me, and pulled out the well-handled email from Christian. As I prepared to write, something about it bothered me and I realized the address at the top was different from the one I had used in my first email to him. It occurred to me that Christian's delay in responding to my first letter might have something to do with the different address and figured, in time, I would find out. Then I opened the computer and began typing.

I wrote about the memories his voice had brought back; the places and events we shared during our last year in school, and how I treasured them for years. It was a sentimental letter influenced, I am sure, by my long talk with Reenie during the night, and the loneliness I had been unwilling to face.

After saving the letter, I closed the laptop and put it on Paul's desk next to his computer. I took the tray back to the kitchen—realized I was dead tired—and dragged myself upstairs. Without much ado, I dropped my clothes on the floor, fell into bed and was asleep before I even thought to close the blinds.

Chapter 13

I awoke to the aroma of baked bread swirling around my face waking up my taste buds, and realized Reenie had been at it again. A look at my travel clock told me it was shortly after one in the afternoon and as I jumped out of bed I yelled down to Reenie I was up and alive.

"It's about time you get that lovely body of yours out of bed and in gear," she hollered.

"I've already been to Luther's to pick up fresh crab legs and shrimp, *and* I just finished baking two loaves of bread."

Needless to say, Reenie doesn't need much sleep before she's back in high gear. It was eighty degrees outside and she was baking bread! Thank goodness for air conditioning.

"Why don't you grab a bathing suit and a towel and let's hit the waves for a quick swim?" she called on her way up to see me.

She dropped down on my bed and said, "I see your computer moved from your bedroom to Paul's desk. Might that perhaps mean some creative writing was done while I slept?"

She laughed and I blushed. At my age I don't blush often, but the thoughts of my letter and the memories it brought back made my color rise, so I quickly agreed to a dip in the ocean.

We met on the deck and, with towels slung over our shoulders, proceeded to the ocean. The tide was on its way out and the water calm, but cold. After daring each other, we dove into the sea. I came up shuddering from the impact of the icy water, but soon my body adjusted to its temperature and I swam back and forth enjoying the ocean until Reenie called for me to come out. She declared she was hungry and I wondered how she kept her figure until I remembered her daily regimen. At home she lives on salads, fish and a lot of fresh vegetables and she is a stickler for a daily work out in her home gym.

Paul still has his firm military figure and wants no fat on his wife. In all other ways, Reenie maneuvers his life and runs circles around him, but when it comes to weight, Paul stands his ground. Reenie lives the phrase "It's in to be thin," and only on occasion deviates from her strict program.

I grabbed my towel and dried off as we walked back to the cottage where I put on one of the many terry robes Reenie keeps in her guestrooms. I too felt hungry and went down to the kitchen for a long delayed lunch.

I found Reenie buzzing around. Next to Swedish silverware, she had placed pottery plates brought home from Italy, linen napkins from Ireland, and glasses from Italy.

"Just because it's a beach house doesn't mean I don't want nice things around," she always said. A bouquet of early summer roses stood in a clear crystal vase in the center of the table, a sign she had visited the florist just around the corner from Luther's Fish Market.

We lunched on thick slices of homemade bread, a variety of the cheeses Reenie brought from her shop, some green grapes, and a fine bottle of Chardonnay—a real feast.

"So, you gonna tell me who you wrote and sent a letter while I slept—as if I couldn't guess," she smiled and popped a grape into her mouth.

I already felt mellow from the first glass of wine. On an empty stomach and without a good night's sleep, it made me a little lightheaded.

"I haven't sent it yet," I said sheepishly. "I didn't want to tie up your phone line in case Paul called and thought I would check with you before I connected to his computer."

"No, you didn't," she grinned. "First of all, and despite not being a 'tecky,' you know enough about computers to know you do *not* need to hook up to Paul's machine in order to send an email. All you need is a phone outlet. Second, you know perfectly well Paul and I don't object to you using the computer or the phone line. Finally, Paul always calls me on my mobile to make sure he always reaches me. Besides, if Paul knew you were using his computer to contact an old love he'd be delighted. He's threatened to introduce you to his cousin Vinnie if you don't get serious about someone soon."

I started to laugh.

"No, you don't understand—he really *has* a cousin Vinnie!" she said; we both laughed and almost choked on wine.

We have watched the movie, "My Cousin Vinnie," together a number of times and often mimic the lines of Morisa Tomei.

"Anyway," Reenie continued after composing herself, "I'm not going to let Paul's cousin anywhere near you. I swear he's part of the Mob and he smokes and drinks entirely too much. Besides, he's not your type."

I started to ask her what my type would be when she sat up straight, wagged her finger at me and said: "Now tell me, just why you didn't send it."

I cut a wedge of Brie and placed it on a small piece of Reenie's homemade bread and thought for a moment. I wasn't entirely sure.

"I think I was too tired to think straight and decided I better sleep on it," I said, hoping this would satisfy her. It did. Reenie agreed it'd been a good idea to hold off for a couple of hours to make sure I said the right things. She didn't ask me what I wrote Christian, just continued looking at me.

"*Only* because you care and are my very best friend, and *only* because I'm not exactly sure what I'm doing, I'll read you the letter."

I wiped off my mouth, brought over the laptop and placed it on the kitchen table. I assured her the letter was a "little personal" but not confidential.

I turned on the machine and brought up the letter.

"My dear friend," I began, translating from Danish to English. "I can't begin to tell you just how delighted I was to receive your email and later your phone call. I'm sorry I wasn't home to take the call, but in a way it was probably as well. Unlike e-mail, a phone call is more personal, and I'm not sure I'm ready for that just yet.

"Your call transferred me back in time, first to a happy period where you were my everything; and later to the time when you broke my heart," I read out loud.

I went on to recall things from our days of dating—events and times that had been special to me. I told him how I met and married Robert, but gave no details about our roller-coaster marriage, only that we were married for many good and wonderful years until Robert's death several years ago. I said I didn't want to interfere in his life and hoped that he and his wife and his children were all doing fine. I closed by wishing him well and told him I looked forward to his next email.

I looked up at Reenie and told her I'd chosen to ignore the reference to "for the time being wife," thinking it was just a way with words.

"It's not," Reenie disagreed. "It sounds to me like he's getting ready for yet another divorce. Not exactly the staying-with-it type is he; but you never know the circumstances," she added

"You're such a romantic," I told her. She disagreed, poured me another glass of wine, and gave me a nudge.

"So send it, OK?"

I felt reluctant and a little afraid of diving into the unknown, but after a few moments' hesitation, and another sip of wine, I made up my mind.

"What the heck; it's not as if I'm asking him to marry me. I'm just trying to re-establish an old friendship. Right?"

Reenie laughed and before I could change my mind, she connected the computer to the phone outlet. "Anytime you are ready, my friend."

As before, I took a deep breath and hit "send." It was done. Fate would have to handle the rest.

Then we emptied our glasses, and after putting on shorts and cotton shirts, went for a much-needed walk.

We arrived back about four that afternoon and agreed we needed showers in the worst way. Before going upstairs Reenie stopped me and said, "Since we're not going out, let's put on our 'gaudy-awful' suits."

She knew I brought it. Among the other essentials in my suitcase was my "gaudy-awful" suit.

Reenie bought us each one several years ago while on a trip to Mexico. They were lightweight sweat-suits, adorned with multicolored fruits, sequences, beads and tassels and featured a picture of Elvis on the back of the sweatshirt. Mine was purple; Reenie's was a tacky aqua. They looked awful.

"That's the whole point," Reenie said when she gave it to me, assuring me her purchase put food on the table for the vendor's family for at least a week. "And since the purchase was made for a good cause," she said, "we should wear them in that spirit."

By now the suits were worn and faded, and though we wouldn't be caught dead wearing them in public, we loved them on our girls' nights.

"I picked up a couple of movies for tonight while I was out shopping," Reenie yelled on her way to her shower. I didn't have to guess what at least one of them was; we're die-hard Sean Connery fans.

"The Medicine Man?" I guessed; it was one of our favorites. The movie with Connery as a doctor working deep in the jungle was about as sexy as we thought a man could get.

"No, I got 'Goldfinger,' so we can look at his younger— but equally sexy body," she shouted just before I heard the water come on.

She had also got "The Witches of Eastwick," another favorite. Jack Nicolson's characterization of the "horny little devil" aka Darryl Van Horne, always sent us into ripples of laughter.

After her shower Reenie prepared her famous crab legs while I set the table. We gorged on crabmeat and convinced each other not to worry about calories since the only other thing we ate was a tossed salad. We discreetly discounted the butter for the fish and bottle of wine we shared.

After diner Reenie brewed some Colombian coffee. I filled the dishwasher and by eight o'clock we settled down for four straight hours of movies.

We planned on shopping in Wilmington the next day so

when the second movie ended, shortly after midnight, we decided to hit the sack.

After I got in bed, I tossed and turned worrying about Christian's reaction to my email. Would he think it was too personal; had I misinterpreted his message? Eventually the previous late night, the swim and long walk—not to mention the bottle of wine with dinner—took its toll and I drifted to sleep to the steady sound of the ocean as the tide rolled in.

Chapter 14

With Reenie at the wheel, we were headed for Wilmington the next morning, when she suddenly turned toward me and said, "I've never met this Christian; I know very little about him, and you've never even shown me his picture. Just the same, I'm beginning to think he might be good for you."

"Get your eyes back on the road, you are driving my car," I ordered.

"You are too funny Reenie. You'll not let me date cousin Vinnie, yet you are ready to marry me off to a man you admittedly know nothing about," I chuckled.

"Not so fast, sister," she said poking a finger at me— never taking her eyes off the road. I knew, without looking, she was giving me that piercing look again.

"From what little I do know about him, he's probably the last man I'd want you to marry. His four marriages don't exactly serve as great recommendations, and since he's a physician, he's most likely very arrogant," she concluded.

I turned my head and caught her impish smile.

"However, at the moment we're *not* planning a wedding and he *has* helped bring out the old, yet new, you. For that I'm most grateful."

I didn't bother to tell her that marriage—at the moment, or any time soon—was the furthest thing from my mind. In the mood Reenie was in, there was no point arguing.

I noticed a man up ahead with a "slow down" sign and watched Reenie quickly maneuver the jeep through the roadwork waving to the crewmembers standing idly by observing the passing cars.

Without batting an eye, she changed the subject and said, "Enough about your old flame; let's hit Wilmington and buy everything in sight. I have a list a mile long and intend to come back with at least half of it. Besides, I'll be starved by noon so we better start planning lunch," she added and hit the accelerator.

We had a great day in what has long been one of my favorite places. A college town, not yet ruined by tourists, Wilmington is filled with wonderful small coffee shops, specialty stores, and a lot of art galleries. We headed for one of the latter in search of a painting for a downstairs room Reenie was planning to convert into an office for Paul. She said she hoped to entice her husband to "really retire and fish, write, and enjoy life at the beach in our 'reclining' years," as she refers to life after fifty. By converting a room to an office, she figured she could breach the gap between his work and retirement. She is, if nothing else, an optimist.

We shopped for nearly two hours and were pleased with our finds. Reenie's haul included new linen for two of the bedrooms, several canvas pillows for the porch chairs, a new set of pottery mugs, a silk blouse and three pairs of sandals. She also bought an original watercolor by a well-known local artist. It depicted a ship in a raging storm and cost more than the average family of four spends on groceries in a month.

In addition to the salt water taffy I promised Becca and a few things for her children, I also found a pair of pewter candlesticks for my den and a small limited print of a tree toad hanging from a green leaf with the most darling grin on his face. It was not the sort of painting I would have bought a couple of months ago, but this morning the impish little frog "spoke" to me and asked that I take him home. I knew it would look charming in the guest bathroom I was in the process of doing over and the price fit my budget. After putting up the top of the jeep and locking our packages and paintings away in the back of the car, we set off for Elijah's.

This old eatery sits right by the water's edge and offers diners a clear view of the bridge spanning the Cape Fear River. From almost any table you can see the Coast Guard icebreaker—when it's in port -and the Henrietta, a small steamship that takes tourists for trips around the harbor. Since the weather was pleasant, we chose to eat on the veranda and both ordered lobster and spinach quiche, the special of the day, with glasses of iced tea. It was a quiet day without many tourists, and we savored the well-prepared meal while observing the many fishing boats and a single yacht sailing down the languid river. Our conversation was easy and carried us through our meal and coffee centering on our purchases and Reenie's remodeling plans.

On our way back to the island Reenie stopped along the roadside at one of the many fruit and vegetable stands and bought vegetables and a basket of fresh strawberries.

"I'm fixing chef salads tonight," she said as we pulled into the driveway at Idle-a-While. "We'll throw in marinated shrimp, add a slice of my bread and call it a meal, what do you say? Then we can pig out on strawberries while we watch Hercules Poirot on the tube later on."

I told her it sounded like a splendid idea and as soon as we came home I rinsed and hulled the berries while Reenie prepared the green salads.

"Soon as I'm done here, I'm gonna change. Then we'll have a fat girl margarita and wait with dinner until later," she said and began peeling shrimp for our dinner. I agreed and went upstairs to put away my purchases.

I came down to the kitchen a few minutes later and after setting the table looked around the cottage for something to do. I was about to offer to empty the dishwasher, when Reenie's mobile phone rang. It was Paul from Texas wanting to know how we were doing. I left the two of them to talk and went over to Paul's desk where my laptop still sat connected to the phone plug.

I thought this might be a good time to check emails from both home and work. By checking now, I could delete junk mail before I returned to work tomorrow afternoon.

I brought up my email and saw I had twelve messages. Most were from my grandchildren containing jokes, I suspected. There was also an Eddie Bauer ad for their summer sale and a note from Barnes and Noble informing me that a book I had sent for was on back-order. Then, at the bottom, I saw one that read: "cpr, subject: hello from France," followed by time and date.

I immediately recognized it as the address I used when I sent Christian's letter the day before. Figuring the time difference between continents, he would have sent the letter long after midnight, his time. It had come in on my machine much earlier but since I hadn't expected a reply that quick, I never turned on my computer until now.

I glanced over at Reenie, saw she was still on the phone, clicked on the note and, with butterflies invading my stomach, read Christian's letter.

"Dearest Anna," it began, "how wonderful to come back this evening and find your e-mail—a great end to an otherwise stressful day.

"First of all, let me say that I am sorry to hear about the death of your husband. It must have been difficult for you. Losing someone close is always hard.

"Just for the record, I am writing you in English; not because your Danish is not good, it is, but I sense you find it easier to write and read in your adopted language.

"Anna, I can't begin to tell you how moved I was by your letter. I have—over the years—also thought back to all the wonderful times we shared before you left; years etched in my mind. At the moment I'm in my hotel room with a glass of good French wine next to my computer and want to give you information about myself—things you might like to know.

"1. I was named chancellor at our local medical university earlier this year and took over the position several months ago. I had decided to give up surgery and was just thinking about retiring when this great opportunity came along. The conference I am at is for the heads of medical universities and is proving very informative.

2. Shortly before I left for this trip, my wife and I agreed to file for divorce. It saddens me, but we have grown apart. She travels a lot and for several years we haven't spent much time together.

3. I know what you look like! After I read your letter, I looked up the web site for your Chamber of Commerce and on the last page found mug shots of the entire staff, including part-time employees. There you were—bright blue eyes, lovely smile, and your beautiful face—looking at me. Anna, you haven't changed—please come back to me! Just kidding. Seriously, you really look just like you did at eighteen, at least to me. I hope we can meet before too long. There is a good chance I might attend a conference at Duke University in North Carolina later this year; I believe that is located just up the road from where you live. Perhaps you will let me come and visit?

4. Finally, I thought it only fair—since I now know what you look like—to let you know how your old love has weathered over the years. So I scanned my picture from the conference program and added it as an attachment. Hope I don't disappoint you. I normally wear contacts, but for professional shots, I usually wear my glasses.

"I must turn in now as I have to be at a seven o'clock working breakfast followed by a round-table session at nine.

"Please write back soon. It is so wonderful to have you back in my life again." He signed the letter, "Much love from your once 'one and only,' Christian."

I clicked on the attachment and within seconds his face appeared on the screen. He looked older, with gray hair mingling with the blond locks I remembered from school; only the glasses were new. Otherwise, it was the same old Christian with his enticing smile staring at me. Old feelings rushed to the surface.

Reenie had finished her conversation with Paul and now stood right behind me. She tapped my shoulder and said, "Excuse me for reading over your shoulder, but he did write in English; besides by now I feel like I'm part of the story."

I assured her I didn't mind; in fact, I was glad she'd seen it.

"Who knows, maybe this guy will turn out to be all right," she said. "You always told me you loved Robert very much but that your life together was like a roller coaster ride at times. Maybe Christian will be able to provide you something different. He certainly seems interested and it appears that neither of you will be attached to anyone much longer."

I agreed there certainly appeared to be interest on both sides of the Atlantic; but she made it sound too simple.

Reenie's reference to Robert and our marriage bothered me. She was right, of course. I had often said my marriage, at times, moved in waves. But she didn't know Robert's background; knew nothing of the letters I had found, or what my trip to Ireland brought to light.

I asked if she was ready for yet another long night and she immediately answered yes. She knew I had more to tell.

"Why don't you call Becca and ask her to keep Tessa one more day. Then call or email the Chamber and tell them you'll miss the board meeting tomorrow afternoon since it's not essential you attend. That means we can stay another day and not drive back until early Thursday."

I took her up on both ideas. Becca was delighted I was having a good time and told me not to worry. She had checked on the house that morning and said everything was fine and that her children loved having Tessa around. I thanked her and called work and left my message on my boss's answering machine. We finally sat down to our shrimp dinner and chatted about our day in Wilmington. We laughed about the silly—and so unlike me—frog picture I bought and discussed, yet again, her changing one of the rooms into an office for Paul and other renovations she was considering.

The conversation also covered the handsome features of young Leonard from the "Mourning Dive" and when I pointed out I thought he had an specially handsome derriere Reenie gave me a resounding "Yes, sir." We both avoided any reference to Christian and Robert knowing we would save it for later.

After dinner Reenie ground fresh beans for our coffee and set out two of her new mugs. It had turned cool late in the afternoon and, as the evening light faded, the cottage felt chilly so Reenie lit the gas logs in the living room. She poured our coffee and we sat down, mugs in hand, and I began telling her about Robert, starting with the time I found his old letters on a day planned for cleaning up old files.

I had carried this story with me for some time and, although Reenie and I had been close since shortly after we met, I had never thought it right to share Robert's early life in Ireland with her or anyone else. Now, however, having told Reenie about Christian, it seemed only fair to tell her Robert's story. We sat in opposite ends of the soft sofa and I began.

I told her how finding the old letters had led to my trip back to Robert's birthplace and my discovery of the events that took place long ago in a small village on the western coast of Ireland.

PART TWO

Robert - The Leprechaun

Chapter 1

"Ok girl, time to get going on preps for that room you plan to convert, and—no stalling anymore," I spoke out loud to myself.

It was a warm Saturday morning in October, the year Robert died, and I had gotten out of bed early to begin the job. As I looked outside, however, I felt the fall colors calling me to come join them. Like sailplanes, the leaves fluttered in the slight breeze just before they reached the ground and became part of an Autumn-colored quilt on the lawn.

I was tempted to go outside, but resisted the urge remembering the promise I made myself the day before. I planned to begin cleaning out Robert's personal papers, sort through his business files in his office, and box and store what was important. It was my intent to convert this space into a second guestroom.

The next day I was going with friends to the mountains to visit the Arbor Lanes Winery just east of where North Carolina meets the Tennessee State line. It is known for its smooth Merlot and crisp Chardonnay and I planned to stock up on these *and* enjoy a meal at the vineyard's famous restaurant. Andre, the French chef—the winery has managed to keep him for years despite constant offers from surrounding eateries—prepares some of the most mouth-watering meals; simple fare with exquisite taste.

71

In order to get the paper work accomplished that weekend, I needed to get it done Saturday, so I turned away from the tempting deck, showered, had an English muffin, a cup of coffee, and went to work.

After a couple of hours of sorting files and discarding papers, I came across an ancient looking accordion file at the back of a bottom drawer. It was well worn and looked as if it hadn't been handled for years.

It was nearly ten thirty so I decided to take a break and was putting back the file when I noticed a piece of copy paper sticking out the back with a typed title at the top of the page. I pulled it out and felt a smile tuck at the corners of my mouth. It was a story entitled "Beach Siesta," and had been one of the term papers Robert wrote the year he decided to take a course in Creating Writing at the University of North Carolina in Charlotte.

As with everything Robert undertook, he worked tenaciously on class projects and, to no one's surprise, received an A. He declared that "for an engineer, that is not too shabby," and let me read a couple of his papers.

I had enjoyed his writings and thought I owed it to myself to take it outside and read while I enjoyed a cup of tea on the deck; deep in my heart I knew I was just hunting for an excuse not to be inside. The room with the file cabinets felt stuffy, and the chairs on the deck beckoned. So, without much of a fight, I gave in and went and settled down with my mug and the file and began pulling out Robert's college papers.

As I read Beach Siesta, I broke into a smile. It was a story based on the first fishing adventure Robert made with our grandson, David, the summer he turned four. They had gone fishing early one morning for "Big Blue," the name Robert used for the bluefish that favors the Carolina beaches, and the two of them came back a couple of hours later, wet from top to toe, without any fish, but laughing over "the one we almost caught." David stood dripping on the floor beaming from ear to ear as Robert bragged about his heroic grandson telling everyone how "David came so close to bringing home dinner." It was one of Robert's endearing traits that he always made children feel proud.

I put down Beach Siesta and reached for another paper and saw, stuck between the college notes, a small group of letters and one faded envelope with stamps from Ireland but no return address. Judging by the brittle rubber band around the small bundle, the letters must have been there for years. The fact that Robert had gone to the trouble of putting them in such an unlikely place made me curious.

I was suddenly distracted by the screech from a Mockingbird in the yard just below me. The bird, known for its clown-like behavior, performed a couple of loops and then, without warning, flew down over the lawn and dive-bombed Tessa who lay quietly on the grass watching the leaves fall. The dog jumped and began to bark, unsure what happened. I laughed and called her up on the deck, gave her a hug, and assured her everything was all right. After a few minutes she flopped down at my feet and almost immediately went to sleep.

I settled back in the chair and picked up the letters and as I removed the rubber band it fell apart. I inspected the envelope, addressed to Robert, and took out two fragile sheets of airmail paper. From the date I saw it was written in the middle of September but the year was unclear.

In a flourishing script, Cecilia, Robert's mother, asked about her son's health, his schooling, and how he was getting along with her sister, Lucy, and her family. She told him his father had hired someone new to work in his shop and that the youngest twins had started school. The children all missed him and she too expressed her sadness at his leaving.

At the end of the letter she told him Mary was going to have Sean's baby and assured Robert that everyone was being kind to his older sister. She knew they had been close and told him not to worry about her; they would all take care of both her and the baby.

I pulled out the second letter and noted the handwriting was the same. Folded inside the letter was a small, faded picture of a baby, dressed in a long gown, and held by a priest. From the content of Cecilia's letter I figured this must be Mary's baby taken the day of his Christening, but the picture was worn and I couldn't make out much of the baby's face. I flipped over the photograph and barely made out the writing: "Father O'Neill with baby Francis."

In this letter Cecilia also told Robert that the arthritis in her hands was getting worse and that soon she might not be able to write. She closed her letter by wishing him God's Speed.

Looking down at the letters on the table next to me, I wondered why Robert had kept them tucked away. That he failed to show them to me might be because they dated back years before we met. The fact that he had kept them at all, *and* kept them hidden, was more of a puzzle.

I picked up the third letter and saw it was signed Nora Sheehan. It was dated sometime after Cecilia's last letter. She told him that his mother's hands were getting worse and that she was helping her sister out with the younger children. She mentioned that Mary and the baby were doing well and not to worry about them. Nora signed her letter, 'your devoted aunt.'

After pondering this for a few moments I picked up the last letter. It was not dated and was written in yet another hand.

It turned out to be from Mary and read: "Dearest Robert. It was kind of you to send the hundred dollars to me. I know you must have worked hard in Uncle Mario's place to earn this. But the money I don't need. I am doing fine and so is the baby. Mam and dad are good to both of us and Aunt Nora is much comfort and strength to me. Please take back the money and use it for your schooling. Make something of yourself and please don't come back. I keep you in my prayers and ask you to keep us in yours; your devoted sister Mary."

I had sensed that Robert was close to Mary while growing up; they were, after all, the only "American children" in the Thornberg family. I thought it was sweet he had sent his sister money. The part I couldn't understand was why she asked him not to come home. The feeling gnawed at me and made me want to go to Robert's home town, find someone from his family, and learn about his early years.

We never had much contact with his family and a few Christmas cards during our early years of marriage were all we ever exchanged. Robert didn't talk much about his relatives in Ireland, and he never expressed any desire to go back to visit. He did finally go home to attend his father's funeral. I was pregnant with Becca and my doctor strongly advised me not to travel. I knew Robert had brothers and sisters, but from the bits of news I had gathered, the older ones had moved away from the homestead leaving his mother and youngest children behind. After his mother died, our connection with Ireland pretty much ended.

The bells from the nearby Methodist church began to chime and I realized it must be noon. I carefully placed the letters back in the file, woke up Tessa, and went inside to fix lunch. After putting down the file on the kitchen counter I made myself a ham and cheese sandwich and poured a beer into a mug. I filled Tessa's dish with fresh water and with her tail wagging, she slurped down the water sloshing it all over the floor. Normally I would have cleaned it up, but I was preoccupied with the letters I just read.

With a canine's instinct, Tessa turned and looked at me. She sensed I was troubled and in her own way wanted to help. I gave her a hug and decided to quit cleaning and instead go outside on the deck and enjoy what might be the last of the really good autumn weather.

After I ate my lunch I felt the beer lull me to sleep and decided that a snooze on the deck might not be a bad idea. I went into my bedroom, picked up a throw and with Tessa at my feet settled down for a nap on the deck.

Chapter 2

An hour later I woke up to the sudden ringing of a phone and reached for my portable. Realizing I had left it inside, I dashed down the deck and into the den in an attempt to catch the call in time. I didn't make it, and as I opened the sliding doors, the answering machine finished its message. I grabbed the receiver and heard a familiar male voice: "This is someone from your past, and I bet you can't guess who it might be?"

His laughter filled the den and, without the caller ever identifying himself, and although it'd been months since I'd heard from him, I knew immediately that this was Robert's cousin Fran from New York.

Francis Xavier Sindoni is the only son of Cecilia's oldest sister Lucy and her husband Mario—the aunt and uncle, Robert stayed with when he came to the States—*and* he's the black sheep of the family. He left the church at an early age, never settled down, and despite his mother's endless attempts at finding "a nice girl for Francis to marry," remains a confirmed bachelor. He treasures being single and more than makes up for this status by keeping company with dozens of eligible, and sometimes not so eligible, women in various parts of the country. He had been close to Robert since their teens and I adored him.

Following twenty years in service, Fran mustered out of the Air Force as a Lieutenant Colonel. Before that, he had played the markets and had great success in both bull—and bear—markets. When he left the military, he got a co-op apartment in Manhattan and went straight to Wall Street. After he retired for good, he bought a large one-story cottage on Hatteras Island and it was here he preferred to spend his time fishing and hanging out with the shrimp fishermen sharing bottles of beer and endless stories.

At Fran's invitation, Robert and I took the children to his beach house during part of our annual summer vacations. The kids loved his cottage, "The White Owl," named after his cheap and favorite brand of cigar. He could easily afford the eight-dollar Cohiba cigars but preferred his "owls."

Whenever we visited, he would take Robert and Patrick out deep-sea fishing, while Becca and I—and Fran's current flame—explored the shops in Hatteras, Avon and Buxton. Late in the afternoons the men would come back from their trip, reeking of fish and bad cigars, and talking about their latest great adventure at sea.

Fran and Robert cleaned and cooked whatever they caught and the evenings were spent savoring fresh grilled seafood accompanied by an abundance of local summer vegetables and the beverage of our choice. And always, Fran entertained us with stories from his military years—some, I am sure, might actually be true.

I had not seen him since the day after Robert's funeral when he left with a girlfriend for a vacation in New Zealand and Australia. I got a crazy card from "The Land Down Under," a few weeks later, but that was the only communications I'd received from him. Until this call, I had no idea of where in the world he was.

"So, what are you doing tonight Anna Elisabet without the 'h'?" he asked, and without waiting for an answer added, "I have tickets to the Hornets game or I'll spring for dinner at Slug's 30th. It's your choice, my dear."

He, of course, knew my answer; he was well aware of my indifference to basketball and weakness for the elegant restaurant with the spectacular view of the city, located on the 30th floor in downtown Charlotte. I asked him where he was.

"At the moment I'm on I-85—just left Raleigh heading for Charlotte for a meeting with an investment banker on

Monday," he explained. On the spur of the moment, he had decided to combine pleasure and business and came down early in order to see me and visit an old pal.

I invited him to stay at my house—I did, after all, have a perfectly fine guestroom that was unoccupied at the moment—but felt a little strange inviting a single man, even if he *was* family. Fran had stayed with us on many occasions while Robert was alive and it would seem prudish not to ask him.

My worries turned out to be for naught. He graciously declined my invitation and told me "I already have a place for the night, my dear." From his raunchy laugh I guessed that his old pal, no doubt, was one of his Southern woman friends; he would spend the night with her.

We agreed Fran would come to my place around six that evening. We would have a drink before we headed for "Emerald City"—our nickname for Charlotte—the growing city rising up in the midst of the flat lands. Fran promised to have me home by eleven; his friend, it seemed, was going to a fund raising event and would not be home until shortly after midnight.

The evening with Fran turned out to be a lot of fun. We enjoyed an excellent meal with fine wines and good service, as we watched the uptown high-rise buildings sprinkle lights all over the city. We savored imported brandy with our coffee and shared memories from our summers at the beach and occasional trips to New York City.

Fran also reminisced about the years Robert stayed with his family. The two were about the same age; had attended college together, and in those four years grew to be close friends. During that time, they toured New York City— adding to their worldly knowledge by exploring museums and art galleries—and made acquaintance with most of the bars that featured jazz bands in and around Greenwich Village.

Over coffee, I asked Fran if Robert ever talked about his

family in Ireland, specifically his older sister. He said, although he and Robert had been best friends, his cousin always stirred away from any conversation about his family and hometown.

"I got the impression something hadn't been right back in Ireland and that he was glad to have gotten away. I always assumed he was jilted by a girl, but never asked him."

I let the subject drop.

True to his word, Fran had me home by eleven and after I waved him goodbye and let out Tessa for a run, I got ready for bed.

My friends picked me up the next morning and we headed for a long day in the mountains and when they dropped me off that evening I was tired. After bringing in Tessa, I was about to sit down and watch Masterpiece Theater when I remembered the folder with the letters from Ireland. I decided to read them again to see if, per chance, they would tell me anything more than before, and went out to the kitchen and picked up the file I'd left.

After re-reading the four letters, I felt no more enlightened and decided to put the file back in the cabinet where I'd found it. They were obviously something Robert had kept for sentimental reasons, and I figured he just never thought to tell me about them.

As I bent down to put away the letters, my eye caught the corner of another envelope lying on the bottom of the file drawer, partially hidden under a folder. It was yet another letter from Robert's Aunt Nora and I quickly opened the envelope, eager to see if what she wrote might cast some light on the other correspondence. It turned out to be a short note with no new information, just sharing with Robert a few events in town. She ended by telling him that his family was doing fine.

I started to put the letter with the others and felt something inside the envelope I hadn't noticed before. It was an old photo. Before looking at the front, I saw an inscription on the back that read: "Francis Sean Keogh with the Staunton twins, Stephen, and Declan, after their first Holy Communion, 1957." I turned it over and saw a picture of three boys around six or seven, standing on the steps in front of a church. They were all dressed in white shirts, black pants and ties, with their hair slicked down; all of them grinning from ear to ear. I had no doubt that the one in the middle was Mary's son, Francis, and starred in disbelief at the curly-haired boy—his arms around his two friends.

His smiling face nearly took my breath away.

Chapter 3

After finding the last letter, I knew I had to go to Ireland to talk with someone from Robert's family—if any were still around—and learn about his early years. During the first part of our marriage I often suggested that we go back and visit his family, but he always had an excuse; we needed to save for the children's education; he was too busy at work, there were things to be done around our house, and on and on until I finally gave up. I realize now, there were things in Ireland he wanted kept from me.

As fate would have it, Tess called from Cornwell a week later and asked me to go with her on a visit to Ireland or "the old sod," as she affectionately referred to it. She wanted to visit old family again and said Tom didn't feel up to the trip.

"Providence," I thought, and told her I would love to go. She planned to leave the following April so the trip would work with my schedule. The Chamber's Spring Arts Festival was scheduled for the last weekend in March and after that, I would have some free time. A trip to Ireland around Easter would be a welcome break.

Tess and Tom are long-time friends from our Navy days in Texas, and Robert and I would always visit them when we came north to see Matt and his family. Tess was with me the time Matt was born, right after midnight, filling in for Robert who was off on a military assignment. We bonded that night and have stayed friends ever since.

She is an amusing and handsome women; tall and lanky with auburn hair and smoke-colored eyes, and possesses an attitude of never-say-die. I decided she was just the person I needed for companionship if I was to go back and visit Robert's native country.

I hung up with Tess, turned on my computer and found St. Francis Catholic Church in Bally Shanee, the town where Robert was born. Nora's letter made mention of the church and I thought it would be a good place to start. The church would have family records and perhaps information about Thornberg family members still in town. The same priest might not be there, but surely someone at the church could help me look up family records.

I immediately wrote to the priest listed as pastor of St. Francis. I told him who I was and my interest in finding information about Robert's family, specifically his sister Mary and her son, Francis. Any information, regarding either or both, would be of great service to me.

A few weeks before Thanksgiving, I heard back.

Coming home from work early one afternoon, I picked up the mail from my box, and on my way in saw a couple of bills, a bank statement, several magazines and some advertising flyers. I was about to throw the mail on the foyer table when I noticed a letter with a foreign stamp stuck between two magazines. I flipped it over and saw the return address: Father Timothy O'Neill, St. Francis Catholic Church, Ennis Kilroy Road, Bally Shane, Ireland. I dropped my pocket book and other mail on the table, walked back to my den and turned on the classical station. Then I sat down in my easy chair and opened the letter. The writing was that of an older person with neat and elegant cursive letters. I figured the priest would be quite old by now; it had been a long time since he baptized Francis.

It was a short and kind letter telling me that Father O' Shaughnessy, the current parish priest at St. Francis, had given him the letter. Father O'Neill wrote that he was retired, but served as priest-in-residence in the parish. He said he would be glad to meet with me when I came over in the spring, but added he was not sure he would be able to tell me much.

"Robert's Aunt Nora still lives in the old village and might be able to answer your questions," he wrote. "She is on in years, but her mind is still quick and since she knew Robert, Mary, and Francis from births, she might be able to help you." Father O'Neill closed by saying he would be glad to tell her I was coming and included her address.

At the bottom of the letter was the telephone number of the church rectory and he invited me to call shortly before I left for my trip.

Chapter 4

Having made up my mind to go to Ireland, I plunged into preparations for Thanksgiving. I'm no cook, but my son Matt and son-in-law, Forrest, are wonderful chefs and Becca makes great desserts, so I didn't worry.

I shopped for days and had everything, including a huge turkey, ready when Matt and his crew arrived from New York Wednesday afternoon. As always, Matt's wife Camilla took charge and arranged chores for everyone and at one o'clock Thanksgiving Day all of us—Patrick had invited Madison—sat down to eat. The tantalizing smells of roasted turkey, sweet potato casserole, pumpkin and apple pies filled the house.

We held hands before the meal and Patrick gave thanks with the youngest children chiming in on the "Amen." After dinner the adults watched football games while the children went outside to let lose some of their pent-up energy.

Friday we drove up to the Blue Ridge Parkway and had lunch in a quaint tavern. Saturday, Hunter Lee had us all for dinner, minus Patrick and Madison who went off to her parents' house, and Sunday Becca served brunch after church.

As they had done since their father died, the kids all went out of their way to fill the void left by Robert's death. I was thankful and felt good—even if a seat did seem missing.

I flew to New York toward the end of December to spend Christmas with Matt, Camilla and their children. Luke and family were going to Georgia and Becca and Forrest had headed for Florida to spend the holiday with some of his family. Patrick had also been invited to Matt's, but a few days before Christmas, he and Madison were invited to go skiing in Aspen with some of their friends. I told him to go ahead—I would be fine with Matt and his family.

Matt called and said the snow had begun falling right after Thanksgiving, and two days before Christmas a fresh batch covered everything in fairytale white. I went sleigh riding with my grandchildren exposing my joints to a whole new set of exercises and aches and laughed my head off when we all careened into a huge bush and tumbled out into a soft-powdered snow-bank.

Christmas Eve, Matt served roast duck, red cabbage, small caramel potatoes and our special almond and rice pudding—all dishes from his childhood Christmas. It was all so familiar and I savored the memories of past holidays. Only when Acy proudly produced an almond she had hid until we all finished, did I recall how Robert made hiding the almond a game for the little ones. It was, however, not the same without him; perhaps it never would be.

After dinner we opened gifts as we had in years past—just one gift each, saving the rest for in the morning—and shortly before midnight we attended midnight service at Holy Trinity Episcopal Church. Camilla's family had us over for a lunch Christmas day, and in the evening we went out in the neighborhood and sang carols. I missed Robert, but it felt good to be back in old surroundings.

While in Cornwell, Tess and I met for lunch and finalized plans for our journey to Ireland. She showed me pictures from previous trips when she and Tom had gone to see his family in County Galway, and I began looking forward to visit this beautiful green jewel located across the ocean from the country where I was born.

One night Matt brought out videotapes converted from old thirty-five-millimeter films that Robert took when the kids were young. As we watched the films, the memories flooded back. One tape showed Robert and the older boys surfing the waves and Becca, Patrick and I building a huge turtle of sand and shells. In another, the boys played in a neighborhood band, while Becca belted out a song, doing her best, at eleven, to look sultry. We laughed and shared Christmas stories long into the evening and after everyone else went to bed, Matt and I sat up for a long time talking about his father.

That night, before going to sleep, I gave thanks for such a great family. No matter what I found in Ireland, Robert and I had loved each other and raised four wonderful children; something we both could be proud of.

Chapter 5

Early that spring, I flew up to join Tess for our trip to Ireland. She picked me up at Cornwell Airport on a Wednesday evening and as we stepped outside were met with snow coming down at an alarming rate. What, until now, had been an uneventful trip suddenly became an adventure as the snowfall turned into an unexpected spring blizzard eliminating all visibility. Tess stopped the car at the first truck stop and called Tom to let him know we would be delayed, and I had visions of spending the night sleeping on one of the benches among the truckers also waiting out the storm.

After a few hours, the winds died down, and within minutes we heard the reassuring sound of the snow plough thundering through, the noise from the big machine bringing us comfort in the midst of the snow-clad landscape. With the roads cleared, we got back on the highway and, at one in the morning, made it to her house where Tom awaited us with steaming hot toddies. As I sipped my drink I said a quiet prayer that the storm not be an omen for what awaited me in Ireland.

My memories of our trip to Kennedy Airport and the connecting flight on Irish airline, A E R Lingus, are somewhat hazy. I do recall staying awake all night with Tess quietly discussing our early years in Corpus Christi when we lived side by side on the Navy base. Like so many other young military wives, we spent a lot of afternoons playing canasta, drinking coffee, and smoking cigarettes—everyone smoked back then—while our children played, and the men were at work.

It rained when we landed in Shannon Airport on the West Coast of Ireland, but by the time we arrived at Aaron's

Bed and Breakfast in Adare, the sun was out. In the aftermath of the rain everything looked fresh, but we were not in any shape to appreciate this green jewel of an island as we dealt with the five hours' time difference and total lack of sleep on the plane.

We rented a car and did a bit of sightseeing the first couple of days. We drove to Killarney to inspect the "Stone of Eloquence" at Blarney. After looking down the cliff, we decided to pass up the chance to kiss the famous stone reasoning we were already blessed with the gift of gab. We also shopped for pieces of Waterford crystal and went to one of Tom's favorite bookstores to look for gifts. After a day on a "pint n' piss" trip—as Tess fondly called our tours of charming area pubs—I felt less nervous and the trip to Bally Shane no longer seemed intimidating.

Before we left on our trip, Tom had called and asked a second cousin, Michael Clohessy, if he would drive me to Bally Shane at the end of our first week. Michael, who was retired, said he would be glad to and told Tom that he would also arrange for me to spend the night in the town's only bed and breakfast. So on a fine April morning, I left Tess for a couple of days—she would spend time with her family—and set out for my trip to Robert's home town.

Michael told me he had a brother in Rathburn Farm, not far from Bally Shane and planned to spend the night at his house; he would come back for me the following day. I offered to pay him for his trouble, but he said, "A pint on the way back will do just fine; I like to drive and look forward to seeing my brother and his family."

The drive took us past sloping fields—broken on occasion by large protruding rocks—and stone fences edging the meadows where cattle grazed, showing not a care in the world.

We drove through quaint villages with town squares where the locals met and passed the time of day; streets lined with thatched roofed cottages dating back to the turn of the century, and I wondered how Robert had ever been able to leave something so breathtaking.

As we drove through the countryside, so different from

anything back home, I nearly forgot my mission—lost in the beauty of the land—and to my surprise arrived in Bally Shane shortly before noon.

The village resembled the others we had driven through—a small hamlet without any sense of urgency. Along the main street, snaking its way from east to west, were similar stores to the ones I had seen in the previous towns: a tobacco shop with its owner sitting outside on a stool enjoying his noon day cigar, a green grocery where loaded wooden crates tempted the buyer with rainbow-colored fruits and vegetables, and a tiny book store with a bin full of well-used books in front.

On the other side of the street a couple of clothing stores displayed fashions dating back a few years, a tavern with small tables outside, and a general store where everything from shoes to pots and pans could be bought. At the end of the shopping section was a tiny post office and far down the street I saw the spire of what I felt sure must be St. Francis Catholic Church.

In the middle of town, Michael turned right onto a narrow side street and stopped in front of Callahan's Bed and Breakfast where I was to spend the night. He helped me out of the car and carried my small suitcase inside, introduced me to Mr. and Mrs. Callahan, and bid me farewell promising to be back midmorning the next day. If he sensed my uneasiness, he was too polite to say anything.

Chapter 6

Mrs. Callahan led me up a well-worn staircase to a small, plainly furnished room. She showed me the bathroom just down the hall and told me breakfast was served between six and eight.

"The tavern serves good and plentiful meals. If you like, I'll let them know you'll be there for supper and if you need anything else, just let me know."

I thanked her and said I would enjoy a home cooked meal at the tavern and took her up on her offer to call the place. As she was about to take her leave, I asked for directions to Nora Sheehan's cottage.

Aunt Nora, it seemed, was well known in town, and I listened as Mrs. Callahan talked about "the good work Miss Sheehan has done for our families in town, helping out whenever a child takes ill or someone needs help."

I asked if she remembered Cecilia Thornberg, Miss Sheehan's sister, but learned that the Callahan's had come to town just five years ago.

"When Mr. Callahan's uncle died he left this place to my husband. We felt a bit of change would be nice and came here and turned the house into a bed and breakfast place," and no, she never met any of Miss Sheehan's family.

Sensing I was anxious to go about my business, she said, "Miss Sheehan lives by herself at the end of the street in a small cottage right next to St. Francis Church. You can't miss it."

Aunt Nora had invited me to tea when I talked to her on the phone—shortly after I arrived in Adare—and I looked forward to meeting her, hoping she might be able to shed some light on Robert's past. We had agreed to meet at one o'clock; it was time to go.

On my way to her place, I walked by the tavern and the general store. Right before reaching the church yard, I saw a series of small and well-kept homes. The last one had a sign by its gate with the name N. Sheehan. It was a tiny house with a neatly kept front yard, with a profusion of spring flowers on the right, and an old apple tree with a small bench beneath it on the left.

Behind the house I glimpsed the ocean down below the cliffs and heard its roar as it hit against the rising rocks. On the far side of the cottage rose St. Francis, the old church where members of Robert's family had been parishioners. It was the church where Robert was baptized and took first Holy Communion and where relatives had been married and buried. Somewhere, amongst its records, I would surely find the names of all the Thornberg family members, including those of Mary and Francis.

Feeling nervous, I knocked on the front door that, within minutes, was opened by an older, friendly looking woman who, with a wave of a hand, invited me inside.

I followed her in and found a sparsely furnished, but comfortable cottage. Well-worn furniture filled the small living room, with green plants and fresh flowers sitting on the window sill. A small crucifix hung on the wall behind the couch along with a picture of the Pope, and several renderings of the Blessed Virgin. A lot of family pictures covered most of another wall; other framed photos sat on a small buffet and I recognized Robert in a couple. A table, in front of a sofa, was covered with a lovely linen tablecloth and laid out for tea.

Nora Sheehan, I had been told, was nearly 90, but you would never know from the way she looked and walked. She was a tiny woman with her hair pulled back in a bun at the nape of her neck and piercing blue eyes that age had not managed to dim. She welcomed me and asked me to sit down. She poured our tea and soon we were sitting down across from each other in the quiet and peaceful room that looked, I am sure, as it had for ages.

For a while we talked about Robert and our children and life in America. Then I told her I thought I detected an ever so slight Yankee accent in her speech. She smiled and said she had lived in America until she was in her late twenties.

"I've also gone back to visit family in New York several times in the past."

Aunt Nora poured me another cup of tea and then she said, "It is only out of respect and memory for Robert and Mary that I agreed to talk to you. Their story, it has been kept quiet these many years and it must stay that way after you leave."

I assured her I didn't intend to discuss this with anyone in town and was, in fact, leaving the next day to go back to Adare. I told her I would only be in Ireland for another week before heading back to the States.

She took another sip of her tea, put down the cup and saucer, and finally began to tell me the story:

When Robert's father, Patrick Thornberg, announced his intention to go to America back in the year 1920 everyone thought him very adventuresome. He was a young man in his mid-twenties working with his father in Bally Shane and doing well.

Patrick Thornberg, Sr.—a descendant of Swedish immigrants that came to Ireland more than a century ago—had always wanted to travel to the country of his origin, but family and business kept him here. He understood his son's desire to travel, gave him his blessing, and after making arrangements for young Patrick to board with a relative in New York City, watched him sail off for 'fame and fortune.'

Patrick did well enough for several years and even when the Great Depression came, he managed to get by. In the spring of 1929, at the age of thirty-four, he met and married my younger sister Cecilia, barely eighteen at the time. We were second-generation Irish Catholics and my parents liked Patrick and never treated him like a foreigner unlike many others at the time. A year after Patrick married Cecilia they had a daughter who they called Mary. "I was always close to Cecilia and was proud when she asked me to be Mary's Godmother," she noted.

At the beginning of 1933, they learned that Cecilia was

going to have another child. Work had begun to fail and Patrick decided to go back to Ireland and work with his father until the Depression was over. They thought it best that Patrick go ahead and begin work, while Cecilia would stay behind with our parents until the baby was born.

"It was decided I would travel with Cecilia—when the time came—and help her bring Mary and the baby over. Then I would stay on and help out until it was good for all of us to come back to the States.

"The baby was born in the fall of 1933 and Cecilia and I sailed off in time to be in Ireland for Christmas. On the day after Christmas the baby was christened Patrick Robert Thornberg, III, in St. Francis Catholic Church in Bally Shane. They called him Robert.

"Twin sons and three daughters followed right after the other and when Cecilia was in her early forties she gave birth to yet another set of twin sons. When the family decided not to return to America, I chose to stay. I was several years older than Cecilia and had no plans or prospects of marrying. I had grown close to the children, especially Mary, my Godchild, and remained so."

Aunt Nora stopped talking, looked me straight in the eyes and took my hand in hers.

"You told me in your letter you wrote me that you and Robert had a 'tumultuous marriage,' I believe that was what you said."

I nodded and said that despite some bad times, I had loved him very much and that the marriage had been good. But I knew he was troubled and for years I thought it was because of me.

She assured me that Robert's troubles were not caused by me or anything that happened in the States, but instead stemmed back to an earlier time in this small town. She told me she wanted to make sure I would accept what had happened without holding anything against anyone.

"You must realize," she said, "that I will tell you the

things I would not ordinarily be telling anyone. But since I decided to meet with you, I think it only right to tell you everything exactly as it was told to me."

I repeated my assurance and without asking if I would join her, she got up and poured us each a glass of port. Then she sat down and continued her story:

"Robert was as Irish as Irish gets, but he never stopped longing to go back to the country where he was born. Throughout his growing years he often asked me to tell him about America and his family in New York and he was always interested in seeing pictures and postcards from my sisters.

"My brother-in-law told him that, since he was born in America, he was still a citizen of that country and could go back any time. He did, however, encourage Robert to finish school before leaving home and Robert agreed to wait.

"Then came that awful time when Mary was preparing to marry. She was a lovely young woman with bright auburn hair and sparkling green eyes. The young man she was to marry was the son of the owner of O'Deas Inn, the local tavern. He was a strapping young lad with red hair, eyes like Mary's, and a temper as good as gold. His name was Francis Sean Keogh; he was called by his middle name.

Robert was sixteen and worked in the tavern after school doing odds jobs and over time the two young men had become close friends. Sean had been seeing Mary since they were both sixteen years of age and the date for their wedding was set. It was to take place on the last Saturday in May of that year and would be celebrated at St. Francis Church with Father O'Neill officiating.

"Mary was to begin work at the O'Deas Inn waiting tables and Sean planned to continue working with his mam and dad in the tavern. Their plans were made; they were full of life and joy, and I was happy for Mary.

"Then a few days before the wedding Sean and Robert went out to celebrate the coming marriage and were headed home early in the morning when something went terribly wrong.

"Sean had a lot to drink that night. Robert tried to stop him from driving home, but Sean insisted he was in fine shape. Robert told me the next day that Sean had gone barreling down the road and as they approached the stone bridge, a mile outside Bally Shane, the lights from a big lorry blinded him and he lost control of the car. The lorry swerved and managed not to hit the car, but Sean collided with the side of the bridge."

"Robert was thrown from the car and suffered a mild concussion. Sean died instantly and we buried him on the day he and Mary were to have married."

The three o'clock church bells from St. Francis tolled and brought me back to the present. I had been so engrossed in the story—sounding like a tragic romance novel—that I nearly forgot Aunt Nora was talking about my Robert and his early life.

Aunt Nora stopped talking and took a sip of port. She put down the glass and said, "That was just the beginning of all that went wrong.

"The night of the funeral Robert got very drunk. No one thought to stop him from drinking, knowing the grief caused by the loss of his friend and future brother-in-law. We knew also of the guilt he felt having survived the accident. Even his father poured him a glass of stout and assured him he was not to be blamed.

"Like the rest of us, Robert watched Mary throughout the day and I saw him worry. She did not cry but instead moved about without appearing to accept what had happened. This only seemed to deepen Robert's concern and guilt and so he kept on drinking. I stayed up and helped Mary to bed shortly after ten o'clock. I retired myself about half past eleven and read my Bible and around midnight I heard Robert as he stumbled into his bedroom up in the attic."

Aunt Nora took another sip of port and said, "Part of the rest of this story Mary told me, other parts are what I think happened. Perhaps, because I knew Mary from infancy, or maybe because I was her Godmother, I was the one she turned to and confided in.

"Some time in the middle of the night Robert woke up and realized someone was with him in bed. Still drunk with the drink, emotions and desire must have started to stir in him. I always suspected he had relations with a local tart from down the Valley since he was the age of fourteen.

"When he turned around he found Mary looking at him with tears streaming down her face. She told him she was so desperately alone and in pain. She cried and said since Robert had been Sean's closest friend and was with him at the time of his death, she needed to be with him on this night when she had buried the only man she had ever loved and ever would love.

"Mary told me that she kissed him and held him in her arms. Still drunk and with desires burning in his young body he pushed aside the fact that this was his sister and took her."

Aunt Nora looked at me and said. "I was raised by unusually freethinking parents back in the United States in the 1920's so talk of sex did not offend me. Although this was not a natural thing to happen, I felt less shocked than just so terribly sad for both of them.

"Later that night, Mary told Robert she had saved herself for Sean and had never been with a man before. Then, after they both cried, they decided to pretend to each other and everyone else that this never happened.

"She said Robert had assured her that God would not send her to Hell because of what she had done. She had always been a good girl and this had been a terrible mistake brought on by their grief. He also begged her to forgive him—and she did—before quietly going down to her own room.

"The next morning Robert, driven by the shame and the guilt, told his father that he wanted to leave, get away from the accident, and start a new life.

"Patrick, recalling his own desire to seek a future in

America, and realizing the troubled state his son was in over the loss of his friend, agreed that perhaps the time had come for him to make a change. He began preparations for his son's leave.

"The next month Robert sailed to the United States to live with Cecilia's and my sister and her family in Syracuse in the state of New York. They enrolled him in the local school. In his off hours, Robert worked for my brother-in-law in his restaurant on the north side of the city."

Aunt Nora stopped talking for a moment and then took a deep breath before she continued.

"By the end of July, Mary realized that she was two months with child and came to me beside herself with the grief and remorse. She told me everything that happened. She had gone to confession but needed a family member to confide in and knew she could trust me.

"An abortion, of course, was unthinkable and Mary talked of going away and giving the baby up for adoption. But the problem of the incestuous act plagued her.

"What if the baby is not right—what will happen some day when the child is grown up and perhaps wants to marry and have children," she asked me. Her guilt was enormous.

"In the end, the two of us agreed that Mary should tell my sister of the pregnancy, but let her believe the baby was Sean's. The neighbors might talk at first, but I felt sure that in time the townspeople would sympathize. They would reason that Mary and Sean were to have been married and that the baby was conceived right before the marriage.

"And that was what she did. She gave birth to a boy whom she called Francis Sean Keogh after the love she had lost. She remained at home living in a tiny house behind her parents and began to study to become a nurse while Francis stayed at home with Cecilia. She never married and lived quietly with Francis and seemed content with a life that included just the two of them."

Chapter 7

Aunt Nora stopped talking and looked as if she expected me to comment. So I began telling her of the letters I had found among Robert's old papers, and about the one Cecilia wrote and told him Mary was going to have Sean's baby.

"From another letter I learned that Mary returned the money Robert sent to her and told him that she did not need it and told him that he must not worry about her and the child and asked him not to come home again.

"There was yet another letter from Cecilia with a picture of a baby I thought must be Francis taken shortly after he was born and then there was the one from you, Aunt Nora, with the boy on the day of his first Holy Communion."

Aunt Nora got up from her chair and went over to the bureau and picked up a picture—her copy of the Holy Communion with Francis right in front.

I looked at her picture and then reached into my pocketbook for a small pouch and pulled out a picture taken at our home the day of Matt's graduation from High School.

Matt stood in back of the picture wearing his black robe and mortarboard, with the tassel hanging smartly to the side of his smiling face, his arms draped over Becca and Luke. And standing in front, with his hand on top of the head of our Airedale Terrier, was our youngest son Patrick—eight years old at the time and small for his age—looking straight into the camera, his dark hair falling down over one eye.

I looked from the communion picture to the graduation picture and saw the same face in the two small boys. They could have been twins.

I handed the picture to Robert's aunt.

"Jesus, Mary and Joseph," she said, staring at the picture of my children and making the sign of the cross. "That little boy is the image of Francis,"

"I remember Robert went to Ireland when his father died from a massive heart attack," I told Aunt Nora. "I was pregnant with our daughter and unable to accompany him."

"I recall that time well," she said. "It was the first time Robert saw Francis and I made sure I was at the Thornberg home when father and son met.

"I saw the shock in Robert's face when he came face to face with Francis and I quickly took him outside and told him Mary needed his help.

"She had just learned she was very ill, with less than a year to live, and did not know what would become of Francis after she was gone. Cecilia was getting old, and with her husband gone she now found herself alone with her hands full caring for the younger children still at home.

"Mary knew her mother would not know how to handle Frances when he got older—having no knowledge of the truth of his birth—and I was not sure how much help I would be since I too was older and just the child's great aunt.

"Robert, Mary and I talked for a long time about Francis, a sweet boy but very slow for his age, and we finally decided to talk to Father O'Neill, in a year or so, to see if the church could help.

"As it was, we need not have worried. A month after Robert returned to New York, the small house, where his sister and son lived, caught on fire early one Saturday morning and both Mary and Francis died in their sleep. It was a terrible thing to happen," she added.

"I remember the call to Robert from one of his younger brothers telling him of the accident," I said. "It came at one o'clock in the afternoon and while listening, his face turned white. I heard him say goodbye and then watched in disbelief as he threw down the phone, turned and screamed to me that Mary and Francis had burned to death. Then he stormed out of the house in a blind rage and did not return until three o'clock in the morning, drunk out of his head.

"Some time after Robert left, I called my friend and asked her if she would keep Matt and Luke overnight. I told her Robert had gone out, not sure when he would come back, adding that I felt a bit under the weather, my pregnancy getting the best of me. Tess loved the boys and willingly agreed to keep them and said she would stop by and drop them off in the morning in time for church.

"I stayed up most of the night worrying about Robert and finally fell asleep on the living room couch. I fully accepted his sorrow and would have understood tears, but I could not understand why the death of a sister and her son would bring on such rage. All I had ever known about Mary was that she was three years older than Robert, had lost her fiancée right before their wedding, and born a child she named Sean Francis Keogh after the baby's father.

"When Robert stumbled in early that Sunday morning, he raved on through tears about how God had punished innocent people, and no attempt of mine to calm or comfort him made any difference. He stood in our bedroom swearing at every saint and heavenly body he could name before finally falling into bed. In despair, I went back in to the living room and went to sleep on the couch. I didn't know what else to do.

"Tess brought the boys back in the morning in time for us to go to Mass. I dressed them and quietly went into our bedroom to ask Robert if he wanted to come with us to church. He turned around and with blood-shot eyes and through clenched teeth told me that he never, ever, intended to set foot inside a church again. Then he rolled over and went back to sleep.

"The boys and I attended service at St. Philips and after church I took the two of them and Tess and a couple of her children out to lunch.

"Robert was true to his word. From that day on he refused to attend church with us. As my pregnancy progressed, I became lax in my attendance and by the time Becca was born I had quit going. A close friend of ours served as vicar at 'All Saints Episcopal Church', in the town where we lived and when, at three months old, our daughter had not yet been baptized, his wife, Isabel, gently suggested that perhaps her husband might perform the ceremony.

"And so, on a hot Sunday morning in August, we had a service as our daughter Becca was christened Cecilia Rebecca Thornberg after Robert's mother. Robert made no objections to my taking her to another church as long as he did not have to be part of it.

"That's why I left the Catholic faith and joined the Anglican Church. I found it encompassed the beliefs of the Lutheran Church of my youth, *and* the Catholic Church.

Chapter 8

I had told my story to Aunt Nora and thanked her for her kindness and care for Robert's family. Before I left, I kissed her cheek and she embraced me, bid me God's peace, and asked me to stay in touch.

From her cottage, I walked the narrow road by the edge of the ocean leading to the small cemetery behind the church. Aunt Nora had given me directions and with a heavy heart I walked between rows of gravestones until I found the one I was seeking.

Looking at the headstone, I saw the two names: Mary Cecilia Thornberg, 1930—1965, and underneath, Francis Sean Keogh, 1951—1965.

From my pocket I took out the pouch that, along with the graduation picture, held a small spoon and Robert's old Rosary—one he faithfully used until the day he learned Mary and Francis had died.

I went down on my knees, dug a small hole in front of the stone, gently laid down the worn beads, and said a prayer for all of us.

After I covered the rosary, I sat down in the grass across from the graves and cried for a long time. I wept for Mary and Francis but mostly for Robert who, for all these years, had kept his sorrow to himself. Mary had had Aunt Nora to comfort her and Francis had been innocent of anything related to his birth. Robert had been alone with the knowledge and I admitted to myself that if, early in our marriage, he had tried to share his past with me, I would have been shocked. Later, after we grew close, I might have understood and been able to help him, but by then it would have made no difference. Robert had carried his burden alone for too long.

I thought of him and our stormy love and felt a longing for him so strong it stole my breath.

I brought myself back to the present and pulled out the last item from the pouch, placed it in my hand and walked down to the edge of the cliffs and looked out over the clear blue waters.

It was a tiny wooden box that held part of Robert's ashes. I had kept it, thinking that someday I would bring this small part of him back to his native home. I flung it out into the sea while reciting from my favorite hymn, "On Eagle's wings,"

"And he will raise you up on eagle's wings
Bear you on the breath of dawn,
Make you to shine like the sun,
And hold you in the palm of his hand."

Chapter 9

I finished my story and sat, still looking out into the darkened room, transporting myself from Ireland and back to Topsail Island and the DeNero cottage where the only sound came from the ocean reminding us of its constant presence.

Reenie got up from the couch where she had sat quietly listening for hours. She came over and gently wiped away my tears—I was unaware I had been crying.

"I don't know for whom I feel most sorry, you or Robert," she said. "He lived with his consuming guilt and you lived in the ignorance of what really tormented him. Most of the time you blamed yourself for his troubled moods."

I hugged Reenie and realized that telling the story, to someone who cared, had helped. Then I got up and went into the bathroom and washed my face.

When I came back, Reenie proposed what turned out to be a brilliant soul-cleansing thing. Still dressed in our gaudy-awful sweat suits, she suggested we put on sneakers and go for a long walk on the beach. I agreed and we locked up the cottage and set out over the dunes down to the water.

The same moon that had shined so brilliantly through the sliding doors in my den—just a few days ago as I listened to Christian's voice—now reflected itself in the Atlantic Ocean bathing the sea in its pale light.

Reenie and I walked arm in arm for nearly an hour saying little, finding comfort in the company of each other. I listened to the rhythm of the steady waves as they were tossed up on the Carolina beach. I thought back to the coast in Ireland where I had reunited Robert with the two people who had sealed his fate, and finally to the shores in Denmark where I had left behind my first true love.

Three beaches—worlds apart—bound by destiny.

PART THREE

Christian-The Knight

Chapter 1

"If you plan to meet Christian at the Central Railway Station at ten, you better start getting ready," Astrid called from inside the apartment.

I smiled, knowing my "big" cousin was just trying to help. From our childhood, she knew I tend to dawdle and she had more than once made sure I got to wherever I was going on time. I was sitting by a small table on the balcony in her second floor condo looking into the profusion of cherry blossoms on the tree in the neighboring yard.

"I just rang and ordered a cab for nine thirty so you still have time, but you really ought to think about getting dressed," Astrid said and stepped over the threshold, balancing a bowl of partly peeled green apples in one hand and a thermo coffee pot in the other. She put down the bowl, poured us each a cup of coffee, and sat down.

"I can't for the world understand why you didn't just have Christian pick you up. It's not as if the good doctor doesn't know where I live," she added with a grin.

Astrid, ten years my senior, still remembers Christian coming to pick me up during the months I lived with her and her husband. I felt a slight pang of guilt as I remembered the time he came here while they were away and I was alone in the apartment for the first time. No sense dwelling on that, so I inquired about the apples.

"I'm making four apple tarts today. Three I'll freeze and

keep for desert for the dinner after my grandson's christening. The fourth is for Lotte, my friend next-door, who helps me with a lot of things."

We shared our coffee in silence, enjoying the company of each other. Then Astrid picked up her bowl and went back inside.

The balcony was off the apartment on Amager—the island just south of Copenhagen—where I had lived with my parents back in the 1950s. It now belonged to Astrid who, after her mother died several years ago, issued me an open-ended invitation to come back to visit Denmark and use her home as base, "any time you feel like returning to native ground."

The previous day had been chilly, but we woke up to balmy weather and decided to enjoy breakfast outside. For once the TV weatherman had been right when he promised warm weather ahead. Judging by this morning's temperature, it was going to be a good day and a wonderful Easter.

It felt odd being back in the old apartment and stranger yet going to bed—the night of my arrival -in Astrid's guest room that once was mine. On past trips to Denmark, with Robert or by myself, I had stayed with my mother's oldest sister Ida—Astrid's mother—but had not been back since she died. By now the only familiar thing in the room was my old chest of drawer, left behind when I flew to a new life in a new world to join my parents in 1959.

My parents had journeyed to the United States in January that year; mother to set up a new home, and my father to begin work at the Danish Embassy in New York City. They resided there until they both died in 1985; my mother from an aneurysm; my father, shortly after, from a heart attack. Dad had worked as a courier at the American Embassy in Denmark but with his life-long desire to immigrate he had applied for a job in New York City.

In the fall, before we left, he received a letter from the Danish Embassy in New York telling him there was a position coming up in February. Strings pulled by my father's boss made it possible for my parents to leave the following January while I stayed behind with Astrid and her husband, Svend, until I graduated from school at the end of June; then I joined my parents.

Astrid and her husband were in luck when they found themselves able to take over our large apartment. They were expecting their first child and were elated to leave their cramped two-room walk-up in the center of Copenhagen and move to our spacious place at the outskirts of the city. Apartments were, and still are, hard to come by in and around Copenhagen—unless you have connections. The fact that they were related to my father, who worked for the American Embassy, carried clout back in the fifties and Svend's position with a prestigious law firm in the Southern part of Copenhagen helped.

Over the years Astrid had made it into a pleasant home for the two of them and their daughter, Anne Marie. She filled the place with antiques she and Svend collected and made it cozy by adding the embroidered pictures and cushions she made. When the exclusive apartment complex converted to owner condominiums some years later, they bought it.

Anne Marie was born late in July the year we immigrated and by then Astrid had converted my girlhood chamber into the sweetest nursery, judging from the pictures she sent us. Anne Marie had long since married and moved out and Astrid lost Svend in a fluke skiing accident early in 1991, so she now lived there by herself.

"I've converted Anne Marie's room into a guest room and even brought up your old chest from the storage room," she wrote when she encouraged me to visit.

My mother and Astrid had been close, and Astrid was like a surrogate mother and sister wrapped into one. As an only child, I attached myself to Astrid early on and after I left Denmark we stayed in touch through visits and regular correspondence. She even came over and spent time with me right after my mother died.

A year ago, Astrid "went modern," as she called it, and

bought a computer, so now we send email across the ocean and keep each other up on family news.

It felt good to be back with her.

Chapter 2

It was a quiet morning, interrupted occasionally by songs from the birds flittering around in the garden next door. I thought back over the past several months to everything leading to this trip to my native country.

The first email from Christian the previous summer proved to be the beginning of a lot of intimate correspondence; you might say we began dating over the Internet as the mail flew back and forth.

Christian called at least once a week—early in the evening my time, and shortly after midnight his time. We talked for hours discussing books, music, plays and concerts we were going to or had already been to, about our children, and most everything else.

Our love of animals was the subject one evening and I told him all about Tessa and her funny habits. Christian said he had owned dogs for years but that his last one died right after he met Brigitta, his fourth wife. Since she was allergic to dog dander, he never got another one and asked me if I could send him one of Tessa's pups when she had some. I told him she was spayed, but promised to help him find one "just as nice" when I came to Denmark.

One Saturday, around one in the morning when I could not sleep and Christian had just arrived home from a trip to Italy and was anxious to talk, we covered our financial situations. He admitted he had more money than he would ever need adding, though he enjoyed a good life, he didn't like waste. I told him I was financially comfortable and was big into recycling and re-use of things.

We talked a lot about old friends and events and pulled up oceans of memories from our dating years; what one had forgotten the other remembered and over time our old attraction resurfaced.

There was, however, one subject we never discussed—

Christian's last letter to me—the letter that caused our break-up in the autumn of 1959. Christian never brought it up and I felt it was too sore a point to discuss; no sense bringing up something that might cause discomfort for either of us. What happened could not be undone or changed and the important thing was—we were in contact again.

We were both anxious to meet and a North Carolina trip to a medical conference at Duke University—so close to my home—in the middle of December, provided an opportunity. Christian called Sunday evening right after he arrived in Durham and told me he had reserved a car for the coming Friday morning; he would be at my house in time for lunch and would stay until the following Tuesday.

I was looking forward to having him stay at my home and spent an entire day getting the house in tip-top shape. I also stocked up on all sorts of good food and wine.

Then a little after midnight on Wednesday, Christian rang and said he had to take a flight back that morning. He explained that the university had just called and told him there had been a murder-suicide on campus a few hours earlier and that two young students were dead. It seemed a young man had strangled his ex-girlfriend and then jumped to his own death, off a dormitory roof.

A university killing is always sad and attracts a great deal of attention, and in Denmark—where few people own guns and the crime rate is extremely low—this was a highly unusual situation. Television crews and newspaper reporters were all over the place and as chancellor, Christian needed to be there to take charge.

With a last minute change, Christian was able to fly home with a stopover in Charlotte. We met at the airport during his two-hour layover and what we discovered after one look, one hug, and one very long kiss, was that after all the years—the chemistry was still there.

Before his plane took off, I promised Christian to come to Denmark around Easter and the next day began making plans for things I wanted to attend and accomplish on this trip. Since I hadn't been back for a while, I decided to make this a long holiday and stay in Denmark an entire month. My boss was gracious about the trip and my time off. He told me to have a good time adding, "Come back with some good European ideas for events for us."

My plans would include the christening of Frederik, Anne Marie's new baby, a healthy and happy little boy who arrived late in her previously child-less marriage. I had been asked to be Frederik's Godmother at the ceremony taking place in Vor Frelsers Kirke and looked forward to the church service and the dinner Astrid had planned following the baptism of her first grandchild.

Our old school would also observe its 100th anniversary during that time with a huge official ceremony and various class parties and dinners. I had finally heard from someone at the school who applauded my comments and invited me to participate. I wrote and told them I was happily anticipating meeting old classmates and perhaps a teacher or two returning for the event.

I would also celebrate my birthday "properly," Astrid said—she planned to see to that.

"In view of the fact that you've not had a proper Danish birthday party since you left Denmark, I am planning a large sit-down dinner for you," she wrote.

Finally, and perhaps more important, I would get to spend some real time with Christian—more than just a couple of hours in an airport.

After we kissed good-by at the Charlotte Airport, early that December day, I drove home to a house that, despite the Christmas decorations, seemed empty. For two days I wandered around my home, feeling misty every time I looked at my sparkling home and well-stocked refrigerator. Tessa did her best to make me feel wanted, but she wasn't Christian.

Then Friday afternoon, right after I got home from work, the most beautiful bouquet of pink roses was delivered. As I un-wrapped the flowers, I found a card inside that read: "My darling Anna, please come back to me. I don't want to not have you in my life." It was signed, "Your Knight in Shining Armor."

I smiled at the gesture. Christian had remembered that pink roses were my favorite and with the awkward wording from long ago, let me know that he too was disappointed we'd only had such a short time together.

Despite getting caught up in the holiday bustle, the effect of Christian's visit lingered and I felt lonely for a while.

Now that I was finally in Denmark, I was unsure where the re-acquaintance might lead and felt less in control this time. Last time we met, I'd been on home-ground with everything familiar around me. This time was different. We were still meeting on familiar turf, but I felt Christian had more control of the situation since I was now a visitor.

Through our email exchange we made plans on when to get together and once I arrived, he had called Astrid's and confirmed our date. He was at a conference in Germany the day I landed, but would return Thursday evening. He offered to pick me up at Astrid's but—for my own reasons—I told him I would rather meet him in the city.

Chapter 3

I arrived at Kastrup Airport earlier in the week and spent the first couple of days poking around my old neighborhood and went for a long solitary stroll through the park just across from my former home.

The afternoon before, Astrid and I had taken a walk on the beach, just fifteen minutes from her home, and as we strolled along the waterfront, we shared memories from our youth. We came home, chilled to the bones but in great spirits, and spent the evening lingering over one of Astrid's famous meatball and leeks dinners. Later we watched Humphrey Bogart and Ingrid Bergman in "Casablanca," while splitting a bottle of good red wine I bought on the way back from the beach.

After breakfast Easter Friday, Astrid declined my offer to do the dishes and told me, "get ready for your date," and then nodded with approval when I came out wearing my light wool suit with the charcoal skirt that fell softly to the middle of my calves. Under the jacket I wore an off-white blouse with a deep V-neck that Reenie talked me into buying. When I tried it on she assured me, "it softens your face and makes you look younger."

I didn't believe any piece of clothing held that much magic, but felt rakishly adventuresome that day and spent a fortune on the blouse. As we left the up-scale store in downtown Charlotte with the silk shirt packed in tissue and fine wrapping paper, we laughed and both admitted, "Vanity, thy name is woman."

I put on square-cut diamond earrings—a birthday present from Robert—and a small platinum locket on a matching chain that fell just to the top of my cleavage. Not knowing what our plans were, I chose black suede high heel boots to complete my outfit.

"As Svend used to say: for an old broad, you look pretty damn good," Astrid told me and winked.

Astrid is a tall, striking-looking woman, who years earlier dazzled young Svend with her chestnut colored hair, high cheekbones, and sparkling cinnamon-colored eyes. He fell hard and courted her with persistence, but it took him more than two years to get her to the altar. Astrid was a determined young woman with a goal and, not until she graduated from nursing school did she give her hand to Svend. He remained ever adoring. By now her hair was steely gray, cut fashionably short, her eyes still sparkled, and she was as sensible and direct as ever. I loved her, and praise from Astrid meant a lot to me, especially in the nervous state I was in at the moment.

I thanked her for the compliment and went out on the balcony to collect my thoughts. I sat down and looked into the neighboring yard, taking in the scent of the early blossoms on the cherry tree. The small apartment building butted up against a private villa and it had been one of the joys of my youth to look and inhale the fragrance of the flowers each spring. I was romantic back then and felt I was looking into a dream full of promises of wonderful things to come.

"Christian and I agreed to meet under the clock at the central train station. He's coming down from Charlottenlund and I don't want him back, just yet, in what used to be my home," I said and walked into the foyer to pick up my trench coat. "Besides, 'Under the Clock,' is where we always met our friends back when we were in school; it's where all good Danes meet," I laughed. Astrid admitted this was true.

The large clock hangs high and central in the century-old railway station in Copenhagen and has been the meeting place for generations of people heading out to the country-side for picnics, hike, and visits with friends and family. Everyone knows where it's located and "under the clock" is part of the every-day language. The only difficulty—when meeting someone there—is finding the person *you* are

114

looking while everyone else seeks out *their* friends.

A sudden honk interrupted our conversation letting me know my ride had arrived and I gave Astrid a kiss and a hug good-by.

"I'll be back tonight—in time to pack for our trip tomorrow—so we can catch the early bus to Freddy and Rie's place," I said, picked up my handbag and headed for the door. My cousin Frederik is Astrid's older brother, and he and his wife, Harriet, called Rie, had invited us down to their cottage—nestled close to the beach south of Copenhagen—to spend Easter weekend.

"We'll see about that," Astrid said handing me a key to the apartment. "Give me a call if things change. I've told Freddy and Rie that you might make other plans," she grinned and gave me a knowing look. I just smiled, shook my head, and ran down the steps and out to the waiting cab.

I approached the car, a Renault of some sort, and stopped for a moment to look at the sign on its side reading: "Amager Little Taxi Company." Then I glanced at the driver, a handsome young man of middle-eastern descent, and chuckled knowing that if my paternal grandfather could see either the car or the driver, he would turn in his grave. Hans Drener founded the company years ago and was, by all accounts, extremely racist. A French automobile driven by a "foreigner" would have set his teeth on edge.

Putting thoughts of grand-papa behind me, I hopped into the taxi, gave the driver my destination and as I settled in my seat, heard raga music coming from the car radio.

I began feeling anxious again so, in order to divert my thoughts, I looked through the driver's windshield and in the distance saw the old bridge, Knippels Bro, that connects the Island of Amager to the old part of Copenhagen. I had walked across it many times with Christian and our friends, coming back from school dances and parties held in the city. A great many years had gone by, but the bridge hadn't changed.

I turned and looked out of the side-window and caught a glimpse of the church spire from Vor Frelsers Kirke adjacent to my old school. I was baptized and confirmed there and, during my school years, had sung with our chorus in the church at the school's annual Christmas concert held the day before our holiday vacation.

Christian and I had gone to the church one winter afternoon to do research on a paper on religious institutions, and another time during our spring break, the year I left Denmark. At that time, we decided to climb the spire in order to get a look at the figure of Christ, at the top.

The first part of the staircase is inside a bell tower; a door at the top floor leads to an outside spiral stairway. Not paying attention to the time, we were caught on the top floor inside just as the large bells began to chime the hour. The noise was overwhelming and frightened me.

Christian seized the opportunity to do what he considered the manly thing and covered my ears with his hands and kissed me until the bells stopped. By the time it was quiet again we had done some serious necking and we never did make it to the top of the spire.

The music in the taxi stopped and the news came on. Apparently not interested in world affairs, the driver began looking for another station. As he did, the start of an old song, "My Prayer," by The Platters—the popular group from the fifties—began playing, taking me back nearly forty years. Then, just as I was reminiscing, the young man reached over to switch the station again; this type of music evidently not to his liking. I quickly tapped on the window and asked him to please leave the song on until it ended. He threw me a sly smile, as if he had read my thoughts, and left the music playing; I blushed.

"My prayer, is to linger with you
At the end of the day.
In a dream that's divine."

Tony William's soft voice floated from the radio to my heart just like it had in the spring of 1959 during many of the dances Christian and I attended. Knowing that I would leave him in just a few months made the words bittersweet.

We had danced to that particular Platters' song at the annual End-of-the-Year-Dance our school sponsored, just before graduation. I had cried as Christian kissed my tears away and assured me, "we will be together always—we *will* find a way."

Chapter 4

During our last years in school, Christian and I were inseparable and considered the "golden couple" among our peers. We broke up only once—more accurately—Christian broke up with me after a heated argument late one evening. It was not the first time we had a fight, but always before, we easily resolved our differences. This time it was serious.

We had, yet again, argued over my not being willing to "go all the way" with him. It had happened on a mild December night, a couple of days before our Christmas break in 1958, when Christian walked me home from the dance studio where we took weekly ballroom dancing lessons with many of our friends.

As usual, we chose to walk home through the park across from where I lived, and as always we stopped and sat down, away from the lights, on a bench partially hidden behind a large tree trunk.

We stopped there almost every week on our way back from our lessons—supposedly to talk for a while—until it was time for us to say goodnight shortly before ten o'clock. My father, though lenient in many ways, was strict about my curfew, and I always made sure I was back a few minutes early.

Long ago, Christian and I discovered that kissing good night in the darkened entry to my apartment complex proved embarrassing; other tenants would arrive home, turn on the light inside the small lobby, and discover the two of us wrapped around each other. So heavy necking is what we usually did on the bench in the dark park. That evening was no different. We had dated for a long time without "going all the way," and, on several occasions during the last year, came close to consummating our love. But always, my fear would stop us.

Admittedly it was getting more and more difficult to

118

keep things under control and Christian's hormones were getting anxious. He would celebrate his nineteenth birthday at the end of January; I would turn eighteen that spring.

That December night in the park was particularly difficult. Both of us were driven by youthful passion. After I stopped him, yet again, he stood up, straightened his clothes and at first was very quiet. Then he turned around and faced me—his eyes flaming.

"You drive me crazy, Anna," he yelled. "You let me touch you and we both get turned on; I get all worked up wanting you so badly and then you push me away. Enough is enough—I can't stand it."

He accused me of being cruel saying I was teasing him. I tearfully told him I was not and that I wanted him just as much as he wanted me. The argument went on and Christian finally gave me an ultimatum: we either have sex, or he would break off our relationship.

"I can't go on like this," he shouted while he stomped back and forth, his arms flailing and his hair falling down over his eyes. I begged him, but he stood his ground. "Either or, the choice is yours," he added.

Fear of losing him frightened me and I pleaded with him saying I was afraid of getting pregnant and confessed that I also felt I couldn't betray my parents' trust.

Christian threw his hands up, turned away from me and stormed off. He stopped on the path in the park near the entrance and turned to look back at me. I stood where he had left me, still crying, trying to compose myself before going home. When I saw Christian stop my heart skipped a beat and I prayed with all my heart that he would come back.

But with one last look at me, he turned around and was gone.

Getting through the days leading up to our Christmas vacation was difficult. Everyone around us was in a festive mood and anxious for the holiday season to start. They all sensed something was wrong—the Golden Couple was suddenly not inseparable anymore; this just made it harder.

Christmas went by in a fog although I'm sure it was a festive time for everyone around me. Realizing it would be our last holiday before we immigrated, our family and my parents' friends went out of their way to make it a festive and memorable time.

My mother saw my pain and consoled me—to no avail. I confided in her, but all she could offer was sympathy; in those days daughters were very much discouraged from "doing anything," with boys.

My father didn't have a clue. He had never been in favor of my going steady with any one and, although he didn't like to see me sad, would have been delighted to learn that my serious relationship with Christian had come to an end.

We celebrated Christmas Eve at my grandmother Aggies' home and spent Christmas day with my maternal grandparents as we had for years. We attended a great many parties with lots of food, fun and singing and I went through it all smiling; feeling lost and miserable inside.

Mid-morning, on the day before New Year's Eve, I decided to go for a walk on the beach. It was a bitterly cold day, the winds gusting and foam forming on the water right before washing up near my feet. I walked along the shoreline and finally sat down on a bench near the edge of the water, vaguely noticing a lone seagull that kept diving into the sea in an effort to catch a meal. Ordinarily, I brought dried bread to toss the birds; today, however, my thoughts were neither on the seagulls nor the waves pounding against the pier.

This bench was one of our chosen spots, placed near the walkway, close to a small harbor. We had sat there many times and watched small sailboats come in, sharing thoughts and feelings.

It was here, several years ago, Christian had asked me to go steady and where we had made plans for our future: We would go on to university; get engaged the Christmas after graduation; begin our careers, marry, and raise three children.

It was also here, a year earlier, I tearfully told him I had to go to America with my parents after graduation. We had both cried and sworn to love each other forever; I would come back—no matter what. Now I was here alone and my whole world—along with my heart—seemed to be crumbling.

The temperature was just below freezing, but for once, it felt good. I wanted to cleanse my soul and think about a future without Christian. But no matter what plans I summed up, the pain surfaced. It was sad enough to leave for the United States at the end of the school year, but the thought of spending the next months separated from the young man I had loved for years was more than I could bear. Tears welled up and I finally turned around and headed back home trying hard not to cry.

I arrived home shortly after two o'clock in the afternoon and realized I had missed lunch but did not feel hungry. I walked slowly up the stairs to our second floor apartment dreading yet another evening without Christian in my life.

As I started to pull out my key, my mother opened the door and greeted me with a big smile.

"I've been looking for you. Quick Anna, go look," she said. She helped me take off my coat and mittens, and led me to my room. I opened the door and there, on my desk, stood the loveliest bouquet of pink tea roses—my favorite kind of flower.

There was a card stuck in the bouquet, and I quickly read it.

"My darling Anna, please come back to me. I don't want to not have you in my life." It was signed, "Your Knight in Shining Armor," a nickname I gave Christian after we had seen "White Christmas" together. My heart soared, and as I re-read the note, I even found room in my happiness to smile at his grammatically incorrect sentence.

I burst out crying from happiness and relief. My mother said Christian had already called to ask if the flowers had been delivered, and told her he would call again. She left my room only to come back a short while later carrying a tray with a mug of hot tea and a cheese sandwich. As she handed me the tray she smiled. She knew that for me it was going to be a good New Year after all.

Within an hour the phone rang with a quiet and hesitant Christian on the line. He begged me to forgive him and asked if I had read the card yet. With a smile in my voice I told him I had and that, "off course I'll come back to you."

He came over and picked me up at six thirty that evening and we went to see Limelight, the sad movie with Charlie Chaplin and Clare Bloom. After the movie we went to a small cafe nearby where a pianist played love songs from the twenties. We sat close, holding hands, and drinking coffee, and talked. We even laughed at his grammar on his card accompanying the roses.

"You, my dear Anna, will be a famous writer some day and use language the right way. I plan on becoming a rich physician with little use for knowing how a sentence is structured; beside, the card expressed exactly how I feel about you."

On our way home, we promised each other to keep our passion reigned in and to find a way not to separate ever again.

It was an extremely happy me that went to a New Year's Eve party the next evening and danced the night away in the arms of my knight. One of the last songs played that evening was My Prayer by The Platters. My prayers had been answered—Christian had come back to me.

The New Year dawned with our hearts in tune and our best intentions in place. We felt so certain we would not succumb to desire until much later and that we would never part again.

We kept the first part of our resolution until shortly after my parents left for the USA. The latter promise we faced several months after I left Denmark.

As soon as the song ended, the young cab driver winked at me and switched back to his preferred station. I sat back in the cab and smiled having no fear that the driver's choice of music would bring back any more thoughts from my past.

The cab suddenly stopped as the bridge opened to let through a cruise ship and I wondered about the destiny of the people on board. Many were outside waving to the bicyclist and pedestrians on both sides of the bridge; it made me think about my destiny and what the weeks ahead might bring. Then the taxi moved and I looked at the cruise ship sail away from the bridge—off to other destinations. I spent the rest of the trip watching the busy city life in my old childhood town observing how much had changed but also—and this was more meaningful—how much remained the same.

We pulled into the railway station shortly before ten and I paid the driver his fee adding a generous tip. Tipping is not usually part of a taxi fare in Denmark, but he *had* allowed me to savor a memory.

I got out of the cab, took a deep breath, and inhaled the atmosphere of the city. I love Copenhagen with its ringing of bicycle bells, the fumes from buses, the honking horns of the cars, and the clatter of any large metropolis.

I looked across the street to Tivoli Garden, the world-famous amusement park located near City Hall, across from the Central Railway Station. It was quiet now, but in another week it would open its gates and from then, until the end of September, the shrieks from the roller coaster and other dare devil rides inside the park, would blend with the street-noise outside its age-old walls.

Tivoli Garden dates back to 1843 and was originally part of a military moat system surrounding the inner city. Most Danes, and thousands of tourists who come to Tivoli these days, pay little heed to its history. Like myself, they enjoy the beautiful park-like atmosphere with flowers in the Hanging Gardens, The Fountains, the Pantomime Theater, and many other attractions, while watching The Boys Guard"—a corps of young boys in red and white uniforms—parade through the park several times each day playing well known marches.

Most everyone, from the very young to the senior citizens crowd, also takes pleasure in the food obtained from any of the numerous vendors, or perhaps enjoys an exquisite meal at one of the many well-known indoor and outdoor restaurants throughout the park.

Children—and a lot of adults—also delight in the variety of rides from the wild roller coaster to the merry-go-round, and young lovers find their way to the Tunnel of Love. I planned to visit Tivoli before going home; maybe I would go there with Christian?

The sharp ringing of a bell—a bicyclist eager to get somewhere in a hurry—made me step from the street up to the sidewalk. I turned around, pushed through the station doors, and headed for *the* clock. It looked down at me like an old friend letting me know, as had the city, that though some things change, others remain forever the same. I was about to find out just how much, if any, the years had changed Christian and myself.

Chapter 5

Christian had already arrived and stood right under the clock looking as tall and handsome as ever. Then he saw me, and his face lit up.

"Anna, darling, it is so wonderful to see you again," he said and without another word, drew me into his arms and kissed me. It was just a short kiss, but I swear my toes tingled.

"Let's head out," he said, took me by the elbow carefully guiding me toward an exit. As soon as we were outside, he turned me around, looked me square in the face, smiled and said, "God, it's great having you here—you look absolutely beautiful." His smile melted me, just as it used to.

"You're acting like a teenager," I told myself and began telling Christian about my trip as he led me toward his car, a silver-colored Mercedes a couple of years old, parked in a no parking zone.

"I know, I know," he laughed as he watched my raised eyebrows, "I'm taking advantage of the 'doctor' sign still on the car, but I knew I would only be parked for a short time. Please don't make me feel guilty," he said and gave me a pouty look. I squeezed his hand as he helped me in the car.

Christian was quiet as he negotiated his way through mid-morning traffic, reaching over occasionally to take my hand. I sensed we were headed north, but didn't know where we were going. Then, as we pulled out of the inner city, Christian looked at me and began talking.

"I thought we would head out to Dyrehaven; it holds a lot of memories for us, and since it's such a mild day it should be nice in the park." He passed a car and continued, "First we'll have lunch at Peter Liebs; I can't guarantee how good the food is since it's been years since I had a meal there, but the atmosphere is still bound to be great."

I said it sounded like a wonderful idea and we proceeded

north toward Klampenborg and the old park. We had gone there many times on picnics with friends and family and often by ourselves, during the years we dated.

As we headed up the coastline, we talked about my trip over, the upcoming christening—I had invited Christian—and our forthcoming school reunion. We both looked forward to seeing old classmates and to visit the school that had been the setting for our young love.

We arrived at the inn in time for an early lunch and Christian asked if I wanted a hot meal or open-faced sandwiches. It had been years since I enjoyed the well-known sandwiches, so I told him I preferred the latter.

When the waitress asked for our order, Christian looked at me, then back at the young woman, and said, "Smoked salmon, beef tartar, and brie on French bread for both of us."

This was what we had ordered when we went here to eat during the last spring I was home. I told him I was impressed he remembered, but assured him I couldn't eat three sandwiches, even if they were small.

"If you can't eat it all, I'll finish it," he laughed and ordered two glasses of Danish Aquavit and a couple of Carlsberg beers to go with the meal. "I'm a hungry man these days," he added with a glint in his eye.

I blushed and thought it was getting to be a bad habit.

We had a wonderful time during lunch. The meal was as tasty as I remembered, and true to his word, Christian ate all of his sandwiches and most of mine. We did a lot of "do you remember ...?" but stayed on safe subjects covering teachers, friends and events not too personal.

We finished our meal and declined dessert in favor of a walk. We decided to come back later for coffee and perhaps dessert.

We walked outside and I inhaled the wonderful scent of the woods. I love this place and especially in the spring when everything is new and fresh.

I had come to the Dyrehaven each spring—ever since I

was a little girl—back when riding to the park on the train for picnics with family and friends was a special treat. I could still taste the milk I had with my meal; milk my mother put in a glass bottle topped with a cork. By the time we ate our lunch it was warm, as was the beer the adults enjoyed. In those years we didn't own insulated coolers or thermos bottles and for years I associated lukewarm milk with picnics, woods, and good times.

The path Christian chose led toward a small lake and as we walked, Christian put his arm around my shoulder while I slipped my arm around his waist, the way we had in the past. We were quiet for a while and then he began to talk.

"Anna," he said, "I've told you a lot about myself in our emails and phone calls. You know I've been married four times, have three children, and you know how my career has proceeded. You also know my taste in music, the books I read, where I like to vacation and much, much more.

"I have, however, avoided writing or talking about my marriages and the women involved. Not because there is anything to hide; I just thought it would be better to tell you face to face," he said.

"You can't but have wondered—'why so many marriages?' and perhaps even thought I must be a terribly unstable man. I want to tell you my story and let you judge for yourself. I'll try to be as honest as I can and give you details when I think they matter."

We reached the lake and found a small cast iron bench with wooden slats, sitting under a large oak tree, not too close to the path and somewhat secluded. It was just like it had been when we came here as young students, but by now the bench was well worn and the tree more than twice as tall. We had enjoyed many serious conversations on this site.

One Saturday, during our last month together, the two of us had found ourselves alone on the bench after dusk. Most of the visitors had packed up their blankets and baskets and left the park for the day, heading for the train station nearby; outside the entrance gate, our bikes stood in the racks waiting for us to return and claim them.

It had been a balmy and warm evening and soon

Christian's caressing hands led us to give in to each other on the soft grass underneath the old oak. A pale rising moon observed us while light filtered down through the tree, its crown in early bloom. The occasional ripple of the nearby lake was the only accompaniment to our lovemaking. It had been wild and sweet, and as we sat down on the bench now, the memory returned.

Chapter 6

The lake was calm this Good Friday afternoon except for the occasional splash made by a couple of ducks diving for food. Near the shoreline, on the far side of the lake, a pair of elegant swans glided side by side while an older couple threw bread out to feed them. It was a picturesque scene— Hans Christian Anderson could not have created a lovelier setting for his fairy tales.

We sat down in the shade of the old oak and I savored the quiet moment with an old love, in the place we had enjoyed together many years ago.

After a few minutes, Christian took my hands and turned me toward him. I sensed this was going to be difficult for him, but I was a caring friend and he knew I would be open to whatever he had to say.

"I finished my early studies after you left and began my internship at Bispebjerg Hospital," he began, "and despite the fact that I missed you, I enjoyed working in this area of town where we spent time together before you left. It reminded me of the good times at your Grandmother Anna's home, playing cards with her and your Aunt Ida, eating apple tarts, and walking our bikes passed the hospital near her apartment, on our way home."

"Then after the letters returned, I finally accepted the fact that you weren't coming back, so I settled down and studied hard. I dated some, but not seriously," he said.

I was about to ask what he meant by the 'returned letters' but decided not to interrupt. He needed to talk, and I could ask questions later.

"At a party, toward the end of my internship, I met Vivian, an older sister of Raymond Jaegerlund, a university friend. The party was held at their parents' home where they still lived. Vivian was an attractive, dark haired art major who, early in the evening, told me she was an aspiring stage actress. We immediately hit it off," he said and gave me a wry smile.

"Vivian and Raymond came from a large bohemian family filled with musicians, artists, writers and entertainers—so different from my own family. Her father was a magician, her mother his partner and the two of them spent most of their time touring Europe with their act. In addition to herself and Raymond, who planned to become a successful writer, there was a younger brother in France—another starving musician, plus a semi-successful older sister on the west coast of Jutland who painted in and around her small cottage. The family was completed by a younger sister, headed for the United States the following year, with aspirations to become a Broadway actress. It was an interesting family, to say the least.

"My parents never approved of Vivian and my father, the mighty supreme-court attorney, especially did not sanction this relationship. I decided, however, that I'd been the 'good son,' long enough and chose to ignore my father. Growing up, I had been the dutiful son; my younger brother Jasper—who you may remember was two grades behind us—was the rebel. At the time I met Vivian, he had, yet again, defied our parents and was off to sea seeking new adventures. My father disowned him and never again mentioned his name around the house.

I decided it was time I too stood up for myself and Vivian and I were married in the garden of her parent's home that summer—without the presence of my mother and father.

"Following my years of intense study, Vivian's theater life seemed exciting and, in the beginning, I enjoyed mixing with actors and directors. We went to some wild parties; smoked pot and drank a lot of wine, and for a while I had fun around these contrary and artistic people.

"After a couple of years, though, I began realizing, we were totally unsuited. I was still studying, working at a city hospital and gone during the day when Vivian was home. She would leave for the theater late in the afternoon and not come home until past midnight or early in the morning. By the time she did get home, I was asleep or back at work at the hospital.

"Vivian didn't like to clean house and hated cooking, and I didn't have time for either. My life was medicine—hers was the stage. I was advancing my own career and couldn't blame her for not devoting her life to our home. I believed I stilled loved her and didn't have the heart to break off the marriage. We had no children—Vivian was not the least interested in raising a family and as it turned out, couldn't have any.

"Toward the end of our marriage, she began getting larger and better parts and she finally landed the leading role in a play that quickly became a huge success. After drawing a full house every night for six months, the producer decided to take the show on a tour of Europe.

"Vivian and I had a serious talk and acknowledged we were headed in different directions. She wanted to be free to travel and devote her life to the stage—I wanted to become a successful physician. We agreed to remain friends, called the marriage quits, and our divorce was quickly finalized. Vivian married her director a few years later and now lives not far from my home. We're still friends and visit from time to time.

"After the divorce, I didn't connect seriously with anyone until I met Karen, a twenty-year-old nursing student at the hospital where I worked. She was a tall, attractive, blue-eyed blonde reminding me of you. I'd been living by myself, was lonely, and wanted to settle down and start a family; so I began a relationship with her.

"After a couple of months, Karen told me she was pregnant and we decided to get married. My parents were delighted. Her father was a well-to-do dairy farmer on the West Coast of South Zealand and felt sure Karen was the sort of girl that would be 'just right' for me.

"Karen gave up her studies right after we married and our daughter, Helena, was born the following winter; Peter came along a year later.

"The first years were good. We got along, had a good life, and enjoyed our children. Karen was busy making a home and caring for the children and I was advancing my career. But I was also away from home a great deal.

"It turned out that what Karen had expected was the life she perceived as that of a doctor's wife with the prestige and luxury it encompassed. At the onset of my career, I didn't make a lot of money and had not yet inherited from my parents, so our budget was tight. Karen also had difficulty accepting the time I spent on research and my long hours away from home. She wanted a social life with dinner parties, theater nights and weekends traveling away from home; she began to resent being alone with the children.

"We started to argue, whenever I was home. Then, realizing we were drifting apart, we did what many others do in that situation—we decided to have another child in an attempt to cement the marriage. Christina was born the following spring and for a while things were better.

"Then, a year later, I came home unexpectedly one afternoon—our two oldest children were in school and Christina asleep in the nursery—and found Karen in bed with, Erik, my old friend from school. I took one look and stormed out of the house, unable to face the situation.

"I went to the hospital and wrestled with what was happening and did not return home until late that night. I confronted Karen who told me she'd been lonely. Erik, recently divorced, worked at our local newspaper; he lived nearby and had begun dropping by early afternoons for coffee; they never meant for it to go this far.

"Karen cried and promised to stop the affair. For my part, I promised not to leave her alone as much and so—for the sake of the children—we agreed to try to make the marriage work. By now I was making a lot more money and we were able to hire a sitter now and then. We even managed a ski trip to Norway with all the children and our marriage appeared to be doing all right.

"Shortly after that trip, I attended a weeklong conference in Sweden followed immediately by a two-week research tour to the United State; then a four-day seminar away from home. When I came back I worked long hours in order to catch up on my work, and without realizing it, fell into the old routine of working late and rarely being at home.

"A month or so later, Karen told me she was pregnant. I'd been out of town the better part of a month and after some quick math I realized this baby could not be mine.

"Karen admitted having started the affair with Erik again; told me she loved him and that the baby was his, adding they wanted to marry and raise their child together. She said she also wanted to finish the nursing career she gave up when we married, and we resolved to get a divorce.

"After some discussion, she agreed to let me keep the children. In turn, I would help her financially so she could start her studies and we parted amiably. Karen moved to a small town near the home of her parents and kept the children every other weekend and during most of her vacations.

A week after our divorce, she married Erik."

Chapter 7

Christian stopped talking, took my hand, stroked my cheek, and continued.

"I tried to raise the kids alone, but they required more attention than I could give them. I still worked long hours at the hospital and finally decided I needed someone to help me run my home.

"I was in a hurry to get things arranged and through an agency hired Paulette, an au pair girl from France. She was younger than I expected, but came with excellent references. Three weeks after she joined our household I learned she was not quite eighteen and after a month I acknowledge that having Paulette in the house might become a problem. I considered letting her go but the children adored her; she cooked like a dream, and kept the house running smoothly, so I decided to keep her. In retrospect, that was an insane idea.

"Paulette soon made it obvious she would like to be more than my house-help. She was tall and slim with long, dark hair worn in a ponytail; I was in my early forties and flattered, but didn't think I needed to get involved with a minor. For several months, I threw myself further into work and spent less time at home.

"Then, a few days before her eighteenth birthday, Paulette asked if I would take her out for dinner, some place nice, to celebrate her coming of age. I thought it sounded like a reasonable request; we'd gone out before, but always accompanied by the children. Karen had the children that weekend and I admit I pretty much knew where this might lead. I also admit to being weak—Paulette was an extremely enticing young woman.

"The night of the dinner she came down from her bedroom wearing a white, clinging dress that left little to the imagination. It was a warm June evening and Paulette appeared to be wearing little, if anything, underneath her dress. She wore her hair piled high and looked older—more sophisticated.

"I had a great evening. Paulette hung on my every word, kept encouraging me to talk, while flirting shamelessly. I'll admit it felt good. Here I was at age forty plus with a young woman who was turning the heads of the men around us. My head swelled.

"Throughout the evening Paulette gave me seductive looks and ran her bare feet up my legs. I had been celibate for some time and was turned on.

"We came home to an empty house and Paulette turned on soft music and fixed us each a drink. Then she came over to where I sat, let her hair down and slipped out of her dress revealing a naked body that would have stopped a clock.

"I carried her to my bedroom and we spent most of the weekend in bed. She taught me things I never knew and I was hooked. Despite her age, she was experienced and admitted to having had an older lover before coming to Denmark.

"I started to come home in the middle of the day whenever I could get away from the hospital and knew the children would be in school. I was addicted to Paulette and sex with this willing young woman.

"Then late one evening, a couple of months later, Paulette came to me teary-eyed and told me she would have to go back to France immediately. She was pregnant, she said, and would have to return to her family; they would take care of her, she assured me.

"I felt trapped and torn. I was not ready for another marriage or the responsibility of another child, but also knew I was not ready to give her up. I suggested she have an abortion; with my connections at the hospital I could easily arrange something safe.

"Paulette refused. She told me she was Catholic and could not consider an abortion. Although she did not observe much other church dogma, she convinced me that she could not commit a mortal sin.

"So I offered to marry her and she admitted that was

what she hoped I would say and gladly accepted. A couple of weeks later, on a weekend when Karen had the children, we were married in a quiet ceremony in a country church just north of here.

A month later, Paulette had a miscarriage.

"I enjoyed our sex life and showing off my young bride, but after a while our relationship began going downhill. Our taste in music, our choice of friends—and the fact that we had absolutely nothing in common to talk about—began driving us apart and after a couple of years I admitted to myself that she was, realistically, young enough to be my daughter.

"I had just begun to face the fact I might be headed for yet another divorce, when Paulette came to me one evening and told me she was leaving. She said she was tired of being married to an old man—that really hurt—and wanted to live her life among people her own age. She packed, left for France within a week, and I soon found myself divorced and alone again."

Christian paused for a moment, looked out over the lake; then he continued.

"By now the two older children were capable of taking care of each other, and look after their little sister while I was at the hospital. So I hired Mrs. Larsen, who was married with a family of her own, to come care for the house and prepare meals.

The children pitched in and helped around the house and, on the weekends they didn't spend with Karen, we cooked together or went out. We had fun and grew close during that time.

"For some years I remained alone. I had an occasional fling when I was out of town, but decided never to get serious again—I was burnt out on marriage.

"It was during this time that both my parents died. My father suffered a stroke, arguing a case in court early in the spring. Mother contracted pancreatic cancer shortly after and died quietly in the hospital between Christmas and New Years the same year.

Mother had inherited her parent's home in Charlottenlund; it was where she grew up, and where she and my father lived for many years taking care of my widowed grandfather. In her will, she left the estate to me and my brother.

"Jasper—by this time living in California—had no interest in the home and no objections to my taking over the house as long as I gave him his share in cash. I, on the other hand, had always loved my grandparent's house.

"I inherited a great deal from my father—who'd left nothing for Jasper—so buying him out was not a problem. He spent money like water and was always broke; receiving half the value of the homestead in cash suited him just fine."

Christian stopped and gave me a sad look. I knew this was distressing and a little embarrassing for him, so I just squeezed his hand and nodded for him to go on.

"I was through with marriage, or so I thought, and Mrs. Larsen agreed to stay on and run my parent's house—now mine. In addition, I hired a gardener and a woman to come in a couple of times each week to help with the cleaning.

"Then, at a conference in Hamburg, I met Brigitta, an attractive woman in her mid-fifties. She was a corporate attorney from Sweden attending the conference as a representative of an English client, and after watching her debate one afternoon, I found myself interested.

"We got along from the start. Sex was not great, but comfortable, and after Paulette, I was ready for the stability Brigitta provided. She'd been divorced for many years and appeared to offer the kind of relationship I needed.

"We shared love of books and theater, enjoyed skiing, good wine and food, and easily discussed our mutual interests. In the beginning, our relationship was fragmented because Brigitte traveled a lot, but a year later she was offered a position with a Danish insurance firm and we agreed to move in together. Six months later we decided to marry.

"I quickly discovered I had made yet another mistake!

"At that time Helena and Peter were attending college and Christina spent a great deal of time with Karen and Erik. Still, the children's easy-going lifestyle bothered Brigitta who told me she did not enjoy being around all the young people who came and went in our home. She also informed me she did not particularly like my parents' home—she found it too old-fashioned—even though she had moved in a lot of her own furniture in an attempt to modernize the place.

"We bought a new bedroom suite when we first moved in together, but shortly after we were married, Brigitte told me she was not sleeping well and decided on separate bedrooms. Only occasionally did she allow me into her bed.

"She felt confined in her job, and missed traveling—I began to miss a regular sex life.

"We were spending less and less time together and it became an empty marriage; but I decided to hang in there; I had my work and my children *and* I'd already been divorced three times.

"I began having problems with my hands. Mild nerve damage had occurred, and I decided to retire from active practice in order not to put my patients at risk. It was just after I made this decision, I was offered the job as chancellor of Horstenberg Medical University and decided it was providence.

"When I told Brigitta about the job offer, she informed me *she* had just been offered an excellent position with an English law firm and would spend most of the next two years traveling in and around London. We talked it over and agreed to accept our new job offers and to work out an amiable divorce. There were no hard feelings—just nothing left to keep us together.

"That, for the most part, wraps up my sorry marital record," Christian said, adding, "The only other thing you might like to know is the status of my children.

"Their situations are as follows: Helena is married and lives with her husband Oliver and their son, Chris, in the southern part of Zealand just outside Vordingborg in a large old farmhouse they have spent a great deal of time and money remodeling. They met at the university they attended, and after they married and settled down, bought a small-animal veterinary business at the edge of town. I see them quite often and they seem to be doing well.

"Christina owns a flat in the city and attends the University of Copenhagen where she is an art major and plans to become a commercial illustrator. She still keeps a lot of her stuff in her old room at my home, including some of her paint material; she stays with me whenever she has a break or feels like getting out of the city. Sometimes she just visits and at other times she comes to paint on the beach or in the woods around here.

"For a while she appeared to be seriously involved with a young engineering student. They even talked about getting married once their studies were over. Then one day she came home rather crestfallen and told me the relationship was over. Seems the young man thought her art was 'interesting' but not anything he wanted her to take seriously. She told me she suspected he'd been more interested in her money than in her. Since then she has, to my knowledge, not dated anyone special," he added with the look of a caring father.

"And then there is Peter," he said and shook his head ever so slightly.

"He started out studying internal medicine at the University of Copenhagen but after a year decided it was not for him. For several years he invested in a couple of entrepreneurial ventures that fizzled out. He is currently studying to become a large animal veterinarian at a university near Oliver and Helena, and says they have indicated it might be possible for him to join the two of them when he is finished with his studies. Helena and Oliver are letting him use the apartment above their office when he's in school, but he also owns a large flat near the center of Copenhagen where he heads whenever he misses big city life."

"My father and mother were both only children and came from wealthy families. When they died, they left substantial legacies to their grandchildren so my children are now more or less financially independent. Both girls are sensible about their money and even Peter was smart enough to invest his money and has managed to hold on to the major part of his inheritance, despite his entrepreneurial fiascos.

"I just don't know about my son. He's drifted in and out of relationships since he was in his late teens; was married briefly several years ago, and engaged twice. For the past several months he's dated a young student nurse named Lisa and I keep hoping they'll get serious and settle down. At the moment however, he still doesn't seem at all sure about the direction of his life."

Christian paused and with a sad laugh added, "I am afraid, when it comes to women, he's a lot like his father."

Chapter 8

Christian stopped talking and we sat quietly for a while. For once I was lost for words. He seemed so sad and I was searching for the right thing to say.

Finally he looked at me and said, "About the time Brigitta left for England, I received the first email from you, Anna. It arrived at a time when I was at an all-time low and felt no one cared."

He looked at me with eyes, deep as pools of amber, and I melted. I knew he had brought some of his misery on himself, and that he might be playing on my sympathy, but I didn't care. He exuded love and warmth—not to mention desire—and at that point in my life, I too was in need of someone to help me go on with my future.

I took his face in my hands and said, "Christian, *I* care!"

His face lit up and he pulled me into his arms and kissed me long and deep. For a moment I didn't think of time or place; I had forgotten how thrilling it was to be held in the arms of a man who desired me. This time more than just my toes tingled.

A small, quiet sound brought me back to reality. I pulled away from Christian, and with a smile, said, "Christian, we've got to stop, and I'm not just saying this to tease you— as you once accused me of doing." He looked surprised so I pulled his ear close and whispered, "This *is* a public park and someone just passed by coughing ever so discretely."

We looked out to the narrow path that went around the lake and saw the older couple, who earlier had fed the swans, walking arm in arm, away from the bench, stealing glances at us. As if on count, we both waved to them and with hesitation they waved back before proceeding with their walk. We turned around, faced each other, and burst out laughing.

"Let's head back to Peter Liebs and have some coffee,"

Christian suggested; and so we did.

Fifteen minutes later we found ourselves the only people in the restaurant, sitting at the table we left earlier. Christian ordered coffee and cognac and asked if I wanted dessert. He told me he was famished and ordered a large piece of layer cake. He said he would share.

While waiting for our order, Christian reached across the table and took both my hands in his and looked deep into my eyes.

"Anna," he said with a slight catch in his voice, "come home with me and stay for a while—please. I'm off most of Easter Week and have made no plans, hoping you would come and spend time with me. We have years of catching up and there is so much I want to tell you and share with you."

Before I could respond, the waitress arrived with our order and distracted us for the moment. When she left our table, Christian picked up his cognac glass with one hand, and my hand with the other. "Please, Anna, come and at least spend Easter with me; I don't want to not have you in my life."

I looked at him for a long moment while a lot of old feelings surfaced. I really didn't have to consider my answer.

Placing both my hands in his I smiled and said, "I'll come back with you for a couple of days, Christian, and we'll see what happens."

Chapter 9

"I seem to have developed this terrific appetite just being around you," Christian said and cleaned up the last bite of the layer cake as I finished my coffee and cognac. I chose to ignore him and instead informed him that if he didn't watch his fat intake, I would tell a "certain heart specialist," I knew very well, about this gluttonous craving for fatty things. He just laughed, paid the waitress, and led me outside.

After we got in the car, I told Christian I needed to call Astrid to let her know of my change of plans and he handed me his car phone. She answered on the first ring and I felt slightly embarrassed as I told her I would not be home that evening.

"I think that's just wonderful," she said as her warmhearted laughter reached me. "Have a great weekend and if you and Christian feel like coming down to Rie and Freddy's on Sunday, just get there in time for lunch."

I thanked her and turned off the phone.

"Now that wasn't so hard, was it?" Christian asked, and kissed my hand. I said no and told him about the invitation to my cousin's summer place in Greve.

"That sounds like a great idea," he said. "I've not been down that way for some time, and I enjoy the drive along the southern coastline."

As we drove—not wanting to discuss anything personal—I asked Christian to tell me about his home and his family.

"Ulrik Plesner, you might remember, was a famous architect at the turn of the century. He designed the house for my maternal grandfather, Peter Valdemar Mathiesen; my mother, their only child, was born and raised there," he said.

"Grandfather was a Supreme Court judge and a stern and dominating man, although he was always kind to me. He encouraged the marriage between my mother, Inga Louise, and my father Christian David Raabensted, the only son of Grandfather Mathiesen's best friend. At that time, father worked as a lower court attorney. Later, he went into partnership with his father and uncle and eventually went on to become a supreme-court attorney. After my parents married they moved to the house on Amager where we lived when you and I attended school in the 1950's.

"When my grandmother died, my mother and father moved into mother's old home to be with my grandfather in order to help him run the large villa. After he died, mother inherited everything and they stayed on.

"I moved here with my parents and stayed until I married Vivian. After I left, my parents kept my room intact, hoping, I am sure, I would abandon life with 'that awful bohemian woman,' and return home to their 'normal' world.

"My brother didn't live there after he became of age. He and my grandfather did not get along and Jasper never liked the place. As I told you earlier, I bought out his share after my parents died.

"I've always loved the house and was thrilled to move in permanently. After I married Brigitta she joined me there and I'd hoped she would come to care about the place.

"In the early part of our marriage she didn't seem to object to the house. Mrs. Larsen and the part-time maid kept the place running so it never interfered with her work.

"After a year, however, Brigitta systematically began to change the furnishings in the house. She put my parents' and grandparents' furniture in the attic and moved in a lot of her own things from her home in Sweden. She also bought some new stuff in order to create her 'own look.' I never complained, thinking that if it made her happy, it was all right with me.

"When she left and moved to London she took her furniture with her and I still haven't filled up all the rooms. I gave several pieces of my parents' furniture to Helena and Oliver when they settled in their farmhouse, including a couple of things that dated back to my grandfather Mathiesen's childhood. I gave Peter the bedroom suite that Brigitta and I bought together, but rarely shared. After Peter moved out, along with other furniture, Christina assured me she wanted to inherit the place and would take whatever was left when the time came," he added with a laugh.

"After Brigitta left, I brought down my grandparent's old bedroom furniture from the attic, had it restored and placed in the master bedroom. I am anxious for you to see the house; I think you'll like it."

I realized we had slowed down and looked out just as Christian pulled into a side street. He drove down the road a few hundred yards and turned right through an open iron gate.

He pointed to the end of a long gravel driveway lined with birch trees and said, "There is the house; it's called 'Valhalla'. Grandfather Mathiesen was very proud of his Viking heritage and was able to trace his family tree back to the early seventeenth century. After the house was finished, he decided to name it after the place where—legend has it—all Vikings go after they leave this earth."

We drove to the end of the driveway and Christian parked in front of the house. As he helped me out of the car, I took a look at the villa and fell in love. I didn't have to be convinced that this was an outstanding home.

Valhalla was a spacious two-story brick home with a wing at each end and gables decorating the third-floor attic. In some ways, it didn't differ from many of the other houses of this type, but the Plesner touch was evident in the details.

At the end of the sloping garden, behind the house, I caught a glimpse of the sea and the clear blue water that offered an exquisite backdrop for this stately old mansion.

Christian parked the Mercedes in front of the detached three-car garage that featured the same tiled roofline as the main house, and age-old oak doors with wrought-iron hinges and latches. By the edge of the sea, I saw a small gazebo, green with ivy climbing over its tile roof. It looked like a place where one could enjoy quiet moments of solitude while watching the ocean play along the edge of the beach.

I felt a slight shiver and realized it had gotten cooler as the day had worn on. The weatherman had been right last night; we were indeed experiencing warm days with evenings that still turned chilly.

We walked up the wide steps at the center of the house and Christian unlocked the front door.

Chapter 10

Just as I stepped inside, a grandfather clock in the foyer struck six o'clock. I looked around and my expectations were not let down—the villa, despite its size, felt inviting with early evening light shining through the windows, bathing the home in a golden glow.

"Let me give you a quick tour of the house so you can find your way around later," Christian said, took my coat, and put it in the hall closet. Then he walked to an old mahogany cabinet, opened its doors to what looked like a stereo system hidden inside, and suddenly music filled the rooms.

"Most everything in the house date back to my grandfather's time, but the stereo system is new. It carries music all over the house," Christian said. "It was one of the first things I had installed after I took over the place," and as we began touring the house, soft jazz followed us.

To the right, inside the entrance, was the living room and right behind that, a study. Both rooms were spacious with high ceilings and tall windows. The first room was sparsely furnished with only a low table between the windows, a couple of Queen Anne's chairs, and a large grand piano at the end of the room. I figured this must be one of the rooms left empty after Brigitta's departure. The comfortable study, on the other hand, still carried the flavor from the days of the old judge who, from his picture above the large, stone fireplace, seemed to watch us with an expression of mixed favor.

Pocket doors led from the study to a large library with a bank of floor-to-ceiling windows allowing a spectacular view of the ocean on the Eastside of the room. Old leather-bound books lined tall bookcases flanking the sides of a stone fireplace and large green plants added freshness to the atmosphere. Comfortable chairs and a leather couch in soft brown hues, filled up the library and made the room inviting. An old armoire in a corner discreetly displayed media equipment including a large television set.

Christian had gone to some length to outfit this space to suit his own taste.

"This is where I spend most of my free time," he said. "I enjoy the large fireplace and since I saw you shiver, I'll light the gas logs so the room will be warm when we come back."

Before I had a chance to look around the library, much less inspect all the pictures on the mantel, Christian led me across the hall into the formal dining room. It was an impressive looking room with pastoral oils of a past era decorating the light brocade walls. Judging by their age and quality, the furniture in the room evidently dated back to his grandparents' time.

From here, we walked through a conservatory where the early evening light was giving the plants their kiss good night, and out to the large country kitchen. Here I saw, what appeared to be, the only new construction ever made to the house—a quaint breakfast nook facing the back garden. I immediately noticed the table was set for two and gave Christian a questioning look.

He grinned, "Mrs. Larsen is an eternal optimist. This is where I take most of my meals, and when she learned I was meeting you, she decided to get the house ready. 'I want to be sure the place looks nice and ready, just in case you bring home this old friend of yours,' she told me on the phone Thursday. She'll not be back until Tuesday morning due to the Easter Holiday—so we have the place all to ourselves," he added and gave me a mischievous smile.

I decided to ignore the remark lest I blush again.

We soon learned that Mrs. Larsen had indeed gone out of her way to make things ready. Not only had she set the table with lovely linens and pretty dishes, she had also filled the refrigerator with all sorts of good food, ready to be eaten, or put in the microwave for Christian and his "old friend" to enjoy.

Christian pulled out a bottle of chilled Champaign and filled two glasses. He handed me one of the crystal flutes, took his own glass and the rest of the bottle, and led me up the wide, curving staircase.

As I walked up to the second floor I looked around. Everything in the house gave off the comfortable feeling of quiet wealth and faded "old money." To the left, at the top of the stairs, was Christina's old room, the one she still used from time to time. Her name was on a couple of pastel paintings hanging above an old dresser holding all sorts of make-up. The room also had a made-up day bed, a desk, and a large bookcase filled with art books. Near the window were a couple of easy chairs and a small table, and in a corner stood an easel next to a bureau with a box of tubes of paints. There was also an old jar filled with paintbrushes looking as if they'd seen a lot of work. The whole room was done in shades of beige and taupe—I felt right at home.

Christina shared a bathroom with the adjacent room that stood nearly empty, save for an old desk and an easy chair. That room led out to a balcony—running across the entire back of the house—with double doors and large glass panes giving you a full view of the ocean.

"This was Peter's room until he left home. When he bought the flat in Copenhagen, he took most of the furniture with him," Christian said.

We went into the upstairs hall again and Christian pointed to the wings at each end of the house.

"There are two guest rooms at each end of the hall, directly above the library and the conservatory. They are furnished, but rarely used. The ones above the conservatory and kitchen served as servant quarters in the days of the old judge and the two at the other end were used by my mother and her nurse when she was a little girl."

"Elsa, the part-time girl, comes in twice a week to help Mrs. Larsen and occasionally dusts them, but for the most part, the rooms are left alone.

"While my children lived here they often had groups of friends over for parties, spending the night, filling up every room in the house—but that was some time ago," he added.

We walked across the upstairs hallway and into Christian's home office. It contained much of his boyhood paraphernalia and took me back in time. His collection of books and jazz records filled a huge bookcase along one wall with a couple of his old Piet Heins' pictures above it. Lined along the top of an old chest of drawers, were several soccer trophies.

"I also spend time in here; I do a lot of my work, write to you, and play a lot of my old LPs," he said. "Some of the stuff here is still left from when mother decorated it after we moved in."

He went over to his desk and picked up a black and white picture set in a heavy silver frame. "You remember this?" he asked and handed me the photograph.

I looked at it and saw Christian's and my own face looking back at me. One of our friends had taken the picture the day we graduated. We stood smiling, arms around each other, wearing the caps we had earned after years of hard work. We had been in love and on the top of the world that day, not worrying about the day when an ocean would separate us. Somewhere at my home, in an old album filled with pictures from my school years, was an exact copy.

"I framed this and placed it here right after I came back from France and read your response to the email I sent you while you were at the beach with your friend, Reenie. It's such a great picture and reminds me of a happy time in my life," he added.

He kissed the top of my head and refilled our empty wineglasses. I took a quick sip and noticed the champagne had begun to produce a new feeling in me—one I couldn't identify—but it was nice.

We went through Christian's bathroom—tastefully decorated in deep greens and eggshell white—into the master bedroom dominated by old oak furnishings. Fine linen curtains fell softly from under velvet valances while faded old wool rugs in golden tones, covered part of the wide plank floor. The four-poster bed stood against the wall, tall and impressive, with a turned down comforter showing off crisp white sheets Mrs. Larsen must have put on before she left.

Suddenly the familiar tones of Jo Stafford's "Tennessee

Waltz" filled the room. We stopped and starred at each other.

"I swear I had nothing to do with this selection," Christian smiled. Then he reached over and took me in his arms and began moving us to the rhythms of the song.

"I could not, however, have asked for a better song to play at this moment," he added and took my wineglass and his own and put both on the dresser next to the bed. He touched my lips lightly with his and then picked up the small gold locket in its slim chain resting above my own heart.

"You still wear this," he smiled and slowly let his fingers slide down inside my silk blouse. My heart began to beat fast and I had no idea how to make it stop.

"I remember the time I gave this to you and every detail of that night." He paused and looked at me with affection. "It was the day of my nineteenth birthday party at Rikke's home, after your parents left, and the anniversary of our first date," he said as his hand strayed further down to cup my breasts.

I admit I just lost it. The effect of the Champaign on a nearly empty stomach—added to the feelings that had built up during the day—brought things to a zenith. I felt a desire I thought had died years ago.

Without a word, Christian led me to the four-poster. He slowly undressed me and gently laid me down on the bed. Then he quickly undressed and with stored up passion, we joined each other for the first time since we were young.

There is something to be said for sex in your late teens— it has vigor and an intensity that rarely comes back. However, making love at an older age with someone I once knew intimately turned out to be an exhilarating experience. Our bodies found a rhythm of their own, and I was transferred to a place of white lights and warm sensations.

When I finally became aware of my surroundings, I heard the clock in the foyer strike.

"I'm famished," Christian said, kissed the tip of my nose, and got up. He put on an old and well-worn bathrobe lying at the foot of the bed and walked over to a closet and pulled out a dark blue robe.

"This is a new dressing gown Christina gave me for Christmas, hoping I would get rid of this one I've had for ages; I never will. The new one may be a little big but it'll keep you warm," he added and gave me a quick hug.

We walked down to the kitchen and began to inspect the dished Mrs. Larsen had left in the well-stocked refrigerator. I took out cold chicken salad, a large cluster of grapes, and some crisp biscuits. Giving me a hungry look, Christian added a plate with cheeses, some French pate, and another bottle of champagne.

Then, with food and plates on a wooden tray, Christian led me back to the library where we settled in front of the fire. Ravenous, we cleaned our plates as if we'd not eaten for years.

I suggested watching television, so we sat close in the large couch and watched most of "Rififi," a movie we had seen in the theater the first year we dated. Around midnight, we went to bed and fell asleep in the arms of each other.

I had not been this content in a long time.

Chapter 11

The aroma of coffee brewing drifted into the bedroom and tickled my nose until I finally opened my eyes and realized I was neither at home nor at Astrid's. A quick glance at the clock told me it was not quite seven in the morning so I settled back in the soft pillows. I heard the shower running and Christian's baritone singing at the top of his voice.

He was entertaining himself with a rendition of "King Christian Stood at the High Mast," an old song we sang as students. It tells the story of the victorious King Christian the Fourth, a brilliant sailor and warrior, who won many battles at sea. One of the most famous paintings of this seventeenth century monarch can be found at Freriksborg Castle. It depicts the king standing on board his battleship, surrounded by smoking cannons and flying bullets with a handkerchief bandaged around one eye—the result of an earlier hit to the side of his face. He was considered quite a war hero, but was also known as the "builder king" of Denmark. He directed the construction of many of the beautiful churches and buildings that add to the scenery in and around Copenhagen.

The singing continued so I jumped out of bed, grabbed the bathrobe, and crossed the hall to Christina's old bathroom. Since I didn't bring a toothbrush, I checked the cabinet above the sink and found some toothpaste I applied with my fingers in order to perk up my mouth. I threw some cold water in my face, dried off, and walked back into the master bedroom.

By the time I came back, the water had stopped and I was just considering what to do about getting dressed when Christian came prancing back into the room looking like the proverbial cat that swallowed the canary.

"You look like a teenage boy who has just had his first sexual experience," I laughed, whereupon he strutted over to the bed and opened up my bathrobe.

With a twinkle in his eye, he said, "Well, I may be a lot older but that's how I feel this morning."

A quick glance at his anatomy left no doubt as to how he felt and I realized that getting dressed right now was out of the question. So we hopped back into the four-poster.

When we finally got out of bed, I firmly announced that I was going to take a shower—alone!

Christian rubbed my hair, laughed, and said, "Fine; you take your shower *alone* and, *I'll* bring you up a cup of the coffee I so thoughtfully brewed earlier. Then we can go for a brisk walk on the beach."

I agreed that sounded like a wonderful idea, but didn't think my suede boots would stand the sand.

"I'll tell you what," he said looking thoughtful for a moment. "I'll find you some knock-around clothes to wear, and after our walk we'll make plans for the rest of the weekend." Then he kissed the top of my head and went down to the kitchen singing "King Christian" at full volume.

I showered, enjoying the pounding of the hot water as it poured from an old brass shower fixture that, like everything else in the bathroom, likely dated back more than half a century. After the long soak, I grabbed a thick towel and stepped out on the terrazzo floor.

While I dried off, I looked out the window to the garden, observing the trees in the side yard. Small leaves, curled around twisted branches, lent the trees an aura of softness and mystery. Spring had arrived and it looked like it was going to be a beautiful day. I felt on top of the world and quickly wrapped the towel around me. Then I padded into the bedroom to see what, if anything, Christian had found for me to wear.

A steaming mug of coffee sat on the stand next to the bed, beckoning me to come and enjoy its fine flavor. In a neat stack on the bed was a pair of faded jeans, a thick white cotton cable-knit sweater and a pair of tube-socks. On the floor stood a pair of well-worn clogs that looked to be near my size.

I was just getting ready to put on yesterday's underwear when I noticed a small cellophane package tucked partly under the sweater. Judging by the wrapping, it looked like expensive lingerie. The label read, "Made in France."

I carefully opened up the package and took out a pair of pretty, if skimpy, white briefs along with a matching lacy bra made of soft silk. Since I felt in a "what-the-heck" mood already, I decided to try them on. The panties were a little snug, but the bra fit and both felt nice. I strutted around in front of the dresser mirror for a few minutes taking in the picture of myself. The brief coverings made me feel like a French maid in an X-rated movie—certainly a new feeling—and I realized that somewhere in the night many of my earlier inhibitions had vanished. I liked it.

I put on the jeans and rolled up the legs several inches. The "one size fits all" socks were perfect, and thanks to their bulk, enabled me to keep on the slightly too-big clogs. The sweater was long but after I rolled up the sleeves, it fit.

In Christina's bathroom I found some make up and dabbed some on. Then I sauntered downstairs to the kitchen and joined Christian who was in the process of making toast to go along with some freshly squeezed orange juice.

"Wow! You look even more beautiful this morning than you did last night," he said and pulled me close for a kiss and a hug. I answered that the previous night must have been rejuvenating to produce that effect on my old face. He just beamed and looked me over from top to toe.

"I see you found everything. I had to dig around in a few drawers to find something I thought might fit you. The pants were some left from Peter's early teens (before he grew another six inches) and the clogs and socks are Christina's. The sweater was mine until I threw it in the dryer a month ago. Mrs. Larsen was off for a few days and I learned that you do not dry cotton on high heat," he laughed.

"And to whom, pray tell, does the scanty underwear belong?" I asked. "Or do you just keep extra sets around for any of your women guests who might be in need of fresh underwear?" I teased and quickly apologized. "Sorry. That's really none of my business."

Christian gave me half a smile, refilled my coffee mug and said, "Well, I bought them for Brigitta on one of my trips to France in the mistaken hope that she might like them. She thanked me kindly, said they were too small and put them away in a drawer where they've stayed ever since."

I felt foolish and quickly changed the subject asking him about our plans for the day.

"I thought we would go for a short walk on the beach to get some fresh air. After that the day is yours, my darling Anna. We can do anything you want, as long as you promise to stay with me."

So we ate our toast—I had half a slice, Christian ate three—and set out for a walk along the sea.

The northeastern coastline of Denmark is rocky; so unlike the long smooth stretches of the Carolina beaches and especially those at Reenie's place on Topsail Island. This shoreline, however, has its own beauty and I enjoyed the brisk walk along the pebbled edges while the salty surf water sprayed my face.

On the way back, Christian asked me what I wanted to do the rest of the day. I had made up my mind to stay with him for a while and realized this would require some clothes and toiletries.

"If I'm going to spend time with you I think, perhaps, we had better go back to Astrid's place and pick up some of my clothes and personal things. After that, I would love to stop by our old school and then walk down to Prinsesse Gade to the park by the old moat. Maybe we can stop for lunch or coffee at the old mill; Astrid told me they've turned it into a restaurant."

I knew I sounded eager, but Christian just smiled and said this sounded fine.

"I was at the mill last winter with some of our old class mates—at our annual pre-Christmas dinner," he said. "We decided to visit the place where the painter kept a studio back in the fifties."

I knew the place well. During our last year in school we had often gone there to study and draw as part of our art classes and had, on a couple of occasions, received advice from the old artist.

Within minutes we reached the border of the long lawn that sloped from Valhalla down to edge of the beach. I took a last look at the ocean and observed a small sailboard glide by before I turned and, with my arm around Christian, went up to get ready for our trip back to Astrid's.

Chapter 12

We rode along with the radio tuned to an all-jazz station. We didn't talk much—just enjoyed being back together. From time to time Christian reached over, took my hand and touched it to his face. It made me feel eighteen again.

It was ten in the morning when we arrived at Astrid's and since it was Easter weekend not many people were about. Christian opened the door to the car and took my hand as we walked to the building. He unlocked the door to the apartment complex, stopped right inside the entrance and started to kiss me. I threw him a questioning look.

"Just once for old time's sake," he laughed.

I tried to nudge him away, but not in time to avoid the surprised look of a teenage girl who came flying in through the entrance wondering, I am sure, just what in the world an old couple were doing necking at the bottom of the staircase. She stopped, gave us a quick smile and said, "Cool," and continued up the stairs humming; we laughed and hurried up to the apartment.

Once inside, Christian picked up the mail and morning paper from the floor in the foyer and placed it all on a small table. I took out my leather duffel bag from the hall closet and went back to my room to put together clothes for the next several days. I reached inside the armoire in my old room and brought out things that would mix and match and be suitable for both dinners and exploring. After a few minutes I turned around and realized Christian had followed me. He stood in the doorway staring at me with an odd expression on his face.

"What?" I asked, "Why are you looking at me in that peculiar way. Do I look funny or something?"

"Anna," he said and was suddenly serious. "It's so odd being back in your old home. Standing here, in this room with you—it's all coming back. Right now I just want to take and pull you down on that narrow little bed and make love to you until we both have to come up for air. You do remember, don't you?"

"I assure you I remember everything in great detail, but after last night *and* this morning, we might want a breather," I said with a smile and asked him to please go make us a cup of tea.

Christian went back to the kitchen and as I sat down on my bed folding things to be packed, I thought of the night, so many years ago, when we had made love for the first time.

A couple of weeks after my parents left for the States, Astrid and Svend made plans to spend the weekend with his mother on the island of Funen, leaving Friday afternoon. Now that they had space in their new apartment, Svend's mother had offered them several pieces of furniture from her home. This included a cradle that had been in Svend's family for generations and they were going down to make arrangements to have the furniture moved.

Astrid was concerned about my being alone, but I told her I had the weekend lined up. I was going to a party Friday night and our clique planned on an outing Saturday. I would spend that night at my girlfriend, Greta's, and Sunday I was to have lunch with Grandmother Aggie.

"You and Svend will be back sometime Sunday," I assured her and added, "I'll be fine —remember I am nearly eighteen."

They left Friday afternoon and, for the first time, I was on my own.

Christian and I met that evening where our two roads joined—our usual meeting place—and took the street car to our friend Rikke's home for a party she was giving in honor of Christian turning nineteen that Sunday. In addition to Christian's early birthday party, the two of us would celebrate the three-year anniversary of our first serious date.

Despite their different backgrounds, Rikke and Christian were the un-disputed leaders of our group. Christian was raised in a well-to-do family and Rikke, or Frederikke as she was christened, came from a working class family with a father who worked as a carpenter at a factory outside the city. Her parents were self-educated and extremely well read. Classical music played on their record-player at all times unless Rikke, or someone in her family, played their upright piano. One full wall of their living room held books, including all the classics.

Rikke's meager background was not reflected in her appearance. She was a stunning girl with long hair the color of chestnuts caught in the sun, and blue, mother-of-pearl, eyes. She was cool and collected and had, for many years, been my best friend.

Most weekends our gang got together in each other's homes since no one, other than Christian, could afford to go out much. We always had fun. The night of Christian's birthday party was no exception. We had potluck dinner that finished with a cake Rikke's mother had baked. Then we played party games, and danced until shortly after midnight when we decided to break it up since we planned to go to Dyrehaven for a winter outing the next day.

Although we usually walked home in order to prolong the evening, Christian hailed a cab as soon as we reached the street. He invited a couple of our friends to share the ride and, although I was a little surprised at the extravagance, I figured it was because this day was our anniversary. I enjoyed sitting on his lap kissing in the dark in the back of the taxi.

After our friends were deposited at their homes, Christian and I rode in silence for the last part of the trip. As soon as we reached my home and Christian paid off the driver, I sensed that tonight was going to be different. Although very much in love, I was still afraid of going to bed with him. But now I was alone—without anyone watching over me—and I decided tonight would be the night I gave myself to the young man I loved.

We went into the dark apartment letting the moonlight guide us to my room and did not speak until we got there. Then Christian took my face in his hands and said, "Anna I love you. I have loved you for a long time and I promise I will never hurt you."

That was all he had said, but suddenly I was not afraid any more. We lay down on my bed, filled with love and desire, and when morning dawned, I had left my virginity behind.

Before Christian left, he pulled out a small package from his coat pocket and took out a gold locket on a slender chain.

"We have years of education and changes ahead of us, Anna, so I know we can't get engaged yet," he said and gently kissed me. "But I want you to have this locket as a constant reminder of my love for you and the happy years we have shared together," and he put it around my neck.

He drew me close and said, "I had the date we fell in love inscribed so you'll always remember the luckiest day of my life."

I felt sure I would never take off the chain with the little heart, having no knowledge of what the coming year would bring.

Chapter 13

The whistle from the teakettle brought me back from my reverie and I went to help Christian take the tea out to the balcony.

Christian took a sip of tea and announced he was hungry so I went back inside to look for some of the shortbread cookies Astrid had baked in honor of my arrival. With a dozen cookies on a plate, I went back and found Christian leafing through the morning paper.

"I want to show you something," he said looking both proud and a little embarrassed.

He opened the paper to the third page and there, above an article, I saw the headline: "Queen Margrete appoints four to Knighthood." I read the short story that included the names of the four so honored and next to the last was that of Christian Peter Raabensted.

I stared at him in disbelief and said "Sir Christian! Why in the world didn't you tell me this sooner? That sort of thing doesn't happen to just anyone. What a wonderful honor," I added and leaned over and kissed him.

He pulled me down on his lap, ran his fingers through my hair, and said, "I received the letter from Parliament a couple of weeks ago. I'm being awarded the 'Order of Danebrog' in honor of some research I did on the advancement in heart surgery," he explained.

"My children all know about it and I've wanted to tell you ever since it happened. But I wanted to wait for the right time. This time and this place seem perfect, and seeing the article in the paper made me decide. By the end of October, I will truly be 'Your Knight' even if I *am* missing the shining armor," he said. "What do you say we celebrate tonight?"

I told him how proud I was and thought a celebration very much in order. He asked to be excused for a few minutes while he made a couple of phone calls, and I settled down in one of the two chairs with my tea and nibbled on half a cookie Christian hadn't devoured.

I had enjoyed sitting here with Astrid a day earlier but it felt really good to be in my old home with Christian again. It not only felt good, it felt right, and I wished it would go on. I heard him laugh and felt a pang of sadness knowing I would be leaving him again in less than four weeks.

"You can't stay, even if he asks you to," my inner voice said. "You have a job; you have a family; grandchildren; friends, *and* a dog. Besides, what would you do with your time in this country for the rest of your life?" I questioned myself.

Before I could come up with answers, Christian appeared looking self-satisfied standing by the French doors leading to the balcony.

"We are really going to celebrate tonight, Anna. We not only have theater tickets, we have front row balcony seats to the opening night performance of The Russian Ballet at The Royal Theatre," he said triumphantly.

I looked at him in amazement. Tickets like that weren't easy to come by.

"'Fess up you scoundrel," I demanded, "who did you bribe and with what?"

"Well," he said looking smug; "Remember I told you Vivian and I parted amiably and have stayed friends. She became a successful actress and has, from time to time, sent me tickets to plays she's in.

"She's pretty much retired now taking only occasional bit parts, but she's married to Richard Vagner, the director of the Royal Theater, and has helped me with tickets before.

"Vivian did say that in return for the favor, she wants to meet you, and I promised we would get together with her and Richard for a drink after the performance. I hope that's ok?"

I assured him I would be delighted to meet anyone who, in minutes, could produce prime seats to a performance I had yearned to see for a long time. I also admitted to myself I would like to meet the woman who—I couldn't help but think—had taken him from me, even if the two of them didn't start dating until long after I went to the States.

"I also made dinner reservations at d'Angleterre, our prime place for French cuisine, so we're going to make a real night of it," Christian said.

It sounded like a wonderful evening—but a long one—and I made, I thought, a sensible suggestion.

"Christian," I said, "It's shortly after eleven; why don't we skip lunch at The Mill and drive back to Valhalla and eat lunch there. There is still enough food in the fridge to still even your appetite," I joked. "After that I am going to need a nap if I'm to stay up past midnight."

Christian agreed this made sense and admitted a nap might not be a bad idea.

"You make me feel like I am nineteen again," he said, "but my body reminds me, I'm not." Then he sheepishly asked, "You think perhaps we could nap together?"

In reply, I gave him a quick hug and kiss before I poked him in the side and said, "Not on your life. I need real sleep!"

I left him to carry the tea things back to the kitchen and went back into my room to pick out a suitable outfit. I needed something special to wear when we celebrated Christian's forthcoming Knighthood *and* opening night of the Russian Ballet Corps.

On the drive back, we decided to come back to Amager the following week and visit our old school. "We have lots of time," Christian said.

I nodded and tried not to think ahead to the end of my four weeks' vacation and a plane leaving with me on board.

Chapter 14

I stepped out of the car at Valhalla and noticed the weather had turned cold again. It was indeed Danish spring with hourly temperatures changes. I realized my trench coat might not be warm enough over my evening dress but decided to worry about it later.

Once inside, I walked straight to the kitchen to prepare a meal while Christian went to check for phone messages and to turn up the thermostat. I had just put everything on the table when he came back and said I had a message on the answering machine. I gave him a questioning look; no one, except Astrid, knew where I was and she had no reason to call me.

"Your friend, Reenie," Christian laughed and led me to the telephone on the desk in the study. "I only listened long enough to hear who it was."

Pushing the button, I noted the call had come in just passed noon—6 am her time. I turned on the machine and heard Reenie's cheerful voice.

"You can run, pal, but you can't hide. Call me as soon as you get this message. Then there was a pause before she added, "*please!*"

Christian smiled and told me to make the call. Then he tactfully left and went out into the kitchen to open a bottle of wine.

Reenie answered on the first ring and without beating around asked, "So, how is it going? Have you fallen in love yet; are you coming back; is he everything you hoped he would be? I woke up this morning and was curious."

"Hello my darling Reenie," I answered and laughed. "And the answers are as follows: one, very well thank you; two, I'm afraid so; three, yes, of course, and four, yes and then some and, by the way, you are a real rascal; how in the world did you find me and what are you doing up this early?"

165

"'Elementary my dear Watson, elementary.' I called your cousin Astrid and got a message saying she would be away for a few days. Since you had told me you were going to spend Easter with your cousin Freddy and had given me all the names and numbers of people and places you planned to visit—paranoid that you are—I called Freddy. The rest was a cinch," she finished.

I heard Christian whistling an old tune in the kitchen and told Reenie I was having an absolutely wonderful time. "Right now, however, I need food and a long nap, but I'll send you an email in a couple of days and tell you about what has happened to date."

Before I could say another word, she interrupted with her sparkling laughter.

"Oh, you *are* having a good time if you need a nap in the middle of the afternoon. That can only mean you didn't get much sleep last night and since you spent it with Christian that's as it should be."

I told her she was irreverent, but I adored her, and for her to get back and take care of my dog I had left in her care. She assured me Tessa was doing fine and was getting spoiled, adding she would check with me in another week. "Meanwhile, I'm anticipating a full report via email."

I told her about the ballet that evening and she said she was green with envy.

"I want details and an autographed program," she said and wished me a good time.

Christian had poured wine and was making sandwiches when I came into the kitchen. I gave him a rundown of the conversation—he knew Reenie through our emails—and understood why she called.

"I'm glad you have a friend like that."

We finished eating and put away the dishes before walking upstairs, hand in hand. At the top of the stairs, I started toward Christina's room.

Christian looked me in the eyes and said, "Please, come and lay down with me. We don't have to do anything. As a matter of fact I'm bushed and not nineteen, so you're safe."

I preferred to sleep next to him, so I shed the jeans and

heavy sweater, put on his bathrobe, laid down and almost immediately fell asleep nestled in Christian's arms.

I woke up realizing someone was playing with the lace on my bra and felt Christian's warm breath on my neck. The old clock struck three so I knew I had slept for nearly two hours. By the time his lips reached the little heart around my neck I also knew that my nap was over, and pulled him closer. I enjoyed feeling alive and wanted again.

Later, I thought how the grandfather clock in the foyer had begun to mark events in Christian's home as I was sure it had for others in years past.

When I heard the clock strike on the half-hour, I told Christian we had to get up if we planned to get ready for our big celebration that evening.

Chapter 15

After showering, I went to the closet and pulled out my new dress and was glad I'd brought it; it would be just right for this occasion. I remembered the day I bought it.

A week before my trip, I had gone with Hunter Lee to the South Park Mall in Charlotte to shop for a few things and was just walking out of a bath and toiletry boutique when she suddenly eyed the dress on display in one of the up-scale stores. She said it looked irresistible and suggested I buy it.

"It is so you, or at least the new you," she laughed and urged me to see if they had it in my size. On a whim, I decided to go along. Hunter Lee talked to the sales lady and with a sly smile—not like her usual cool self—handed the dress to me and said, "You just never know."

It was an elegant two-piece crepe dress in midnight blue with a flowing tea-length skirt. The top fell just below my hips, had slightly flaring, long sleeves and an *extremely* low-cut neckline.

"Just right for showing off your fabulous chest," my daughter-in-law said.

Hunter Lee was raised very much a southern belle and would never say boobs or breast. It wasn't part of her Georgian upbringing to use anything but 'refined' language. She did, however, have excellent taste in clothes and had never led me astray. So without blinking an eye, I wrote a check for an exorbitant amount as Hunter Lee assured me, "Mother T, that dress will knock someone dead."

Back in Christian's bedroom I put on some of my own fine lingerie—Christmas presents from Reenie—adding a garter belt and dark stockings and decided to check on Christian before I continued my dressing. I put on Christians robe, tied the belt around me, and went down to look for him. I found him in the kitchen fixing a snack of cheese and apples, wearing a starched, high collar shirt, the pants of his tuxedo, and a pair of black patent leather shoes. As I entered, he turned around with a sheepish grin on his face swallowing a bite from the brick of Havarti sitting on a butcher block on the counter.

"I'm going to put on at least twenty pounds if you stay in my life," he said and wiped his mouth before coming over to give me a kiss.

"I seem to work up an appetite for everything in sight whenever I'm around you," he added and pulled open the bathrobe.

He looked at me with a pronounced leer and said, "I love you in that bra and garter belt; especially if that's all you plan to wear. However, I'm not sure it will pass the dress code at the Royal Theater tonight."

I gently pushed him away and told him I was just checking on him and wanted a drink to take up while I finished dressing.

"I'll gladly oblige you," he said and found a bottle of club soda in the refrigerator, poured it into a glass and handed it to me. Then he walked upstairs with me.

"I'll finish dressing in my office and leave you alone so we can get out of here on time. Our dinner reservation is for six o'clock but I would love go in early and take the scenic road," he added. He gave me a friendly pat on the rear and I went back into his bedroom and finished dressing.

I came down half an hour later and the look on Christian's face, accompanied by a whistle, was well worth the amount I spent on the dress. Admiration showed in his eyes as he said, "I hope the Queen stays home tonight since the audience, most certainly, will look at you instead of her."

"Flattery will get you everywhere," I joked. Just the same, I was pleased. The dress did look good on, I admitted to myself, and I owed my dear daughter-in-law a big 'thanks' for her excellent choice and for talking me into buying it.

In the hallway, I reached into the closet to take out my

trench coat but Christian stopped me.

"The temperature has dropped considerably, and you'll freeze in that coat." He reached back into the closet and brought out a mink cape.

"It was mother's," he explained. "My daughters won't wear it since both are avid wildlife preservationists," he said. "I bought it for her a few months before she died, but she never got to use it. I'd be pleased it you'd wear it tonight."

Being practical—and not against furs as long as they were from an era when no one was concerned about killing animals—I let Christian help me with the cape. The softness of the fur and the silk lining felt comforting, and luxurious. I glanced at Christian, who looked elegant in his tuxedo and black light wool overcoat, and smiled. It looked like the "golden couple" was back, albeit slightly less golden and a lot grayer.

Within minutes, a cab pulled up in front of Valhalla and as I walked down the front steps to the car I recalled the strict rules regarding driving and drinking in Denmark. Any person, caught "driving under the influence," not only receives a stiff fine but often has his car impounded. The automobile fatality rate in this country is low and they very much intend to keep it that way.

Christian explained that, like most Danes, he takes taxis when going out for an evening that might include alcohol. He asked the chauffeur to take the long way and the driver willingly agreed; then we sat back and enjoyed the scenic ride along the coast as the car took us into the heart of the city.

We arrived at d'Angleterre, one of the oldest and most elegant dining establishments in Copenhagen, right at six o'clock. I had been there with my parents on several occasions before moving to the States. The most memorable time was the day of my confirmation when my parents entertained forty family members and friends at a dinner in my honor.

Visitors from all over the world can be found among the

guests in the graceful dining rooms where, on weekend nights, most of the women are in evening gowns and the men in dark suits or tuxedos.

The walls are covered in off-white brocade, and French provincial furniture fills the many dining rooms. The tables hold fresh flowers in cut crystal bowls placed on thick damask cloths laid with heavy silver and crystal glasses and the well trained wait staff whisks about catering to their customers.

This evening a young man in coat and tails sat at the grand piano, softly playing tunes dating back to World War II. The only other sounds were the hushed voices of the guests and silverware touching fine china.

The Maitre'de led us to our table and Christian ordered scotch and water "with just a little ice for the lady;" he had indeed studied my emails carefully and knew my likes and dislikes. During dinner we recalled a few anecdotes from school, and that night's performance.

"I have to confess that ballet is not my chosen form of entertainment," he admitted, "but I knew you loved it and it is, of course, the Russian Corps that everyone ought to see at least once," he added and raised his glass to toast.

The Champaign topping off our dinner was stimulating, and I felt in a festive mood. Having recently made love to a man I cared for—after several years of celibacy—probably added to the feeling.

Following dinner, we walked across the street to the theater that sits majestically on Kongens Nytorv opposite the restaurant.

Once inside, we were shown to our seats on the second tier balcony. From the faded, plush-covered chairs, I observed the orchestra and the interior of the age-old theater. I had come here as a young girl with my grandmother Aggie to matinees, and sat in back row seats while she explained the music or ballet we had come to see. She was a wonderful teacher and artfully taught me music appreciation without ever making me feel she was instructing.

I sat back in the seat, took Christian's hand, and reminded myself that I must thank Vivian.

Just before the curtain went up, a discrete drum roll sounded from the orchestra pit. The audience rose and I looked across the theater and saw the Danish Queen, Margrete II, accompanied by her oldest son, Crown Prince Frederik, enter the royal box. She nodded gracefully to the audience and then to the orchestra before taking her seat. Then we all sat down to enjoy a breathtaking performance of Swan Lake.

The meeting with Vivian and Richard Vagner turned out to be more fun than anticipated. Vivian was witty, outspoken, and charming; Richard proved knowledgeable on every aspect of the theater, and throughout the evening entertained us with back stage stories spiked with a dry sense of humor.

We had met them in the lobby right after the performance and without any prior introduction Vivian planted a kiss on Christian's mouth and hugged him. Then she grabbed my hand and said, "I always wondered why Christian married Karen and now I see; she's the spitting image of you."

The remark made me feel a little uncomfortable, but Vivian just went on to chat about the ballet and the plans for the summer season. We walked down the sidewalk, away from the old theater and entered one of the many small bistros in Nyhavn, a place no self-respecting woman would have gone to back in the fifties when Nyhavn had been the setting for drunken sailors, brawls, and fights. Vivian must have seen my surprised look and explained it had been renovated some years ago and was now *the* place to go; we quickly settled down to drinks inside the small cafe featuring a jazz combo.

Shortly after midnight, Christian told Vivian and Richard we had an early trip scheduled the next day and needed to get home. I still felt on top of the world, but realized I needed sleep if we were to join Freddy, Rie, and Astrid for Easter lunch the next day.

Vivian kissed both my cheeks in theatrical fashion and as we left, she asked me to call "so we can meet and have lunch in town." She liked me, she said. She also pointed out that she and Richard lived just a couple of blocks away from Valhalla in "a monster of a house" and that it would be easy to get together. Richard rose and gave me a hug and while Christian helped me put on the cape, I assured Vivian I would like to see her again.

Once outside, Christian hailed a cab and soon we were sitting in the back seat of the quietly moving automobile passing stores—closed for the night—and apartment buildings with scattered lights telling us who was asleep and who was still up enjoying this cold, but lovely, spring night.

Chapter 16

As soon as we woke up, Christian announced he was starved and offered to make us a "big breakfast." I declined. After the drinks and meal I consumed the evening before, all I wanted was coffee. I also knew how Rie cooked and wanted room for the delicacies she was bound to serve.

Christian offered me the use of his bathroom and tromped across the hall to the one adjacent to Christina's room. After my shower, I put on my charcoal suit and a light blue turtleneck sweater, added my amber pendant, platinum loop earrings, and the large marquee diamond ring Robert had given me to celebrate his first year in business for himself. I put on heels but threw a pair of loafers in the canvas bag I planned to take with me. I knew Freddy's passion for walking and wanted to be prepared for the stroll I felt sure he would suggest. I recalled getting caught once at their cottage in a pair of good shoes that had to be retired after seawater, salt and sand ruined them.

We took off for our trip shortly before ten even though we were not expected until one o'clock and the drive to Freddy's took less than two hours. The reason for the earlier departure was a favor I had asked Christian. It was one that would puzzle most Danes, but one my American family and friends would understand—it was Easter Sunday and I wanted to go to church.

Most of the churches in Denmark sit nearly empty year round, but do draw small congregations on Christmas Eve and Easter Sunday. "The Poinsettias and the Lilies," our old priest in New York used to call those attending church only on those occasions. This year, however, the turnout might be greater. According to Astrid, church attendance was suddenly becoming popular so perhaps we would not be alone this morning.

Years ago, like most young persons in Denmark, I had

not been much of a churchgoer and Christian had given me a questioning look when I suggested we go. I told him I attended service on a semi-regular basis at home and would like to visit the century-old Lutheran church located thirty minutes from Freddy and Rie's cottage. The church was a historic landmark, featured years ago in a classic Christmas movie that still played every holiday. Christian knew it would add an hour to our trip, but was more than willing to oblige. He conceded, "a little religion probably won't hurt," adding he too would like to visit the famous church.

On the way Christian told me the church was recently featured in a popular Danish magazine and as a result had attracted a great many tourists. We arrived at St. Gertrude's just as the bells tolled and were lucky to find two empty seats near the back.

The organ suddenly broke the silence as an old familiar hymn thundered into the hall echoing off the ancient white, chalk walls. We all rose and joined the small choir in a song of praise. It was a nice service with a predictable sermon that focused on "go forth to rejoice and love your fellow man." I felt somewhat self-conscious; I already felt joyful and was more or less sure of loving the fellow man sitting next to me. Somehow, I didn't think that was what Pastor Andersen had in mind that morning; so to make up for my smugness, I left a generous offering on my way out. Then I shook hands with the minister and told him I enjoyed his sermon.

Right after we left the church, Christian pulled into a gas station and as he filled up the tank, I looked out the window and saw two small children eyeing a poster picturing ice cream and candy. The sight rang a bell and I panicked, realizing I had forgotten to bring a hostess gift for my cousin and his wife. You do not visit someone in Denmark without bringing a house gift (usually flowers or candy) even if they are relatives. Not taking a gift to your hosts is just not done. I was also bringing Christian, who had never been to their home, so the slip-up would be two-fold. I rolled down the window and told Christian about my faux pas and to my great relief he pointed to a shopping bag on the back seat.

"Have no fear; your knight has come to your rescue. Since I'm visiting your cousin for the first time, I knew I needed to bring a little something," he assured me.

"Just before you came down for coffee this morning, I went into the study and found a small box of Cuban cigars that one of my former patients gave to me a couple of months ago. At the time he gave them to me I didn't dare ask where he got them; I also didn't have the heart to tell him I rarely smoke.

"I've kept them in a humidor, so I'm sure they are still good, and since you told me Freddy smokes, he'll probably enjoy them.

"They're in the bag along with a box of Swiss chocolate I bought at the duty free shop in the airport on my way back from Germany earlier this week. I usually try to keep a couple of boxes on hand for when I'm asked out."

With relief, I sat back in the car and in a short time we pulled up in front of the gate to my cousin's summer place.

I've always enjoyed visiting "Easy Rider," the vacation cottage Rie and Freddy have owned for years, named after a well-known American movie. It welcomes you and makes you feel it's been sitting there just waiting for you to come along. Built at the turn of the century, it has an aura of quaintness from a time that enjoyed a slower pace.

Over the years, Freddy and Rie have modernized the cottage and turned it into a year-round home where they enjoy spending the major part of their time. They only head back to their condominium outside Copenhagen to check on things now and then, and at Christmas when their entire clan gathers for one of Rie's famous holiday meals.

They had named the place in honor of the trucking firm Freddy owned and operated for years. He and his wife Harriet raised a great group of children and Astrid told me that their three boys now ran "Easy Rider Trucking." Freddy officially retired several years ago, but still drops in to see "how things are doing," whenever he's in town. His hard work and dedication in his younger years paid off and some of the profit from the company provided the capital, and later the upkeep, of their summer-home.

I looked forward to introducing Christian and my family to each other.

Chapter 17

No sooner did we get out of the car before Freddy charged through the cottage door, a big smile on his face, hands outstretched to welcome us. Fast on his heels was "Sissy," Freddy's Golden Retriever, jumping, barking and wagging her tail, letting us know she too was glad to see us.

"It's about time you two got here," Freddy bellowed and swallowed me in his embrace. "I'm starved and Rie will not let me touch as much as a radish."

"Anna, my love, you look even lovelier than the last time I saw you," he said, planted a kiss on my cheek, and tossed my hair. I smiled with delight realizing my oldest cousin hadn't changed a bit.

Freddy is in his seventies but seems years younger. He is six foot two and if ever anyone looked like a Viking, he does. With a full head of snow-white hair, matching full beard and steely blue eyes, he looks like a brother to Holger Danske, the mythical Danish hero who, according to the legend, sits and waits to come to the rescue of all Danes during war or other danger. The statue of Holger is located in the dungeons of Kronborg Castle in the northern part of Zealand.

During World War II, Freddy had been a member of an underground movement in Denmark. They called themselves: "Sons of Holger the Dane," and to the frustration of the German Army—and great delight of all the Danes—they had excelled in sabotaging many an enemy plan.

"Come in, come in," Freddy beckoned and put his arm around my shoulders, practically carrying me into the house. I have adored him for years and didn't resist. Sissy, ignored by her owner, chose instead to jump up and lick Christian's face displaying an immediate and undying affection and, for the rest of the day, she never left him.

"Will you put that girl down Freddy, and get your silly dog off our guest," Rie laughingly reprimanded her husband as she came to the door.

"I don't know why I let you out to greet anyone—you are hopeless," she added and shook her head. Then she gave him a devoted look and welcomed us to their home.

After fifty years of marriage, Freddy and Rie, a tiny woman in her late sixties who barely reaches her husband's chest, still treat each other like newlyweds. She bosses him around; he teases her and usually just laughs and swings her around and kisses her. That ritual settles most of their disagreements and it makes them nice to be around.

"I'll put Anna down as soon as you ring the dinner bell, Rie," he laughed and let me go. Christian assured them that he loved dogs and didn't mind Sissy's attention.

Astrid came out to greet us, shook her head at her brother and sister-in-law, and took our coats.

"Do come in Dr. Raabensted," Rie said, "and pay no attention to my husband, he always did have a soft spot when it came to Anna."

Christian, who until this point had looked amused, jumped into action and produced the cigars and box of chocolates for his host and hostess. Both gifts were accepted with pleasure.

"I'll be damned if those aren't Cuban cigars," Freddy said. "I've not seen any in years. I know you can't legally bring them into the country so I won't ask you where you got them; I do hope you'll join me and smoke one after lunch, Dr. Raabensted," he added with a big heartfelt laugh

"Please, call me Christian, and I'll be happy to smoke one later. Incidentally, I have no idea where the cigars originated," Christian said and threw me a bemused look.

"I don't care if you burn expensive and illegal cigars, as long as you smoke them outside the cottage. I'll enjoy my chocolates while I watch you both ruin your lungs," Rie said with a small huff.

"Don't take my wife seriously," Freddy told Christian.

Then he laughed, and threw his wife a kiss as she went back into the kitchen to see to our lunch.

"Well now," he said rubbing his hands motioning for Christian to follow him, "let's all just have a little something to whet the whistle while we wait for Rie to feed us."

The two men, followed by Sissy, went over to a corner cabinet where Freddy kept a small bar. After serving Astrid and me each a glass of dry sherry, he and Christian settled down with whisky and soda and began discussing the upcoming soccer match between Denmark and Sweden, two arch-enemies.

With drinks in hand, Astrid and I went out to offer Rie our help, but she declined with a wave of her hand saying she had everything under control and was just putting the finishing touches on her dessert.

"You two go sit down and catch up. We'll be ready to eat in about fifteen minutes—or as soon as Flemming arrives" she said.

Flemming is Rie's younger brother who evidently had been invited to join the party for lunch.

Astrid and I took our drinks and went out to the closed-in veranda facing the ocean. The view from there was idyllic on this clear Easter Sunday with barely a wave stirring. The cottage is about a hundred yards from the beach with nothing but low dunes in between. On the horizon, sailboats passed by, and near the edge of the water, a couple of swallows were executing acrobatic dives.

I dropped down in a comfortable rattan chair, sipped my sherry, took in the splendid scenery, and waited for Astrid to begin talking. I sensed she was trying not to sound nosy, but knew she was curious.

I didn't have long to wait.

She fiddled with her glass, looked out at the dunes, stole a look at Christian, before she finally turned and looked me straight in the face.

"So how are things going as if I couldn't tell by the looks of you," she smiled. "I take it you're getting along just fine with Christian and that I'll not see much of you during your vacation."

"We are indeed getting along just fine," I told her and paused for a moment. "I'm just not certain where we are heading. Christian and I have made plans for the next several days, but I'll be back and help you with the preparations for the Christening next weekend."

Astrid was about to comment when Sissy began barking letting us know that company had arrived. We rose and walked outside into the courtyard to greet the final guest.

An old, black and well-kept Volkswagen pulled up next to Christian's car and a somber man stepped out dressed in a dark-gray, three-piece tweed suit, and a smart-looking red bow-tie.

It was Flemming, and even if I hadn't known he was expected, and though I hadn't seen him for years, I would have recognized him; he hadn't changed one bit.

Flemming, a confirmed bachelor in his early sixties, is small of stature like his sister and as neat and dapper as Hercules Pierot, right down to his upturned mustache. He taught ancient history at the university in Koege, and had done so for several decades. Astrid had told me his students often joked and said he too was a left over relic. Flemming possessed the greatest sense of humor—something his appearance belied—and his pupils loved him and never failed to include him in most of their festivities. He always made an excellent dinner companion, and I looked forward to being with him again.

Freddy and Christian came out to join us, and Freddy made introductions. Flemming gallantly kissed the hands of both Astrid and myself and led us inside. Without asking, Freddy fixed Flemming a very dry martini with a twist of lemon, went out to tell his wife her brother had arrived, and could they *please* eat? A few minutes later, Rie came out from the kitchen carrying a basket of hot rolls and announced lunch was ready and "please be seated."

I looked at the table, beautifully set with green pottery plates on a blue and white patterned linen tablecloth, green cut glass goblets at the tip of the knives, and blue and green-checkered cotton napkins on the plates.

Rie had picked white and yellow daffodils from her garden and, with the flowers, brought in a bit of spring. They were placed in a bowl at the center of the table flanked by white candles in tall, red earthenware candlesticks.

On our plates was an arrangement of tender pieces of lobster on top of an all green salad served with the crusty rolls she just baked. From here on we worked our way through delicately boiled shrimp, marinated herring, smoked trout, roast beef and ham served with fresh vegetables and tasty sauces—one delicious morsel after another until I had to stop. My appetite had returned, but I was still not prepared to consume large portions at any meal.

The conversation flowed during lunch—covering sports, weather and politics. Then, just as we were about to finish, the topic of Christian's knighthood came up.

"Did I read in an article in yesterday's paper, that you were just named a knight Dr. Raabensted?" Flemming asked.

Rie and Freddy, who only get the local newspaper at their cottage, looked with interest at my companion and asked for details.

Christian admitted that yes, he, along with three others, had been selected to receive the honor, adding that the actual ceremony would not take place until sometime in the fall.

"A knight!" Freddy exclaimed as his face lit up. "Well I'll be damned!"

Then he winked at his wife and said, "Hey, Rie, we practically have royalty in our house today. With Christian here being a knight and Anna almost a duchess, we're certainly entertaining high society this afternoon!

"You did know that Anna's grandmother on her father's side was a Prussian duchess, didn't you," he asked after he caught Christian's questioning look.

"Your grandmother Aggie was a duchess?" Christian looked at me in disbelief. "You never told me that."

"No, no, not Mrs. Wiinter," Freddy said. "Mrs. Wiinter was indeed a fine and elegant lady but she wasn't aristocracy," he explained. "I'm talking about Anna's real grandmother, Clara. Before she married old man Drener, she was Duchess Elisabet Augusta von Ludwig including a couple of other names I can't remember."

I looked down at my empty plate and thought back to all the unspoken truths, the pretending, and many outright lies that had been so much an everyday part of my life while growing up. At times I had been uncertain as to what *was* the truth.

Rie, sensing the awkward silence, announced that lunch was over and encouraged everyone to get up and stretch after the meal.

As he rose from his chair, Christian looked at me, confusion written all over his face. We were growing closer day by day and yet I knew there was so much he didn't know about me. For a moment, I was lost for words not knowing how—or in what way—to respond.

Chapter 18

I didn't have to worry long. Freddy, totally unaware of the pregnant moment he'd created, thanked Rie for a great Easter lunch and got up from the table. The rest of us chimed in and thanked her for a wonderful meal, praising her culinary skills. Freddy kissed Rie and offered to help her in the kitchen, but she laughed away his offer and said he broke more dishes than he cleaned. "Just take care of our guests," she said and began clearing the table.

Astrid immediately joined her sister-in-law, and suggested I join the men while she helped Rie in the kitchen. So, I left the table and followed the men into the living room.

Sissy, who during lunch had slept—gently snoring—behind Christian's chair, got up and walked closely behind her newfound friend. I was still antsy about Freddy's reference to the 'duchess,' unsure what he would say next. Freddy rarely lets a good story go untold and this one, I sensed, was one he would love to tell.

Christian and I sat down together in the big couch facing the dunes with Sissy right in front of Christian.

Freddy poured cognac all around; then went over and picked up an old photo album and a picture from the top shelf of a bookcase next to the window. He pulled up a chair next to Christian and put the album on the table.

The frame held a faded picture of a group of men standing next to a taxi outside a large brick building. All were dressed up, looking as if they just came from a party.

Freddy handed me the photograph and I looked at it with surprise. I had been to their cottage many times, but had never seen it before.

"Rie found this picture, last fall while cleaning out some boxes at home, and had it framed as a surprise for me. I really like it and decided to bring it to the cottage since we spend most of our time here. It was taken in the summer of 1945 and reminds me of good times in my younger days. That's me with the big grin and my arm draped over the shoulder of your father, Alex Drener," he said pointing to a tall, good-looking man. I recognized him, of course, but said nothing.

"That's your grandfather, the stern-looking Hans Drener, standing by the door of his brand new automobile wearing a fedora and holding his walking stick. The two dark-haired men to the left are your uncles, Karl and Axel. They both married before the war and each had a couple of sons—but no daughters," he said and gave me a significant look.

"Later, the brothers moved away and I lost touch with them. I heard, through the grape-vine, that their younger sister, Clara, became some sort of an entertainer. Supposedly, she had an affair with a young foreigner while she was on a trip to Germany but, as far as I know, she never married him."

He stopped for a moment and took a sip of his drink before pointing back to the photograph.

"The picture was taken after an anniversary party of your grandfather's business. He used to own the Amager Little Taxi Company. Maybe you remember?"

I just nodded.

"Anyway, we all had a good time celebrating that day; the war had just ended and the taxi business was picking up again.

"I went to work for him right after I got out of the army and stayed with the company until I went into trucking. I kept contact with the family for a number of years but never, of course, let your father—that is Nels Wiinter—know of my connection. I knew him enough to keep *that* to myself."

Freddy took the picture and put it back on the bookshelf. Then he came back and picked up the album, opened it and flipped the pages until he came to a photo of a young woman dressed in an evening gown. She was posed on a chair with a handsome, somewhat older, man standing behind her; she looked to be about seventeen or eighteen years old.

"Anna," he said, "that's your paternal grandmother Clara. The man standing behind her was a duke or something she was supposed to marry. The story goes that she got involved with Hans Drener, who was the handsome head coachman at her father's estate. He drove her carriage home one night after she had a fight with her fiancé at his home; I'm not sure I got all this right," he added.

"Anyway, sometime later, she discovered she was pregnant and rather than face the shame of an illegitimate pregnancy, she eloped to Denmark with your grandfather. He had an older brother living just outside Copenhagen, and he helped him get started in the coach business."

"Old man Drener never would let your grandmother talk about her early life after they were married, but she did tell her only daughter—your aunt Clara—about it and she, in turn, told me. I had a little crush on Clara at the time and we dated briefly," he said.

He looked at Rie who, with Astrid, had joined us. "That was long before I met you my dear."

Rie smiled and Freddy turned back to Christian and continued his story.

"Then one day I arrived early for dinner at the Drener's house, and found Anna's grandmother alone, except for the maid who let me in. When the girl went back to the kitchen, Mrs. Drener asked me to come into the living room. She took me aside, served me a glass of port, and handed me this album. She expressed her hopes that someday I would be able to pass it on to you, the daughter of her favorite son and her only granddaughter."

Freddy paused and finished off his cognac. He patted Sissy's head, topped off Christian and Flemming's glasses, and noted I had barely touched mine. He re-filled his own glass and went on.

"I'd heard from Clara that your grandmother was born a duchess, but this was the first time I actually saw pictures from her days in Prussia," he said. With a wink he added, "For an aristocrat, she was quite a dish."

He continued, this time addressing his comments to me.

"Your grandmother had given up hope of ever seeing

you again after your mother divorced Alex and married Wiinter, but she thought someday, when you were older, I might be able to pass this album on to you. So I took it home and put it away and forgot all about it until Rie discovered the album in the same box where she found the anniversary picture."

Freddy flipped the page over and at the top of the next one was a photo of that same young woman wearing a white evening gown. She was with a group of young women, all dressed like her, sitting on either side of a man standing erect with a saber-like cane in his hand and an elegant plumed hat under his arm.

"That's Kaiser Wilhelm of Germany," he said pointing to the only man in the picture.

"According to your grandmother, that picture was taken during the annual ball the Kaiser gave in order to introduce aristocratic young ladies to his court."

Throughout Freddy's story, Christian sat quietly listening—I remained mute. Christian and I had been so close during the years we dated, yet, he had no knowledge that Nels Wiinter—who he had known as my farther—was my mother's second husband who married her and adopted me when I was only five. Since any mentioning of mother's and my previous life was a forbidden subject in our home, I never dared talk about it, not even with Christian. But despite the deception, I very much remembered having another grandmother before Aggie Wiinter.

Chapter 19

Sensing an uncomfortable situation, Flemming stood up and suggested we all go for a stroll to walk off some of Rie's sumptuous lunch. Freddy, who is always ready to hike along the water, quickly agreed and Christian said he would also like to stretch his legs.

"I want to be able to do justice to the dessert I eyed in the kitchen," he said and stood up.

Rie begged off saying she preferred to stay home and relax while the rest of us went for a walk. Freddy hugged her and laughed.

"I know—you just want to take your little afternoon snooze and nibble on that good Swiss chocolate Christian brought."

We all chided him saying that Rie had more than earned a rest after preparing the splendid meal we just enjoyed. Astrid conceded she would also like to relax, and as the rest of us got ready for our walk, the two settled down with comfortable crocheted blankets in a couple of the chaise lounges.

I put on my trench coat and changed into the loafers I had brought, and soon we were walking along the strand by the edge of the crystal-clear waters. This part of Denmark has clean, wide beaches with sand ruffled by the waves, and I remembered my summers spent here with my mother, Astrid, Rie and a couple of my cousin's children. They had been happy days, yet all along I had carried the burden of memories from my early years, knowledge I wasn't supposed to have.

As we walked, Freddy regaled us with tall tales from his trucking days while Flemming provided entertaining anecdotes from his job at the university. Sissy pulled guard duty and never left Christian.

All the time we walked, Christian held his arm tight around me and never broached the subject of the Drener family. He must have sensed this was something I was not ready to talk about.

We arrived back at the cottage, now filled with the aroma of coffee and something delicious just out of the oven. The men had built up appetites, and dozens of shortbread cookies—and a considerable portion of the layer cake covered with whipped cream and filled with strawberries—soon vanished. I settled for a cup of coffee. I told Rie I still had clothes I wanted to be able to wear, but the truth was, I had lost my appetite realizing there were things I needed to tell Christian if we were to further our relationship.

After coffee and dessert, we spent time in sociable conversation that brought me up to date on the whereabouts of Freddy and Rie's five children and great number of grandchildren.

Christian, with three children and just one grandchild, told his host he was impressed with the size of Freddy's clan. This caused Freddy to fill the room with a raucous laugh.

"After three sons, we finally figured out what caused them! Then we thought we would have one more, just for fun, and by God, if Rie didn't bless me with twin daughters!"

Rie looked at him affectionately and said, "And two more spoiled girls than Annelise and Annebeth, you'll never find."

Astrid, quick to defend her brother, immediately pointed out that the two girls, by now in their thirties, were "two of the nicest young women you ever want to meet."

Freddy just beamed.

It was getting late and Christian and I began preparing for our trip back north declining Rie's offer to stay for a quick little meal before leaving, and Freddy's offer to "spend the night, we have plenty of room and Rie puts on a great breakfast."

While Freddy went to get our coats and Christian

exchanged university research gossip with Flemming, Astrid pulled me aside and said she would not be back home until late Tuesday.

"I plan to stay at Easy Rider for a couple of days and do some visiting and shopping with Rie before I catch the train back." She assured me she would not need my help until Thursday afternoon and told me to have a great time.

With promises to Rie and Freddy to come back again, Christian and I drove off with Sissy following us, running along the car barking and sending him longing looks.

"You really ought to get yourself a dog," I said.

"You're right. I'd almost forgotten just how nice it is to have one around; perhaps we could look for one together," he said.

We arrived at Valhalla sometime after eight o'clock and promptly raided the refrigerator for a light meal. We opened the kitchen window and shared our food in the kitchen nook while enjoying the mild breeze blowing in from the ocean. Christian ate the better part of a cold chicken and a cucumber salad; I picked at some cheese and apple wedges. We finished our meal, closed the window, and went into the library.

During our trip home from Rie and Freddy's cottage we had talked about safe subjects and Christian never asked about the Drener family. Now, sitting in the library on the couch by the warming fireplace with steaming mugs of coffee in front of us, he put his arm around me and said,

"Anna, I realize there are parts of your background I don't know and I have no intention of prying. But, please know I'm here to listen, if and when you want to talk."

I nodded and said perhaps I would tell him the story another day. "Right now I would just like to sit quietly with you in front of the fire and enjoy the rest of the evening."

He looked at me, smiled and said, "In that case, I know just the right thing for us to do tonight," and for a brief moment I thought he was considering seducing me on the couch; and, although it might have been enjoyable, I wasn't sure I was in the mood.

As it turned out, Christian had something else in mind. He went over to the Armoire, pulled out a tape from one of the shelves and put it in the video player. Then he came over to me, smiled as he sat down, and wrapped his arm around me. Within minutes the credits to "White Christmas," came on the screen and soon the film began to roll.

"I know this isn't the right season for this movie, but I think it might be the right time for us to see it. We can watch Bing Crosby, as Sir Bob Wallace, court his Lady Betty, and I'll sit here as your old—soon to be real—knight, and protect you from whatever evil lurks in the crevices of your mind."

Then he kissed me.

The movie turned out to be just the right thing to watch. We stopped the tape at the point where Rosemary Clooney leaves on the train for the city, having been let down by *her* knight in shining armor, and made ourselves mugs of tea to which Christian added a generous shot of bourbon.

By the time the movie ended, I was in a mellow mood and had, for the moment, put all my family relations behind me. When we finally went to sleep in the big four-poster, I was only aware of being with a man I felt closer to each moment.

Chapter 20

I woke up alone in the bed and, when I looked out the bedroom windows, noticed the weather had turned dismal overnight. The sky was grey and a battering wind was playing games with the plants on the front lawn.

Out toward the main road I saw the birch trees—lining the driveway—swaying like two rows of drunken sailors ready for muster.

I decided to go look for Christian, threw on a robe, and found him in the kitchen in the process of setting out plates and cups on the table. He met me with a smile and a hug and told me he had woken up early and thought he would let me sleep in.

"You seemed exhausted last night, and I didn't want to wake you. But I did ride my bicycle to our local bakery to pick up freshly baked breakfast rolls, while trying to work off some of Rie's baked goods," he laughed.

I complimented him on his exercise and we sat down to eat the warm rolls, lathering on butter and thick slices of cheese accompanied by scalding coffee and fresh juice. We finished, and I put the dishes away, gave Christian a kiss, and went up to dress for the day.

After my shower I put on Christian's thick white sweater, my own jeans and Christina's clogs and felt snug and happy. All thoughts of the Drener and Wiinter families were temporarily buried and I almost skipped down the stairs and into the kitchen.

"So, what do you say we go for a walk?" Christian asked as he finished emptying the dishwasher. During breakfast we decided to postpone our trip out to Amager and our old haunts since the weather was not going to be particularly nice, and the weatherman had promised sun the next day.

"Surely you jest," I said and gave him a look of disbelief. "It's nasty outside. Besides, you promised we would look through old family albums some time, so I can see how you looked during the years we were apart, and also see pictures of your children.

"First we go for a walk—doctor's orders," he joked. "Christina has a hooded, lined rain slicker you can wear and the fresh air will do us both good. Then I promise we'll light the fire in the library and look at pictures for as long as you like."

Despite the rain, the ocean looked spectacular with waves crashing against the low boulders, piled on the shoreline, while the sea foamed like a mad dog ready to attack.

The truth was, I enjoyed a walk in this sort of weather, and Christian remembered. Years ago we had often walked in the rain when he came over to see me on a wet Saturday or Sunday afternoon. Although the beach near my old home doesn't have boulders, it does offer spectacular waves during high winds and rain.

So off we went and enjoyed an invigorating walk.

As we approached the house on our return, my face drenched with the spray from the sea, I noticed a small red car parked in the driveway. I thought perhaps I'd misunderstood Christian and that Mrs. Larsen had come back to work this morning rather than the next day. Christian didn't comment, just kissed my salty face before we went inside.

We approached the back door leading into the kitchen and I heard a teakettle whistle emitting a piercing sound just before it stopped on a sad little half-note.

We went in, hung our coats in the mud-room and, as I entered the kitchen, saw the back of a young, blond, women standing by the stove. She was dressed casually in jeans and a sweatshirt with "University of Copenhagen" written on its back.

She turned around as we entered, starred at me and said, "My lord, you look just like mother."

193

Although caught off guard, I figured this must be Christina. Not only was she obviously at home in the place, she also resembled me as a young girl.

She came over, gave me a quick hug, wrinkled her nose, smiled and said, "Clinique Aromatic Elixir—my favorite," a reference to my signature fragrance. Then she turned to her father, threw her arms around Christian and gave him a hug and a big smile.

"Dad, if I was studying psychology instead of art, I'm sure I could come up with a term for this particular phenomenon. It is, of course, not Oedipus, but surely Freud has a name for a man who keeps company with a woman who resemble the mother of his children," she said and gave him a mischievous look.

This time it was Christian's turn to blush.

"I never thought your mother looked more than a little like Anna," he started.

Christina just smiled, poked his arm and said, "Well, at least you have good taste."

She turned to me again and I was taken by her warmth and openness. Blue eyes sparkled from a sweet and angular face framed by thick wheat-colored hair that hung half way down her back. She had her father's nose but in most other ways she looked a lot like me at about that age. It felt uncanny.

She offered me a mug of hot tea before she continued.

"Anna, I am *so* glad to meet you. Dad has told me so much about you I feel I already know you. And you do resemble my mother and therefore, I suppose, myself," she added with laughter that filled the room.

Unsure of what to say, I just smiled and thanked her and took the mug of tea she offered me.

Just then the phone rang. Christian answered, talked for a few minutes, turned around and said, "I'm sorry ladies, but I have to go over to the University for a couple of hours. There seems to be a problem with the plans for the visit of the Chancellor from the University of Stockholm next week; they need me there."

It was about eleven o'clock and Christian said he would

be back before long and take us out for lunch to a restaurant of our choice. Since I was ignorant of the local places, I looked to Christina for help.

"All right dad; if you promise to take us to Henry's Fish House tonight instead of lunch, we'll let you go."

She turned to me and said, "You'll love the place. I've enjoyed it since I was young and my grandparents used to take us. It's been there for ages and the owner is like an old friend of the family."

She gave her father a quick peck on the cheek and said, "I've already inspected the refrigerator and seen the mountains of food left by dear Mrs. Larsen, so I think we can manage lunch. And if you are not back in an hour, we'll start without you."

Christian gave us each a hug, went out the door, and within minutes we heard the soft purr of the Mercedes moving down the long driveway out onto the main road.

"Well, here we are," Christina said and picked up her mug. "Let's go down to the library and talk."

I nodded and followed her.

"I've been anxious to meet you ever since last December when I picked dad up from the airport—the week of the murder at the University."

We reached the library and Christina sat down in one of the easy chairs next to the couch; I took a seat in a corner of the sofa. Then Christina put down her mug and began talking.

"As you can imagine, it was a very difficult time for everyone at the university, especially for dad. He was under a lot of pressure and had to deal with the press, the students, and the staff. He also had the sad job of talking to the parents of the two dead students. What do you say to parents who've just lost their only daughter to a violent murder, or to someone whose son has killed an innocent person and then taken his own life?"

I told her I couldn't imagine how difficult this must have been.

"My classes were over for that semester and, since dad was obviously upset, I stayed around for a week until things began to quiet down. During the evenings we sat and talked by the fire and he told me about you. About how he had loved you years ago and how he was so happy the two of you had found each other again.

"He showed me the picture of the two of you at your graduation and talked about how anxious he was to have you come to Valhalla this spring."

She stopped for a moment and looked me in the eyes, adding, "He's also shown me some of the emails you sent him."

She laughed at my startled look and said, "Just the ones with stories about your children and grandchildren—the ones that weren't too personal. I think he just needed to share his joy with someone, and I am an interested listener," she said and gave me an assuring smile.

She took another sip of tea and looked at me as if she expected a response. I felt uncertain about what to say.

"I too am glad to have found him again," I said hesitantly. I still hadn't really come to terms with how much I cared for Christian.

"Are you in love with him again?" she asked and immediately covered her mouth and apologized.

"Forgive me—that was insensitive of me. You've only just met me, and that is such a personal question. But I feel like I already know you, and he's been hurt a lot in the past, even if he did set himself up for a fall on several occasions," she said with a wry smile.

"I'm just looking out for him," she added. "He is such a dear and loving man."

I was beginning to really like this young woman who obviously loved her father very much and, while weighing my words, said, "Yes, I think I *am* falling in love again, but don't you dare tell him. We've been in touch for nearly a year through email and long telephone conversations, but we've actually only spent a couple of days together since I arrived. The hours in Charlotte airport last December hardly counts, so it really is much too early to talk about love," I

196

said trying to convince both Christina and myself.

"Your father promised we could look at family pictures," I continued in an effort to change the subject. "Perhaps you might show me some as long as he's not here."

Realizing I wanted to avoid any further intimate talk about her dad, she said that looking at photos was a great idea.

"I always love seeing old pictures of my family and haven't looked at them in a while, so let's do it."

She excused herself and went into the old study and came back a few minutes later with four large albums. She laid the first one down in front of me and went over to light the fireplace.

"We won't have to look at each and every picture. We can flip past many of the pages, but this should give you the history of the Raabensted family," she said, and sat down next to me on the couch, took a last sip of her tea, and opened the first album.

Chapter 21

The grandfather clock in the hall brought us back to the present.

"It's one o'clock and by now dad must have grabbed a bite to eat at the university cafeteria," Christina said.

"Let me go out and fix some lunch. You just sit here Anna, look at pictures and enjoy the fire. I'll come and get you when lunch is ready."

She asked if I wanted beer or wine with lunch and I told her some white wine would be nice.

Before she left, she handed me an album we had not yet inspected and I sat back in the couch prepared to look at more photos.

Among the pictures I'd seen so far, were several of Vivian as a young woman—pretty and piquant. She had aged more than Christian, I noted. Late night hours in the theater had taken their toll, though I suspected she had undergone several nips and tucks by an expert plastic surgeon; she was still a *good* looking woman.

A picture of a group of children, standing around a swimming pool, had also caught my attention. It was from one of Cristina's early birthday parties. Vivian had arranged a pool-party for Christina and had invited Peter and Helena and a few of their friends to join Christina and hers.

The younger children looked directly into the camera, but several of the older boys focused their attention on someone at the side of the pool; I couldn't blame them. The center of their attention was an eighteen or nineteen year old version of Brigitte Bardot—the French sex kitten from the 1960s—wearing the most miniscule white bikini I had seen to date. I didn't have to ask who this vision was. From what Christian described a couple of days earlier, I knew this had to be Paulette. Christina concurred and I understood how Christian, a wonderful man with a weakness for lovely women, had been enticed—any man would have been.

I had asked Christina if she ever heard from Paulette.

"We actually met a few years ago when she came back to Denmark for a few days," she said.

"By that time she'd become a well-known model and was here on a photo shoot in Tivoli. After she got here, she called one morning and invited all of us to lunch at her hotel."

She laughed and said, "Dad asked Vivian to go with us to meet her—he refused to go near her. Not that he was worried about seeing her—he was long over that—but Brigitta, his wife at the time, would have had a fit if she knew he was mingling with a French model, especially one he'd been married to."

I saw only one picture that included Brigitta. It was taken at Christmas and showed her standing next to Peter by the fireplace in the living room. A striking looking woman, she was tall, slim hipped, and the personification of an iceberg. Christina quickly passed over the picture noting she'd never especially cared for Brigitta—"a cold fish," she said, and had gone on.

We had also looked at photos of herself and her siblings from their later years, but the pictures that really interested me were the ones with Karen.

I took a closer look at the album she handed me before going out to fix lunch, and felt sure it would include her mother. Judging from the age of the covers, this one went back further than the others.

I opened the album and on the first page found a studio picture of the woman who had born Christian's children and who evidently had attracted him, in part, because she resembled me.

I looked at the photo as objectively as I could and finally admitted that Vivian and Christina were right; Karen *did* look a lot like me.

The photograph showed Christian and Karen at what must have been Christina's christening. I figured Karen would have been around twenty-seven. I had a similar picture of Robert and I at Patrick's baptism and the resemblance was striking. I had no idea what to make of this other than Christian had fallen for two similar-looking women.

Just as I decided to leave this puzzle alone, Christina came in to tell me lunch was served and I joined her for an excellent cold pasta salad served on lettuce with fresh tomato wedges. To this she added a basket of heated rolls, left over from breakfast, and an excellent bottle of white wine from her father's wine cellar.

After she lit a couple of candles on the kitchen table, she went out to turn on the sound system and as she came back, Benny Goodman's "Body and Soul," filled the room. She evidently inherited her father's taste in music.

We spent the next couple hours getting to know each other. She was, in many ways, like Patrick in her joy of art and nature and I sat back and delighted in her youthful enthusiasm.

Sometime after three, Christian walked into the kitchen where we still sat nursing our wine. We had been so absorbed in our conversation that we hadn't heard the car pull up.

"So how are my two girls doing?" he asked and came over to the table and gave us each a peck on the cheek.

"Where on earth have you been?" Christina asked while she cleared our lunch dishes. "I called the university a while back, trying to reach you, and they said you left some time ago."

Christian looked a little embarrassed and said he'd met Richard Vagner on his way out of the university and the two of them had gone to lunch at The Blue Dolphin in downtown Charlottenlund.

"Richard invited us over for dinner tonight, but I told him I had promised to take the two of you to Henry's Fish House. Instead, I agreed we would come over for drinks later."

Christina noted she needed to run into town and pick up

a couple of paintbrushes. She said she would return in time to change for dinner, and a few minutes later we saw her little red car go down the driveway.

As soon as his daughter was gone, Christian gave me a big hug and a kiss, and told me he had deliberately looked for an excuse to leave us alone in order for us to get to know each other.

"So tell me, how did it go? I was hoping the two of you would enjoy each other's company. I know I am prejudiced, but I think she's a great young person; even if she is a little over-protective of me," he laughed.

I agreed, and told him we had spent several enjoyable hours together but avoided telling him the part about whether or not I had fallen in love with him again.

Chapter 22

The weather started with dreary skies that morning, but took another April turn during the afternoon. Although it was still a little cool, the sunshine now poured through the kitchen windows. We decided to go for a walk along the beach and I grabbed some of the bread left over from breakfast and lunch and brought it along for the seagulls. We walked arm in arm along the beach while the sea birds dove near us in efforts to supplement their evening meal with a bit of carbohydrates.

Christian asked if I had enjoyed looking at family pictures and I assured him it had been a real treat. "You look just as handsome now as you did back then," I laughed.

"That piece of flattery will entitle you to champagne any time you wish," he responded giving me a smug look and with a laugh added, "having my front teeth capped after Paulette told me I was an old man, probably helped."

I smiled; then asked him what would be appropriate to wear that evening, and he said the attire for Henry's was casual. I reminded him we were going to Vivian and Richard's later.

"It's still casual, but if you prefer to change into something other than jeans, that's fine; I'm wearing corduroys and a sweater."

When we arrived home, Christina stuck her head out from her room and I saw she had changed into a long red and black plaid skirt, an oversized black sweater, and a pair of huge clunky shoes favored by the younger generation.

I picked out my charcoal skirt, added a red cable-knit sweater and pulled on my black high-heeled boots. Then I put on the heart-shaped locket Christian had given me years ago.

As I came out of the bedroom Christina greeted me with a slight whistle.

"Not bad! Not bad!" she nodded in approval. "*And* I see you have on the locket dad told me he gave to you—the same one you are wearing in the graduation picture on his desk.

"Good sign," she added, winked, and took my arm as we walked down to join Christian.

Eating at Henry's Fish House was a great experience. The restaurant was right next to the harbor—with a view of the boats in their slips—and as we sat down at an alcove table, we observed fishermen on the pier still trying to get a catch before the sun went down.

We had smoked trout, the specialty of the house, and a pitcher of the popular "Carlsberg Ice," a variation of the old beer; new since I had last been home.

There actually was a real Henry who owned the restaurant, and as we entered the place he came over and congratulated Christian on his appointment to knighthood.

"I read about it in the paper the other day and have been proud to tell my customers, that you're an elite customer of mine," he said. He motioned for a waiter and then addressed Christian with a broad smile.

"I hope this doesn't mean we won't see you any more, in this humble place, sir."

"You are the proprietor of one of the best restaurants along the coast and serve the best trout in the entire kingdom," Christian assured him, "I merely have a title," he laughed, and asked the owner to join us for a drink.

Henry sat down with us for a few moments and Christian made the introductions. We shook hands and Henry gave me a puzzled look—you could almost see the wheels spinning. I knew he must have met Karen in the past and was obviously making comparisons, but was too discrete to say anything.

Our dinner arrived, and as Henry stood up to leave, he told us that drinks were on the house in honor of Christian's new title.

It was shortly after eight when we left for the Vagner house and after Vivian's description of their home as "a monster of a house," I was anxious to see what it looked like.

"You're in for a treat," Christina said, "The Vagner house, or 'Troll Haven,' as it's called, has been featured in many magazine in Europe, and not just because Vivian is a famous actress. The home is huge and ultra-modern with everything, including the temperature of each room, the water fountain in the front of the house, the music system, and much more, operated by electronic panels located throughout the house. Since Vivian never had children, she sort of adopted me, and I've spent a lot of time there."

We pulled into the driveway and at the end I saw a large house, displaying more glass than I had ever seen in or on a house.

The Vagner residence was only a couple of blocks from Valhalla, but it might as well have been on another planet. The two homes both faced the ocean and sat on large lots at the end of long drives, but that's where all similarity ended.

"Richard bought the lot some years ago, after the former house burned down," Christina informed me as we pulled up to the front door. "Then they had an American architect design the place to meet their specifications."

Before we could discuss this further, Richard and Vivian appeared in the doorway and came out to welcome us. Richard wore a brocade smoking jacket, the type you usually associate with old Vincent Price movies. Vivian had on a jersey toga in bright red, and a multi-colored headscarf. I was glad I'd changed out of my jeans.

"Come in, come in, and have something to drink" Richard said as Vivian put her arm through mine and led me into a vast foyer and down a marbled hall toward the back of the house.

We passed rows of rooms, most of them decorated in black and white. On one wall, in what looked to be an office, I noticed a painting by Hans Tyrrestrup. I had seen pictures of his work in a Danish magazine and liked his colorful abstracts.

The evening passed as we discussed everything from theater to politics. As Danes go, the Vagner's were conservative, but by American standards no Danes are even remotely to the right of any party in the United States.

Right after ten o'clock, Vivian suggested we go to their home movie theater and watch a copy of a French movie recently released. It was a risqué film, light and amusing and way beyond R-rated; but I'm sure I was the only one who blushed and thanks to the darkness no one noticed. Shortly after midnight we bid Vivian and Richard good-by, but not before I had promised Vivian the two of us would get together "real soon."

When we got back to the house Christina got ready to drive back to her place in the city, but Christian reminded her she had consumed more than her share of wine and would be better off spending the night in her old room. She agreed, kissed us both good night, and said she would most likely be gone by the time we got up in the morning.

I felt a little self-conscious going into the master bedroom with Christian—with his daughter just across the hall. Christian laughed and reminded me "Christina is a big girl."

Then he turned down the light and began to undress me, highly inspired, I am sure, by the French movie we just watched and it was some time before we finally kissed good night.

Chapter 23

We woke up Tuesday morning to the sound of a vacuum cleaner being run in the downstairs hallway and I guessed Mrs. Larsen had arrived. Just as I sat up, the clock in the hallway struck nine and already this energetic woman was busy at work while I was still in bed—I felt pampered.

Christian pulled me close and suggested we take our showers together. I swatted him and told him—in no uncertain terms—that with good and faithful Mrs. Larsen in the house, there was no way I was going take part in Act II of last night's movie. Who knew when she would decide to vacuum the upstairs rooms? He chuckled and obediently went across the hall to Christina's bathroom making sure it was empty.

I dressed in khakis, a navy cashmere twin set and loafers. I put on my locket, surveyed myself in the bedroom mirror, decided I looked all right and went out to meet Christian.

By now the noise from the cleaner had stopped and I detected the faint smell of bacon frying. As we walked downstairs to the kitchen, I heard someone singing a World War II tune I hadn't heard since my mother used to entertain me with songs from that era. As we entered the kitchen, the singing stopped.

"I know you Americans like bacon and eggs for breakfast," Mrs. Larsen said without any introductions, her back turned to us tending the skillet. "So I thought I better fry you up several slices."

She wiped her hands on a kitchen towel hanging next to the stove, turned around to greet us, and stopped dead in her tracks.

She looked like she was about to say something—by now I was getting used to being likened to Christian's second wife—so I just smiled. I realized, having worked for the family for many years, the housekeeper would know Karen.

But after staring at me for a moment she just snapped her lips together, stuck her hand out, smiled, and said, "I'm Kaja Larsen, and you must be Anna. Why don't the two of you sit down and I'll serve you breakfast."

After that, I didn't have the heart to tell her I usually don't eat bacon and promptly downed two slices, one scrambled egg, and two cups of coffee.

While we ate our breakfast, Mrs. Larsen went out to hang laundry in the backyard. I threw Christian an inquiring look but, before I could ask the question, he said, "I know, I know. Why doesn't she just throw things in the dryer and save herself the extra work?"

With a shrug he added, "Several years ago, I bought one of the biggest and best clothes dryers for her to use, but Mrs. Larsen is old school and believes things are 'much fresher if they are air-dried.' She flatly refuses to use the perfectly good machine."

Mrs. Larsen, finished with her chore, placed the small bag with clothes-pins at the end of the clothesline, picked up the empty basket, and came back inside.

I looked at the sheets hanging side by side on the line stretched between poles outside the kitchen window. As I observed them flap like sails in the wind, I realized how lucky Christian was to have engaged such a good woman.

"So where are you off to today, Dr. R?" she asked, then picked up the breakfast dishes, placed them in the sink, and poured the two of us and herself another cup of coffee.

Christian told her we were headed to Amager to take a look at our old school and visit other places from our youth. He inquired about Christina, and Mrs. Larsen informed him that his daughter had left just as she had arrived.

"That child probably didn't eat a single thing before she left," she said with a pained look, and I realized how Mrs. Larsen, in many ways, had been like a mother to Christian's children. It warmed my heart to see the pride she took in taking care of his home and family.

The day was sunny and mild outside but as we prepared to leave I picked up my trench coat—just in case—it was still April.

We were headed out the front door when Christian asked me to wait a moment. Then he went to the middle door of the garage, opened it and disappeared. Soon after, I heard an engine, other than the Mercedes, being revved up, and minutes later he drove out in a racing-green Austin-Healy, with a big grin on his face.

"So that's what's behind door two," I laughed and got into the passenger's seat. "And just what might be behind door three?"

"A big riding mower and a large assortment of tools and other equipment the gardener uses. There's also sleds and snow shoes and a surfboard Peter brought back from California the year he was there as an exchange student; plus an assortment of the children's old bikes, including *my* 10-speed I ride now and then.

"The Austin is my toy I like to play with on occasion, and today is a perfect day to air it," he said with a wink, and kissed my hand.

He suddenly became serious, turned to face me, and took my hands.

"This is probably neither the time nor the place to tell you, Anna, but I want you to know I love you—I think I never stopped—and after receiving your first email a year ago, it became clear I still do. I hope, so much, you feel the same way?"

Before I could answer he put his hands up in defense.

"Don't answer me now. Just give it some thought."

Then he patted my cheek and gave me a light kiss. I smiled back. I wasn't certain how I felt, but was beginning to have a fairly good idea.

Within the hour we arrived at Christianshavn, the southern section of Copenhagen where I was born and raised and where I later attended school. Christian parked the car on a side street by the canal, just up from our old school.

We walked arm in arm down the street passing Vor Frelser's Kirke where the sign outside indicated the church would open for visitors at two o'clock.

"Let's tour the school first," I suggested.

On the outside, the old building looked just as it had when we were students; same old red brick walls and doors still painted green and it felt strange walking through the big green portal leading into the schoolyard realizing some things had changed.

"The school won't be in full session right now, since it's still part of the Easter break, but some students will be there, doing research," Christian explained.

When we were students, the school closed Easter Thursday and stayed locked until the end of our Easter vacation. Christian had been invited back to take part in a symposium a couple of years ago, so the changes were not new to him. I, on the other hand, had not been back since I graduated in 1959.

I noticed right away that the three big chestnut trees, in the courtyard, were gone.

"The trees fell prey to disease, a few years back," Christian explained, "in their place we now have some Danish birch trees."

The old flagpole still stood in the center of the courtyard where we had walked around during recess, but the bike racks were new, and an old shed, used to house the teachers' bicycles, had been torn down allowing a better view of the north wing.

The more significant changes, however, were inside the main building where walls had been removed—and some classrooms completely done away with—in order to create several large rooms.

Colorful paint had been applied to the walls—gone was

the horrid pale green from our school days—and new metal railing had replaced the ancient wooden one. The former barren walls were now hung with modern paintings, apparently done by the current crop of art students. When we peaked into what used to be the teacher's lounge, we saw it was now a small cafeteria, open to both staff and students.

One thing, though, remained unaltered in forty years: the smell inside the school halls. There is something about the blend of commercial cleaners and young perspiration that seems to permeate all high schools the world over. You could take most people, bring them to a town where they had never been, blindfold them, and place them in a school hallway during any given school year. Without ever hearing a student laugh or talk, they would know instantly that they were standing inside an educational institution for young people.

Despite the changes, it still felt nice to be back. A couple of students came out from what was now the library, dressed casually and a bit funky like most young people—some with spiked and colored hair. I realized the fifties dress-code had gone by way of the old chestnut trees, and couldn't help but think of my last year in school when girls were finally allowed to wear slacks to class. The rules, however, had dictated that "they must be tasteful in appearance and not worn too tight" and jeans, or "cowboy pants" as they were called, were a "no-no."

On a bulletin board, outside the cafeteria, we saw a note announcing the school's hundredth's anniversary with graduating classes from 1955 through 1960 grouped together at various events. The anniversary celebration would begin with a dinner-dance Friday evening at a nearby convention center—new since I was in school.

The following day "...the big formal celebration will take place at the school with Prime Minister Frederikke (Rikke) Bergdorf—Class of 1959—giving the keynote speech," I read out loud.

Christian nodded, "Since arrangements for all other events are left up to the members of each class, I talked to Benny and he has sent out schedules and information regarding plans for our class. I'll fill you in when we get home."

I told him I really looked forward to seeing Rikke again and asked him if they ever ran into each other. He said they'd met at charity dinners a couple of times in the past.

"We spoke briefly, but didn't have a chance to catch up, so I'm looking forward to seeing her and her old boyfriend, John, again. They didn't marry, of course, but he and I, you may remember, were best friends in school.

"How about you and Rikke?" he asked. "Did you stay in touch since graduation and have you seen her during any of your past trips?"

I told him the two of us corresponded for some time after I moved to the States and on one trip back years ago we managed to have dinner.

"I followed her political career for years, through newspaper articles Astrid sent me, but just about the time I moved to North Carolina, Rikke accepted a position as an aide to the Ambassador in some Far Eastern country and we lost track.

"Then on a flight home, after my last trip, I found her address in a magazine article on the plane and as soon as I got home, sent her a letter and an update of my life including pictures of my family, hoping she would respond.

"The magazine article went into great details about her private life so I know she married an anthropologist—at least a dozen years her senior, previously married with a couple of grown children from his first marriage—but you probably know all that.

"Rikke *did* answer my letter and I've since learned about her career and family, including the fact that she and her husband have chosen not to have children," I said.

I was about to tell him we still exchanged letters and that Rikke had written and asked me "and your date" to a party she was giving, at her place, after the Saturday celebration at our school, when the old school bell rang—and I lost my thought.

Although the schedule at the school this week was different, due to Easter, students now flooded the halls, many carrying their lunch bags heading for the cafeteria—all so young and full of energy. I stood for a moment and observed them, listening to their chatter about upcoming dates, their plans for the weekend and what they were doing after school that day. They may have worn clunky shoes, tight pants and spiked hair, but they sounded just like our group, decades ago.

Chapter 24

By now it was after one, and without fail, Christian announced he was hungry and suggested we go to the Old Mill for lunch. I readily agreed. I hadn't been there since our school years, when it was the home of a well-known artist, and I looked forward to seeing the place again.

As we walked to the restaurant, I suddenly realized we would pass right by my grandfather's old business—the old Drener building that had advertised "Amager Little Taxi Company" on the front wall.

Over lunch, I would tell Christian the tale of my two fathers; and, as long as I was airing family skeletons, I would tell him other things that, for years, had been stored in the back of my mind.

As we neared the end of Prinsesse Gade, I spied my grandfather's old place—a three-story red brick building. At one time, the family's living quarters occupied the two top floors with grandfather's business offices on the street level. I knew he had died years ago and since none of his sons were interested in continuing the business, it had been sold to a man who bought it with the stipulation that he could keep the established company name.

I knew Christian recognized the name from Freddy's story but he never said a word, just held me a little closer and began to tell me about the Old Mill.

We arrived within minutes and—judging by the outside—the mill had not changed much since we had come here as students in the late fifties. As we approached the place, a gust of wind stirred the mill's blades and they began moving slowly on their axle as if to wave us closer. It was a splendid structure, painted white with a narrow red door leading into the base of the building and deep-seated windows that kept one from looking in.

It was a picturesque sentinel near the edge of the waters.

Save for a small tasteful sign to the right of the building depicting the unoriginal name, "The Old Mill," it looked in every way as it always had. Once inside, however, the changes were apparent. The bottom floor was given over to a large dining room and kitchen while a couple of smaller and more private dining rooms were located on the second floor. The downstairs was full of professional people conducting business over lunch and a few elderly couples lingering over their mid-day meal.

Christian asked to be seated on the second floor and we were led upstairs and shown to a table in a small room that afforded us a view of the water separating the Isle of Amager from the inner city.

Our waitress arrived and we decided to try the special of the day—a tempting shrimp and pasta salad. Christian also requested a large bowl of potato chowder for himself and a basket of assorted rolls for us to share. He ordered a chilled Riesling and told the waitress we would decide on dessert later.

While we waited for our lunch, we chatted about our time spent painting outside the mill, the fun we had in the wintertime skating on the nearby lake—whenever it was declared safe- and about the friends we both hoped to meet at the school reunion.

When our meal was served, we noted that the other lunch guests had left and we found ourselves alone in the small dining room. Christian dove in and ate his meal with gusto; I picked at mine. I knew the time had come to fill him in on my background, the part he never knew about during our dating years.

"Christian," I began, "there are things about me I think you ought to know. But before I start, I want to give you the answer to your question from this morning. Yes, I love you too," I admitted, and gently stopped him from commenting.

"I loved my husband very much, even through our difficult times. We had a good marriage and I will always treasure that part of my life. The love I have for you is different but, in its own way, just as strong."

I paused for a moment, looked him, and said, "I'm not

sure where all this is taking us, but before we get more deeply involved, there are things concerning myself and my family I want to share with you—things that have influenced my life."

I stopped for a moment and looked down at the meal in front of me. My salad was tasty, but I was not hungry and pushed the nearly full plate aside and played with my wineglass as I talked. This was a complicated story, but I felt I owed Christian the truth.

I began by telling him about my mother's first marriage; how she met and married Alex and about the Drener family and the attraction the lively family had held for her. I told him about my father's alcoholism that finally led my mother to divorce him when I was five. I filled him in about my grandmother Clara and let him know how I had loved, and never forgotten her. I told him the parts of her story that Freddy hadn't known and how I missed seeing her after my mother married Nels Wiinter—immediately after her divorce.

"Nels knew he couldn't have children and adopted me right away and forbade any mention of the Drener name; he wanted everyone to think I was his own," I explained.

I told him about starting school at Christianshavn where he and I met and fell in love; a school located just up the street from the home of my former family and how, over the years, I wanted so much to visit them, but was too afraid of my new father's anger, should he ever find out.

For more than an hour, I filled him in on a past that had been my burden for years. At some point the waitress came back and Christian ordered coffee and brandy. When it arrived, I took a large sip of mine.

Looking down at my hands, unable to face Christian, I told him about Nels and how he had loved me too much; how he had done things to me that were not natural, and how this sort of abuse emotionally damaged something inside of me.

It was a part of my life that was difficult to talk about. It included events that had gnawed away at me for years and were something I had never shared with anyone, not even Reenie.

But I was falling in love with Christian, who had bared his soul to me. I felt that, for the first time in my adulthood, it would be all right to let it out and perhaps free myself from the guilt and shame that comes from abuse, even when it's clothed in love.

As I spoke, Christian quietly held my hand. By his presence, he gave me the support and encouragement I needed in order to let go of the heaviness I had carried in my heart.

When I finally finished, I glanced out the window and saw the cars in the parking lot were glistening wet. While we had eaten, an unexpected rain shower had drenched everything. It was still coming down, although by now the rain had turned into a drizzle. I was glad Christian had left the top up on the Austin Healy. He was familiar with Denmark's unpredictable weather.

Christian got up from the table and said he thought it was time to leave and suggested we go visit the church that by now would be open. He paid for lunch, helped me on with my coat, and led me outside. He guided me over to the edge of the lake where he took me in his arms, the mist wetting his face ever so slightly.

"Poor little Anna, so much to hide, and so much for you to carry by yourself. No wonder you became upset with me when I sent you the letter suggesting we date others until you came back. You must have felt you were once again being let down by someone you loved and whom you believed loved you."

I tried to answer, but couldn't.

Just as quickly as it had started the rain stopped and as we walked toward the church the sun began to peak through the clouds. Right before we reached the light at the intersection of Havne Boulevarden and Prinsesse Gade," Christian turned me toward him with a questioning look on his face.

"Does this, by any chance, have anything to do with you

sending the letters back to me?" he asked.

"I have no idea what you're talking about," I said and starred at him.

Then I recalled the letters he had mentioned when he told me his own story in Dyrehaven the previous Friday.

Just then the light changed, and Christian took my arm and led me across the street.

As soon as we got to the other side he turned to me and said, "Never mind about the letters right now. Tonight, I have something I want to show to you. Right now let's go visit the old church."

Then he put his arm around me and we went down the street and into Vor Frelser's Kirke that by now had opened its doors to the public.

No one else was inside, save for a custodian collecting a donation in return for a brochure about the church's history and inventory. We looked around the large entrance hall, studying many of the old historic documents on the walls, before we finally went inside and up to the age-old baptismal font—a carved and sculptured marble piece with a golden canopy—where I had been christened many years ago. We also inspected the choir section where we sang as young students every Christmas, and then walked along the outside isles admiring the paintings and tapestries decorating the walls.

An organist had come in and was practicing a lovely piece by Bach. So we sat down in a back pew and held hands listening, as the music billowed out from the wall-sized pipe organ, floating out over the pews, penetrating the interior of the century old place of worship. As the music rose, I felt my burden starting to seep away.

The church bells suddenly struck four and Christian and I turned and looked at each other trying hard to suppress our laughter. It had been the four o'clock bells that caught us in the church tower years ago; we both remembered the incident. When the bells stopped tolling, the chimes in the church tower began to play their hourly tune and I felt as if I had been to confession and received absolution.

I took Christian's hand. Together we went outside into the spring day and began our walk back to the parked car. By this time the sun had returned and was casting a soft light over the ancient tile roofs and down on the graying locks on Christian's head. I felt at ease again.

"We have no plans for tonight," Christian said as we pulled out into traffic. "Mrs. Larsen promised to leave a meal ready at six o'clock. Then, after dinner, I have some important things I want to show you. And, *after that*, I suggest we watch an old movie while we neck in the library," he said in a voice full of mischief.

I gave him a quick hug and told him he was a reprobate.

"The devil's gonna get you," I laughed.

Joining my laughter—and in his best imitation of a Southern accent—he told me: "no, the good Lord's on my side, of that I'm sure, 'cause, I've done found me a good woman and I've done changed my ways."

We left and headed home but—as it turned out—our plans would, yet again, be changed.

Chapter 25

We left Christianshavn shortly after four and arrived at Valhalla a little before six, having stopped at a small shop to pick up a wine Christian wanted to try.

As we drove down the driveway toward the house, I saw a navy-colored Jaguar parked in front of the villa near the garage. The driver had not yet stepped out and whoever it was, obviously shared Christian's love for expensive cars.

"Peter is here," Christian said eyeing the automobile. "I had no idea he was coming tonight. I'm sorry Anna; I had hoped for a quiet evening together. Peter is a wonderful young man and I'm sure you'll enjoy meeting him, but I'm afraid you and I will not be able to talk privately," he added.

I got out of the Austin and assured him I was delighted to meet yet another one of his children.

"Our talk can surely wait a while longer," I said.

As we spoke, the door of the car opened and a tall, blond, good looking young man stepped out of the car. Dressed in boots, tight jeans and a huge Icelandic sweater—both thumbs hooked in his pockets—he sauntered over to meet us.

"Dad, it's great to see you,'" he said and hugged his slightly shorter father. Then he turned around, bent down, took both my hands, and gave me an appraising look from top to toe.

"Christina certainly didn't exaggerate," he smiled approvingly. "Not only do you resemble mother, but like her, you're an extremely good looking women."

I wasn't sure whether all young people nowadays were as outspoken as Peter and Christina or whether having money of their own gave them an edge on frankness. In either case, they surely didn't hesitate to tell it like they saw it.

I smiled, a little embarrassed but, before I could think of

a reply, he turned to his father and without further ado said, "Lisa left me yesterday and I felt a bit down this morning. Then Christina called mid-morning and told me all about Anna being here, and since I'm on my Easter break, I thought I'd come up and check out this lovely lady for myself."

He winked at me and threw me the same devilish smile his father used. With his chiseled face, deep-brown eyes and straw-colored hair, Peter looked like a slightly taller and younger Christian; the resemblance was unmistakable.

Through it all, Christian stood quietly by my side, but after Peter's last remark he put his arm around the shoulder of his son and invited him to join us.

"I'm sure Mrs. Larsen has cooked enough food for all of us and if you're in the mood for a movie, a drink, and some good conversation later, you are welcome to stay the night."

"I'll take you up on the meal, the drink and the conversation, but I have a date tonight around ten o'clock with one of Christina's friends, so I'll pass on staying over. I *am* starved, however," he added, and with that we headed for the house.

Mrs. Larsen had outdone herself. The table was set with a heavy damask tablecloth, good bone china, and delicate crystal glasses. Fresh daffodils floated in a bowl in the center of the table and scattered, from one end to the other, were tea lights in small votive candleholders. She had turned on the fire in the library and from the kitchen wafted the aroma of what promised to be a great dinner, presently being kept warm in the oven.

After freshening up, I took over in the kitchen and began plating our dinners while Peter selected music and Christian tended to wines. Then we sat down to eat.

Like his father, Peter was a charming conversationalist and I enjoyed our dinner. Afterward, we went into the library for coffee and some excellent cognac while father and son took turns telling episodes from the time the children were young, outdoing each other with witty stories.

Shortly after nine, Peter stood up and said he was heading out. As he prepared to leave, he invited us to come down and visit him at his upstairs flat in Vordingborg, "in case you have plans to drive down to visit Helena in the near future. It's no Valhalla, but it's quite nice."

He gave each of us a hug, was out the door and gone, and we were suddenly alone again.

"Easy comes, easy goes, seems to be the story of his love life," Christian said.

"I do hope he finds a young woman some day and settles down. For that matter, I hope Christina will find someone to share her life and love with," he added in a father's voice.

We went out to the kitchen, loaded the dishwasher, poured what was left of the coffee into a pair of mugs and went back into the library. The late news in Denmark comes on much earlier than in the States, so we sat down and enjoyed the last of the fire, watching what was happening in the world.

Since there are no commercials on most Danish television channels, all the shows come on at odd times and after the news was over we watched a comedy show that ended at eleven thirteen.

By then I felt worn out. It had been an eventful day, and I told Christian I was dead tired and needed a good night's sleep. He allowed that we *had* packed a lot of things into the past few days and admitted that he too could use some rest.

We went upstairs and shortly after we turned in, I heard Christian's even breathing and realized he was already asleep.

Although I was tired, sleep did not come right away and I lay in the large bed for some time listening to the fluent rhythm of the ocean as its water washed up against the pebbled beach at the foot of the Valhalla lawn.

For the first time in a long time, I didn't feel sure just where I belonged. Home was still North Carolina where my children were. I knew they loved me and I them, but I also realized they no longer depended on me. They were all involved in their own lives, were doing well; none of them truly needed me and I was beginning to feel that Christian did.

I also realized that, but for a twist of fate, I might have ended up in this bed, in this house, years ago had I not gone to the States with my parents. There was no way I could know for sure, but I conceded it was a distinct possibility. I further acknowledged that I too could have ended up as yet another one of Christian's marriage casualties. Who knew?

I heard the clock in the foyer strike twelve thirty but fell asleep before it struck again and slept soundly through the night.

Chapter 26

Right after we got up the next morning, Christian told me he wanted to take me to Gilleleje, an old fishing and vacation village up the coast where he knew of an old tavern he felt sure I would enjoy. I remembered the town from my childhood and was excited about a visit to the place.

"The food is great and the view spectacular," he said. So we settled for coffee before we left, kindly refusing Mrs. Larsen's offer to fix another American breakfast.

Despite the sun shining, it had turned cold again and I put on a pair of light wool camel-colored slacks and a heavy handmade black turtleneck sweater I bought on my trip to Ireland with Tess. Christian said we might do some walking, so I borrowed a pair of Christina's lace-up boots and a scarf and threw on my trench coat.

We were in the foyer, about to leave, when Christian asked me to excuse him for a few minutes while he went upstairs.

I sat down in one of the two winged chairs flanking an ancient desk in the hallway and leafed through the morning paper Mrs. Larsen had brought in when she arrived. I figured Christian had gone to his office, perhaps needing to make a call to the university, or had a letter he needed to mail, and gave it no further thought. A short while later he came skipping down the staircase tucking something inside his jacket. Then we were on our way.

Shortly before ten o'clock we arrived in the old town and Christian parked the car in a small parking lot beside an age-old, one-story, half-timbered inn. The Lilliputian tavern featured white chalk walls and ancient timber, a weathered thatched roof, checkered curtains in the windows, and spring flowers just beginning to bloom filling wooden buckets on either side of the front door. It was called "The Inn by the Sea" and sat edged between the road and the ocean offering a spectacular view of the North Sea. The smell of bread baking greeted us as we entered and the staff, dressed in replicas of centuries old costumes, welcomed us.

Christian asked to be seated by a window at a corner table somewhat off by itself. He ordered hot tea with lemon and scones with the raspberry jam—a specialty of the inn.

A pretty young woman wearing her hair in long thick braids brought out our meal and I suddenly realized I was hungry *and* thirsty. The good sea air was aiding my appetite and by now, the coffee at Valhalla had worn off.

The tea was steaming hot and of a fruity variety I didn't recognize, but immediately enjoyed. I buttered a scone adding a small amount of jam and relished the late breakfast meal.

The place was enchanting and as charming as Christian had promised. The food was good and the view out the window made me feel as if I had stepped into a children's storybook.

I watched several sleek boats steer toward the harbor, their sails fanning in the wind. It was mid-morning and it appeared that several of the sail-sports people were planning a mid-morning bite to eat at the tavern.

I turned around to take another sip of my tea and saw Christian reach into his jacket pocket to bring out what looked like two old airmail envelopes edged in red and blue stripes.

You don't see the thin parchment stationary much anymore, but when I first began corresponding with friends and family, after I arrived in New York, that sort of envelope always meant a letter from home.

I looked with surprise at the envelopes as Christian silently slid them toward me.

"These are the letters I've been referring to Anna," he explained. "By now, I realize you may never have seen them, and I'd like to talk about them, if you don't mind."

Picking up the first one, I saw it was addressed to me.

The postmark, barely visible, read October 23, 1959.

"Go on, read it," Christian said. Bewildered, I pulled out two thin sheets of airmail paper and read the letter addressed to me from Christian.

It started by Christian telling me he was sorry he ever suggested we date others the last time he wrote and went on to say he missed me and was willing to wait until I was able to come back to him. He added that he realized leaving my parents would not be easy, but assured me he would wait. The rest of the letter was filled with news about his studies and our friends.

At the end he begged me to forgive him and then he wrote, "My darling Anna, please come back to me. I don't want to not have you in my life." It was signed, "Still your knight in shining armor—I hope."

"This came after I began dating Robert; trying to forget about you," I said feeling confused.

"We had a post office box near our apartment in New York City, and my father picked up the mail on his way home each night. I can't imagine why he didn't give this to me. And if, for some unknown reason, my mother and father didn't want me to have it, why did they return it to you instead of just throwing it out?"

"Anna, if they'd just gotten rid of the letter they would know I would write again thinking the letter might have got lost. By returning it, I'm sure they meant for me to believe you wanted nothing more to do with me," he added, and looked at me with sympathy.

"If, as you say, you were dating Robert at the time, they probably hoped you'd forget all about me and settle down in the States and remain near them. Frankly, you can't really blame them."

I picked up the other letter, dated six weeks later and pulled out a single sheet of paper. It was another note with Christian asking me to please write to him, if not to continue our correspondence, at least to let him know that I really did not care about him anymore. It made no reference to the first unanswered letter.

"Right before the second letter came back I tried to call you—that took some doing. First I had to go to the embassy and find a friend of your dad's to get your phone number. Then I had to order the call. You may remember that back in the 50s you didn't just call overseas. Finally I had to muster up courage to call. But I did, because I truly wanted you back in my life.

"So I called one evening around midnight here, or six o'clock in the evening your time, and your father answered the phone.

"He told me you wanted no more to do with me and was, at the moment, out on a date with someone you'd been seeing for a while. A few days later my second letter came back—unopened, so I reasoned you had decided to permanently write me out of your life and had found someone else and never planned to come back to me."

"Christian, you do realize that I never saw, or knew anything, about either of these letters *or* your phone call," I said, my voice shaking.

"I do now," he nodded and reached over and stroked my cheek.

I knew there were some very dark sides to my father, but I also knew that in his own way he had loved me. But to do this!

"I just can't believe he would deliberately hurt me," I said feeling tears welling up.

"They knew I was terribly upset when I received the letter from you suggesting we date others. I took that to mean you no longer wanted me. Mom was very understanding and dad at least pretended to care. Why did they do this to me?"

"They *did* care, Anna, but I also feel sure they wanted you to remain in the States," Christian said.

"I realized after we connected and began to e-mail, that you would have been pregnant with your oldest son at the time my last letter arrived. Your parents knew you were expecting a baby and probably returned my letter—out of what they considered kindness—in order not to complicate matters."

Logic told me that Christian might be right, but I kept hurting. I stood up and told Christian I needed to get out of the inn. He said to go on ahead while he paid for our meal.

I went outside feeling confused, with a million thoughts storming through my head. I had dated, thrown myself at, and finally married Robert because I felt abandoned by Christian, and had entered a marriage filled with feelings of rejection. Christian had hurt me and my insecurity was inflamed.

Because of that, I had assumed for years that the only reason Robert married me was because I was pregnant. It did not occur to me—until many years later—that we might have married anyway. Since I knew nothing about Robert's trauma going back to his years in Ireland, I always interpreted his distress as regret over having had to marry me.

"Oh, Christian," was all I could say when he joined me on a bench at the end of the lawn where I sat watching the boats maneuver in and out of the harbor.

"I didn't mean to upset you, Anna, but I thought you ought to know I didn't just abandon you. It was insensitive of me to suggest we date others, but I never meant for it to sound like I wanted to leave you. I only thought that we needed to go out and take part in life until we would be back together. I realize now that I didn't make that clear. I never meant for us to part permanently.

"I almost wish I hadn't showed you the letters. I've kept them all these years for sentimental reasons as a remembrance of my first real love. I don't want you to be upset, and especially not with your parents. Whatever they did, they meant well," he said and put his arms around me, and for some time we sat still without talking.

"No, Christian," I finally said, "I'm glad you showed me. We both have things we're not proud of from our pasts.

I think if we are to continue our relationship, no matter where it leads, we need to do so with a clean slate."

He nodded and held me close, and as I observed the water play with the anchored boats, and the seagulls dip down for a catch, I let my mind absorb all the new information.

I decided we needed a break. I threw Christian a smile and suggested we head back to Charlottenlund and on the way stop at Kronborg for a visit with Holger Danske.

"You're kidding, right?" he said. "You actually want to play tourist and go and see the old guy down in his dungeon?"

"And when did *you* last go pay your respect to our old hero?" I teased him in an attempt to lighten the mood.

Christian admitted he hadn't been to the age-old castle since he and Karen took the children there one summer, long ago.

"We didn't actually make it to the dungeons. Right before we went down, Peter threw up all over his clothes— too much ice-cream, I think—so we never got any further than the formal halls upstairs."

He broke into laughter. "Church on Sunday, castles on Wednesday," he mocked good-naturedly. "I can't wait to see what the rest of the time with you will be like," he added and gave me a kiss on the tip of my nose and with that we hopped into the Mercedes and became castle bound.

By the time we reached the historic castle I felt better and chose not to think about the two returned letters or how, had I received them, it might have changed my life.

Chapter 27

We had a wonderful time touring Kronborg, the old bastion sitting at the eastern most point of Sealand in the town of Helsingoer looking across the sea to Sweden and its counterpoint castle in Helsingborg. Though the Swedish stronghold is pretty much in ruins, the Danish castle—the setting for Shakespeare's "Hamlet"—looks much as it did hundreds of years ago.

As we walked through the large rooms admiring the fine furniture, we occasionally looked out the tall, narrow windows facing the ocean and caught sight of ships sailing by. Eventually we found our way down to the dungeons where we located Holger of the ancient legend. The statue actually only dates back to 1907, but looks as if it's been there for centuries—a solitary and imposing figure located between the stark, vaulted walls. He sits with his shield to the left of him, bent over as if in deep sleep, just waiting for an occasion to wake up and come to the rescue of all Danes.

Somewhere between the dungeons and the parking lot, Christian declared he was starved and within half an hour we discovered a small seaside tavern.

During our meal, I reminded Christian that I had promised Astrid I would be back the next day.

"I really want to catch an early morning train so I can be of help."

He gallantly offered to drive me back, but I reminded him of his morning meeting at the University. "The meeting you emphasized requires your presence. Besides, I'll see you Saturday at the Christening of Anne Marie's baby. I think we can manage to be apart that long," I laughed.

He pretended to pout, then smiled, and agreed he might

just possibly survive being alone for a couple of days.

As we pulled away from the restaurant, Christian popped in a tape and within minutes the smooth voice of June Christy dominated the sound waves. "Love Does Not Live Here Anymore," she sang and Christian reached over, took my hand and brought it to his lips and said, "Thank Heaven that's not true."

Looking out of the car, I watched the clouds sail by overhead. They moved and changed shapes, much in the same way our lives had during the past several days. Christian and I were growing closer by the minute, but too many events and revelations had been crammed into a short time. I needed to digest it all, so I just gave him a smile and sat back and enjoyed the ride.

Although it was slightly cold outside, we rode with the windows down in order to enjoy the fresh sea air and by the time we pulled into the driveway the sun was back, shining from a cloudless sky, bathing the house in its golden light.

Elsa, the part-time maid, was just coming out from the house and waved to us as we pulled up to the garage. After letting me out, Christian went over to talk with her for a few minutes while I went inside to the kitchen.

Mrs. Larsen was just putting something in the oven holding promises of being delicious. Before she left, she instructed me on how to serve the dinner and we spent the evening, lingering over our meal before going in to the conservatory, where we sat and watched the sun go down and disappear behind the calm waters.

After Christian lighted the logs in the library, we played a game of backgammon before watching Murder on the Orient, with Peter Ustinov, and around midnight we headed for bed and spent some time in the old four-poster enjoying each other.

We had avoided any talk of the two returned letters since leaving the inn, and as I lay in bed, waiting for sleep, I decided it was a chapter in my life I could do little about. I am a fatalist and decided that there must have been good reasons why everything happened the way they did. I had spent some heart-sore times with Robert, but we had also shared a deep love and some wonderful years together. Now, in my later years, I was given the opportunity to reconnect with a man I once loved and who still loved me—I had no reasons to complain.

As I drifted off to sleep, I heard waves pound against the shoreline as a storm gathered, and heavy rain began hitting the windows facing the ocean. I turned my back to the storm and, as I snuggled deeper under the soft comforter, gave thanks for all the good things in my life.

The rain was still coming down as we drove to the Charlottenlund train station the next morning, so Christian pulled up near the entrance as close as it was legally possible.

"I can handle things from here," I said, kissed him good-by, and told him not to get out. Christian said he would be at Astrid's promptly at three Saturday afternoon. From there we would drive to Vor Frelser's Kirke where the youngest member of my Danish family would become a full-fledged member of the Danish Lutheran Church. The baby would be given the name of his father and that of his great maternal uncle.

I watched Christian drive away and as he turned to wave, I felt a tug in my heart and was glad I would see him again in just a few days. I picked up a cup of coffee from a nearby kiosk and went down the steps to the platform where my train was due to arrive in a few minutes.

On schedule, the train pulled into the station and, as I boarded, recalled the first time Robert and I visited Denmark and decided to take the train to visit Freddy and Rie.

My aunt, with whom we were staying, had given us the train schedule and Robert figured we could easily make the eleven o'clock morning train arguing we probably had a margin of five to ten minutes on either side of the arrival time. My aunt and I tried to tell him that the trains in this country ran on time and there would be no leeway.

"The train will arrive, as scheduled, wait exactly two minutes to allow passengers to get off or board, and be gone by three minutes past eleven," Aunt Ida told him.

Robert did not believe it, basing his opinion on what he was used to in the States.

So, we had watched the train pull out of the station just as we came down the steps leading to the platform a few minute past eleven o'clock. Robert had looked at his watch, turned to me, smiled in amazement, and said: "It's exactly three minutes past." From then on, he never doubted that Danish trains do indeed run according to schedule.

Chapter 28

I took a taxi at the Central Railway Station, and watched the windshield wipers on the cab go at a steady pace. When I arrived at Astrid's, I quickly paid the driver and ran for cover managing to get inside the apartment building just as the rain started coming down in buckets.

As I let myself in, I heard my cousin singing, "Tuppen og Lillemor," an old tune from our childhood. Then the song stopped and Astrid came out from the kitchen wiping her hands on her blue-checkered apron, flour decorating her nose.

Without concern for my damp coat, she greeted me with a smile and a big hug.

"Lord, I'm glad you are here to help Anna—even if you can't cook," she chuckled.

I started to object but she kept laughing and cut me off before I could get in a word of defense.

"Aunt Lilli was one of the most wonderful and charming women I've ever known, but cooking wasn't one of her talents, so naturally there were no skills for her to pass on to you. It seems your mother got the charm, and my mother inherited the cooking talent in their family," she added matter-of-fact and went back into the kitchen to continue her work.

"Grab an apron and start shelling peas in the blue bowl on the table," she directed and from then until one o'clock we worked steadily side by side while I filled Astrid in on what had happened, the last couple of days.

There were, however, a couple of things I chose to leave out. I didn't tell her of my confession to Christian regarding my father and his relationship with me, nor did I tell her about the two letters I never received. There didn't seem to be any point, at least not at this time, and perhaps not ever. I reasoned those two subjects probably ought to remain a closed chapter.

I *did* tell her about meeting two of Christian's children and getting to know Christina, and she loved hearing about the ballet and my visit to Vivian's place.

"I've always enjoyed watching Vivian on stage, and I've been fascinated by several of the magazine displays of Vivian's home. Now I have the inside scoop to share with my friends."

I entertained her with an account of the visit to our old school telling her of all the changes that had taken place. I mentioned that we had lunched at the Old Mill and elaborated on our trip to The Inn at the Sea ending with our paying proper respect to Holger Danske.

"Sounds like the two of you made a trip around the world in eighty days or less," she laughed and asked if I'd told Christian about Grandmother Clara. I said I had.

"I am sure Freddy had no idea that he was broaching a sensitive subject that day," she said; "my darling brother has a heart of gold—and is one of the most wonderful men I know—but sensitivity is not one of his strong points. Rie gave him a royal chewing out after you and Christian left Sunday and he, of course, had absolutely *no* idea what she was talking about.

"By the way, I brought back your album and put it on the desk in your room. I learned from Freddy who several of the people in some of the photographs are. I'll share it with you later. I looked through it a couple of days ago and among the many photos, I found several of your parents. There is even one of you from the day you were christened. You were held by your Aunt Clara, your father's sister, the one your grandmother made sure was given her chosen name. Clara, by the way, did later become quite a famous singer."

She stopped talking and eyed me carefully before she continued.

"You do know that Clara was your godmother, and not my mother, as you were told?" she asked.

I thanked her for bringing the album back, and admitted that, yes, I had learned about Aunt Clara being my actual Godmother.

"I told the whole tale to Christian who found the story fascinating," I said.

Then I gave her a brief account of Christian's four marriages.

"Well, well," she said, "he doesn't exactly sound like the stable kind to me. But you never know about the details and circumstances, do you?"

I told Astrid that Reenie had expressed the same opinion, adding that even Christina had admitted that her father had "set himself up for failure" on several occasions.

"Sounds to me like a man who very much loves women, but maybe still needs to do some growing up," Astrid philosophized. I admitted she might be right.

"Christian being such a softie for women might, in part, be due to the vow he made to himself as a young boy—to never hurt any woman," I said.

Astrid gave me a questioning look and I explained.

"One night while we sat and talked, Christian told me that his father used to verbally abuse his mother. Any little thing would set him off and he would tear into Inga, Christian said. She was a shy and reclusive woman, unable to put up any self-defense against his father; the smooth, cold, and extremely successful barrister.

"As a young boy, Christian often stood outside his father's study, feeling helpless listening to his father verbally tear his mother to shreds until she finally whimpered and cried. After that she would cringe and retire to her room for several days.

"He said he'd made a vow—when he was just a boy—to never treat women badly. So he's gone on loving one woman after the other without ever making it work," I told her.

"Just the same, you are losing your heart to him again, aren't you?" she inquired quietly and before I had a chance to comment she continued.

"Anna, if you were thirty or forty, with children still at home, I would tell you to be real careful and move slow. But you're not thirty or forty even, and if you love Christian that's really all that matters, isn't it?"

I looked at her while she paused to pull a sheet of

cookies from the oven and put them on a cooling rack.

"Well, yes, I just don't know what to do about it," I said.

Astrid, ever the practical one, reached into the refrigerator, brought out a plate with opened-faced sandwiches she had prepared earlier, along with a bottle of chilled wine, and said, "Let's have some lunch and talk about it."

She had already set the table in the dining room and we soon sat in the comfortable apartment listening to the rain drum on the balcony outside, while we enjoyed a fine meal and the company of each other.

Astrid poured Riesling into stemmed, finely etched crystal glasses dating back to our grandmother's home, and I took a sip of wine, leaned back in the chair and expressed my concerns over possibly leaving my family behind, giving up my life in the States.

I expected her to agree that, indeed, there was a catch to the situation. Instead, my sensible cousin put down her glass and faced me.

"You might consider the fact that you both have enough money to travel any time you want to. That means you do not have to be stuck forever in either country—away from your own family—in case you decide to throw in your lot with Christian."

She drained her wine and refilled both our glasses. She made sense, I admitted, and I felt better having received, what I considered, some sound advice.

After lunch we worked together for another couple of hours, and then sat down with a cup of tea in the living room for a well-deserved rest. Just as we finished our tea, the rain stopped and the sun came out and we decided to go to the grocery store to pick up a couple of items we still needed.

The rest of the day, and all day Friday, Astrid and I spent either working, going for walks, or just relaxing. The rain picked up again Friday afternoon and it felt cozy being in Astrid's home, reminiscing and talking about her plans for the party on Saturday.

We also spent some time looking through the pictures in Grandmother Clara's album and found several photos of my grandmother who, Astrid assured me, I resembled. Among the photos were also some childhood pictures of my biological father, Alexander, with his brothers and younger sister.

Christian called both evenings and we talked at length as if we hadn't just spent time together.

When he rang Friday evening, he told me he had wrapped up most of his work and would be able to take several days off the following week. He wanted to take me on a visit to meet his daughter Helena, her husband, and their baby, and I told him I would be delighted to meet yet another of the Raabensted siblings.

I got off the phone and told Astrid our plans.

"After meeting Peter and Christina, I can hardly wait to see what kind of person their older sister is."

Late that evening, I took time out to write Reenie a long email on Astrid's computer, bringing her up-to-date on all I had done during the week I had been gone. I only hinted at some of the conversations with Christian, not wanting to go into details over the Internet. I knew she would understand.

By now she knew nearly everything there was to know about my life with the exception of the letters I never received, and my real relationship with my adopting father, Nels.

Saturday afternoon I found myself in my old room dressing and preparing for the Christening of little Frederik. I had gone out on the balcony earlier and with satisfaction noted that the day was going to be my kind of day—quite balmy and a little cool, with the sun peeking out from behind clouds resembling soft whipped cream.

I put on a lined silk, cream-colored pants-suit—brought for the occasion—and accented it with a long scarf in shades of taupe, black and cream. I added my diamond earrings and ring from Robert, and a thin diamond bracelet left from the days when the "tennis" bracelets were the rage. The outfit would be just right, not only for the occasion, but for the weather as well.

Shortly before three o'clock Christian rang the doorbell and while I let him in, Astrid gave the apartment a quick, but unnecessary, look-over. After our ardent work the previous day, she found everything to her liking—the place fairly sparkled. The tables were set with her best china, heavy silverware, and crystal. Bouquets of freesias and anemones filled several vases, and candles stood in silver holders, ready to be lighted as soon as we came back.

Astrid had hired her weekly cleaning lady and the woman's teenage daughter to come and help out with the party so she would be free to fuss over her guests.

The Christening was a lovely event. Anne Marie and Torben were all smiles as they arrived with their baby dressed up in the old family baptismal gown, passed down from generation to generation.

Everyone in our family had worn it at their christening, ever since it was made for my maternal grandmother back before the turn of the century. It is a delicate, long and white lace frock with two different muslin undergarments. One is blue, the other pink and the color worn depends, of course, on the gender of the baby. I have a framed picture of my mother as an infant in the gown and another one of her holding me wearing the same gown. It felt wonderful to stand by "my" baptismal font in Vor Frelser's Kirke holding this newest member of our family clan.

Later that afternoon newly christened Frederik Torben Tangelund slept soundly in his portable crib in his grandmother's bedroom while twenty adults gathered at Astrid's tables for a fabulous dinner. This was followed by coffee, an assortment of after-dinner drinks, and the overwhelming amount of pastries and other delicacies Astrid had prepared prior to the event.

Christian spent some of the time talking with Freddy and at one point I saw the two of them on the balcony, in the company of Freddy's oldest son, Mika, enjoying a couple of the Cuban cigars Freddy had brought.

Around eight, we said goodnight to Astrid and told her we had a trip planned early the next day.

"Christian and I are heading to the southern part of Sealand tomorrow, to visit his oldest daughter and her family," I said while Christian helped me put on my coat.

I told Astrid I planned to stay with Christian's family overnight. After that, I would catch the train to Als (a small island off the eastern coast of Jutland,) to spend a few days with friends I had not seen for a while, adding I would be back, Friday morning.

"You have the keys to the house, and you know your way, so come back whenever you like. I'll be home until Tuesday; then I'm taking the train to Roskilde to visit our old pastor from the city. He and his wife settled there after he retired a few years ago, and they've invited me to come up and visit with them for a few days. I told him I was uncertain about your plans and could not commit to a specific time, but now that you have re-connected with Christian, I feel safe leaving you," she added and gave me a hug.

The drive back that evening was relaxing, and I felt better than I had in a long time. Coming face to face with the two missing letters had taken off yet another layer of guilt, doubt and insecurity. I was grateful for the way things from my past were starting to clear up and felt I could begin to look back without the angst that used to haunt me.

Since it was still relatively early in the evening when we arrived at Valhalla, we exchanged our party clothes for jeans and sweaters and went for a long walk on the beach. The rain that drenched everything in the days before had cleared the air and the walk on the moonlit beach was invigorating.

Christian told me the house had seemed lonely without

me, and that Mrs. Larsen had complained to Christina, "The doctor is just moping around."

We came back, fixed mugs of hot chocolate and spent the rest of the evening in the library listening to recordings from the forties while hashing over all the things we had experienced since I arrived.

Chapter 29

We left Valhalla around nine thirty the next morning facing a mild spring day with lazy clouds drifting along in the slight breeze and everything looking fresh and green. After leaving the suburbs, we drove through the inner city that was taking its time waking up this Sunday morning. As we passed a bakery at the edge of town Christian assured me he would perish from malnutrition if we did not stop within the hour for a meal and we agreed to pull in at the first "charming inn" along the way.

This caused us to arrive a little late at the home of Helena and Oliver but, as it turned out, our lateness was hardly noticed.

Shortly after one o'clock, we pulled into a gravel driveway leading to a weathered, but well-kept, thatched-roofed house, and as the car slowed down, I took in the view of the captivating homestead.

The old, yellow farm house was fairly isolated, with no neighboring homes. Open fields flanked the well-kept yard. Out in front—in the cobblestone courtyard—the Danish flag snapped in the breeze making the scene look like a picture postcard.

As we pulled up in front of the house, four dogs of various sizes charged out from behind the building and barked their greetings. A pair of German Shepherds ran through a large rain puddle in the middle of the yard and jumped up and placed their paws on the Mercedes, while a Terrier of mixed breed—and a very pregnant Schnauzer—kept circling the car.

Christian got out, gave them all friendly pats on their heads and shooed them away before they had a chance to do serious damage to my slacks. Close on the heels of the dogs followed a young man carrying a toddler.

"Hello Oliver!" Christian cried out, and took my arm and led me toward his grandson and son-in-law. Christian hadn't told me much about his oldest daughter and her family and I admit I was somewhat surprised when the tall, handsome, ebony-colored man came over to meet us. He looked to be somewhere in his thirties and was carrying a sweet looking toddler in his arms.

"And how are you Chris?" Christian asked gathering up the little boy as he reached out to him.

"Chris this is Anna, a very special lady, and Anna, this is Christian Oliver Wilson. He will be two next month, and is my first and favorite grandson. Not only is he handsome and well behaved, he's also my namesake," he said with pride.

The little boy looked at me, flashed me a wonderful smile and held out his arms—my heart melted; he obviously knew a grandmother when he saw one, and knew he would be safe with me. His skin was the color of coffee ice cream, and he had deep brown eyes and soft curly hair. He looked at me and picked up the locket on the chain I was wearing while he chatted away in a mixture of English and Danish.

"We are trying to make him bilingual," Oliver laughed and reached out his hand for an introduction.

"I am Oliver and you must be Anna. Peter told us about you already. Do come inside," he added and I noticed he spoke Danish with a distinct British accent.

Oliver called the dogs over and put all of them, save for the Schnauzer, inside a fenced-in area to the side of the house. When he came back I saw he walked with a slight limp.

"I'm so sorry, but Helena isn't here right now," he said.

"We received an emergency call a little more than an hour ago. A dog got hit by a motorcycle just the other side of town. There is no other vet around, so Helena went to tend to the animal," he explained.

"I would have taken the call, but I did a bit of damage to my knee, working in the yard a few days ago. I can walk okay, but the doctor recommended I not drive for a week or so. Anyway, Helena will be home soon. Our lunch is ready and the table is set so if you are famished, we can start without her."

We confessed having stopped for brunch on the way down and were not yet hungry.

"So if it is okay with you Oliver," Christian said, "We'll wait for Helena."

We walked inside and Oliver suggested we leave our luggage in the hallway until later.

"Helena will show you your room when she gets back," he said, and took us through a corridor leading to a terrace in back of the house.

Mitzy, the Schnauzer, had followed Christian since he got out of his car and—like Freddy's dog —now planted herself right at his feet. I gave him a significant look; he acknowledged the hint, and reminded me I had promised to help him find a dog.

Oliver led us to a modern-looking outdoor table circled by big teak chairs cut in straight lines and filled with soft, stark white cushions. The seating offered a view over the sloping back lawn, yielding to newly plowed fields off to the left. To the far right was a windmill—its blades slowly turning.

We played with the baby for a while and then our host excused himself and went into the house. A few minutes later he came back, carrying a small tray with frosted glasses filled with ice and a pale green liquid.

I took a taste of the icy concoction made of lime, lemon, vodka, and a touch of something Oliver claimed was his own secret. I told him it was delicious and just what I needed.

"Please enjoy yourself while I take Chris inside. He's already had his lunch and it's time for his nap," he said.

He picked up his son from his grandfather and swung the boy around producing the warm laughter only children make—the kind that reaches right into your heart.

We watched them disappear and for a moment everything was quiet. I looked over at Christian leaning back in the cushioned chair and saw him observe me in a bemused way.

"You never gave me any background on your son-in-law. Not that it matters. Oliver is a charming and hospitable man; I just never saw any mixed marriages in this country when we were growing up. I *am* glad some of the prejudices have begun to go away," I said, adding, "I'm afraid we still have a long way to go in the States."

"I guess I wanted to see your reaction," Christian admitted. "It wasn't meant as a test, but if it had been—you passed. I never, for a moment, thought you would find it surprising, but Helen and Oliver have had several American clients who seemed outright offended by their marriage. Helena tends to be on the defensive and is wary, especially of anyone from the States.

"I may not have told you earlier that Oliver was born in London. They met as veterinary students at a University in England, where Helena had chosen to further her education.

"They fell in love and were married right after Oliver finished his graduate work. He did some additional studies for a year until Helena received her degree. Then they came to Denmark and stayed at Valhalla for a couple of months. They finally settled in Vordingborg where they bought this farm and their practice from Dr. Jakobson, an old vet getting ready to retire. He stayed on for six months until Helena and Oliver got the hang of the practice. Then he moved into a retirement complex at the center of town. As far as I know, he still drops in at the clinic now and then.

"Oliver is an only child, born late in his parents' marriage. His father, Oliver Wilson—called Ollie—served with the diplomatic corps in England. When he retired, about a year ago, he and Oliver's mother decided to move to Denmark in order to be near their only son and his family. Chris, needless to say, is the apple of their eyes.

"Ruby and Ollie settled in Klampenborg—near me—rather than in Vordingborg. After visiting me on several occasions, they found they really liked the northern coast of Sealand. Ruby also confided that part of their reason for buying a home in close proximity to mine, was so it would be convenient for Helena and Oliver to call on all of us at the same time whenever they found time for a visit. She told me she preferred not to live too close to the children, in order to not get in the way."

Christian smiled and added, "I also happen to know Ruby enjoys being able to hop right on the train into Copenhagen. They had a chauffeur all the years they lived in England and Ruby never learned to drive. They are several years older than us and are two of the nicest people you ever want to know."

As he finished talking, we heard a car approach and I looked and saw a Volvo station wagon pulling up by the garage. Just then Oliver came out carrying a pitcher of the potion we were drinking. He placed it on the table in front of us and went over to greet Helena.

Unlike Christina and Peter who, with their angular faces and blonde hair, both resembled their father, Helena looked entirely different. Although tall, she was slight of build with a heart-shaped face, eyes like emeralds, a small rosette mouth, and nearly jet-black hair pulled back in a ponytail.

I detected a slight resemblance to Christian's mother Inga, but she really looked more like a feminine version of Christian's maternal grandfather, the old judge who looked down from the wall above the fireplace in the old study. With something near determination, she walked straight toward me, shook my hand briefly, and offered me a nod and an icy smile.

"You've met Oliver I see. Good! Well I'm sorry lunch was delayed, but duty called. I'll go and wash up and then we can all eat."

She turned, gave her father a quick peck on the cheek and without hesitation, walked toward the house, leaving me feeling like something the cat dragged in.

Chapter 30

A while later we were seated in the dining room enjoying an excellent lunch of green salad tossed with smoked salmon, homemade oat bread, plus assorted imported olives and farm-market pickles.

The interior, in contrast to the ancient exterior, was furnished with ultra-modern furniture featuring a lot of chrome and glass, mixed with a few antiques—most likely from Valhalla. Two faded wool rugs, in shades of white and beige, covered part of the light wooden floors otherwise left bare. Several large abstract oil paintings—rendered in bold red and orange—provided the only color in a home that otherwise exuded a pleasant, but chilled atmosphere. I decided that Oliver, who seemed warm and open in contrast to his wife, must be responsible for acquiring the paintings. I later learned from Christian that his son-in-law actually did all the paintings.

We had no sooner started lunch before Oliver turned to me and said, "I just cannot get over how much you look like my mother-in-law. Peter called early this morning to let us know he would be joining us later this evening, and told us all about you and the remarkable resemblance."

He turned to his wife for acknowledgement but found none.

"I don't see why all of you are making such a fuss," she said, and gave me a frigid look; then she addressed her father and husband.

"Mother is slight of build, taller than Anna, and a little younger, I think. There may be some resemblance around the eyes," she added looking straight at me, "but other than that, they really look quite different."

Having finished her judgment she turned and offered me another glass of wine. Stung by the remark—and by now feeling short, fat and old—I meekly said, "Thank you," and took a sip from my refilled glass.

Oliver, obviously sensing his wife's hostility, quickly changed the subject and asked Helena about the dog she had just treated.

As night becomes day, Helena changed and engaged in an animated account of her emergency call. It was obvious she enjoyed her work.

"This was a somewhat bizarre call. I actually saved a dog that in a short while may be sent to the pound," she said and laid down her knife and fork.

"The woman who owns the dog is the younger sister of one of our friends. She is called Amanda and her husband is Kurt. They are a pair of veritable retread hippies who, despite their young ages, look and act as if they've been frozen back in the 60s and then brought back just before the start of the new millennium. They rent a place a couple of miles outside town—a rundown farm, actually—where they grow and sell vegetables and herbs. She does some weaving and makes all the odd looking clothes they wear. He is a fair carpenter and we've had him do some repair a couple of times both here and at the clinic."

She stopped talking and took a sip of wine before continuing.

"They recently decided to join a kibbutz in Israel. They'll be leaving in a few weeks and will be gone for two or three years. They don't own much, but they do have two wonderful golden retrievers they bought about a year ago. I've given the dogs all their shots and gotten to know both animals. About a month ago, Kurt told me they just learned, they were not allowed to take the dogs along. Amanda's' sister has agreed to take the female but the other dog—the male that just got sideswiped by a motorcycle—will have to be turned over to the animal shelter, unless they find a home for him soon."

She had turned toward her husband during the last remark but, before she could continue, Oliver held up a hand and interrupted her.

"Don't even think about it Helena," he laughed. "We already have four dogs and Mitzy is about to bless us with another litter. We do *not* need another animal."

She looked resigned for a moment; then a smile brightened her face, and she looked at her father.

"Dad, you really ought to have a dog for companionship, living all by yourself. You've always loved dogs and they you," she added with a voice so unlike the one she had used with me.

"You've not had one since Buddy died, right before you married Brigitta, and this dog is a really nice animal. He is well behaved, housebroken, and just a little over a year old; you could easily train him."

"Christian, Helena is right," I said, seeing a chance to score brownie points with his daughter.

"A dog would be so nice for you at Valhalla and I'm sure Mrs. Larsen would enjoy the company of a good dog during the day."

I received what I determined was an ounce of approval from Helena and decided to push on.

"What's the dog's name?"

"It's 'Dog' and isn't *that* original," Helena said with obvious disapproval.

"The female is called 'Girl' but Birgit, Amanda's sister, told me she fully intends to change it to something more appropriate. You can surely come up with something better if you decide to take him. He'll be ready to leave the clinic in a couple of days," she said and beamed at her father.

"Oliver is going to visit Ollie and Ruby next week; he could bring him over," she urged.

Christian, obviously feeling trapped, agreed he would think it over and promised to let her know before we left in the morning.

Just as our lunch ended, the baby woke up. After feeding him a snack, Helena suggested we go for a walk. During our lunch the weather had turned cool and misty, but in Denmark that never deters anyone from going for walks. With a great number of inclement days, you would be housebound for weeks if you let sprinkles of rain keep you from going outside. As Oliver said, while all of us put on raincoats, "There's no such thing as bad weather, just inappropriate clothes."

He put the baby in a pram, pulled up the carriage hood, covered the blanket with a waterproof sheet, and off we went for a long hike along a nearby lake, accompanied by all the dogs, except Mitzy.

I was glad I'd decided to put on sensible slacks, a crew-neck sweater over a thin white turtle-neck, and Christina's old boots. I felt appropriately dressed and received an encouraging smile from Oliver, as we sat out on our walk.

An hour or so after we arrived back at the house, Oliver fed the baby and put him to bed for the night—but not before he had spent a lot of time playing with his grandfather. It was a side of Christian I had never seen, and I enjoyed watching the two of them.

Peter arrived just in time to join us for a before-dinner drink and we all sat around the table in the spacious kitchen and talked, while Helena prepared our evening meal of clear soup, cheese and asparagus quiche, a green salad, and crusty bread. With this, Oliver served an excellent German white wine.

Afterward we settled in the living room where a streamlined wood burning stove created a warm atmosphere. We enjoyed dessert consisting of coffee, fruit and imported crème-filled chocolates. I ate everything I was served so as not to offend my hostess. I knew I had better take some antacids before retiring, and plan on a lot of skinny food the next couple of days. After we watched the news on TV, we spent the rest of the evening listening to Peter entertain us with stories from his years in California while Oliver filled in with anecdotes from their veterinary business. Karen, or my likeness to her, was not mentioned again.

Around midnight, Christian said that he planned to drive me to the train station early in the morning, and would then head back to the university for an afternoon meeting. We bid Peter farewell and I said goodnight to our host and hostess.

With Helena just down the hall, I absolutely refused to

do anything more than kiss Christian after we got into bed. He just chuckled and playfully nibbled my ear.

"It'll be a long time until Friday," he said and we both laughed and quietly made love muffled by the featherbed, and my fear of being heard.

As we prepared to sleep, I questioned Christian about his oldest daughter.

"Am I being overly sensitive, or was there a visible coolness from Helena toward me all day?"

Christian put his arm under my back and drew me close.

"No, I too felt her reserve coming across the room, and I think I know part of the reason," he said and gently kissed me.

"Helena has always been a serious person. She never quite forgave her mother for not taking her and her sister and brother with her when she left to marry Erik. Oh, she was happy enough to be with me, but I think she felt rejected by her mother—consequently they are not close. Peter, always a carefree soul, was perfectly content to stay with me, and Christina, who as I am sure you noticed, is the type who is happy most anywhere.

"At a young age, Helena decided she was the reason Karen and I married. When the marriage didn't work out, she took on some uncalled for guilt."

While he talked, I lay quietly and watched as the moonlight and spring breezes gently played with the soft curtains. I told myself that I could not win over everyone. I was not a part of Christian's family and therefore should not be concerned whether or not all his children approved of me. Two out of three wasn't bad anyway, I reasoned. Then I nuzzled against the soft skin at the nape of Christian's neck.

He let out a sigh and concluded, "The fact that you *do* resemble her mother probably makes it difficult for Helena to warm up to you. I'm not a psychologist, but I *am* sure it is nothing personal," he said and gently stroked my hair.

Right before I fell asleep, I whispered, "Don't forget to make arrangements for the dog to come home to Valhalla. I'm sure we'll think of a proper name."

Chapter 31

I sat in the train around ten thirty the next morning and watched pastoral scenes, each one pretty enough for framing. We passed rolling hills where well-fed cattle leisurely grazed on slightly sloping fields. A pair of colts bolting around in a large corral just on the edge of one small village caught my attention. From my window, I observed plowed fields with dark brown furrows holding promises of summer, and small towns tucked in between the open acres, observing that the backside of most of the houses looked more or less alike and charming on this clear and bright April day. I went down to the dining car and brought back a cup of tea, made myself comfortable in my seat, and reflected on the stay with Helena and her family.

We woke to the sound of rain drumming on the roof that morning, but by the time Christian drove me to the train station, the rain had stopped and the sun begun to show its face. With blue skies above, it looked like the day ahead would be much like a North Carolina spring day.

The morning had gone considerably better than the previous evening. Helena had set things out for breakfast while Katrine, the young woman who came in around seven-thirty to take care of Chris, fed the baby. We enjoyed a simple breakfast of soft-boiled eggs, toast, and juice, and chatted fairly amiably about the weather, the baby, and their work. Afterwards Christian and I went upstairs to pack while Oliver and Helena left for the clinic.

We kissed the baby good-by, said farewell to Katrine, and drove to Helena and Oliver's animal clinic to meet "Dog." He, of course, turned out to be absolutely irresistible. He took one look at us and despite some pain to his leg, limped over and licked our hands. It wasn't much of a sell.

"I'm afraid I'll have to take him home," Christian said with a deep sigh. "If I don't, I'm sure Anna will refuse to speak to me ever again. But he can't just be called dog," he said and shook his head.

He asked me to think of a name and without batting an eye I said, "'Sir Bob Wallace,' 'Sir' for short."

Helena looked at me as if I was totally nuts and I quickly explained.

"The dog would be named after the main character in the movie 'White Christmas,' and in honor of your father being knighted this fall," I finished.

"I like the name and it's certainly an improvement over Dog—so Sir it is," Christian said.

At that time I didn't dare mention to Helena that the name actually was a referral to my long-time name for her father—"My Knight in Shining Armor." In my heart I knew this wouldn't play well, so I remained mum.

Helena bid me farewell in her usual cool way, but did manage a small and sincere smile. Then she went over to kiss her father goodbye and told him they would be in touch. She would let him know when Oliver would bring the dog to Valhalla.

The train suddenly slowed down and came to a halt and I looked out and saw we had pulled in to a small country station; so I took time out from my reverie to observe the passengers board the train. They included a couple of young mothers with babies in strollers, several students with knapsacks on their backs and smiles on their adolescent faces, a few tourist-looking middle aged couples plus one single businessman carrying his all important briefcase. Within minutes we were on our way again.

I took another sip of my tea; watched the enchanting scenery fly by, and thought of Christian, who had seen me to the train.

He had bought me the morning paper and a box of

chocolates for my host family on Als. Then, despite people looking, he kissed me thoroughly good-by.

"My darling Anna, please come back to me. I don't want to not have you in my life," he said and grinned.

I had given him my most winning smile, trying not to look embarrassed in front of a large group of teen-aged students filling up the station, carrying day packs, and getting a kick out of two old people kissing in public. From their chatter I learned they would be joining me on the train, heading for a class trip to Odense on the island of Fuen, to visit the home of Hans Christian Anderson.

I waved goodbye to Christian and was relieved to see the students head in the opposite direction toward the end of the long train where a couple of cars had been reserved for their group. I enjoy being with young people, but listening for hours to the mixture of sound emanating from tape players and the boom boxes they all seem to carry, can be tiring.

The train pulled out of the station, and I began to anticipate seeing my young friends on Als—the "M & Ms" my family called them—and reflected on our friendship that started years ago.

Magnus Madsen, or Mole as he is called, married Marin Mortenson right after she returned from North Carolina where she had studied at the university in Charlotte. Becca, a freshman there, had met Marin in the college cafeteria, and as soon as she learned Marin was from Denmark, she immediately felt it was her sworn duty to bring her home. During all her school years, she had brought home a variety of foreign students for dinner or weekend stays, and for years we entertained dozens of Scandinavian young men and women who were here as part of various studies and exchange programs.

With the exception of one student, a girl who had to be sent home because she had gotten herself pregnant, we enjoyed all of them. They in turn seemed happy to discover a little bit of home, so far away from home, even with strangers.

From the first time we hosted Marin, she had seemed like one of our clan and when her mother came over to visit her at Christmas she had stayed with us since Marin's host family did not have a spare room. After Marin returned to Denmark, we kept in touch with her and her parents and shared Marin's pain when her father died.

Robert, Becca and I even flew over to be part of the celebration of her marriage to Mole, and when the two of them decided to visit the states, they used our home as a base while touring the entire USA.

Marin and Mole had said from the start that they wanted to have a large family, but after Marin delivered triplet girls they decided that three was enough. The girls, Mette, Melena, and Manne were near teens by now and turning into handsome young women, judging by the pictures Marin sent me.

Mole taught physics at a near-by junior college, and Marin filled in as a substitute teacher at the local elementary school whenever someone was sick, on leave, or on vacation. With the generous five weeks of vacation allotted all Danes, no matter where employed, Marin could pretty much choose how and when she wanted to work.

She had sent me a letter and told me she had taken the entire week off to spend time with me, and I looked forward to some "girl time" with her. Despite the difference in our ages, we shared a relationship that was a combination of sisters, mother-daughter, and plain close friends.

Chapter 32

The train pulled in to their town early in the afternoon and as I stepped away from the railroad car, leather duffel slung over my shoulder and pulling my small suitcase behind me, I saw Marin waving a small Danish flag at the top of the station stairs leading up to the street-level platform. I hurried up the steep steps and fell into her embrace. Then she picked up my duffel and put her arm around me as we went out to the parking lot.

"Mole will not be home until five-thirty tonight and the girls are headed for riding lessons right after school, so we have the next couple of hours to ourselves," she said with a big smile and gave me another hug.

She loaded my luggage into her little utility vehicle and set off for their house located at the edge of town.

On the way, we chatted about my trip and family in North Carolina and in fifteen minutes we pulled up in front of the old house they had lovingly restored and made into a place where friends feel at home. The front garden was in bloom with tulips and daffodils creating a border of color against the pale yellow sides of the stucco home bathed in midday sunshine.

Their two Labradors and one of their cats, came from behind the house to greet us. A fat, white bunny sat in the window twitching its whiskers as if to offer me its own greeting.

I pointed to the rabbit and Marin laughed and said, "That is Minnie the Moocher, the girls' latest addition to our menagerie,"

Then, just before unlocking the front door to the house, she stopped, took a hold of my arm, and looked me straight in the eyes.

"Anna, I'm so glad you are here," she said and gave me yet another hug.

"It's been way too long and I have something important to tell you; something I didn't want to cover in any of my emails."

"You are not going to tell me that you and Mole are divorcing, are you?" I said, half in fun, while giving her a quizzical look.

She burst out in her throaty laughter and said, "Lord no, I'm afraid we're stuck with each other for eternity. Let's get inside and have a cup of tea and a piece of my lemon cake—or lunch if you're really hungry—and then I'll tell you all about it."

Within minutes we were sitting inside their enclosed sun porch amidst wicker furniture enhanced by Marin's homemade, big flowery cushions and colorful afghans. I looked out at their peaceful backyard and enjoyed the mint tea as I waited for my friend to tell me her "something important."

I was savoring a small piece of cake, having declined lunch in favor of my hostess' tasty homemade baked goods, when Marin took my hand.

"Anna—we are going to have another baby," she announced without any lead up.

Before I could utter a word, she went on.

"Please be happy for us and don't tell me you think I'm crazy. My mother and her sister are up in arms because it's been twelve years since the girls were born, *and* I will be in my mid-thirties by the time the baby arrives. My doctor has assured me that I'm in great health and my ultrasound indicates the baby—only one this time—is going to be just fine."

She is blessed with a sunny disposition and a positive attitude, and you just can't help but feel better when you are with her.

I smiled and took her hand.

"Marin, I think that you and Mole having another baby is absolutely wonderful. Since your doctor has assured you you're in good physical shape, there seems to be no reason to worry. I also think you are one of the best mothers I've ever enjoyed knowing. Any baby raised by you is a lucky child."

Marin squeezed my hand and looked relieved—apparently satisfied she had my support. Then a mischievous expression surfaced on her face and I guessed she knew what my question was going to be. I admit that I couldn't resist and asked if it was going to be a boy this time.

"Nope, that little gene is not anywhere in our family," she said with a twinkle in her eye.

"Besides, Mole is nuts about girls and I don't care what it is as long as it's a healthy baby.

"But, you'll never guess what we are going to name her," she said and gave me a significant look.

"Well, considering the Ms in all of your names, and the fact that your dogs are named Max and Mindy and your cats Mopsy and Mick; I would venture to guess you are going to call her Mary, Margrete or Molly, perhaps?"

She gave me a slow gentle smile and poured me another cup of tea before she spoke.

"No," she smiled, "we've decided we have enough 'Ms—this one is going to be called Anna Marie—after you."

If someone told me I had just won the lottery I could not have been more pleased, and I gave her a hug and thanked her.

We spent the rest of the afternoon talking about the new baby, what it would entail having a little one around again, and everything else under the stars, until it was time to think about getting dinner ready.

Shortly after five I heard crashing sounds coming from the hallway and in minutes, the door flew open and three girls poured into the living room looking, as always, like exquisite reflections of each other. Without thoroughly studying each one and observing their different characters, it was impossible to tell who was who of these pretty blue-eyed blondes.

The girls ran over to hug me, all talking at the same time.

"Anna, it's so great to see you!"

"How long are you staying?"

"Did you bring pictures of your grandchildren and your dog?"

"Do you know we're going to have a baby sister?"

I laughed at their enthusiasm; then we did a group hug.

"Now, will you give Anna a break and go to your rooms and change out of your riding gear and wash up before dinner. Then come back down and set the table, make the salad, and feed the animals," Marin instructed her excited daughters.

I received a peck on my cheek from all three and watched as they bounded up the stairs leading to their rooms as excited conversation drifted back down to the suddenly quiet living room.

The Madsen household is a lively one and I spent the next four days enjoying myself. Every morning after Mole and the girls left for work and school, Marin and I went for long walks with the dogs, strolling along the ocean—a short ways from their home—and came back to sit and talk over tea or coffee.

One afternoon when Marin sat crocheting on an afghan, I told her about Christian and our relationship and how we seemed to be growing closer. He called every evening and I felt I needed to share my happiness *and* my concerns with her. Marin listened quietly while I talked and then she advised me in much the same way Astrid had.

"First of all, I am delighted to hear that you might be making a change in your otherwise solo life. I know you loved and still miss Robert, but you really are much too young to spend the rest of your life alone. Christian sounds like he really loves you and from the way you look, I dare say you share that feeling.

"You should, perhaps, move forward slowly. On the other hand, you no longer have children at home, so enjoy your life, and if it feels like love, go with it."

Then she broke out in laughter and asked me to keep her informed "when something serious happens."

I enjoyed the times alone with Marin and the evenings

when we gathered as a family. A couple of times we played board games and one night the girls entertained us by singing old Danish songs while Marin played the piano and Mole strummed his hollow-body guitar.

One afternoon I helped Marin bake bread to be sold at a fund raising event at the girl's school and on an especially warm evening, we all went wading in the ocean. Afterwards, we hurried home and settled down in front of the television sipping warm drinks, laughing as we watched videos from the time Mole and Marin stayed with us and toured the States.

Before the girls left for school, the day I was leaving, they made me promise I would come back the following spring in time for their confirmation ceremony and party. Then they gave me a figurine of three little bunnies dressed in pink and said, "Now you'll always have something to remind you of us and how much we love you."

I assured them I would keep the bunnies in my den— always. Then they grabbed their backpacks, ran out the door, got on their bicycles, and were off to school.

While I packed, Marin came into my bedroom carrying the afghan she had been working on.

"I stayed up last night after you went to bed to finish this. It is your birthday present, a little early," she said.

"After looking at pictures of your home, I think the colors are right for your den so I hope you can find a use for it."

I thanked her and told her it would always be part of my den and a wonderful reminder of my "other Danish family."

I found a space for the afghan in my suitcase, finished packing, and bid Mole goodbye with promises to return again "real soon." Then I got in their car with Marin who drove me to the train station.

"The baby is due in September," she said while driving, "and the Christening will be sometime late November. So, in case something permanent develops between you and

Christian—and you decide to come back—I sure would love to have you attend the event with him," she said with a big smile.

"The girls—all three of them—are going to be the baby's Godmothers, but we would all love to have you be Baby Anna's honorary Godmother."

I told her I would be honored to accept "in the event I am here."

We reached the station and I thanked her for all the love and care she and her family had given me. Then I gave her a quick hug and promised to let her know how things progressed with Christian.

"Just go with it," she said and smiled.

By this time I didn't have to tell anyone that I was falling in love with him again—they all knew. But from falling in love to loving someone forever is a long jump, one I wasn't sure I was ready to make

Chapter 33

It had been a great, but busy time with the Madsen family and soon, the gentle rhythm of the train lulled me to sleep and I didn't wake up until the train pulled into the Central Railway Station in Copenhagen a little after one. I looked out of the window, pulled down my suitcase from the net above the seat, and realized I was hungry. All I'd had for breakfast was a container of yogurt and a glass of orange juice, planning to eat something on the train. Instead, I had slept most of the way and missed a meal.

I gathered my luggage and headed up the stairs for the main hall thinking I would grab a hot dog at one of the many vendor carts outside the train station. This way I wouldn't arrive at Astrid's starved, causing her to make a fuss.

As I walked toward the exit, someone suddenly came up behind me and grabbed my suitcase. I took hold of my handbag and turned ready to slug whoever it was, only to find myself face to face with Christian. He put his hand up in defense and burst out laughing. Then he sat down my luggage, embraced me in a bear hug, and lifted me off the ground.

"Lord above, I've missed you Anna," he said and gave me a kiss, making my toes tingle like the first time we kissed! He let me go and I looked at him with a mixture of confusion and delight.

"Why are you here and not at the university—and how did you learn about my arrival time? I thought our plan was for me to go to Astrid's and for you to pick me up tomorrow morning in time for our trip to Sweden?"

"Hold your horses woman, and I'll tell you all about it, but first let's get out of here," he said and let go of me after yet another kiss.

He picked up my bags and put his arm around my shoulder as we headed for the car—this time parked

261

legally—in the parking lot across from the Tivoli Gardens.

"First of all, let me assure you that Astrid is fine," he said, causing my immediate alarm, and I started to ask questions.

"No, no don't interrupt, let me finish," he said as I inquired just why Astrid should not be fine.

"She rang me up yesterday from Roskilde where, as you know, she's visiting her former pastor, and told me she had tripped over a branch and twisted her leg during a hike. It's not serious, but the doctor suggested she keep off her feet for a few days and her host family is apparently more than delighted to have her stay. She instructed me to tell you not to worry.

"She also asked me to please look after you and I assured her I planned to take you to Valhalla and would be more than happy to take real good care of you," he said and squeezed me tight.

"I also promised we would check on her apartment, and water the plants, and offered to do whatever else was needed," he said with a grin.

"You see, I am trying to influence your family so they'll think I'm someone nice, and a real asset in your life."

I gave him a friendly push and told him I was starved and really wanted a hot dog from the nearest stand. Next, I wanted a shower and a chance to get into some other clothes after sitting in a train all morning.

So we found a hotdog stand and stood alongside a couple of police officers on a late lunch break, and with great gusto, consumed hot dogs with everything on them. Then we headed for Amager.

On the way, Christian filled me in on the plans for the weekend and gave me an update on the reunion plans. It was wonderful being with him again and I realized just how much I had missed him.

After we arrived at Astrid's apartment, Christian, in an attempt to prove to me he was aware of shared responsibilities, offered to water the plants. I thanked him and asked him to fix us a cup of tea since he'd done so well the last time. Right now I needed to shower and change clothes. After that, I would repack so we could drive to Valhalla.

I went back to the bathroom where I had showered throughout my youth and enjoyed standing in the warm water. I put on my bathrobe, and walked out into the small hallway that connects the bedrooms at the back of the house and walked right into the arms of Christian.

"Anna, darling, I've missed you so," he said, as he stroked my still damp hair.

"Do you think, maybe, we could try out that little bed in your old room," he said and kissed me.

I didn't need convincing. I too had missed the physical contact we had enjoyed at Valhalla, and for a while we joined each other as only two old loves can.

We were not significantly larger than we had been when we first came together in my bedroom, but we had been decidedly more agile in our youth. So in the aftermath of love, while trying to get up from the narrow bed, we laughed as we took a look at ourselves in the low bedstead.

"I think I need a beer more than a cup of tea," Christian said and got out of the bed pulling me up into a hug. I gently pushed him away and sent him out into the kitchen to get us our refreshments; I quickly dressed in slacks, a light sweater, and my well-worn loafers.

A while later we were on the balcony, each with a Tuborg, enjoying the fine spring weather. We talked about plans for our weekend excursion to Sweden where we had visited with our families as youngsters, but never before with each other.

He sat swirling his beer, playing with the bowl of pretzels he had found in the kitchen, gave me a curious look and said, "Have you given any more thought to our conversation the day we went to our old school? I'm not talking about what you told me about your family history, but about the fact that we still love each other?"

I assured him I had thought a great deal about it, but

added that I still was not sure what we should or could do about it.

"Look, Anna, we are not kids anymore, so let's be frank," he said. "I know I have a terrible track record as far as marriage goes, but I also know that I've always loved you and want nothing more than to spend the rest of my life with you, if only you feel the same way."

I thought for a moment and then I took his hand in mine.

"Christian, we have packed an awful lot of things into a very short time. In the heat of the moment I could tell you 'yes,' and feeling as I do right now, that's what I want to do."

He started to interrupt me with an enthusiastic smile, but before he could comment, I continued.

"Please let me finish, because this is not the easiest thing to tell you. I have never been one to rush into things and right now I feel I need to go back home to North Carolina and take a look at my life. I need to figure out what is best, not only for myself, but for the two of us."

He looked disappointed, so I went on.

"The past couple of weeks with you have been wonderful, and I would like nothing more than to go on like this. But I do have a family and a life back in the States, and until I sort things out there, I would not be the companion you want and deserve."

Crestfallen, he kissed my hand and said, "Will you at least promise to think about it and not wander out of my life again?"

I assured him that no matter what I decided to do, I would, in one form or another, stay a part of his life. I suggested we put the subject on the backburner for a while and just enjoy our time together.

"Does that mean we can go back into your room again?" he joked.

I just gave him a swat with my napkin and got up to take the tray with the bottles and glasses back into the kitchen.

I cleaned up the few dishes, threw a few things into my bags; then we left for Charlottenlund.

Mrs. Larsen was off that day, so Christian exhibited his

culinary skills for our dinner and made great gourmet omelets, served with a bottle of chilled champagne. We spent the evening in front of the fireplace talking and listening to the wind as it began to slap tree branches against the French doors while the sea started to roar at the foot of the lawn.

Chapter 34

That morning, when we returned from our trip to Sweden, we discovered that Mother Nature, in charge of the Scandinavian countries, had decided to put a definite end to the pleasant spring weather in order to show us what else she could do.

From early Monday until Wednesday noon, a cold rain poured down without ceasing, making it unpleasant to do anything outside.

I rode with Christian to the University right after lunch to see his work and meet some of his colleagues. We had coffee at the university cafeteria and while Christian worked in his office, I went to the library and did some research on Prussia at the turn of the century. I wanted to learn more about my Grandmother Clara's homeland, but found little.

Tuesday morning was spent poking around Valhalla looking at old family pictures found all around the large house. I dallied for an hour or so over coffee with Mrs. Larsen as she filled me in on stories about the children and Christian.

I was also privy to some juicy gossip about Elsa, the maid, who according to Mrs. Larsen "shares an apartment with at least two other women, if you know what I mean." She also told me about her speculations regarding the comings and goings of "the stealth gardener—Hector," who kept the grounds immaculate, but was hardly ever seen. Many nods and shakings of her head had me convinced that Mrs. Larsen also attributed various strange habits to this man who I had yet to meet—if indeed I ever would.

She also found every excuse possible to quiz me about my feelings for her beloved employer. I dodged her questions for a while and was saved as Christian came home to a lunch Mrs. Larsen took great pleasure in serving us.

In the afternoon, I went to Christian's upstairs office and

checked my email and sent off several notes to friends, family, and co-workers in North Carolina.

Wednesday morning, right after Christian left, Oliver arrived with Sir as we had definitely decided to call the dog. Before he left, he handed me a leash, vitamins, food dishes, and a huge bag of organic dog food.

No sooner was Sir inside the door before he took a complete tour of the downstairs sniffing every object, finishing his explorations by plumping down on the rug in front of the fireplace in the library. Lying there he truly looked as if he was born to this manor. As I watched him, I felt a pang of guilt having left Tessa behind, but consoled myself with the fact that my dog was having a wonderful time at Reenie's place romping around with the DeNero dogs.

A few hours later the rain finally stopped and the sun began to show its face. After looking out the window, I wanted some fresh air and decided to take Sir for a walk on the beach and was headed for the ocean when Christina pulled up in her car. She waved to me and immediately saw my companion and, for both the dog and the young woman, it was love at first sight. He followed her around like she was his mother and after our walk went with her to her old room while she gathered up some painting material.

Despite Mrs. Larsen's protest, Christina suggested we go to Henry's for an early lunch, so we hopped in her little red car, headed for the place and enjoyed some of the best fish chowder that ever touched my lips.

We lingered over our meal discussing everything from dogs to art. I told her about Patrick's efforts and she shared some of her feelings and experiences about her own work. We left around one thirty and drove straight to Valhalla where she let me off in front of the house. She explained that she had a late afternoon class and with a wave, she was off for the city.

With Christina gone, Sir decided I was his new best friend, and began following *me*. He even stood on his hind legs and inspected my work when I sat down at Christian's desk with the books from the University library to continue my research on the area in Prussia where Elisabet, Augusta, Theodora, Fredericka, Von Ludwig, aka Grandmother Clara, was born. I found a little information about the area in general, a few names linked to the family, but not much that was of real interest to me.

I abandoned the research and decided to write something a little more substantial to my children. I had sent home postcards from Amager and Als, but felt I needed to provide them with some minutiae on what was happening in my native country. Only to Reenie did I write about my feelings for Christian. There would be time enough—after I got back to North Carolina—to gather my whole clan and get their reaction and input. That is, after I had a chance to come to terms with how I really felt about our relationship and future with or without Christian.

Chapter 35

Just when we thought the good weather was back, a hailstorm hit without warning shortly after breakfast Thursday morning. It arrived with a force that bent young trees to their knees, made the old established birches sigh with pain, and had Mrs. Larsen in a complete dither.

"How will Dr. R be able to come home for lunch? And how is my grand-daughter going to be able to ride her bicycle home from school in that weather?" she worried.

"Furthermore, the dog will not be able to go outside for a walk, and I cannot hang out the laundry with all this hail coming down. Oh, this is just a mess," she lamented.

I assured her, "everything will be fine."

"This gale will soon blow over—they usually do," I said, trying to sound convincing; but it was not until the storm finally broke—right before noon when the sun peeked out— that she was finally herself again.

Christian came home right after twelve and we sat down to an early meal in the kitchen. We were about to finish, when the phone rang and Christian got up to answer while Mrs. Larsen and I cleared the table.

He handed me the phone and said it was for me.

It turned out to be Vivian inviting me to go with her into Copenhagen that afternoon "to inspect a few of the stores at the center of the city." She said she could be right over and I told her I would be delighted to go.

Christian said he planned to stay a little late at the university since his work had been interrupted by a power outage caused by the morning storm. He encouraged me to "go and spend some money."

"If you see anything you like, buy it," he said and pulled out a credit card.

"Just charge it to me. I want you to enjoy yourself. You might even find something for the reunion coming up."

I gave him a quick peck on the cheek, but declined his kind offer to max out his card.

Vivian pulled up in front of Valhalla right before one o'clock in a bright red Ford Mustang from the late 1960s. She came into the kitchen dressed in a stunning light wool pants outfit—it out-priced anything I ever owned—and after greeting Mrs. Larsen, gave Christian a peck hello and took my arm.

"Let's go shopping," she said.

I went upstairs to get my handbag and, within minutes, we were on our way toward the ancient capital.

"Where in the world did you get this car?" I asked as soon as we were on the road. "You just don't see many of these around at home—let alone in Europe."

Most American cars are much too expensive for almost anyone overseas and with the price of gas, quite astronomical in Denmark; they are not cheap to drive either. But in Vivian's case it was the vintage of the vehicle and not the price of the automobile that puzzled me; she could have owned almost any expensive European car she wanted.

She negotiated a sharp turn that took us onto the highway, and explained.

"My youngest sister, Lillian, and her family live in South Hampton, Long Island. She's lived there for years and I usually visit her at least once during the winter season.

"Right after graduating from school, she went to the States to work as an au pair in the Stanford household on Long Island. She hoped to go from there to Broadway. Instead, she fell head over heels in love with Porter, her employer, and he with her. His marriage was on the brink at the time and to make a long story short, his wife and a son, from *her* former marriage, left within a year, and Porter married my gorgeous sister. She was mad about him then, and still is.

"Porter and Lillian decided to wait a few years before having children and Lillian began studying drama. Like me, she loves the theater and she actually became a stage actress appearing in several off-Broadway productions. Shortly after her marriage, I flew over during the theater season, and after that, I started to come over each year to catch her in one of her performances and take in the shows and shops in New York City.

"Lillian and Porter have two children now, but she still acts a bit, and whenever I visit, we take in a couple of Broadway shows and preview some of the new movies. We also attend lots of theater parties and simple neighborhood get-togethers, if you can call the mingling of Long Island estate owners' simple. That crowd sure knows how to party," she added.

"I really like the States, but there is nothing like good old Denmark—except for cars. I truly love big American cars and especially the older high-powered convertibles."

As if to demonstrate, she did some fancy maneuvering that took us around a fallen tree lying halfway out on the road; a casualty from the morning storm. Not only did Vivian like powerful cars, she also knew how to drive them.

"During one of my trips to New York, my famous brother-in-law, Dr. Porter Stanford, showed me the 1967 powder blue Mustang convertible he just bought. I took one look, fell in love and decided I must own one," she said.

"Porter is years older than Lillian and a dear soul. He is a renowned plastic surgeon, specializing in facial reconstruction and has improved the looks of a lot of actors we both know and love—the Stanford Nose is famous. He also does wonderful things with other parts of the face suffering from the pull of gravity," she said touching her chin while winking at me.

"Anyway, Porter helped me locate another Mustang while I worked to convince Richard that this was not just a fabulous automobile, but also an investment

"So here we are—driving my little red bomb," she laughed, patted my arm, revved up the engine, and pulled out into the passing lane.

She asked me about our weekend plans and when I told her about the school reunion she got excited.

271

"Richard was also graduated from there, so we are attending," she said and asked if I knew that the Prime Minister was giving the Keynote address at Saturday's big event.

I assured her that, in fact, Christian and I, along with others from our old group, were invited to her penthouse for a party she was throwing later Saturday night.

"I forgot you were classmates," Vivian said.

I told her Rikke had been my best friend during all the years we attended the school.

"We have corresponded for years, and when I wrote and told her I was coming to the reunion, she invited me to come to her party," I said.

"Watch out for the press and the security guys," Vivian warned. "Rikke had a threat on her life not long ago from some group objecting to her liberal views, particularly those on women's place in government. Ever since the Prime Minister of Sweden, Olof Palme, was assassinated on his way home from seeing a movie—back in the late 80s—our government takes all threats seriously; even in our peaceful little Denmark. So at the moment, the press surrounds her and security guards are all over the place."

"I assure you it is my intent to stay out of the way of both the media and the bodyguards as much possible," I said.

I was about to ask her about the threat to Rikke when Vivian commandeered the Mustang into a parking area right next to the Royal Theater across from two large department stores near a string of upscale shops.

"Richard is out of town today, so we can use his parking space," she said by way of explaining her luck in getting a prime spot in a city known for its lack of parking places.

We sat for a few minutes in the car while Vivian rummaged through her purse and finally pulled up the parking permit she needed in order not to have her car towed. As I got out of the car, Vivian asked me what I planned to wear to the big dance at the reunion, switching subjects as quickly as she switched driving lanes.

"Let's discuss your dress before we set out on our shopping trip," she suggested.

I explained that I planned to wear the dark dress I had worn to the ballet.

Vivian conceded and said, "It's a gorgeous dress and looks great on you, but since you will be in the company of the Prime minister you really ought to wear something sensational. Besides Rikke *always* wears black," she said.

"You'll want to wear something contrasting since you're apt to be pictured next to her in the papers."

I dismissed that possibility, but thought it might be fun to have a dress from Copenhagen. Vivian agreed and led me to one of the shops she favored.

We spent a lot of time laughing and getting to know each other while we tried on dresses. I could see why Christian had fallen for her years ago—Vivian was a lot of fun to be around.

After some discussion, I settled on a full-length ivory silk gown. Vivian assured me that "it makes you look like you are forty, ten pounds thinner, and ready for an audience with the queen."

I was sold and without batting an eye I handed over the small piece of plastic that makes shopping possible most anywhere.

Around four o'clock, we decided to end our shopping trip with a cup of tea at a pub located in the cellar of a quaint old building a block from the dress shop, near the canal that runs alongside the theater. Few people were there at the time, and we were quickly seated in a booth near a window.

I had just taken a sip of my tea when, out of the blue, Vivian looked me in the eyes and gave me a wicked grin.

"Sooo—how did you like the ice queen," she asked. "Christina told me you went to visit Oliver and Helena, and I just wondered how that went."

I was somewhat reluctant to tell her about my discomfort during the time I spent with Christian's oldest daughter and told her about Christian acquiring a dog. When that didn't satisfy her, I elaborated on the beautiful baby, Oliver's good looks and talent, and the farm in general.

"Not so good, eh?" she finally laughed recognizing my attempts at avoiding the issue.

"You are dodging my question, Anna," she said, "but I can imagine the visit anyway. Helena, on a good day, is as cool as ice and always has been. With you showing up on the arm of her father, looking incredibly like her mother, I imagine you got the frost treatment. Am I right?" she asked with an ounce of sympathy mixed with good humor.

"She never has liked me," Vivian said, not waiting for me to respond. "From the way she treats me on the occasions we meet, you would think I was the one who took her father away from her mother and not the other way around.

"Well," she drawled, "actually Karen didn't do that; but I prefer to think so. It sounds more dramatic."

Then without further explanation, Vivian ordered drinks, some Brie cheese, and a plate of fruit.

"I just remembered Christian told me he plans to take you out for dinner tonight, but you'll probably not eat until after eight, so I think we better have some refreshments now. Otherwise, he'll think I'm trying to starve his new love," she said with a wink.

"Honestly, you would think Christian was raised in the United States," she said and laughed. "He never misses a chance to eat out. I remember from my visits there; no one there ever cooks anymore."

Somewhat embarrassed about the reference to Christian's "new love," I jumped on the issue of cooking and eating out. I assured her that, though no Julia Childs, I *could* put decent meals together, and that the majority of people cooked a lot of their meals.

Then I dove into the grapes and nibbled on the cheese. Vivian took the hint, changed the subject and began to entertain me with tales from the theater.

An hour later we were on our way home.

By now it was long past six and as Vivian drove down the long driveway, Christian pulled up in front of the house in the Mercedes, his work at the University evidently just finished.

After helping me put away my purchases, we dressed for the evening and drove north along the cost to dinner at Kysten's Perle, one of the oldest and most luxurious restaurants on the East Coast, where we enjoyed a fine meal and a breathtaking moonscape over the ocean.

Chapter 36

It had been a wonderful vacation up to then, and the rest of my time in Denmark turned out to be just as good, but it went by much too quickly. The reunion was an absolute smash. We encountered the 'muscle men' following Rikke around for protection and made the front page of several Danish newspapers. Evidently, no world crises came in over the wire that weekend and the Prime minister hamming it up with old friends at her class reunion was the big news.

The Saturday before my trip home, I celebrated my birthday, a day early, at a party at Astrid's. It started at six with cocktails, followed by a sit-down dinner for twenty. Rikke and her husband were among the guests—with a security guard outside the main door. My cousin Freddy - of course - flirted shamelessly with Rikke all evening. Rie just humored him. At the last minute Astrid had asked Marin and Mole to come over and, despite the late invitation, Marin told me they were delighted to be part of the party.

Astrid, by now well recuperated, had gone out of her way to make this a memorable evening. The dinner was superb and was accompanied by wine that flowed freely. Everyone arrived in taxies—they knew about parties and driving.

Along with all the speeches and songs—done in Danish tradition—I received several thoughtful gifts; among them a small pastel of the Valhalla beach Christina had painted; a newly finished and autographed book from Rikke, and from Astrid I received a lovely needlepoint pillow.

We danced until 11:30. Then Astrid served "midnight food," and after that, we danced some more until I finally gave up just before two o'clock in the morning.

I thanked Astrid for my "real Danish birthday party" and after promising to stay in touch with everyone, Christian and I left.

We slept 'til nearly ten Sunday morning and I awoke to sunlight dancing on my face. I started to get up, but Christian insisted I stay in bed while he went down to the kitchen to fix us breakfast.

"Remember, it's your birthday today," he said.

A while later he brought up a tray holding breakfast for two, a lovely bouquet of pink roses, *and* a small elegantly wrapped package.

Before he handed me the package he took my hand and said, "I hope you'll enjoy this gift and keep it without feeling any kind of obligation."

Judging by the size of the gift, I had a fair idea of its content, but was still surprised, to find a stunning full-circle diamond eternity ring.

"It's not meant as an engagement ring, Anna, but I hope you'll consider it 'I wish you would come stay with me forever,' sort of ring and wear it in that spirit," he said and put it on my finger. After kissing him "thank you," we postponed breakfast and celebrated my birthday by making good old fashioned "whoopee."

The rest of the day we spent walking on the beach, playing with Sir, and finished my birthday with a late dinner at Richard and Vivian's. After coffee and dessert, Vivian gave me a small antique rosewood box inlaid with ivory.

"Keep all your pictures from this trip in it as a reminder to come back and see us all again. I suspect that'll be sooner rather than later," she teased.

Christian hoisted his glass and said, "Hear, hear."

The last days of my trip were enjoyable, but sad. Knowing I was to leave at eleven o'clock Wednesday morning, Christian took time off from the university.

Monday, we went out to Astrid's to pack and say farewell. While Christian settled himself on the balcony with the morning paper, I asked Astrid to help me pack. I wanted some time alone with her.

"Please come back soon," she said, "and remember what I told you; go slow but let your heart lead you. I believe Christian is a fine man and that the two of you could be good for each other."

I promised her I would think about it and told her to give my love to our family, "Please thank all of them for everything they did to make me feel so welcome and at home."

Chapter 37

As the plane took off from Kastrup Airport Wednesday morning I found myself, for the first time ever, not doing a white-knuckle grip on the arms of my airplane seat. I was too busy searching my pocketbook for a tissue to wipe away my tears.

I looked out the window, but could not see Christian. I knew he was standing at the end of the gateway area watching the plane take me back to the United States as it had in 1959. But it was different this time; we both knew I would see him again.

I had promised—no matter my decision—I would fly back in October and be there when Queen Margrete the Second bequeathed him Knight of the Order of Danebrog. I told him I wanted to be with him when he become my real 'Knight in Shining Armor.'

The morning of the day before I left, we had gotten up before seven to find tempting sunshine inviting us outside. Before Mrs. Larsen arrived, we took Sir down to the beach and walked for more than an hour along the water that, on this day, was as calm as a soft blanket, covering the multitude of life beneath its surface.

You could see clear to Sweden and we reminisced about the weekend we had spent there, agreeing that, "Someday we'll make the trip again." It held a promise for the future.

After breakfast Mrs. Larsen packed us a picnic and in high spirits we took off in the Austin-Healy and headed for Dyrehaven. We walked for hours and ended up by the lake sharing our meal with the swans and a couple of ducks.

At one point, one of the elegant birds swam away leaving the other looking sad. When I cast out some bread, however, the other swan quickly returned and joined its mate.

"I'll take that as an omen that you too will return to me," Christian said. I just laughed and told him that the departing swan must be male since it's well known that the way to any man's heart is through his stomach. He threw me a growling look and pulled me closer.

We stayed up late that evening talking about the past and the future. Christian did his best to persuade me to stay and I assured him that the past month had been one of my happiest in many years.

"But what would I do with myself over here?" I questioned him. "You and I have had such good times together, but you have your work, your research, and your lectures to keep yourself busy. I can't just go shopping with Vivian every day or hang around Valhalla with nothing to do. I enjoy talking to Mrs. Larsen and Christina, when she comes to the house, and I also love walking the beach with Sir, but that still leaves me with so much time to myself."

He started to object but I held up my hand.

"Christian, let me go home and think about this. I need to talk to my children, to let them know that if I do come back to you, I won't abandon my family in the States. I need to put some distance between this fairy-tale country and my world at home, but I assure you I want to keep you as part of my life forever, in one form or another."

We finally went back to Valhalla and after a quiet evening in front of the fireplace, went up to the old four-poster and made love as two who might never meet again. Then we embraced and finally fell asleep wrapped in the arms of each other.

The plane was now above the clouds and my attention turned to the small package Christian had handed me just before I left. We had been sitting in the airport bar drinking a Fernet Branca, an Italian drink that promises to keep away butterflies in your stomach.

Christian had looked searchingly at me and said, "I hope you will continue to wear the eternity ring as a reminder that I love you."

Then he pulled out the small package, gave it to me and said, "This is not a going away present, it's a 'til we meet again' token that I hope you'll enjoy. Take it out after the plane is in the air and you are comfortably seated and—I hope—thinking about me and all we shared this past month."

He walked me to the gate and handed me an upgraded ticket to first class, something he had taken care of without letting me know.

"I want you to have a comfortable flight home so you'll be encouraged to come back," he said with a melancholy smile.

We kissed for a long time, much longer than two people our age ought to in public. Neither of us cared nor, for that matter, did anyone else around us. They too were busy saying their own good-by.

The stewardess brought me a glass of white wine and peeked at me while I opened the package. It was a small Bang and Olufson tape player and a set of earphones and on the top was a card with Christians' well-known words written to me.

"My darling Anna, please come back to me. I don't want to not have you in my life," signed, "Your Knight in Shining Armor."

There was a postscript that read, "Please hit track seven and listen; it's the song I most want you to hear."

I put on earphones, pushed the on button, forwarded to track seven, and sat back to listen. Then, as a tear slowly rolled down my cheek, a smile began to form on my lips and, with my heart beating faster, I listened as Tony Williams sang to me:

"My prayer, is to linger with you,
At the end of the day, in a dream that's divine –

Heidi Thurston

My prayer, is the rapture in bloom,
With the world far away,
And your lips close to mine"

PART FOUR

Anna - The Duchess

Chapter 1

"Lord, you're hopeless Anna. No one but you would use a bread knife to cut up vegetables," Reenie said, giving me an amused look.

"I know, I know, you're just using it because I already had it out to cut bread and you don't want to dirty any more dishes than absolutely necessary," she said, and broke into peals of laughter.

Before I could defend myself she grinned, shook her head and added, "You're just hopeless in a kitchen."

I meekly responded the way I usually do when someone takes a stab at my anal-retentive habits and lack of culinary skills: "Well, I do set a pretty table and fix a nice salad if I may say so. Besides, when dinner is done the kitchen will be clean and *very* few pots and utensils will be left to wash," I added triumphantly. When you're a lousy cook you need to bring up all your other talents.

Reenie, who had heard all this before, conceded it was true, and requested that I finish my "nice" salad and go ahead and set a "pretty" table.

It was the middle of June, just before the tourist season started and Reenie and I were at Idle-a-While again for some R and R. We had arrived early that day and spent the

283

morning and part of the afternoon dealing with various workmen, as Reenie made arrangements for work to be done at the cottage.

While I was in Denmark, Reenie had finally convinced Paul to spend more time at their beach house. As a result, Idle-a-While was adding another room with adjacent bathroom for Paul to use as an office. Reenie had also decided they needed a roof over the deck at the end of the boardwalk and benches built near the edge of the dunes.

We were just now getting ready to enjoy our dinner, "Shrimp a la Reenie," and I was doing my best to help.

I went outside and collected a bouquet of the enchanting black and orange flowers that, despite all odds, grow in the sand dunes along the Carolina Coast. I have no idea what their names are and just call them "cheer-me-ups," because they look so perky and full of life in an otherwise wind-bleached terrain. I added a few stalks of broken sea oats, a couple of other interesting looking branches I found lying in the dunes, and proudly placed them in a small earthenware pitcher on the dining table. As I finished the salad, still using the bread knife, I felt I had redeemed myself.

"You've been home for more than a month and you've not stopped running since you stepped off the plane," Reenie had said a few days earlier.

"Let's take one of our mini vacations and head for the beach day after tomorrow. I'm going down anyway, to meet with carpenters and electricians and make final arrangements for the renovation of the cottage. I also want to pack away a lot of things in order to make the work easier for the workers."

I quickly agreed to tag along and help out, and packed my over-night bag with essentials.

We had decided to take along Tessa and Reenie's two retrievers and at the moment the three dogs were snoring in harmony on the deck. I admitted to myself that Reenie was right—it had been a bit hectic over the past several weeks; this would be a welcome break.

I arrived home and started work at the beginning of May and immediately got caught up in the marathon it takes to prepare for the Chamber's Arts and Craft Festival. This year, the Board of Directors had decided to extend it to a day and a half, instead of the one day affair it had been in the past, so a lot more preparation was needed.

I worked around the clock, grabbing quick lunches and dinners on the run. A couple of nights, when I managed to scrape together a few hours off, I took refuge with Becca and Forrest. They took in both Tessa and me and on occasion kept her overnight so I didn't have to rely on help from my neighbor's son, David, who had just started an after-school job.

Right now I was thoroughly enjoying myself; I was by a beach again, listening to the ocean with my best friend—my devoted dog at my side—and back in Denmark there was a man who loved and wanted me as part of his life. Now all I had to do was make up my mind about what *I* wanted to do with my future.

We finished dinner and were just getting ready to enjoy Reenie's special raspberry mocha coffee when she stood up, looked at her watch, and swore an oath worthy of a sailor.

"I forgot to pick up my prescription I called in earlier to the pharmacy up the road," she said.

"I need the pills before going to bed, so I've got to run out and get them before they close in a half hour. If not, my hormones will stomp all over me tonight.

"No need for you to come along, I'll be back as soon as I can. Just stay here and keep an eye on the dogs and have some coffee," she said.

"*And* as long as I'm out, I think I'll run up to the Piggly Wiggly at the top of the island and pick up some of that good frozen yogurt we both like and a bag of low fat cookies so we can indulge ourselves and still feel virtuous.

"I'll also check and see if the video store has a copy of 'Thelma and Louise,' or a Sean Connery movie we've not seen in at least six months," she added, grabbed her car keys and was out the door. A few minutes later I heard the sound of the new Volvo station wagon—bought while I was in Denmark—roar out of the driveway.

It was suddenly quiet as the cottage enveloped itself in the peaceful sounds of early summer beach evenings. A few gulls were squawking near a shrimp boat coming in late after a day at sea, and as always, there was the mesmerizing sound of the ocean.

Reenie would be gone for at least half an hour so I poured a cup of the newly brewed coffee, and went out to join the dogs on the deck. Despite the cool morning, the latter part of the day had turned Carolina warm and at the moment the temperature was pleasant.

I noted that the tide was going out and watched the beach grow wider with each receding wave exposing clean stretches of sand while the Sandpipers ran along picking out shells, scurrying away from each new wave rolling in.

I thought about my arrival in North Carolina after leaving Christian and our whirlwind romance behind. I was trying to put some order in my feelings and needed to bounce all my thoughts off Reenie and get her sensible and down to earth take on everything. I also felt I needed to talk over the things from my past—things that still nagged at me.

In my suitcase was the photo album Freddy gave me and I planned to show it to her and get her input.

I had said little to my children when I came back home; just acknowledged that the trip had been a great success and told them of the many places and people I had visited. I briefly mentioned having united with Christian, but had been careful not to wear the eternity ring after I got home, lest they wonder. Since none of them knew much about my early years in Denmark, or the fact that I had left Christian behind years ago, they didn't read anything significant into it. They were more impressed with my evening in the company of the Prime Minister of Denmark and the fact that I had appeared on the front page in several Danish newspapers. And, of course, they wanted to hear all about my visit with all the M & Ms.

Up to this point, Reenie and I had spent hardly any time alone, so I had yet to tell her the details of my time in Denmark. This beach trip was, in part, meant to help me sort things out and make a decision regarding my future—with or without Christian.

I reached down and patted Tessa on the head and like a faithful friend, she responded with a lick on my hand before curling up against Coal and Sukie who were both breathing softly making gentle whistling sounds.

I took another sip of coffee and thought of my arrival in Charlotte a little over a month ago.

Chapter 2

Reenie met me at Charlotte International Airport where I arrived shortly after nine in the morning, on my first day back. My connecting flight at Kennedy the evening before had been delayed due to engine trouble and I spent the night in New York City in one of the upscale, high-rise hotels, courtesy of the Scandinavian Airline System.

I had been much too tired from my trip over to appreciate the view from the thirtieth floor of the hotel located in one of the most exciting cities in the world. I had phoned Reenie and told her of the delay, and after a quick shower, called room service ordering a glass of wine and an all-green salad that I enjoyed before pouring into bed.

After a fitful night, I woke up early the next morning longing to see my family.

It had rained in New York City when I left the hotel at seven that morning and the air, for a change, had been quite cool. When we landed at Charlotte Airport, however, I was met with eighty five degrees of scorching heat; quite a change from the Big Apple, and even more so from the tepid—to outright cold—temperatures I had experienced in Denmark.

Looking cool and composed despite the draining heat, Reenie greeted me. Energetic as ever, wearing a brand new turquoise safari outfit, she quickly organized the pick up of my luggage and maneuvered us toward the exit of the airport terminal.

"Heavens, so soon you forget just how hot May can be in Charlotte," I sighed, feeling my slacks begin to stick to my legs as we walked across the street to the adjacent parking deck.

Before I could adjust to the stifling heat, we were inside the new car where Reenie hit the AC and handed me a cold bottle of water from a small cooler she always keeps in her car. In minutes we were heading north on I-85 toward home.

"As soon as we get to your house, we'll replace these bottles with tall glasses of gin and tonic," she assured me.

"I stocked your house with enough groceries to keep you going for at least two weeks including fresh milk—*and* several bottles of tonic," she grinned.

In forty-five minutes we arrived at my home and as I entered the foyer I was greeted by a crisp lemony scent wafting from the inside. I immediately recognized the fresh fragrance of furniture polish and realized Reenie must have arranged for Debra, the cleaning lady we have shared for years, to come and prepare the house for my homecoming.

"Your home has been closed up for a month and I knew you would enjoy a clean smelling house," Reenie said as she walked in right behind me.

"Debra cleaned your house, made up your bed with fresh linen, and gave the windows a good washing," she added and came over and gave me a hug.

"Welcome home, my dearest friend," she said.

Then she went over to my bar cabinet, took out gin and went out into the kitchen to fix us each a drink. As I heard the ice clink in the glasses and the fizz of the tonic, I began to relax and dropped down on the living room couch. I took off my shoes, pulled my feet up under me, and let Reenie hand me a tall clear drink topped with a fresh slice of lime.

"Despite your emails and our one short phone call, I have missed you terribly and want to hear all about your trip. But I can only stay a short while today," she said and took a small sip of her drink; I nearly inhaled mine.

"Paul's mother, our darling Sarafina, has *again* taken 'seriously ill' and we must fly up and visit mama," she said and gave me an exasperated look. The animosity between Reenie and her mother-in-law was a subject rarely discussed, but I knew that feelings on both sides were strong and unfavorable.

"I put a couple of bottles of Paul's best champagne in

the fridge yesterday, but unfortunately I don't have time to stay and enjoy the bubbles with you. After I get you settled, I'm off," she said with a sigh, and dropped down on the couch.

"I told Paul that as long we have to make the trek up north, we're going to make it a real trip. After spending the mornings on Long Island with mama, we are going to do New York City properly. I need a new summer wardrobe, and I want to take in several Broadway plays. So unfortunately I can't stay and gab with you since I must get home and pack. But when I get back from New York—and between you and me, I think the old lady just wants attention again and is calling in all her cards—the two of us will plan a girl's trip to Idle-a-While so we can talk endlessly. I want to hear all the dirty details," she laughed, "especially about your darling knight," she said giving me a mischievous look.

"We'll most likely be gone a couple of weeks, and I'm taking along my computer and will stay in touch. *But*, I want to wait and hear your story when we're face to face."

She took my hand and ran her fingers over the Eternity Ring.

"Obviously *something* really important happened or you wouldn't be flashing three-carats of diamonds on your hand. Don't tell me anything now; I want to hear everything—in great detail—and that, I'm sure, will take some time.

"I've told your kids you wouldn't be home until late this afternoon, so they won't disturb you for a while. I'll bring Tessa over tomorrow morning on our way to the airport. Take care of yourself and do go in and look in your Sanctuary before too long," she added with a devious smile, and got up to leave.

"I received a directive in the mail from someone special a couple of days ago, and fulfilled the request yesterday. I trust it'll meet with everyone's approval," she laughed.

Then she was gone and I went out to the kitchen and replaced my empty glass with a glass of orange juice before making my way back to the den.

The room greeted me with the subtle and quiet atmosphere I had missed. It felt good to be back. Something, however, had been added—the most beautiful bouquet of pink roses resting in one of my crystal vases sitting on the top of my desk.

I smiled and went over to read the card sitting in the middle of the flowers. I was fairly sure who had sent the bouquet and also what the card would read—I was not let down. Christian had written what I was beginning to consider his 'code words' and I smiled as I read the message while inhaling the sweet fragrance of the bouquet.

Then, as I was about to stick the card back in, my eyes caught a small arrow at the bottom of the card indicating that something was on the back. I quickly turned it over and read it; then I laughed out loud. Christian was pulling out all the tricks he had up his sleeve in a valiant effort to convince me to come back.

I put the card on my desk next to my computer and decided to write him a long note as soon as I was settled in. Then I put my new' Platters' tape in the tape recorder and, while the music swept the room, I unpacked and reminisced about the wonderful time I had spent with Christian. In many ways it had been like a dream and I knew that sooner, rather than later, I would have to look seriously at the relationship and its impact on my life.

After the last of the suitcases were emptied and put away, I turned on my computer, ran my fingers over the diamond band, and began writing Christian.

Chapter 3

The quiet engine of the Volvo brought me out of my reverie. I got up from the deckchair as Reenie came up the steps, and offered to help her put the few groceries away. She told me "no thanks," took a pill from the prescription she had gone to pick up, and joined me on the deck with a mug of coffee and a look of mixed pleasure.

"The video store was extremely non-accommodating. They didn't have 'Thelma and Louise' or *any* Sean Connery movie, so I decided not to pick up any videos. Instead, let's just sit here for a while and enjoy the view. Later, we'll get serious and talk and you'll fill me in on everything that took place while you were in Denmark. Then you must tell me about your future plans because I'm absolutely sure that something important happened on your trip. You look different, and lovelier, if I may add."

I smiled and reached over and squeezed her hand. It was good to be back in the company of a friend with whom I could share my innermost feelings. There was so much to share.

We sat quietly together and watched the sky turn a blush coral, as a spectacular sunset took over the evening.

After the sun had set, Reenie suggested that we go into the kitchen and exchange the coffee cups with tall glasses of fat margaritas. Then with glasses in hand we went back outside, into the velvet darkness where the only light came from the nearby lighthouse sweeping its beam across the ocean before disappearing, only to come back and remind us of its ever present guardianship.

Suddenly we heard thunder rumbling up along the coast. I sat up straight in my chair and Reenie assured me that the weatherman *had* forecast thunder and perhaps some lightning.

"But relax—it's hitting way north of Wilmington and there'll be no storms here," she added.

I fell back in the chair and turned to Reenie and asked, "Do you remember that late afternoon, right after Labor Day a few years ago, when that freaky storm approached us?"

She nodded and I recalled with a certain anxiety the onset of that late summer storm.

Robert and Paul had both been out of town on business and Reenie and I had taken time off to drive down to Idle-a-While for a few days of late summer sun. As the storm approached it put a dark haze on everything and we had a cold dinner by candlelight since a sudden lack of power darkened the cottage.

"I remember we stood inside the kitchen during the height of the storm early in the evening and watched as great waves curved around the pier and then smashed up onto the shore," I said, recalling the terror I felt.

Later on, despite my fear, and coached by the ever-daring Reenie, we had put on rain slickers and gone outside near the pier to take in the spectacle of the violent storm. Saltwater splashed our faces and drenched our clothes and then, just as quickly as it had arrived, the storm quieted down and left us with one of the most spectacular skies I've ever seen.

"Lord, I would hate to be here during one of the real hurricanes," I had confessed and Reenie assured me that so would she.

"We leave long before any serious storms hit and have our maintenance crew come and board up the place," she told me as we looked up into the star-filled night.

"It's bad enough to sit and watch the storm on television, but to be here would be truly terrifying."

As the distant thunder rolled and lightning cracked the sky, I assured Reenie that Hurricane Hugo, the strange storm that cut inland back in 1989, was more storm than I ever wanted to experience.

"Our home suffered only slight damage, but having to be without water, for nearly a week, was no picnic," I told her.

"And now you fill your bathtub at the first call for heavy rain," she laughed and reached over to pat my hand.

"You are, and always will be a worry-wart, and that's part of what makes you the person I love," she said.

It was getting cold, so we woke up the dogs and went inside, choosing not to turn on the lights. Instead, Reenie lit the gas logs and several candles. I decided Reenie was right—it was time for us to get caught up on my trip to Denmark—more specifically, my reunion with Christian.

During that evening—and long into the night—we talked as secrets were shared, and a friendship that had been tight for years, was sealed for life. By the time the early morning dawned, I felt better and will remain forever grateful to my friend for her honest opinions, and unquestionable support.

We began by going through the first pages of Grandma Clara's old picture album, the ones that showed her as a young girl at Kaiser Wilhelm's' Ball, and the one of her with the young count to whom she had been promised.

Reenie commented that Grandma Clara, sitting next to the tall and handsome uniformed man, looked so lovely with her Mona Lisa smile, with no attempt to conceal her happiness.

"You actually look a lot like her," she said.

Chapter 4

I thought back to the first time I was told of the resemblance. Then I began to tell Reenie the story of my paternal grandmother, the Duchess Elisabet Augusta Theodora Fredericka von Ludwig, known simply as Clara.

I had just turned five when my mother left my father, Alex Drener, in order to marry Nels Wiinter. I was old enough to never forget Alex, my father, or my paternal grandparents Drener, but my new father had other ideas. Nels could not father children, so he decided to make me his—and his alone. He adopted me immediately after their wedding and mother and I were both instructed to never again mention the name Drener. Going forward we were to pretend that Nels was my biological father.

As you can imagine, that put an awful burden on a five-year-old, for of course I couldn't just forget about them, and I never really got over the guilt. The fact that mentioning them was taboo made it even harder not to think about them. You know yourself that when someone tells you *not* to think about something—well that is just like a pass to keep on doing it.

I honestly tried to forget, but without success. I would find myself in a restaurant with my parents or at the home of friends just minding my own business. Then someone would serve pastry with sugar and toasted almonds and the fragrance would transport me back to a time in my grandmother's home where my mother and Alex would sit drinking coffee and eating cake at a family gathering. The guilt would set in as I realized I was being bad thinking about my first family—the one that wasn't supposed to exist.

"Why didn't your mother object?" Reenie interrupted, and quietly filled my wine glass.

"My mother never argued with Nels," I said. "She had already been through one divorce, and did not want to initiate another one, especially from a man her family looked up to and admired. Remember, this was an era when men, for the most part, ruled home and family," I answered.

Reenie nodded in agreement, and I returned to my story:

When I entered Christianhavn's Gymnasium, things took a turn for the worse. The school where I had been accepted was located at the outskirts of Copenhagen, just a block from the Drener home. Each year only sixty students were accepted into this fairly new combined high school and junior college and I had felt so honored when, due to my high grades, a letter arrived inviting me to attend; I knew it was a real coup. It was not until a late fall day, during my first year there that I realized the location of my new school might cause problems.

Our art class was on its way to paint an old mill at the moat surrounding Copenhagen when I suddenly froze in my walk. My girlfriend, Rikke, asked if I was all right and I lied and told her I had a cramp, probably caused by my "monthly visitor." I'm sure she didn't believe me. She said I looked ashen and ought to go back to school, but I told her I would be fine and continued walking.

What had caused my moment of shock was a sign across the street; a sign that in big block letters read "Amager Little Taxi Company," with the name "Drener and Sons," written underneath.

All of a sudden my first five years flooded back. I recalled a time surrounded by a large family, cigar smoke, beer and coffee being served, and myself sitting on the lap of my beloved paternal grandmother Clara. The memories had filled my head, but this feeling was immediately replaced by my infernal guilt. Like a trooper, however, I acted as if nothing had happened, reminding myself that, 'that family' did not exist anymore.

"That was a horrible thing to do to a child," Reenie said and took my hand. "You can't just make someone forget the first five years of her life."

I agreed, but told her that, over the years, I had learned to deep six my first family and kept it up until something happened—the year before I left for the states.

From time to time, the school's music department invited artists to come and entertain the faculty and student body. Toward the end of April—right before I turned seventeen—we learned that a well-known singer, Thea Ludwig, would present a program the last Friday of the month. We found this especially exciting after being told that Miss Ludwig had been born near our school. Although she mostly toured in Germany and France, and rarely made appearances in her home country, it seemed she was in town on some personal business and had agreed to sing at our school.

As it happened, my parents were going out of town for a week on a business trip leaving early that Friday morning. I had made plans to stay at Rikke's following the evening's performance and with my grandmother, Aggie, for the remainder of the week.

Somehow, with the excitement of the preparations for their trip, I never got around to mention Ms. Ludwig to my parents, so it was never discussed.

The afternoon before the performance, Christian and I, plus Rikke and her boyfriend, John, along with an assortment of other students had volunteered to help decorate the girl's gymnasium for the performance. While the boys set up chairs, the girls put up bunting and placed spring flowers on small tables along the walls and stage and by the time we left for home to get changed, the place looked very festive.

* * *

Ms. Ludwig was a hit with both students and faculty and—during the first part of her program - entertained us with well-known arias. Then after a break, she sang a couple of cabaret numbers and ended her performance with, "Love Letters," from the movie of the same name.

Being young and in love, I took the song seriously. Christian and I knew that, in little more than a year, we would be separated and that love letters would have to "keep us near while apart." During the song Christian put his arm around me, drew me close and wiped away a solitary tear that had run down my cheek. Fear of embarrassment won out over my urge to cry and I turned my attention to the performer.

Ms. Ludwig, who appeared to be in her mid-thirties, was a tall, slender woman with shoulder-length, jet-black hair, a heart-shaped mouth, velvety brown eyes and porcelain completion. She also had a voice that captured her audience.

The decorating committee was promised an introduction and brief meeting with Ms. Ludwig after the performance, so we went over to the teachers' lounge where coffee, dessert, and assorted drinks had been set up for everyone to enjoy while meeting informally with Ms. Ludwig.

I was surprised when, after a while, she came over and began asking me questions, but I was too flattered to think much about it until she quietly pulled me aside and gave me a card with the address of an apartment building not far from our school.

"Anna," she said, apparently knowing my name, "I've learned from your literature teacher, Mr. Andersen, you aspire to become a journalist. I have to leave here shortly, but am willing to give you an exclusive interview for your school newspaper. Please come and see me at my place tomorrow morning around eleven o'clock. I also have something I would like to discuss with you."

She took my hand, looked at me for an endless moment while a tiny smile curved around her lips, and asked that I not mention the invitation to anyone. Then, after saying good-bye to the headmaster, she was gone. I turned around and saw that our student group had gone back to clean up the gym and went over to help them.

I'd been too flabbergasted to ask this celebrity any questions, but was honored that she had singled me out. I did not immediately find it odd that Ms. Ludwig had asked me not to mention the private interview to anyone else. At this stage in my life, I had become an expert in keeping secrets, so I kept the knowledge of the appointment to myself, and just discussed her performance with Rikke as Christian and John walked us to her home.

Chapter 5

I took a drink from my glass, as Reenie encouraged me to continue my story, and I did.

Shortly after nine o'clock Saturday morning I finished breakfast and thanked Rikke's parents, Mr. And Mrs. Bergdorf, for letting me stay the night. My grandmother Aggie didn't expect me back from Rikke's until late that afternoon and with guilt tugging at my conscience, I told Rikke and her parents that I needed to be back in time for lunch. So, I grabbed my coat and overnight bag and quickly left before my face gave away the deceit and walked down the street to board streetcar Number 10 heading for Amager and Ms. Ludwig's apartment.

It was a morning with sunshine, a slight breeze, and the smell of spring flowers filled me with a sense of well-being. The air was clear and as I stood on the open back-end of the streetcar, I took in the many tree-lined streets with their unfolding leaves peeking out from their winter sleep. Red and white tulips filled flower boxes outside many of the older homes and the fragrance in the air was heady.

Still, my stomach was in knots. A small voice located deep in my chest kept telling me that I was stepping outside the safe wall I so carefully had created over the years—a wall that kept away outside hurt and blocked out inside pain. I chose to ignore it and decided to have a good time. There really wasn't anything wrong with interviewing a well-known singer was there? Surely, my parents could have no objections to this visit; after all, they knew of my desire to become a writer. Although they planned a career for me as a teacher of literature, they were willing to humor me during my school years. Both of them were certain I would "settle down" and marry, after I finished my education. Perhaps, they said, I could work for a while until I had children and then become a full-time mother and housewife like most other women in the 1950s. I would always have my education to fall back on "should something happen," they felt—much like other parents of that generation.

After stepping off the streetcar, I took out the card Ms. Ludwig had given me the night before. I confirmed her residence in an up-scale section of Christianshavn, near the moat and about ten minutes from my school.

I arrived at the front door of the four-story building dating back before the turn of the century, and pressed a button next to the Ludwig name. It signaled my arrival and I was immediately buzzed in.

Once inside, I stood for a moment on the tiled marble floor noting that the uneasy feeling had returned to the pit of my stomach. I glanced around and saw a caged-in elevator straight ahead. Without hesitation, I walked inside and pressed the button for the fourth floor penthouse apartment. I felt like a trapped bird inside a gilded cage, and thought briefly of pushing the "down" button as soon as the elevator reached the fourth floor. I quickly changed my mind when it stopped—a slight rattle indicating the trip was over—and saw Ms. Ludwig standing by the door leading into her home. She came over to greet me as I stepped off the elevator and one look at her radiant face made me forget all about leaving.

"Anna, how very nice to see you," she said, smiled and took my hand into her own strong and slender hands guiding me through the entrance into her apartment.

Little did I know that my world, as I knew it, was about to change.

Chapter 6

I entered a home where understated opulence ruled. Old oriental rugs covered wooden floors, a heavy silver bowl filled with roses stood on an old buffet, crystal candlesticks graced antique furniture, and walls were covered with aged tapestry and dated oil paintings. In a corner stood a grand piano, its lid closed, holding a large selection of silver picture frames.

What captured my attention, however, was a large oil painting above the gas-lit fireplace. It dominated the room and showed a young woman dressed in white lace, seated on a gold-framed chair with a blue velvet seat. Her gown was of a simple cut that flattered her slim figure; her only piece of jewelry was a single strand of pearls.

While staring at the picture I couldn't help feeling I'd seen her before. She didn't resemble Ms. Ludwig particularly and yet, she looked familiar.

Up this point Ms. Ludwig had not spoken. She just kept an eye on me, wearing the amused expression I recognized from the previous evening

"You're admiring the picture, Anna," she said, the smile lurking just behind her dark eyes, and I assured her I thought the young woman in the painting was beautiful.

"The portrait is of my mother and was painted when she was about your age. She was a lovely and fair-haired woman. None of her children look like her," she explained. "We all favor our father who had hair black as coal and eyes nearly as dark."

Then she led me to the grand piano and picked up a small silver frame and held it close for a moment.

"Anna," she began, "I have a confession to make. I brought you here under false pretenses. Oh, you can still have your interview," she said defusing my questioning look, "but there are others things about me I want to tell you;

things you'll not want to use in your story."

She moved the picture away from her body, looked at it briefly, handed it to me, and watched as I stared in disbelief at the old photo. It was a studio picture of a group of people and included an attractive older woman standing to the left. Next to her stood a young dark-haired woman, somewhere in her late teens, and by her side was a dark haired man who resembled her, but looked older. All were formally dressed and all were smiling. Seated in front of them, on a low and ornate chair, was a young blonde woman holding a baby dressed in a christening gown.

I stared at the woman with the infant, felt a chill, and moved closer to the fireplace. The photo showed the same woman and baby—in a bronze frame—sitting on a shelf on the étagère in my parents' apartment. Our picture, however, did not include the three people standing.

The woman was my mother and the baby she was holding in her arms was a little girl who that day had been christened Anna Elisabet Drener.

I was looking at a picture of myself.

Chapter 7

"You've got to be kidding," Reenie said looking at me with disbelief. I shook my head and told her I too had been struck dumb when I saw the picture.

It was just past eleven and the storm had long since passed. The stars were out, and the beach bathed in the light from a full moon. The three dogs had gotten restless during the last part of my story, and I suggested we take them for a walk.

Reenie put on a sweater and I grabbed one of her old sweatshirts lying at the end of the couch. Coal and Sukie bolted ahead and were already running in and out of the waves by the time we reached the beach. Tessa, perhaps sensing my uneasiness, remained by my side.

"Ok," Reenie said, as we walked toward the pier, "so you were the baby in the picture and the young couple must have been your mother and Alex Drener—your real father. Then who were the two other women, and why was that picture in Ms. Ludwig's home?"

I put my arm through hers and continued.

I stood in Ms. Ludwig's home that morning and felt as if I'd been struck by lightning. I was five when my mother divorced Alex Drener, and I *did* recognize the man as my father and the older women as my Grandmother Clara. In that picture she didn't look that much different from the last time I saw her, but I questioned my aunt about the young woman.

"Anna, she said, that's me in the picture; I'm your father's only sister, your aunt, and also your Godmother. My real name is Clara Theodora Drener. I use a short form of my middle name and part of my mother's maiden name for the stage." Then with a little nervous laugh she added, "Papa never did approve of my singing career and would not allow me to use the Drener name."

Suddenly—after pretending for so long that my first family didn't exist—I was face to face with the woman who had held me in her arms when I was christened in Vor Frelser's Kirke. I had a million questions to ask and no idea where to begin.

At that point Ms. Ludwig—or Aunt Clara as I now knew her—realized my confusion and led me into an adjacent room where a small table had been set up for tea. I immediately recognized the pale yellow teacups from my childhood visits to Grandmother Clara's home. They were the same cups she had used when she let me drink coffee laced with lots of milk and sugar. I looked around the room and began recognizing several things from my grandparent's home; things previously buried in my subconscious.

Aunt Clara poured tea, invited me to sit down, and offered me a sandwich. I declined. I was not hungry, just starved for information, so I kept standing.

"Anna," she began, "I cannot begin to tell you how wonderful it is to finally have you here and see your lovely face again. I have been hoping to see you, ever since Nels Wiinter adopted you and Alex gave up his visitation rights; it nearly broke your Grandmother's heart. But Alex was going through a bad time with his drinking, and was rarely sober. It took a year before he realized what he had done and then he tried to contact your family. He was told by Nels that if he ever tried to get in touch with you, he would call the police on him."

I nodded, for I knew very well that my adopted father would not have hesitated to do whatever it took to keep me away from the Drener family.

"Alex, I am sorry to say, was charming, but weak," Clara continued, "and he just gave up the fight. For several years he turned back to the bottle for solace. He sought refuge in the arms of a number of women, all of them with small children, until he finally fell in love and married Tornhill who used to work in Papa's business office. They had no children, and the fact is Alex never got over losing both you and your mother."

Then Aunt Clara showed me the other pictures on the grand piano.

"Both your uncles are older than your dad; I am the baby," she explained and pointed to a couple of group pictures.

"That is your uncle Karl with his wife and three sons at one of our company picnics," she said and pointed to a tall, slender man seated with his family beneath a large oak.

She picked up another photo, also with a father and two teenaged sons—judging by the similar looks of the three dark-haired men.

"This one was taken at the same outing and is of your uncle Axel and his two teenage sons. Axel's wife died when the boys were young and he never remarried. After his boys finished school he went to Prussia, to the home of mother's parents, who by then had made contact with their daughter and her family and were glad to have one of her sons in their midst. A few years later Karl, his wife Josephine, and their sons followed. I see them whenever I perform anywhere near there. So you see, with the exception of me, you are the only Drener girl; and of course, you are no longer a Drener," she sighed.

I looked briefly at the pictures and then asked her about my Grandmother Clara—where was she, how was she? Did she still remember me? There were oceans of things I wanted to know.

Suddenly a clock on the mantel struck twelve and I turned and walked over to look at it. My aunt asked if I remembered the clock and I told her that, indeed, I did. It had sat on the mantel in my Grandmother and Grandpapa Drener's home in Prinsesse Gade. It was a lovely clock, and as a child it had fascinated me. About the size of a shoebox, it was made of cherry wood, with ornately carved leaves and blossoms on its side and top. It chimed a short note on the half hour and a sweet tune on the hour.

"Mother asked me to give it to you, if I ever found you," she said running her fingers over the wood carvings. I would let you have it now, but I suppose you might have a hard time explaining it to your family; your mother is bound to recognize it. Maybe *some*day I'll be able to take it off my mantle and give it to you; we'll just have to wait and see."

She touched the fine wood again and, for a moment, looked sad.

"What you don't know," she continued, "since no one told you the story because you were just a little girl then, is that this clock not only is beautiful; it is also very special.

"Sometime, I will tell you all about my mother but, for now, it's enough for you to know she was born in Prussia to an aristocratic family, married Papa, her father's coachman and, with Papa, ran away to Denmark.

"She left Prussia in a rush—before daylight—with Papa hurrying her along. She packed in haste and was only able to take one trunk along. In it she had packed some of her simplest clothes knowing that all her satin and silk gowns would be of no use in her new life.

"But she could not bear to leave the clock behind. It was a birthday gift from her grandfather whose favorite she had been. So she hid it in the trunk and did not tell Papa about it until much later.

"She took all of her jewelry, but sold most of it later in order for the two of them to get started in their new country. She *did* keep the pearls—the ones she wore in the painting—along with the mantle clock and a photo album. I haven't seen the album since I was young and it may have been lost when she packed and moved in with me. In it were pictures of herself as a young girl and later pictures of our family, including some of you and your parents. She showed it to me many years ago, but as I said, I have no idea what became of it."

I turned to Reenie who was giving me another questioning look, and told her this was indeed the album back at Idle-a-While. What Aunt Clara hadn't known, was that Grandmother Clara handed it to Freddy long ago and that he, in turn, gave it to me when Christian and I visited him in April.

Reenie nodded and encouraged me to continue.

I began bombarding my newfound aunt with questions: "Was it by accident you found me? Are you married? Do you live here all the time? Where is Grandmother Clara?"

I didn't know where to stop so I finally sat down and faced the woman who—just moments ago—had turned from being a famous singer and stranger, into my aunt.

She asked when I had to leave and I told her my Grandmother Aggie expected me back around four, adding she lived only half an hour away.

"I know exactly where she lives and have known for a long time," Aunt Clara said as I sat there, more amazed each moment. This woman—who I had not seen for years—appeared to know a lot about me.

She gathered the tea things and said, "Let me put this away. You go out on the terrace while I fix us something cool to drink; I'll join you in a moment. The weather is warm enough and the view is splendid—you'll see."

Chapter 8

I walked through the French doors to the penthouse terrace and sat down and took in the view. To my far left I could see the tall spire of Vor Frelser's Kirke and, next to it, the rooftop of my old school. The old tollhouse—where everyone used to pay a fee when entering the Island of Amager—was to the right; now it served as an ice-cream booth. Christian and I had stopped there many times, on our way home from school, pooling our money to buy a cone.

Down below, flowed the tranquil waters of the moat, with a large flock of ducks, and a solitary swan currently sailing along on this peaceful morning. It was a gorgeous view from anyone's home; I was still trying to take in the fact that my aunt owned this exclusive apartment.

Aunt Clara came out, sat down, and continued to tell me about my family.

"Anna, it saddens me to tell you that your father, my brother Alex, is dead; he died several years ago from cancer of the liver. Until his death, he loved you; I want you to remember that."

I nodded. Though we never mentioned the Drener family at home, I *had* seen his brief obituary notice in the paper.

"When he died, your grandmother kept up a strong front—just as she did after leaving Prussia and her former life—but the death of your father, her favorite child, was very hard on her.

"I told you my two other brothers have gone to Prussia and are now living near the von Ludwig estate. Should you ever want to meet them, I can easily arrange it."

The thought of seeing more family was exciting, but I knew full well I would never dare make arrangements to meet them. Just being here with Aunt Clara was enough to make me shudder, thinking of my father's reaction, should he ever find out I was in contact with my first family.

"I guess that probably would not be such a good idea right now," Clara said, maybe knowing about Nels Wiinter. She changed the subject and went on to talk about my grandparents.

"Your Grandfather, Papa Drener, died in an accident some years ago and since no one was interested in continuing the business, it was sold, along with the name and the building. After that, your grandmother moved in with me and until a year ago, was an active women playing bridge, participating in club work, and cooking many of our meals. She lived here with our part-time housekeeper and did a great deal of entertaining, especially when I was on tour."

She looked sad for a moment; then told me her mother had a bad fall last December and while in the hospital, developed complications and contracted pneumonia. She died right after Christmas

My eyes began tearing; for years I had hoped—in some way or other—to meet my grandmother again, but before I could think about it any further, Aunt Clara continued.

"We talked about you frequently, Anna; more often than you can imagine. For although you were taken away from us—largely due to Alex' drinking, I'll admit—you remained in our hearts. You were such a sweet little girl who, even at an early age, often entertained us with songs and stories."

A flash of memory brought back a scene from my past and a slow smiled formed on my lips.

"You're right. I do remember sitting on Grandmother's lap at someone's birthday party singing, 'I am a Gypsy and hot is my blood,'" I said.

I looked at my aunt who must have recalled the incident. Then we both laughed and for a moment the tension faded.

"It was a popular cabaret song at the end of World War II and was part of my repertoire," she said. "You spent a lot of time with us and you would come and stand next to me and listen while I practiced my songs. We were all amused by our little blued-eyed darling singing a passionate love song."

It had been among the memories I was forced to bury when my name had changed to Wiinter. I suddenly felt terribly sad and cried out, "It wasn't fair to try and make me forget all about you."

"Anna," Clara began, seeing my pain. "Nels loves you—perhaps not always in an appropriate way—but he does love you. In many ways he must be a good man since you have turned out to be such a special young woman; try not to judge him too hard."

I listened and knew she was right. Then I realized she talked as if she knew my present life; how could she?

"We have followed your life ever since you started at Christianhavns Gymnasium," she said, apparently reading my thoughts.

"What you don't know is that your literature teacher, Mr. Andersen, was a close friend of Alex. Your mother never knew him since he taught school in Jutland during the years she and Alex were married, but the two of them were friends since grade school.

"Mr. Andersen has kept us informed and brought us class pictures so we could follow you growing up. He even told us about your confirmation, when, and in what church, it was to take place. We were, of course, not invited, but Alex and I went to the church and sat in a back pew watching you. Nels and your mother never saw us and we left before the ceremony ended. We sent flowers but did not add a card," she said with a smile.

"I do remember a beautiful bouquet of white roses arriving without any card," I said. "Mother thought it got lost or that the flowers were delivered to us by mistake. But she was too busy that day arranging for the guests coming to our house that evening after the formal dinner at d'Angleterre."

Suddenly Grandmother Clara's clock chimed and I realized I would soon have to leave. Sensing my dilemma Aunt Clara came to my rescue.

"Anna," she said rising from her chair," you've had a shock today and I think we'll end our visit now. If you leave now, you can go for a walk along the moat before you go back to Mrs. Wiinter. That will give you time to digest everything and enable you to meet her without giving anything away."

I followed her into the living room and turned—full of questions.

Before I had a chance to ask, she said, "Perhaps it was wrong of me to approach you, but after mother died I felt the need to reach you. In another year you will go away to the States—oh yes, Bent Andersen told us that too—and then I'll lose my chance to ever see you again."

I started to protest but she continued. "Anna, I desperately hope you'll come and see me again. Some personal matters will keep me here until the beginning of summer. Whenever you have a chance to come here, perhaps when your parents are out of town or away, please call or let Mr. Andersen know. Just tell him you have some free time and he'll make sure I am here to see you," she said.

"Anna, we don't have that much time left for each other. Please grant me this. I promise I'll make sure no one else knows about it and cause you trouble. I hate to ask you to lie to your parents but it was never fair of them to keep you away from us," she pleaded.

"I want to tell you about your father and your grandmother and her life at the time the painting was made. I think you will want to know," she said trying hard to stay in control.

Then she stood back and looked at me—her eyes pleading. I could not refuse and told her I would be happy to come back.

"I always knew Mr. Andersen liked me," I said. "I just had no idea why he took such an interest. I'll let him know from time to time when I can visit. It won't be often. I am no good at lying and I'm not often alone. But I promise—I'll try."

Clara wiped away a tear, gave me a slight hug, and kissed my cheek farewell. Then, just after I walked out the door, she called me back and handed me a typewritten sheet.

"This is information about myself you can use for your story since that was, after all, the reason you came to see me," she said; smiled and waved me goodbye.

Chapter 9

"If I didn't know better, I'd think you were making this up," Reenie said. She shook her head and gave me a baffled look.

We were sitting on a bench at the end of the main pier, overlooking the ocean. The dogs ran back and forth sniffing the boards where—earlier in the day—fish had been cut up and cleaned. Deciding to head for the cottage, we left behind the orchestral sound of pinball machines and other games coming from the arcade near the pier.

Once on the beach—wrapped in the embrace of a quiet breeze—we took off our sandals and, despite the cool weather, walked at the edge of the water. After a while Reenie asked me to continue my story.

"I admit that part of my life does sound like it belongs in a romance novel. Sometimes I wish it did; it was not the easiest life to live," I said and kicked a shell into the ocean only to have Tessa run out and retrieve it. It was a small conch, and I knew that Reenie was collecting them to fill bases for a couple of lamps for her oldest daughter. I picked it up again and I put it in her hand and, as our hands touched, realized we were both getting cold.

As we approached the cottage I suggested we get out of the late night chill before I continued my tale. Reenie agreed and called the dogs. They came bolting up from the ocean, shaking salt water all over us, before running up on the porch where they flopped down by the front door.

Once inside, Reenie put on a pot of tea while I took out big mugs and a bottle of rum deciding perhaps both of us needed a strong drink. Reenie re-lit the logs and with the toddies in hand, we settled down on the couch facing the fireplace.

I took a deep breath and continued my story.

I did a lot of thinking while staying with my grandmother Aggie. It was hard not to tell anyone about my discovery, but I knew this had to be kept from others. I loved Christian with all my heart, but I thought it unfair to tell him about Aunt Clara and then require him not to tell anyone. So during the next week I acted as if nothing had happened and, when my parents returned, accepted the fact that this was yet another secret I had to keep.

A week later Christian and his soccer team were scheduled for an out-of-town soccer match, leaving right after school. So, the day before, I sought out Mr. Andersen and hesitantly asked him to tell my aunt that I could visit her that afternoon. I was careful to refer to her as Ms. Ludwig and turned three shades of pink while talking. He acted matter of fact and said he would take care of it; I told my parents I would be at the library doing some research for a paper.

* * *

The morning of my visit I dressed with care, but my attire could not conceal a churning stomach. I hated deceiving my parents, but I wanted to know more about my birth father and his family, and knew of no other way to find out.

I left school, having wished Christian good luck on the upcoming match and immediately went to the public library. After checking out a couple of books I left, making sure no one saw me; then hurried down the few streets to the home of my new-found aunt.

I was very nervous when I rang the bell, but Aunt Clara's quiet presence quickly made me feel at ease. She led me to the living room and served me tea and pastries before she began to fill me in on her life and my paternal background.

"Anna, she began, "First I want to tell you about your grandmother and her family. You are, after all, still her granddaughter; no matter that your mother remarried and you were adopted. The blood that ran through your grandmother's veins also runs through yours; I think it only fair you know."

"You might have wondered about grandmother's painting above the fireplace—it's certainly not something the average young woman has made—and also how it came to hang in my home," she said and poured us each a cup of tea.

She took a sip from the porcelain cup, closed her eyes for a moment and then she told me my grandmother's story:

"Mother was born on a large estate, in the northern part of Prussia. Her parents were the Duke and Duchess Heinrich and Elisabet von Ludwig and as the youngest—and only girl—of five children, she grew up in luxury; pampered by servants, tutors, and her personal maid."

"At eighteen, toward the end of the last century, she became engaged to an officer: Count Ulrik Vanderschnell, twelve years her senior, serving in a regiment under Kaiser Wilhelm.

"The Vanderschnell and Von Ludwig families were distant relatives with bordering estates. The marriage had been arranged years ago and their engagement was announced on her birthday during a gala event attended by several hundred friends and families. Their wedding was set for the following year on the day of her nineteenth birthday.

"Then, a couple of months after the engagement, the couple had an argument. Clara had a little too much wine during a dinner dance and, unaccustomed to alcohol, got tipsy and flirted with her fiancé's younger brother. This embarrassed Vanderschnell and he lectured Clara on her responsibilities as his fiancé and future wife. He then packed her into her carriage, and told the coachman to drive her straight home.

"Mother told me she left in tears and anger and when Papa, who was her father's coachman, stopped along the way and joined her inside, she let him. He then began to comfort her, pulled out a small flask and gave her a strong drink to calm her down."

Aunt Clara stopped for a minute and looked very serious.

"Mother was an honorable woman, but she was naïve and unworldly and when Papa proceeded to seduce her, she really did not know what was happening until it was too late.

"Papa told her he was in love with her and had been for a long time even though she was stations above him. She, in turn, thought she had been punished unfairly by her fiancé and one thing led to another. As the result, mother found herself pregnant a couple of months later. She felt both unable and unwilling to tell her parents about it and instead asked Papa to take her away. He offered to marry her and she quickly agreed; anything to avoid a confrontation with her father and Ulrik.

"She later realized that her new husband had entertained hopes of her family giving her money to help them get started in a new life. Instead her father washed his hands of her. Not until he died did her mother send word to Denmark asking her daughter to come home, but by then, Papa wanted nothing to do with mother's family.

"When mother and Papa left Prussia, her family was never to be mentioned. Papa would not let her talk about her background and pretended to everyone that she had been a poor farm-girl he had rescued. Her pearls and the mantle clock are the only things Papa let her keep; he never knew about the photo album. Mother never talked to the boys about her family but, after I grew up, she took me aside several times and told me her story, showing me pictures of herself as a young person.

"After Papa died, mother finally got in touch with her family who gave her the painting that she, in turn, gave to me," Aunt Clara said.

I sat in the quiet surroundings of the elegant apartment and listened in amazement to my aunt tell me about my grandmother. For years she had dwelled in my mind as a warm woman who had loved me, cared for me, and sung to me; but she in no way resembled an aristocrat. It was like a fairy tale, only it was a real life story—and it was a part of *my* life."

I stopped my story and looked at Reenie who, with a twinkle in her eye, said, "Thelma, I knew from the moment I met you, I was dealing with royalty."

Then we both laughed.

Just then clock struck midnight, "the witching hour," Reenie called it, even though we both knew the clock ran several minutes fast.

"I'm hungry," she claimed. "Let's make ourselves peanut butter sandwiches and have a glass of milk before you continue this fascinating tale of yours;" so we went to the kitchen to fix our snack.

The three dogs woke up and, after stretching and scratching, joined us in the kitchen where Reenie dug out some dog goodies from under the sink. Then we all went back into the living room.

"I can tell you one thing that came out of all this, Reenie—I made a vow to myself after I got married to never, ever, ask any child of mine to tell lies or force them to keep secrets," I said to Reenie. "I knew how hurtful it was and it was not anything I ever wanted to pass on."

I felt tired before our snack, but after my last swallow of milk I was awake again and ready to continue. I picked up our plates and glasses, took them out and put them in the dishwasher, then came back and dropped down in a corner of the couch, opposite Reenie and continued.

Chapter 10

By the time Aunt Clara finished telling me about my grandmother's background, I realized it was time to head home before my parents began worrying about me. I promised my aunt I would try to come back soon and left in a hurry after giving her a hug and a kiss.

I was trained to live with deceit, so hiding my newly encountered aunt from my family was not difficult. I had long ago learned to dodge questions and avoid conversation that might give me away. That, however, did not keep my guilt from constantly nagging at me, sometimes making me feel like a trapped animal. I had not sought out my old family, but neither had I ever forgotten them. Now I was living in both worlds and it was not always easy.

Nearly a month passed before I was able to go back to my aunt. Our school vacation began at the end of June and I knew I would have no chance of seeing her during the summer. As always, I was going to spend several weeks of vacation with my Aunt Lidda and Uncle Gustaf, and Aunt Clara had told me she was going to Prussia to spend her summer with her brothers and would not be back in Copenhagen until late August.

Then, right before school ended, I asked Mr. Andersen to call Ms. Ludwig to let her know I would be able to visit her the evening before school ended. My parents were leaving that morning on another business trip and would be gone for several weeks. They knew school was over in another day and that I would stay with grandmother Aggie before leaving for my vacation. I had, however, spoken with my grandmother earlier, and she told me she was going out for an early dinner and on to the theater with a friend that evening. She did not anticipate being home until around midnight, but figured I would be with Christian so thought nothing of leaving me; I was, after all, quite grown up, she said.

318

I did not dispute her, nor did I tell her that Christian was headed for a soccer training camp the same day. As far as everyone was concerned, I was going to be with someone, somewhere, and that is how I found myself with a free evening.

Mr. Andersen approached me later that day and quietly told me that Ms. Ludwig had asked me to come for dinner at seven o'clock and I told him to please let her know I would be there.

Christian came by my grandmother's home in the afternoon on his way to camp, and as he kissed me goodbye, he promised to come visit me at my uncle and aunts' home. Then he was off and, with an anxious heart, I dressed for the evening and left my grandmother's around six thirty."

* * *

I had a wonderful time that night. We dined on the terrace enjoying one of the long Danish summer evenings when it stays light until nearly ten o'clock and never really gets dark. I don't remember the meal only that it was enjoyable, but it could have been burned hamburgers and I would still think of that evening as special.

After dinner, Aunt Clara brought out pictures of my parents from before I was born. They included several from their wedding with my mother looking radiant standing between Alex, my tall and handsome father, and her sister Ida, who had served as her only attendant. There were others from family events I never attended, several from my christening, and some from my early birthday parties. The pictures brought back memories from the happy times in my early years.

After looking at the photos, Aunt Clara took my hand and said, "Anna, your parents were very happy when they were first married. Alex gave up drinking until a couple of years after you were born and they were model parents doting on their little girl.

"Then your father took up with his card-playing friends again and the drinking habit followed. They fought—he made promises he didn't keep—and one day your mother had had enough; she was tired of Alex never being home. To complicate things, she had met Nels at a party and had fallen for him. He was tall and good-looking, came from a cultured and educated family, and offered her the stability she felt she needed. So she divorced Alex and started a new life with Nels. We all understood, but were heartbroken when Alex so easily gave you up for the adoption. As I told you before, you were the only girl in our family and we all loved you."

* * *

Aunt Clara and I said goodbye shortly before eleven that evening with promises of meeting again after school started. I spent the summer, first with my aunt and uncle, and the last part of my vacation with Christian, making plans for our future and enjoying my life. I put Aunt Clara at the back of my mind and for a while the whole episode seemed more like a dream.

We returned to school in mid-August and as soon as I saw Mr. Andersen, it all came flooding back and I began looking for a chance to meet Aunt Clara again. In the beginning of September, he privately asked me to stay after class telling me he had a message from Ms. Ludwig—he never called her by her given name. Alone in the classroom, he told me Aunt Clara was ill and had gone to Prussia for treatment—staying with her family. She would not be back until later that year.

In a way, it was a relief. It freed me from going behind my parents' backs, but at the same time I missed the link to my early years. Then on a Friday, late in November, Mr. Andersen pulled me aside after class again and told me my aunt was back and that she very much wanted to see me. She had told him she had something she wanted to give me and could I come to see her the coming Monday after school?

Without batting an eye I told him yes and immediately began wondering how I could arrange a visit. It would be December when I saw her and knowing she had something for me, I thought it would be nice to bring her something too. She had given me so much and I decided I wanted to bring her a special Christmas present.

Fate was on my side.

Christian came to me a couple of hours before school was over and told me he was not feeling well. He said he was sorry because we had planned to do some shopping together after school that afternoon, but I told him to take care of himself and go home to bed. Wheels were spinning and after trying out different schemes in my head, I decided to go shopping by myself at the large bookstore just a block from our school.

I found the store all decked out for the holidays. It was decorated with Christmas elves, wreaths of straw and lots of greenery, and the scent of pine permeating the store created a festive atmosphere. I had shopped there alone and with Christian many times before; it was one of my special places to visit.

As I browsed through the store, the owner came over to help me and we quickly located at a copy of James Jones's book, 'From Here to Eternity,' I planned to give Christian for Christmas. We had seen the movie together and liked it, and since he was an avid reader, I knew he would enjoy it.

I also found a small leather-bound book by Emil Aarestrup, a poet I especially liked, and decided to give this to Aunt Clara. Then I picked up some elegant stationary for both my grandmothers and a new fountain pen for my father.

After I paid for my purchases, I asked the owner if I could wait and pick up the gifts on Monday. He agreed and said he would have them wrapped and ready and even waited to put away my order until I wrote an inscription in the book for Aunt Clara.

* * *

That evening, I checked with Christian who, it turned out, had the flu and was told by his doctor to stay in bed for several days and keep away from other people

I attended a holiday event at the Embassy with my parents Saturday evening and went for a long walk with my mother Sunday morning. When I came back from my outing, I called Christian to see how he was doing and he told me it would be Tuesday before he was allowed to return to school. I was sad that he was sick and missed being with him, but this did make it easier for me to visit Aunt Clara.

I got ready for school Monday morning and told my mother that since Christian would not be in school that day, I would do a little Christmas shopping after school. Knowing my penchant for early shopping, she just smiled and told me to go ahead. My guilt surfaced, but was quickly put to rest. I felt I was not doing anything wrong.

My classes went by in a hurry with me somewhat distracted. My classmates, who were used to always seeing me and Christian together, kidded me and said they figured it was the absence of him that caused me to be so absent minded. I went along with them; it was an easy way out and I did, of course, miss him. Only Mr. Andersen knew the truth, but never gave me away. As a matter of fact, his class was our last for the day and he let us out early because, he explained, he had a lecture to attend somewhere. I wondered.

I left school in a hurry and at two o'clock entered the bookstore, paid my bill, and put all my packages in a small shopping net. Then I walked quickly to Aunt Clara's taking care not to be seen.

Chapter 11

When I got off at the penthouse floor, I saw her front door had been left ajar and heard Aunt Clara calling me into her living room where I found her sitting by the fireplace with an afghan covering her legs.

In Denmark it gets dark early in December and by now the apartment was in semi-darkness—save for the light from the fireplace and a small lamp on a side table. She rose slowly from the chair and held out her arms, and when I embraced her I was shocked to feel how thin she had gotten. I stepped back and looked at her and saw the gaunt look on her face, the thinning hair, and the protruding cheekbones. All that remained of her old looks were the wonderful dark eyes and her sweet voice.

She let go of me and motioned for me to sit in a small chair across from her. Then she spoke.

"Anna, my dearest, as you may realize, I am not well. I have, in fact been sick for some time. When we met at your school last spring, I was here in order to undergo tests having previously been diagnosed with a form of leukemia and given less than a year to live. That is one of the reasons I finally mustered up the courage to contact you."

She reached over and wiped away tears that had been begun to roll down my cheeks. I was speechless. This couldn't be. I had just found Aunt Clara and now I was going to lose her?

"My dear little niece, don't cry. You'll be going away to another country soon and it might be years before you come back. I have had many wonderful months getting to know you and I can die in peace now. I promised mother that someday I would make contact with you; and now I have; you have brought more joy into my life than you can imagine."

"This is not fair," I said—a selfish youth. I was losing an aunt; Aunt Clara was losing her life.

She smiled her Mona Lisa smile and said, "Anna, I have no one else close to me anymore. I have neither a husband nor any children; my mother is gone, and my career is not fulfilling any more. I have had a good and exciting life and been privileged to have shared part of my life with a couple of men who truly loved me. One was too young to marry at the time we met, and the other was in a marriage that could not be broken."

She reached out and took my hand in hers.

"As a bonus, I have been fortunate to have you near me for a while. I can't complain and am ready to meet my maker when the time comes."

I was speechless.

"Let's have some hot chocolate with scones, and then I have something for you," she said.

She asked me to roll over the tea table when, without any sound, an older woman appeared with a tray set with a silver pitcher, cups, and a laced plate holding baked goods.

"This is Simone," Aunt Clara said, "my housekeeper and my friend who graciously takes care of me; especially now that I'm unable to do much."

"The two of us go back a long time my dear," the housekeeper said as she looked at me. 'I've taking care of Miss Clara since she began her singing career and traveled with her all over Europe. Someone had to look after this darling woman," she added and stroked Aunt Clara's cheek.

Then she sat down the tray and vanished as quickly as she had appeared.

We sipped our hot drinks, and for a while just enjoyed the company of each other and the warmth of the fire. Then Aunt Clara put down her cup and pulled out something from behind her chair.

"You may consider this an early Christmas present, but it's really an inheritance," she said handing me a slim package wrapped in gold paper, tied with a green silk ribbon.

I took the package and put it my lap. Then from my shopping net I pulled out my gift for her—the little book that the bookstore owner had wrapped so carefully in paper covered with hearts.

"Please open yours first," I said, feeling afraid to receive a gift from her; it seemed too intimate. I also realized I had no idea how I was going to explain this gift to my parents.

Clara quickly un-wrapped the poetry book I had bought her and opened it to the front page.

"Oh, I just love this, Anna. Emil Aarestrup is among my favorite poets. I particularly treasure his poem, 'To a woman I love.' It reminds me so much of the first young man I truly loved."

I was pleased with her reaction and began fingering my own package.

"Hurry up and open it," she encouraged and in one quick motion I untied the ribbon and tore open the paper. It revealed a black velvet box and when I opened the lid I let out a gasp. Inside was a single strand of pearls. I looked from the pearls and up at Grandmother's picture.

"Yes, those are the pearls your grandmother wore in the picture; I know she would want you to have them."

I stood up, holding the necklace tight in my hand and went over to embrace her. I whispered 'thank you' with gratitude for both the gift and for giving me back my early years.

Clara suddenly broke into her wonderful deep laughter and said, "I would love to give you your grandmother's picture but I think that might cause uproar in your home. I'm having it sent back to Prussia to the family estate. My oldest cousin, Edwin, lives there now and is in the midst of restoring the place. I know he'll appreciate the portrait.

"The pearls, I believe, you can keep and save in a safe place. Someday soon you will have your own life and your own place and you can wear them then. You can even tell your mother that your boyfriend gave them to you, although she might realize they are antique and much too expensive a gift for a young man to give someone. I don't know what to tell you, but you are a resourceful young woman and I'm sure you'll think of something," she said.

After our exchange of gifts, we visited for a while. At times, we were just silent—listening to the sound of the crackling fire. A little later, Simone came back in and took away the tray and I realized it was time for me to go. I hated to leave my aunt, but felt I had no choice.

As always, Aunt Clara sensed my uneasiness and with some difficulty stood up and walked over and put her arms around me.

"Anna, I know this is hard for you. I am so sorry I gave you troubled news. You must leave now; I *will* be all right. Simone is a former nurse and helps administer my medication. In a few days the two of us will take the train to Prussia where I will spend the holidays with my family. They will all be delighted to hear news about you—I'm sure it will be an exciting time," she said in a voice I now recognize as one trying to convince someone else that everything is just fine when indeed it is not.

"I have just begun treatment with some brand new medicine and I feel sure that I'll soon improve. I plan to be back in February and then we'll visit and talk and have a splendid time," she said and sat down by the fire with an exhausted look on her face.

I chose to believe her. I was young and it was easier to think we would meet again, and that she was on her way to getting well. I bent down and kissed her goodbye and she held me tight for a long time before she finally let go.

With a last look, I waved to her, picked up the box with my pearls, and carefully placed it in my net with the gifts I had purchased earlier. Simone, who had come back in, walked me to the door.

"I promise you Anna, I'll take good care of her," she said and patted my arm. I knew she would, and I tried hard to believe I would see both her and my aunt again after the holidays.

Chapter 12

It had started to snow while I was at Aunt Clara's Penthouse, but since the curtains had been drawn, I hadn't noticed. Flakes fell softly and already an inch of "packing snow," had accumulated. The younger children, and some of the bigger kids, would have fun the next day. I remembered being in the first grade and, seated on my satchel, sliding down the nearby bunkers—left from the Second World War—on my way home through the park near my home. With my friends, I too had enjoyed the snow.

My mind returned to my aunt and my long-ago family and I nearly walked into a car as I stepped off the sidewalk to get to the isle in the middle of the street where the streetcar picked up passengers.

I was a little dazed. There was so much to take in. First the news that my aunt might be dying, realizing that there was nothing I could do to help her—not even stay in touch with her. Second, there were the pearls, safe inside their box in my shopping net that I clutched close to me. How was I to explain them? Where could I hide them?

I turned my attention to the snow gently falling, transforming darkened street scenes into fairytale pictures. Maybe we would have a white Christmas? It didn't happen often. We seemed to have mostly rainy and cold holidays, but I would be spending the days with Christian and my family and I looked forward to sharing the lights, the warmth, and the joy of the season with those I loved. I would put the pearls in the bottom of my bureau and thoughts of Aunt Clara would have to put on hold for a while.

A few weeks later I got into the big argument with Christian, the one that separated us for days and nearly ruined my holiday. Our make-up right before New Year's felt euphoric and in the midst of this, I'm ashamed to say, I forgot about Aunt Clara. The endless packing of my parents' things to be shipped ahead to New York followed this festive period.

No sooner was the apartment empty, save for the bed and dresser in my room, before Astrid and Svend moved in and I spent as much time helping them settle into my old home as I had helping my parents prepare to leave.

* * *

After New Year's Eve, came the realization that I would be leaving in a few months and I didn't really think about the Drener family. As a result—a month after my parents left—it came as a surprise when Mr. Andersen asked me to stay after school one afternoon. Christian had left school, for a dental appointment earlier that day, so I did not plan to walk home with him.

My long-time teacher looked serious and I immediately knew something was wrong.

"Anna, I have something sad to tell you," he said. Then he asked me to sit down at my desk—I told him I preferred to stand.

"Your Aunt Clara died just a week ago," he said, using her given name for the first time. "She was at the family home in Prussia with her oldest brother at the time. He is the one who called me. I am so sorry to have to tell you this. I know both of you had hoped the new medication would help her but, in fact, it did nothing to improve her condition."

Feeling sad and guilty for not having thought more about her during the last month, I started to cry. Mr. Anderson put his arm around my shoulder and gave me his handkerchief. Then he led me to a chair next to his and began talking to me.

"I knew Alex, your father, for many years, Anna. He had a lot of weaknesses, but he did love you and your mother very much—so did your Aunt Clara. Having you in her life, during her last months, meant more to her than you can imagine. She died in peace, surrounded by family.

"Right before she left for Prussia, she gave me something to give to you as she feared she would not see you

328

again. I have kept it until now—wanting you to be alone and
without your parents around—in order for you not to have to
worry about it. By now I am sure you have settled in with
your relatives and have a place to keep this gift until you
decide what to do with it."

With that he brought out a large shoebox and handed it
to me. It was a plain box that at one time had held hiking
boots and I wondered briefly whom Aunt Clara had known
that wore boots that large. I would never know. I opened the
box and found grandmother's clock—the one from her
childhood home in Prussia.

"It was very important to your aunt that this be passed on
to you, the only girl in the family; I hope, someday, you'll
find a place for it in a home of own your."

Starring at the clock, I worried about what to do with it
when it came time to join my parents, but decided to push
that thought aside for now. Astrid never looked through my
things and it would be safe as long as I stayed with them.
Later, I would think of something. One thing was certain,
though—I could *not* take it with me to the States.

I thanked Mr. Anderson, not only for bringing me the
clock, but also for all his help in bringing me in touch with
Aunt Clara. He just smiled.

"Your father was my best friend. He and I go back a
long way and over the years, he did plenty of favors for me.
I'm glad to have done something that would have pleased
both him and his mother."

Just then the janitor came into the room and Mr.
Anderson quickly resumed his role as my teacher and picked
up a couple of books from his desk.

"Now Anna," he said, "these are the books I
recommended as research for your report. You can find
copies in the school library tomorrow." Then he winked at
me and sent me on my way.

I decided to walk home, pulling my bicycle in order to
prolong the time before I arrived home. I told myself that
from now on, my life would be less complicated—a naïve,
but youthful thought. I decided to be happy. Aunt Clara had
been at peace and she had cared enough to give me her most

precious heirlooms. I had Christian who loved me, and parents that cared for me. Surely, I would find a way to make it all work and be with Christian forever and at the same time please my parents. It *had* to all work out."

I stopped talking, went over and sat down next to Reenie and took her hand in mine.

"Reenie, thanks for listening. I feel like I've cleansed my soul and ridden myself of a lot of baggage weighing me down for years. You now know Robert's story; you know about Christian; and now you know all there is to know about me. You also know about my father's and my relationship. Being able to share all this has lightened the burden," I said.

"All I need from you now is advice on what to do next. I loved Robert and I love Christian, but going back to marry and live with him is a big step and a decision I have struggled with for a while. So will you please tell me what to do?"

Reenie looked up as the grandfather clock began to strike—announcing the early hour.

"My dearest friend," she said, "I think it's time for this Thelma and Louise to go to bed. You've given me a lot to think about and ultimately you *know* you have to make the decision yourself. I'm sure you will make the right one. We both need to sleep on this, so let's hit the sack and get up early and invade the Mourning Dive and catch some of Leo's great coffee and his latest raunchy joke."

Chapter 13

At seven the next morning, I awoke to the noise of a crew of construction workers starting their work on the restoration of a place just down the road from Idle-a-While. Metal ladders clanked against the side of the cottage, radios blared out country music with a couple of the men singing along making it utterly impossible for anyone to sleep. Even the early morning birds seem to have taken refuge further down the beach.

I got up and called over to Reenie, moving about in her bedroom across the hall, and suggested we skip showers and head down to Leo's place.

Reenie agreed, "We can dive into the ocean when we come back if we feel we need to be watered."

Minutes later we stepped out from our rooms, took one look at each other, and burst out laughing. Without intending too, we had dressed alike in white slacks, white sandals and green t-shirts Reenie had brought back from her recent trip—displaying the words: "I Love New York." We decided not to change, agreeing Leo would love it.

In ten minutes we were at The Mourning Dive where our friend sat at the counter reading the local paper, sipping a cup of coffee from his old chipped mug, while young Leonard worked the grill.

The minute the owner saw us, he jumped off his stool and came over to give Reenie a hug while throwing me a grin.

"Leo, you salty old dog, how've you been?" Reenie asked, gently undoing his bear hug.

"Well, if it isn't Dolce and her Danish pastry friend dressed like the Bobbsey Twins. What a double treat for an old man," he said and shook my hand and patted me on the back.

"Well, I'm better now that my true love is here," he said

331

and in a melodramatic voice added, "Oh, Dolce come and live with me. I promise to make you a happy woman for the rest of your life."

Reenie laughed, "Okay Leo, but before we make plans to cast our lots together, you can have that gorgeous nephew of yours make me a batch of your famous French toast with a side order of Canadian bacon before I starve to death."

The charming nephew—with the distracting butt— smiled and began dipping bread in an egg mixture before slapping the pieces onto the grill. Leo faked a pout and returned to his coffee, mumbling something about being replaced by a young "whipper snapper." Then his pout turned to a grin and he came over to our booth, poured us both mugs of coffee, made kissing noises to Reenie, and finally went back to reading his paper.

During our breakfast Reenie and I talked about her trip to New York and her impossible mother-in-law, Sarafina DeNero.

"She keeps telling us she is dying and I know damn well she'll outlive all of us. She is plain too mean to ever leave her children—especially her precious Paul. Besides, she loves the drama and having all of her children rush up to her Long Island place, whenever she has the least little ache," she added with a look of disgust.

"I love Paul more than life and I know he loves me, but I honestly think—if he had to choose, between me and his mother—I'd come in second."

As if to spite Paul, she popped a huge piece of bacon into her mouth, knowing that had he been with her he would make a reference to her cholesterol count, telling her to watch her fat intake and weight.

"Ok, ok," she said with her old Reenie smile, "I know he means well, and I was only kidding about choosing between the old lady and myself, but he does dote on her and—oh my Lord—in her eyes, he can do no wrong."

By now it was after nine thirty and Leo was cleaning tables and setting up for the next morning when he would greet early fishermen with a truly good cup of coffee.

We paid our bill and Reenie gave Leo a hug goodbye while I stole a look at Leonard's tight bottom. To my embarrassment, he caught me looking and threw me a grin.

It had started to rain and we hurried back to Idle-a-While since we had left the dogs outside in the fenced-in yard. We were greeted with welcoming barks from Tessa, Suki and Coal who, after being let inside and fed, settled down near the fireplace and within minutes were asleep.

Reenie began emptying the dishwasher while I put things away. Then she turned to me with one of her determined looks.

"Ok, it's time to finish your story and come to a decision. Before we leave tomorrow, you need to make up your mind about whether to stay here with your family and miss Christian, or fly to Denmark and be with him and learn to live with missing the kids. It's not an easy decision, but one I think you need to make—and soon. Indecision is worse and I believe whatever choice you make, will be the right one for you."

Chapter 14

The noise from down the road was absent as the rain had forced the construction crew to take refuge inside their vans and trucks. The only sound was the constant roar of the tide coming in and the rain beating steadily on the roof; in the corner of the living room, the grandfather clock kept ticking almost to the rhythmic breathing of the three sleeping dogs.

Reenie settled down in the couch and looked at me with a determined look.

"Ok Anna, so you were on the way home with the clock in the box. What came next; what became of the clock; and what finally happened between you and Christian?"

I sat down in a chair near the window, tucked my feet under and looked out at the waves that grew in size only to smash against the shore and dissolve. I love the ocean and always have. It has soothed me for years and provided me with strength ever since I was a child. It was ironic, I thought, how this same ocean had separated me from the one man I loved only to bring me across its waves to another man I would come to love. Right now it seemed to urge me to make up my mind on which side I wanted to spend the rest of my life.

I turned my eyes away from the sea and back to the room, faced Reenie, and resumed my story.

I arrived late that winter day at Astrid and Svend's home carrying the box with grandmother's clock. I called out to Astrid who was in the kitchen preparing dinner. She came out of the kitchen, handed me a cup of coffee, and told me Svend was in court and was not coming home until later. She inquired about the shoebox and I told her it was some papers from school I was bringing home. If she doubted me, she never let on, and I went into my room and put the box in the back of one of my dresser drawers.

Christian called shortly after I arrived home. He said the Novocain he had in the dentist's office, was finally wearing off, and could he come over and see me. Astrid told me to invite him for dinner since there were just going to be the two of us, and twenty minutes later he arrived—the effect of the Novocain gone—hungry as a bear.

By the time I went to bed, I had made up my mind not to think about the clock for a while. Right now there were other things more important requiring my attention: Easter was right around the corner and Christian and I, along with Rikke and John, were going on a camping trip during our break. We planned to bike thirty miles to a campground by the beach outside Copenhagen. Then, there was my birthday—a little later—with a big 'to do' planned by Astrid, and of course the end-of-the year school dance. Studies for final examines would also take up a lot of time and ever present loomed my departure date for America scheduled for the end of June. I tried hard not to think about that.

Christian and I went about our lives together trying not to mention the eminent separation until a week before I had to leave. It was St. Hans Aften, (St. John's Eve) a night when everyone who lives near water—and that included most Danes—comes down to the beaches where big bon fires have been prepared for a couple of days.

Every June 23rd—for hundreds of years—Danes have gathered stacks of wood, piling everything, from fallen branches to worn out furniture, in heaps along the beaches. Then, without formal invitation, people from all over gather around at dusk and watch as the fires are lighted. By ten o'clock it is nearly dark and you can look up and down the beach for miles and see the long line of flames. Then Danes, of all ages, form circles around the fires and sing 'Vi Elsker Vort Land,' or translated—'We Love Our Country,' the song they have sung for centuries. It glorifies St. John and expresses their thanks for the warmth the fire brings to them. It is quite a moving event.

On this special evening, Christian and I found ourselves holding hands and singing along with our friends when I suddenly realized we might not celebrate this event together for a long time. We moved away from the group and sat down in a sand dune, away from our friends. I began to cry, clinging to Christian as if he was the only thing that could save me. He tried to calm me, but was just as upset.

When I finally quieted down, we made a vow to stay true to each other. I told him I would come back in a year; I would *make* my parents realize I needed to be with him. By that time the fires had died down, a full moon casting its spell; so we lay down on the cool sand and, clinging to each other, made love.

The last few days flew by and then on a windy morning we stood—looking desolate—with our arms around each other in Kastrup Airport, surrounded by Astrid and a handful of friends.

When we finally kissed goodbye, most of our friends were teary eyed and Astrid cried openly. Then I ran to the end of the ramp unable to turn around; I could not bear to look at Christian, not knowing when I would see him again.

We were hours into the flight before I stopped crying, and had finally fallen asleep from exhaustion.

"Reenie, I can't begin to tell you how wretched I felt. At the time, I knew I should be looking forward to seeing my parents again, but all I could think about was that I had left Christian, and honestly didn't know when, or if, I would ever see him again. Had it been up to me, I would have told the pilot to turn the plane around and bring me back to Denmark. I knew my father and his strong will; it would not be easy to convince him to let me go back, at least not until I was twenty-one and of legal age.

"Someday, I'll show you the picture taken of us right before my plane took off. You can sense our pain and almost feel the quiver of my lips, and if you look real close you can see tears running down my face. You never saw two such miserable looking young people."

Chapter 15

The rain stopped and I saw the sun reflecting in the small pools of rainwater in the birdbath outside Idle-a-While. Down the road, the sound of sawing and hammering had resumed and country and western songs drifted our way from the worksite. Our dogs, that until now had been sleeping, woke up stretching and yawning in that all-relaxed way dogs do.

I wanted to be outside and enjoy the rain-freshened air and suggested we go sit under the awning where the deck chairs were dry. Reenie agreed and brought out the cushions.

"Grab a couple of Frescas from the fridge on your way out. It's too late for coffee and too early for gin and tonic," she said and settled amongst the cushions.

I brought out the drinks leaving them in the cans; we both like the extra fizz you get when soda is left inside aluminum cans. I kicked off my sandals and sat down across the chair from Reenie.

"There's not really a whole lot more to tell you, except one important fact I learned when talking with Christian this past April. It concerns a couple of letters. Oh, yes, also what I did with the clock." Reenie gave me a questioning look and I assured her I would get to that part shortly. Then I picked up on my story again.

Back in 1959 I landed in New York City, and was swept off in a limousine to my parents' apartment—a beautiful flat with a view of Central Park from several rooms. The Embassy had leased the place for my parents and even my mother, who had not been all that keen on the move, seemed to have settled in. I was shown my own room where several pieces of my old furniture were already in place and my father told me we would shop, for whatever else I needed, the following week. What I needed, of course, was Christian, but I didn't tell him that; like a good daughter, I just smiled, but my heart was crying.

Mother told me that my father had recommended I take the summer off to get to know my new city. "Then you can start at one of the universities in the fall, if you like, or your father can help you get a job at the embassy. It's up to you dear," she said a few days after I arrived. My father suggested I just help my mother around the house and take my time deciding what to do. "There's no need for you to rush into things," he stressed.

I lived for mail from Christian who, at first, wrote two or three letters each week. Dad brought home the mail in the evening, having picked it up at his post office box near the embassy. I would grab my letter and retire to my room where I would sit by a window reading it over and over, kissing his signature.

I spent my days investigating the city, visiting the New York City Library, the Museum of Natural Science, the Frick Museum, and any other museum I could find. Often, I walked over to Central Park bringing along my writing materials, and when I was not writing letters or re-reading Christian's, I wrote short essays on my observations of New York, the people in the park, and small love poems I tucked into my letters to Christian.

Then one day in early September, I received a letter from my friend, Elsa, who wrote to tell me she was engaged and planning her wedding for the following summer. She hoped I could attend. She chatted on about her plans and then at the end she wrote, 'Oh, by the way, I saw Christian at a party dancing with Ursula—remember she was a grade behind us. Is there anything to that? Have the two of you broken up?'

I felt my stomach turn and my throat tighten. Then I told myself Elsa was a busybody and to ignore her remark. A letter from Christian arrived the next day and, although he didn't sound quite as lonesome as before, he wrote that he loved and missed me. So, I decided to ignore Elsa's letter.

However, on an unusually hot and humid evening at the end of September, I received—what I later would refer to—

my 'dear Jane' letter. Christian wrote that he thought we should date others and not just sit at home until we could be together again. He hinted that he was having some doubts that I was ever coming back."

I got up from my chair and went over to sit on the porch railing. Reenie looked at me, her eyes flaring with indignation.

"I thought Christian was supposed to be such a nice guy. He just dumped you?"

"Yes and no," I told her.

He told me his friends had been kidding him about sitting home alone all the time and said it couldn't hurt to go out; besides they didn't believe I would ever come back. They told him they thought I should have stayed in Denmark in the first place. So for a while he agreed with what they said, and wrote me that letter."

Before Reenie could say another word, I told her about the two letters Christian had shown me. How he quickly discovered going out with other girls did not lessen his missing me; how he had sent me a letter asking me to forgive him for suggesting we date others, and that he would wait for me, no matter how long.

"So why on earth didn't you go back and marry him?" Reenie said and looked at me with surprise.

I told her how I'd never received the letters. That my parents—most likely my father—had sent them back marked "Refused, return to sender," so Christian would believe I didn't want to see him again.

"Christian told me that he did *not* give up hope until the second letter came back. By then, he felt rejected and assumed that I had gone on with my life and wanted nothing more to do with him.

"The first letter, you realize, would have made a difference, but by the time the second one arrived, I was pregnant with Matt—by then, it would have been too late."

We were interrupted in our conversation when Sukie suddenly started to bark. Reenie tried to hush her only to discover someone approaching the house from a truck parked in the driveway. It was one of the contractors she had spoken to the day we arrived asking if he could look over the pier and take some measurements. He added that he would begin work the following week.

Reenie spoke with him for a few minutes discussing what was to be done and we watched as he went on toward the pier.

Then she turned back to me.

"And that's how you came to stay here and marry Robert," she said more as a statement than a question. She sat down next to me on the rail and put her arm around me.

"I'm so sorry for all the angst and guilt you have had to live with. A lifetime of that doesn't seem fair. But sometimes life's not about what we plan, but about what we make of it, and you certainly made a good life for yourself and your family. You've also made all the difference in my life—and for that I am grateful," she said, patted my arm and went back to sit in the chair. Then she picked up her soda and took a sip.

"Anna, part of the reason we came to Idle-a-While was so you could make a final decision as to where and with whom you wanted to spend your future. I think you'll be able to do that without any input from me.

"Listen to your heart and let go of all your old anxieties. Don't let the guilt you've carried around for years ruin your life as it nearly did Robert's. The two of you were not responsible for a lot of the things that happened in your lives. You deserve to spend the rest of your life without regrets," she said.

We hugged each other, called the dogs and set out for a final walk on the beach.

Chapter 16

After our walk, Reenie cleaned out the refrigerator and put together a lunch with leftovers. Then we packed up fragile things and stored them to keep things from being damaged during the upcoming construction.

Reenie and Paul were headed for a trip to Europe the following week—part vacation, part business trip—and would not be back until sometime late July. With all the work to be done at the cottage, none of their daughters planned to come down for a while; Idle-a-While would have no visitors while repairs and improvements were being made. Reenie planned to come down for a week at the beginning of August to furnish and decorate the new quarters and then the whole DeNero clan would descend on the place as they had for years.

We decided to go out for dinner and walked the short distance to the island's only pizzeria where we shared a vegetarian pizza and a small pitcher of beer before going back to pack up the last things.

Before going to bed that evening, Reenie asked me to show her the rest of the photos in Grandma Clara's album. I had already put it in my suitcase and went back to my room to retrieve it while Reenie poured us each a cup of coffee.

We dropped down on the couch and I showed her the other pictures of the Drener family. There were some of my father and his brothers as teenagers and several from weddings and confirmations, but only three with Aunt Clara. One was from my christening and in it her face was partly turned as she looked down at me. Another was from someone's wedding but she was only eight or nine with pigtails, so I was unable to show Reenie just how lovely a woman Aunt Clara had been.

While looking at the last picture of Aunt Clara, taken at her confirmation at age fourteen, Reenie commented that

341

Clara looked vaguely familiar. She studied the picture for a few moments before going on to other pages, while I explained whom the various other family members were. She enjoyed seeing the photos of my parents and was properly impressed by the one of my grandmother at Kaiser Wilhelm's ball.

I was about to close the album when a small picture fell out from behind a photo of my Grandparents taken at what looked like an anniversary party. It was pasted on the back page of the album and one of the corners had come loose causing the picture to fall out. Why it'd been there, I don't know. It turned out to be a studio photo of Aunt Clara— perhaps one of several used as promotional pictures—taken during the early years of her singing career. She looked to be in her early to mid-twenties and was as striking as I remembered her. I handed the picture to Reenie, telling her how delighted I was to finally be able to show her my once famous aunt. She picked up the photo, studied it for a moment. Then she turned to me with an astonished look on her face.

"My Lord, I don't believe this! I can't be one hundred percent sure, but I would bet my last dollar this is a copy of the same picture Uncle Vincent showed me a long time ago and told me he had carried in his wallet for years!"

I looked at Reenie and realized what she was saying.

"You mean *my* Aunt Clara might be *your* Uncle Vincent's first love? You got to be kidding. We might actually have been related!"

We stared at each other, laughed, and then we hugged.

"Anna, we couldn't be closer if we actually were related," Reenie said and looked serious for a moment.

"Let's not tell Vincent. He's happy with Babe and I think she's going to be the one to share the rest of his life. There is a remote chance that Clara may *not* have been his first love—though I seriously doubt it—and telling him about our discovery would serve no purpose. I think this is *one* secret that won't hurt either of us."

So we agreed to keep the possibility of our "nearly-being-related" to ourselves. As Reenie assured me, it was one secret I surely could handle without guilt.

I put away the picture album and we finished packing. Then we went out on the deck to bid the ocean one last farewell before turning in for the night.

We left early the next morning and spent the ride home singing along with Aerosmith, Led Zeppelin, and The Rolling Stones—Reenie invigorated from a trip to her haven, and me with a lighter heart and my mind made up.

After I arrived home, and before I unpacked my bags, I poured a glass of wine, headed for my den, and sat down at my desk. I read the card from Christian's bouquet, the one that greeted me the day I arrived home. Then I took a sip of wine, pulled out a tape and popped it into the tape recorder.

As the music began, I put down the card, sat down at the computer and wrote Christian. I told him about my decision while listening to the words written by Victor Young and Edward Heymand so many years ago. They were the same words Christian and I had listened to on the fateful night when I first met Aunt Clara again:

> "Love letters straight from your heart,
> Keep us so near while apart.
> I'm not alone in the night
> When I can have all the love you write
> I memorize every line
> And I kiss the name that you sign,
> And darling then I read again, right from the start,
> Love letters straight from your heart."

After the song ended, I picked up the card and read it again. Then I smiled, for the card, and the words on it, were like a key—one that, when turned, enabled me to enter and finish an affair of my heart that began back in the late 1950s.

For, of course, I went back to Christian - how could I not?

Chapter 17

After the weekend with Reenie, our conversations about Grandmother Drener and Aunt Clara—the same woman we were reasonably sure had been her Uncle Vincent's first true love—I finally admitted to myself that I wanted Christian as a permanent part of my future. The pink roses, and the accompanying card I received the day I returned home, sealed the deal.

I wrote him, and in his own words told him, "My darling Christian, I'll come back to you. I don't want to not have you in my life—I'll forever be your duchess if you'll continue to be my knight."

An hour after I sent off the email, he called.

"I'll be in the airport tomorrow to greet you with a truckload of pink roses. Just hurry up and pack."

It took all my persuasive power to convince him it would take a couple of months for me to arrange things and join him with a clear conscience.

Then, having made up my mind, I wasted no time—I wanted to be with Christian. So I called my children and asked them to come for a weekend family summit. I wanted their support and understanding if I were to make such a major change in my life.

Later, that first evening after they all arrived and the younger children were in bed, we sat around and talked long into the night.

"I want to tell you about Christian," I began, "about how we knew each other long before I came to the States, and how we reunited through the Internet and finally met again on my trip this past spring.

"Please have patience," I asked as they all began asking questions. I explained to them that the love I had for their father was in no way diminished by my feelings for Christian. What I felt for him was something old and different.

"Christian and I care deeply for each other, perhaps in the special way that happens if you have loved, lost, and finally found the other again."

When I finished talking, they all assured me they understood.

"We'll miss you terribly when you leave," Becca said with tears in her eyes and the boys nodded in agreement. Patrick said he would visit me as often as possible.

"But you have to promise to come home for all special occasions—confirmations, round birthdays and new babies, mother," Matt said, eyeing his wife. Everyone laughed and Camilla swatted him with one of the sofa cushions assuring all of us that she did *not* plan any future babies.

I promised I would try to attend all special events and come home often. Then they encouraged me to "give your life another chance."

Hunter Lee, adventurous as ever said, "It really will be nice to have you in Denmark. I always wanted to visit Scandinavia and purchase things in all those delicious little shops."

Luke just shook his head, smiled at his wife, patted my hand and told me they would come over whenever they could. I promised Hunter Lee I would scout out the good stores and immediately thought of the places I'd gone with Vivian.

"If you like, Becca and I can keep an eye on the house and keep it up until you decide what to do about it," Forrest said and put his arm around Becca who, still looking sad, nodded in agreement.

"I would be grateful for that Forrest," I told my son-in-law and turned to my daughter.

"Becca, you can drive my Mazda in place of your dilapidated old Ford, when I'm gone. I don't plan to take it with me."

Becca squeezed my hand and smiled while the boys laughed and said they thought it sounded like a fair trade

Patrick came over and hugged me and said, "Mom, I'll help you get ready for your trip and I might consider leasing the house if the rent is cheap enough. Madison has applied for a better position at University Medical Clinic, and if she gets it—and I think she will—we'll be a lot closer to it from here."

I told him I was pleased for Madison and assured him there would be no rent.

"I would, however, appreciate you also taking care of your father's Jeep. I'm not ready to give it up, and I might consider having it shipped over."

Finally Matt came over and sat down next to me. Ever since he was a boy he had been protective of me, taking my side when needed, and after Robert's death had accepted his role as the patriarch of the Thornberg family.

He put his hands on my shoulders and looked me square in the face, "We all love you mom and we'll miss you terribly, but we are all going to be fine. We have each other and we don't want you to live alone anymore."

Then he pulled me into his arms, and I cried; then the girls cried while the boys tried hard *not* to. Finally we all laughed at each other, ending the weekend on a high note.

The next week, I started to pack and ship things to Christian. It was decided Patrick would live in my house. I didn't like leaving it empty and didn't feel right about renting it to strangers. The other three were fine with this arrangement and were glad I didn't want to sell our home.

One of the last things I did was make arrangements for Tessa to come with me to Denmark. Becca and Patrick both offered to keep her but I told them I needed someone from my past to go with me on this new venture and that she was the only one not attached to anyone other than myself.

And so, on a bright morning early in September, Reenie drove me to the airport and with a final "Goodbye Thelma,"—"Goodbye Louise," we tearfully parted promising to visit each other and to call and email regularly.

On the plane over, I admitted to some doubt, but Christian's smiling face and welcoming arms in Kastrup Airport quelled them in a hurry.

I felt I had finally come back to where I *now* belonged.

PART FIVE

"Happily ever after?"

Chapter 1

"You look so content in this place," Becca said and sipped her tea, "Valhalla is such a beautiful house and I love your study with the view of the ocean."

She got up from the couch and, with her mug in hand, walked over to the French doors and looked out over the water.

A little earlier, she had brought up a tray with tea and a small plate of shortbread cookies, just out of the oven.

I sat back and observed her as she watched a cruise ship sail by filled, I was sure, with happy holiday travelers.

"Mother T, I still can't believe how much this study resembles your Sanctuary at home, with the exception, of course, the splendid view of the ocean," Hunter Lee had said in her sweet southern drawl when she came up earlier to say goodbye before going downstairs to join the rest of the family for a trip into the center of Copenhagen.

The study has an oak desk holding a computer and a printer. An old leather chair and footstool sit in a corner near an ancient sea chest that serves as a coffee table and next to the chest is a comfortable chair used when Christian or

348

others drop in for an afternoon cup of tea. I even have an inviting couch—draped with a big thick blanket—made for afternoon naps.

"Is that the afghan Marin gave you for your birthday a few years ago?" Becca asked when she first saw it. I told her that indeed it was.

Along the walls, I have two large bookcases filled with assortments of reference books and copies of selected authors. The shelves also hold a conglomeration of family photos, green plants and other collectibles including the little figurine from the M&M girls and Robert's old silver box—still filled with notes and old movie tickets.

On one shelf is an array of seashells picked up on the Valhalla strand and other beaches Christian and I have visited. There are even a few shells from Topsail Island and a small piece of Connemara rock from Galway, Ireland.

I recently accompanied Christian on a business trip to Scotland, and after that we had gone to Ireland to visit Galway and Aunt Nora. I had kept in touch with her through letters and she seemed genuinely delighted to see me again—this time on a much happier occasion. Nora is getting on in years, but she is still going strong, just moving a little slower.

On the walls, I've hung several of Christina's pastel paintings of scenes from nearby woods and a few of Patrick's beach scenes made while he stayed with Reenie and her family at Idle-a-While for a few weeks last spring.

My study is a large and airy room from where I can look down over the dormant, sloping lawn to the dark waters of Oeresund where ships pass by during the day. I also have the daily pleasure of watching seagulls entertain me with their boisterous scrapping as they leap around the edge of the water forever seeking morsels they know have been left by me during my early morning walks.

One of my most cherished pieces in the room, however, sits on top of my bookcase and looks at me every time I enter this room.

Christian and I were sitting in the library on a fall afternoon, reading the Sunday papers, not long after I moved in, when he suddenly jumped up and hit his forehead with the palm of his hand.

"Anna, I nearly forgot; I have a really big surprise for you."

Then he grabbed my hand and, looking excited, dragged me to the top floor of Valhalla.

All out of breath from the hasty climb, we entered the dust-covered attic and Christian immediately went over to forage around the wooden boxes near the gabled window at the southern end of the loft. I had had no occasion to visit the attic in the short period I had lived at Valhalla, so this was new to me.

While he searched for whatever it was he was hunting, I wandered around the attic. With amazement, I looked at old paintings, antique chests and beds, boxes overflowing with old curtains, cushions, hats, lace-up boots and other paraphernalia any antique dealer would love to have.

Suddenly, Christian let out a yell and with a triumphant look produced an old shoebox, one that once held someone's hiking boots. He pulled open the lid, laughed, and held up my Grandmother Clara's clock—the clock she brought with her when she left her family in Prussia many years ago.

"Okay, Miss Anna, I've kept this for you, forever it seems, and now I want an explanation and the story about this old, and I'm certain, valuable clock.

"I'd forgotten all about it. For several years I stored it with my things in the back of a closet in my room in my parents' old home. Later, when they moved to Valhalla, the box was moved with my belongings to my room here and I put the box in the attic. It wasn't until just now, when I saw an ad in the paper for an antique sale with a picture of some old timepieces, that I suddenly remembered yours. A vision of you giving it to me the week before you left flashed through my mind," he said and handed me the intricate old clock.

"I remember giving it to you, not knowing what else to do with it as I was about to leave and join my parents. I recall making you swear to keep it for me until I came back and never tell anyone about it," I said, delighted at having it returned.

We had closed up the attic and gone back down to the library and spent the rest of the afternoon in front of a warm fire reminiscing, yet again, about times past. By then, of course, Christian knew all about the Drener family but I recalled a few other tidbits I had overlooked, including receiving the clock from Aunt Clara via our old literature teacher.

On the way down from the attic, I gave him a kiss and, with the greatest pleasure, took the clock to my new sanctuary and placed it on top of my bookshelves.

That night, just before going to sleep, Christian took me in his arms and quietly whispered: "Anna, I treasured you back when you gave me the clock to keep for you, and I treasure you now, even more.

"Let's invite your whole family over for Christmas," Christian had suggested the next day. "We have the room and I'll help pay for the tickets," he offered.

So I called my family with the invitation, and to my delight, they all accepted.

"It took some re-arranging of everyone's schedule," Luke told me when we greeted them in the airport, "but thanks to a few miracles, and a lot of prayers, we managed to get here, even if Hunter Lee *did* insist on bringing everything but the sink along," he added with a laugh.

In order to accommodate that many people, Mrs. Larsen has been coming in at dawn every morning helping me get things ready. Right now she's in the kitchen showing Matt's wife, Camilla, and Becca's Lizzy how to make Danish Christmas cookies. She is also preparing all sorts of dishes for both Christmas Eve and Christmas Day and by now the entire house is filled with titillating aromas making their way up to my second floor hide-away.

Chapter 2

It's the afternoon of December 23—Little Christmas Eve as it is fondly called in this old Nordic country, and I'm upstairs in Peter's old room that we turned into my study at Valhalla. I take Becca's hand and for a while we talk about Robert, her beloved father; a man I married under stressful circumstances, but who I came to love deeply.

Shortly before, Hunter Lee had ridden off with most of my family, I'd heard the faint noise of pots and pans clanging and oven doors being opened and closed. A little while later Becca came up to join me.

With the holiday aromas making their presence known, we begin to talk about family Christmas dinners celebrated when the children were young.

"Remember how dad always hid the almond in his cheek if he found it in the Christmas dessert. He would pretend not to have it, and it was years before I realized it. He sure did make Christmas special for all of us with his enthusiasm and sense of humor" she says.

I agree with her. Robert, when in the mood, exuded more life and fun than most others and could be the life of the party when the spirit struck him. He would fall back on his Irish brogue and entertain us with stories and songs from "the old sod," as he affectionately called his place of birth. Those were the good days and as the years went by, there were more of those than of the dark days when things from his past would haunt him and leave him silent and remote.

We finish our tea and Becca picks up the tray. Then just before she leaves, she puts down the tea things and comes over and takes both of my hands in hers.

She strokes my cheek and says, "Mom, I know you

loved dad very much and will always keep him in your heart. But he's been gone for some years and I'm happy you've found someone to be with. You seem so much like you old self and you look beautiful and content," she adds with laughter in her eyes and her voice.

We hug and she tells me she'll come up and get me in time for dinner.

This morning, Christian took most of my family for a trip into Copenhagen to look at the Christmas decorations in the big department stores. He plans to show them the many street vendors and singers, decked out for Christmas, entertaining the holiday shoppers with songs and play along the long walking street running from City Hall to the Royal Theater at the center of the city.

"I'm also going to treat all of you to McDonald's hamburgers," he promised as they were leaving.

The children all thought it would be neat to eat American fast food in another country, and the younger ones were anxious to check out the Danish treats in the Kids' Meal bags.

"Go easy on the French fries and watch out for your arteries, or there will be no goose for you on Christmas Eve," I threatened him. He just laughed.

I watched as all of them piled into the two mini-vans Christian had hired for the trip. They looked like part of the opening scene of the movie, "Home Alone," with tow-headed children and hats everywhere.

Camilla, ever the organizer, assigned everyone a "buddy" so no one would get lost; like me, however, she chose to stay behind. I blessed Christian for taking the family on this trip, but he had assured me it was a treat. He seems to be having a wonderful time, sharing Christmas holidays with my children and grandchildren.

Matt and his crew arrived from New York several days ago and spent the first day unpacking and exploring Valhalla and its grounds. The next morning, he took his family on a tour around Copenhagen.

While in high school, Matt spent a summer in Denmark staying with Astrid and Svend while he explored my native city and had told his family he wanted to show them some of the places and things he liked; they had taken off for the trip with great anticipation.

Their outing had included a trip to Runde Taarn with its circular stone stairway, a ride on the train into the city, and eating Danish hot dogs from a street vendor; a treat they all enjoyed. They had also made a visit to the harbor to see the famous Little Mermaid. Matt's eleven-year-old twins, David and Danielle, were not impressed and told me they couldn't figure out what the big fuss was all about.

"She's just a little naked lady sitting on a rock out in the water," David reasoned.

"I thought she'd be at least half as big as the Statue of Liberty. She's kind of cute, but she sure is puny," Danielle added.

Perhaps in time they may come to appreciate the loveliness of the statue depicting the sweet diminutive heroine from Hans Christian Anderson's famous fairy tale.

My North Carolina children, Luke and Hunter Lee with their children Luke Jr., twins Jackson Lee and Mary Margaret, and little Annabel Grace, arrived the day after Matt as did Becca and Forrest and their children, Charlie and Lizzy. The children rarely experience snow in the south, and they spent most of yesterday outside in the vast garden making snowmen and snow angels. They tried out a couple of the old sleds and even Peter's old surfboard found in the garage, and shrieked as they went down the lawn toward the icy edges of the ocean. We only have about four inches of snow but it's enough for the children to enjoy and for us to call white Christmas.

Acy flew over right after her semester was through and arrived more than a week ago. Peter, who is staying at his flat in the city during the holiday, offered to pick her up. The two of them have been gadding about the city and our suburb ever since, checking out pubs and small, funky shops where they are looking for Christmas presents.

Patrick joined us a month ago at Christian's insistence. It seems Madison broke off their long-time relationship early this fall telling him she felt their lives were headed in different directions. He called and said he felt "sort of lost," and Christian suggested he come over and stay with us for a while in order to "get away from it all."

"I know how Patrick feels," Christian said with a bittersweet laugh. He too had been left by women before and knew what it was like to suddenly be alone.

Patrick's work has actually begun to sell. He had a showing last summer where several art critics called him "a gifted young artist with a unique flair for blending colors." Someone else wrote, "Young Thornberg has a unique talent and is someone we should keep an eye on."

Since he arrived at Valhalla, he's constantly been down on the beach painting or up in the attic drawing. Vivian bought two of his drawings and says she is "mad about his work," and is planning a private show for him right after New Year's.

I look out the French doors and see him sitting near the water drawing. It's much too cold to paint, but he insisted the icy sea butting up against the snow-covered beach "is too compelling not to put on paper." Christina, who is doing some sketching, has accompanied him. They've brought along thermos bottles filled with hot chocolate provided by Mrs. Larsen, and have set up their gear just inside the gazebo. Tessa and Sir, who never seem to care how cold it is outside, are with them. The dogs seem happy as long as they can romp around and be with people.

I open the French doors slightly and for a few minutes look down at the two of them. We invited Christina to come out and meet Patrick soon after he arrived, in order that the two of them could get to know each other. Christian thought my son might enjoy having a person his own age around, especially someone with whom he could share his love of art. I agreed. I have cared a great deal about Christina since we first met and felt certain she would be a good influence on Patrick and that she, in turn, might enjoy being with him.

They hit it off immediately and spent their first evening by the fire in the library talking into the night and were still there when we got up for breakfast the next morning. Since then, they've spent much of their time together painting or drawing and taking the dogs for long walks on the beach or in parks near Valhalla.

The odd thing is that they look so much like Robert and me when we were young. Patrick is so like his father and, from what everyone tells me, Christina resembles me at that age. It's a little eerie, but fate often plays strange tricks.

Chapter 3

I've had fun this month decorating the house for Christmas. We shopped for weeks collecting presents for our large combined family and by now the study is stacked with wrapped gifts waiting to be opened Christmas Eve and Christmas morning.

We flew to North Carolina last year and spent the holiday at Luke and Hunter Lee's home in Charlotte. This year, however, I wanted my children and grandchildren to experience an old-fashioned Danish Christmas. The only deviation from my childhood traditions was putting up and decorating a tree—early—like we do in the State.

"Danes do not even look at a tree until a few days before Christmas," Christian told the children a couple of days ago, "and we usually don't decorate it until the morning of the twenty-fourth," he added; they listened with disbelief.

Christian and I had compromised. He would buy a Danish Christmas tree right before the twenty-fourth. In return, he searched, and through Oliver, found a farm that delivered a nine-foot tall blue spruce two weeks ago.

I called Becca at the beginning of December and had her pack up all my old ornaments and send them to me via express mail. We bought dozens of strings of small white lights and by now have the most glorious looking tree decorating the corner of the living room. We light it every night and sit in the otherwise darkened room and enjoy the reflections of the soft lights in the silver and gold decorations.

On today's trip the children will pick out our Danish Christmas tree on their way home. The trees are quite sparse with few and separated branches, and to Americans they look like a Charlie Brown Christmas tree.

"After dinner we'll put up the tree in the library and decorate it," he promised. "Then you'll all see that the sparse branches serve the tree well. Not only will we decorate it with garlands of small Danish flags and baskets filled with candy, we'll also put on real candles that will be lit Christmas Eve."

The children were skeptical.

Tomorrow evening, the twenty-fourth, is the "biggie" in this country. We'll start the celebration by attending the four o'clock service at St. John's Lutheran Church—just down the road. Only a few of us will understand the liturgy, but a Lutheran service is not that different from an Episcopal and some of the hymns are actually the same. Many Danes go to church on this day, mostly out of tradition, so the church will be full and with children in attendance, the mood will be festive and filled with anticipation.

Right after the service, we'll head home for a huge and elaborate dinner consisting of goose, red cabbage, caramel potatoes and an assortment of Mrs. Larsen's specialties. Like Danes, all over this country, we'll conclude the meal with a light and fluffy rice pudding loaded with chopped almonds and whipped cream and several of the younger children will be "surprised" to find whole almonds in their desert—the adults having made sure that the younger children each find one. This will entitle them each to the traditional prize—a small marzipan pig sporting a red ribbon around its neck.

I introduced this Danish Christmas custom to my family and, with Irish luck, Robert found the almond in his desert on most Christmas Eves. He used to hide it inside his cheek until everyone had finished, triumphantly produce it with a laugh, and claim the prize he always shared with our children.

After the meal we'll all gather behind the closed doors in the hall outside the library and wait while Christian goes in alone and lights all the candles on "his'" Danish tree. Then, when the candles are all lit, he will turn off all other lights and throw the doors wide open. We will join him and, as Danes have done for many years, we'll watch the tree in all its glory ablaze with candles lighting up the room. Joining hands, we'll circle the tree and walk around it singing Christmas songs, this year in both Danish and English.

Finally Santa Claus will arrive, as he will all over the country about this time of the evening. This year Peter, whom the children don't know that well yet, will excuse himself right after dinner to "run an errand" and will reappear, unrecognizable, all donned up as Santa in a red suit and white beard carrying a big sack filled with presents— one for each child and perhaps a candy-cane or two.

I know that David and Danielle and Luke Junior will fail to buy the Santa bit, but I fully expect the younger children to be surprised and delighted.

We'll assure them that the American Santa will come during the night and also leave presents under Nana's Christmas tree for them to find in the morning.

Helena and Oliver with Chris and his new baby sister, Ruby Leigh, will join us for dinner Christmas day along with Ruby and Ollie.

The house will be busting in its seams—I can hardly wait.

Chapter 4

Last night we all gathered in the living room and Matt sat down at the grand piano and played Christmas songs as we all practiced for Christmas Eve.

We did "Noel, Noel," and then "Silent Night," first in English and then in Danish with Christian, Christina, and Peter joining me. "I Saw Mommy Kissing Santa Claus," followed "Santa Claus is coming to Town;" then we paired up and sang "The Twelve Days of Christmas." We concluded the singing with a rousing rendition of "Rudolph the Red Nosed Reindeer."

Even Mrs. Larsen—who has worked for us full time ever since her husband passed away a year ago—joined us in "Rudolph" when she brought in hot chocolate and some of her Danish Kringle, a form of flaky pastry that melts in your mouth.

In the midst of drinking her cocoa, Hunter Lee made us laugh, telling us about her teenage niece, Millicent, from Georgia, who had only one huge wish for Christmas.

"She told me she would gladly give up all other presents in hopes that the 'Millennium bug' not wipe out her hometown. She is a junior in high school and is afraid she will miss out on her first prom, if her home town goes under."

Later, Matt and Camilla and their two youngest walked the short distance to Vivian and Richard's place where they are staying during their visit. Vivian graciously offered to host my oldest son and his family, realizing Christian and I would run out of rooms with both families joining us. She gets Matt to play her baby grand and claims to have a great time in their company.

Even with eight bedrooms, Valhalla is not large enough to accommodate our group. Luke, Hunter Lee, and their children are occupying the old servant's quarters; Becca and

Forrest and their children are in the nursery wing. Patrick sleeps on the couch in my study, Peter is on a cot in Christian's office, and Christina is sharing her old room with Acy.

The formal dining room with all the leaves in the old table, and the kitchen nook, are in full use.

Tonight, after dinner, we'll gather around the big spruce and celebrate Acy's twentieth birthday. It's hard to believe she's that old. I still remember the day I first held her, looking at Matt—so young at the time—wondering how her life would turn out; seems she's done just fine.

By special request from the birthday girl, Mrs. Larsen is making Acy's favorite: spaghetti and meatballs, complimented by homemade garlic bread. We have bought several bottles of Chianti, and early this morning, Hunter Lee prepared enough salad to feed an army.

Astrid will join us and bring cannolis, one of her specialties made from a recipe she picked up on one of her many trips to Italy. She and Svend came over to the states for Christmas the year my oldest granddaughter was born and she has always held Acy dear.

A couple of weeks ago, I had Grandma Clara's pearls restrung and put in a small velvet box and plan to give them to her after the party is over. It seems only right that this precious old piece of jewelry be passed on to my oldest grandchild. I know she will treasure it. She doesn't know the history of the pearls—yet—but before she goes back to the States, I plan to tell her the story about the Duchess—her great, great grandmother.

New Year's Eve the older adults are invited over to Richard and Vivian's for a catered dinner and dance, funny hats, and fireworks at midnight. Mrs. Larsen has graciously agreed to stay behind with the younger children, and Peter, Acy, and Patrick are going with Christina into her flat in the city for a big celebration with her friends.

It is wonderful to have them all here in this marvelous old home hosted by a man I love more each day.

Do we plan to marry? I'm not sure. Christian loves me, of that I'm certain. Even after four marriages, he declares he's ready to add a wedding band to my Eternity Ring and keeps telling me he is most willing to make the trip down the isle—one last time—anxious to make me Lady Raabensted, wife of Sir Christian.

I just don't know. We are happy as it is, going about our lives, sharing time and love. Christian retired from the University this fall but keeps busy as a consultant, does lectures, and plans to write several books on his specialty. He is also busy raising roses in the conservatory and keeps a small pink bouquet next to my computer at all times, even during this season of pine and poinsettias.

We've gone back to the states several times. Last year, we spent part of the summer at my home in North Carolina while Patrick stayed at Idle-a-While painting, letting Reenie mother him like the son she never had. I joined them for a couple of days while Christian attended a conference at Duke University. Then we visited our children near Charlotte before ending our trip up north, seeing Matt and his family.

Reenie has already reserved a large three-story place on the beach for us for a month next summer. It sits just down the road from Idle-a-While and sleeps an army—at least thirty people—and we plan to bring my whole gang out there along with Peter and Christina. Helena and Oliver and their children also plan to join us for a week on their way to Disney World.

Patrick plans to stay on in my home in North Carolina and should his situation change—and it well might—I'll make a decision. A lot of good memories are tied to that home and I still like having a place in the States to call my own.

So for right now, I think Christian and I will just go on "living in sin," enjoying our life together.

The chimes on Grandma Clara's old mantel clock just struck six—it's a little fast—and I hear the girls downstairs getting things ready for dinner. A while ago Patrick and Christina packed up their gear and went for a walk and I see the two coming back from their stroll along the beach, arms wrapped around each other—her blond head resting on Patrick's shoulder while his curls falls to touch her head. The two dogs run ahead of them, in and out of the water like two happy seals, oblivious to the temperature and the young people who are beginning to find each other.

The minivans carrying my family returned a short while ago from their trip to the city. After they got out of the cars, I watched as the children all helped haul a tall, if sparse, tree into the house. They boys all argued over who actually selected the tree while Christian, looking like the happiest man I ever saw, walked into Valhalla hand-in-hand with Annabel Grace and Mary Margaret.

The younger grandchildren do not remember Robert and apparently think Christian is another grandfather; I'll make sure, some day, to tell them about Robert who loved his children and grandchildren with passion.

Chapter 5

I've turned off my computer; I don't intend to use it again until after the holidays. Right now I'll join my family downstairs and luxuriate in the company of Christian and all our children. Becca is calling me from the bottom of the stairs. I answer back, "I'll be right down," and take one last look out over the winter sea, watching as the ocean surges among the soft ice at the edge of the shore.

I reflect on the waters off the coast of Ireland where Robert's life took such a sad turn. Beating against the cliffs near Bally Shane, the waves will continue to pound on the ancient stones, smoothing their surface and eventually wear them down. The water means no harm; it only follows its natural flow like the waves inside Robert who fought his demons, and has by now, I believe, found peace. I think of him—a man who was a wonderful father and who, through our many years of marriage, became my lover, confidant, partner, and friend. He'll always have a special place in my heart.

My thoughts linger on another beach—the one near my childhood home—where I wandered, so long ago, carrying my own turmoil. I've sorted out my feelings for Alex, the man who gave me life; my Aunt Clara, with whom I finally united; and my mother who also suffered, knowing the double life we lived.

Ultimately I think of Nels, my father, who raised and loved me far too much and in ways he shouldn't have. He too bore his pain—aware of his flaws. In my heart I have forgiven him and hope he, like the others, are at rest.

Finally, I recall the North Carolina beach where Reenie and I walked, talked, and took things apart before putting them back together. It was on that calm and lonely strand that I finally came to terms with my life and my future. I'm grateful that the shadows and secrets were brought out and finally put to rest.

Before I leave my quiet Danish sanctuary, I pick up the little card again. I keep it next to my bouquet of pink roses where it sits—like a daily inspiration—with a message that reminds me of the way fate became the hunter. By now, the card is worn—having been handled and read many times over the past several years. It's the one from Christian; the one I found stuck in the bouquet of roses the day I arrived back in North Carolina after re-uniting with him in my native country.

It's a plain little card that Christian wrote and sent to Reenie, prior to my arrival back home, asking her to put it with the roses. It reads the familiar words: "My darling Anna, please come back to me. I don't want to not have you in my life," and is signed, "Your Knight in Shining Armor."

This tale has taken many turns—including a couple of side trips—since I began my story, and the conclusion didn't unfold itself until I connected with Christian through the Internet. It is nearly at an end.

I hear the clock in the foyer strike as I draw the curtains to close out the cold, and prepare to join my family downstairs. I flip the card over and with a smile read the message that Christian, in a valiant attempt to get me to return to him, added on the back. It simply says:

"Come back to me and write the novel you always wanted to pen. Write the story about the Duchess, the Knight and the Leprechaun."

And that's exactly what I just finished doing!

THE END

On Eagles' Wings—a devotional song composed by Michael Joncas, a priest, in 1979 after Vatican Council II, when the Catholic Church began using vernacular hymns at Mass. Its words are loosely based on Psalm 91 and Isaiah 40:31.

"My Prayer"—composed in 1926 by Georges Boulanger with lyrics added by Jimmy Kennedy in 1939.

"Love Letters"—a 1945 popular song with music by Victor Young and lyrics by Edward Heyman. The song appeared, without lyrics, in the movie of the same name, and was nominated for the Academy Award for Best Song for 1945.

Anna's Family

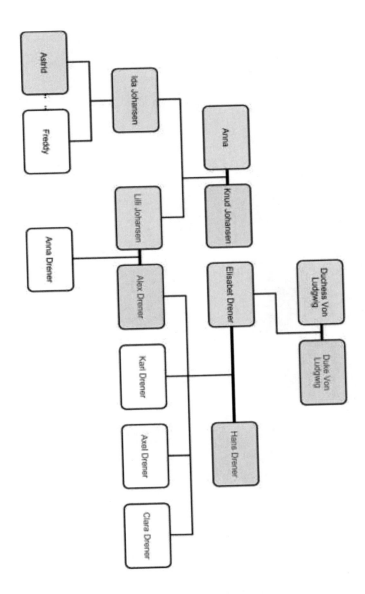

Anna & Robert

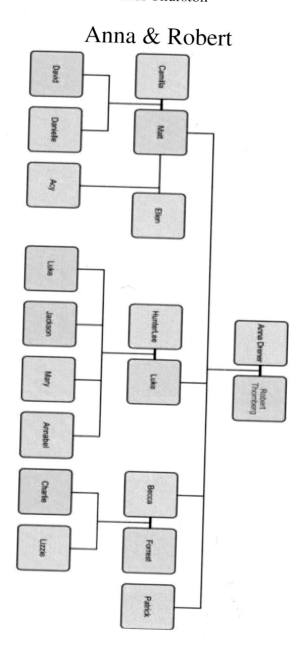